VLADIMIR OBRUCHEV

SANNIKOV LAND

Fredonia Books
Amsterdam, The Netherlands

Sannikov Land

by
Vladimir Obruchev

ISBN: 1-58963-867-0

Reprinted from the original edition

Fredonia Books
Amsterdam, The Netherlands
http://www.fredoniabooks.com

CONTENTS

"I SAY IT EXISTS!"

The first half of the meeting called by the learned society to hear the reports of members of an expedition that had searched for Baron Toll and his companions, who had disappeared, was drawing to a close. On the rostrum near a wall on which hung big portraits of the titled patrons and past chairmen of the society was a naval officer, who had made a daring voyage in a whale-boat, crossing the Arctic Ocean from the New Siberian Islands to Bennett Island, the last place where Baron Toll was known to have stopped. The speaker's manly, weather-beaten face was in the half-shadow cast by the green lampshade, which directed the light of the lamp to his notes on the rostrum and on to his naval uniform with its gold buttons and medals.

At a long table covered with green cloth sat members of the society's Council, all of them eminent scholars or famous travellers who at that time happened to be in the northern capital. The chairman was in the centre. His eyes were closed; it seemed as though the speaker's soft voice had lulled him to a light sleep. The small hall was filled to capacity.

The speaker had already described the efforts to find the lost expedition, the difficult journey during which the heavy whale-boat had to be drawn on dog-sledges from the mainland to the New Siberian Islands over the ridged polar icefield, the summer spent on Kotelny Island in waiting for the ice to break, the rough passage along the shore, and the bold crossing to Bennett Island. He drew a picture of that dreary, eternally ice-bound island, and related how his party found Toll's little hut and the things he had left in it, together with notes describing the island and ending with the words: "We are leaving for the south today; there is enough food for about twenty days. All of us are well."

"Thus," the naval officer declared, speaking in a louder voice, "on October 26, 1902, Baron Toll, astronomer Zeeberg, and two hunters, the Yakut Vasily Gorokhov and the Tungus Nikolai Dyakonov, left Bennett Island and proceeded south across the ice towards the New Siberian Islands. But they never reached their destination. We know that because our search did not yield a single trace. What happened to these courageous travellers? I have no doubt that they perished on their way to the islands. You know, of course, that towards the close of October there is no daylight in those latitudes—only two or three hours of twilight around midday. The frosts are severe, registering a temperature of 40°C below zero; violent snow-storms are frequent. But the sea is not completely covered with ice and is full of unfrozen patches of water. The travellers

8

might have fallen into one of these patches during a snow-storm. Or they might have perished from exhaustion, over-come by hunger and the frost in the struggle with the hummocks, as they had no dogs and were compelled to drag the sledges which were loaded down with canoes and equipment. Or, finally, caught in a storm, they were drowned during the polar night while trying to cross the unfrozen sea in their frail canoes. One way or another, they found eternal rest on the bed of the Arctic Ocean, but, as I have tried to prove to you, Sannikov Land, which Toll searched for for so long and in vain, does not exist."

The speaker descended from the rostrum. His conclud-ing words had dismayed his listeners. Suddenly, a loud voice was heard from the back:

"All the same, I say it exists!"

There was a stir.

"Who said that? Who is this crank?" people asked.

The chairman looked round sternly and rang his bell. When order was restored, he said impressively:

"Ladies and gentlemen, I move that we rise and observe a minute's silence in memory of the courageous men who lost their lives in quest of knowledge: Baron Toll, astron-omer Zeeberg, and hunters Gorokhov and Dyakonov."

Everybody rose.

"The meeting will be resumed in a quarter of an hour."

The people sitting along the side aisles quickly made for the exits. Members of the Council surrounded the speaker, while the stout figure of one of them—Academician Shenk, the well-known explorer and the organizer and adviser of Baron Toll's expedition—was seen squeezing through to the back rows.

"I should like to speak to the gentleman who is so confi-dent Sannikov Land exists," he said in a voice loud enough to be heard above the shuffling of chairs and the hum of conversation.

In response to this invitation, a young man in a black blouse detached himself from the crowd closely packing the aisles. His swarthy face was furrowed with the fine, tiny wrinkles that are caused by summer heat, winter frost, and stormy winds.

"I said it and if need be I'll say it again," he declared, approaching Shenk.

"Come to the library! It is impossible to talk in this crush!" Shenk said, giving the impetuous young man a piercing look from under thick brows.

Taking the stranger by his elbow, Shenk led him through a side door to the premises at the back of the library. This was the society's office.

It was quiet in the office. The academician sat at the secretary's desk, motioning his companion to the other chair. He lit a cigarette and said:

"I am listening. I should like to hear what you know about Sannikov Land."

"First permit me to tell you who I am," the young man replied. "For five years I was a political exile in a village called Kazachye in the mouth of the Yana River. In that land of bears, or, rather, polar bears, I became friendly with the local hunters. They are a rough and ignorant lot if measured by the standards of the metropolis, but when you get to know them you find they are kind, stout-hearted men. Every spring, when the days grow longer and the ice is still firm, they go to the New Siberian Islands for mammoth tusks, which they find there in great numbers. Some of the hunters have seen Sannikov Land clearly and are quite sure it exists."

"That is not convincing enough!" Shenk remarked. "You

know from what the speaker said that the mountains Sannikov and Toll saw are nothing but huge ridges of ice and that in order to be seen from Kotelny Island the mountains of that imagined land must be at least 2,200 metres above sea level. It's hard to believe that there are such high montains in the Arctic Ocean."

"That's a surmise and not a fact!"

"Besides, before disembarking on Bennett Island, Toll searched futilely for the island in his yacht, the *Dawn*, which passed close to the place where this land is supposed to be."

"That only proves that this land is farther north and not as close to Kotelny Island as was thought by Sannikov and others who saw it but did not estimate the distance correctly," the young man objected.

"I agree with you there," Shenk said, "but the fact remains that apart from this, you will agree, very questionable evidence, we have nothing, or, to be more exact, nothing definite to go by except the information that birds migrate somewhere to the north."

"Why do you think that indication is insufficiently definite?" the young man asked in surprise. "Wrangel wrote about it, Mydel confirmed it, while from the local population we know for certain that in summer vast numbers of birds live on the northern shore of Siberia except in two places—the first is between the Khroma and the Omoloi rivers, and the second starts some fifty kilometres west of Cape Yakan and stretches to Cape Rirkaipi.* In these places the number of birds is insignificant but the people there see birds flying farther north."

"From the western stretch the birds fly to the New Siberian Islands, while from the eastern—to Wrangel Island," Shenk insisted.

"That is what people thought, but it is not true. Wrangel Island is very high and rocky and is covered with snow almost all summer. There are too few places on it where birds like geese and ducks can nest. But we are more interested in the western stretch."

"Yes, and from there the birds fly to the New Siberian Islands."

* The Chukchi name for Cape Severny, which is now known as Cape Schmidt.—*Ed.*

"Yet only a small number spends the summer on those islands. Most continue their migration northward in great flocks. I've had that confirmed by many hunters in Ustyansk, Russkoye Ustye, and Ozhogino, who have been to those islands. Sannikov was also aware of it. The migratory birds include white geese, eider, a few species of ducks, snipe, goldfinches and others that feed on plants. The inference is that in the north there is a piece of land that is big enough and covered with vegetation."

"Quite right. And that land is Bennett Island," Shenk noted. "From the notes left by Toll we know that that island is the summer home of two species of eider, one species of snipe, bullfinches, five species of gulls. . . ."

"But neither geese nor ducks are mentioned!" the young man laughed. "They, you know, make up the biggest contingent of migratory birds. That is characteristic! Didn't you notice that in his notes Toll says he saw an eagle flying south to north, a falcon flying in the opposite direction, and a flock of geese heading southwards from the north, that is, returning from this unknown land to the continent at the end of the summer."

"True," the academician acknowledged.

"And Toll adds that because of the mist he could not tell where these birds came from. He did not see any land last summer either, during the attempt to find Sannikov Land."

"What a good memory you have!" Shenk exclaimed.

"I listened attentively to the report, and Toll's notes only confirmed my belief in the existence of Sannikov Land and that it lies farther north than was presumed. That is what made me speak up so categorically. As for Bennett Island, you heard it too, it is too small and too blocked up with ice to be a shelter for a large number of birds. Toll corroborates this point. Bullfinches, snipe, gulls, and two species of eider are its only summer visitors.".

"But land situated farther north, say around the 80th parallel, must have a heavier coat of ice. Consequently, it likewise cannot provide food for many birds."

"In that case, where *do* those silly birds fly?" the young man said with a burst of laughter.

"I really don't know! Perhaps across the North Pole to Greenland, although that is improbable," Shenk replied with a shrug.

"But can't we suppose that due to some especially favourable conditions, Sannikov Land, in spite of its position amidst the ice of the Arctic Ocean, has a warmer climate than Bennett and the New Siberian Islands lying south of it?"

"That, if you'll excuse my saying so, is simply fantasy. Except for the migration of birds, we have no grounds whatever for such a supposition."

"Can't the ground be heated by a volcano?" the young man insisted, "or hot springs?"

"Your hunters and navigators would have noticed the smoke long ago. Do not forget that during his drift in the *Fram*, Nansen also passed the place where people think this mysterious land is, and saw nothing."

"But have you heard of the strange disappearance of a northern people called Onkilons. Harassed by the Chukchis, they left the mainland with all their herds, and nothing more was ever seen of them. Nobody knows where they are."

"Yes, I remember Wrangel, Nordenskiöld, and Mydel gathering information about them. But ethnography is not my subject...."

14

A bell rang in the library, interrupting the academician. Shenk rose.

"I must go and hear the next report. But your ideas interest me. We must have another talk. Come and see me in the evening a week from today. Here is my address."

Shenk took a visiting-card from his wallet and gave it to the young man, adding:

"I'll see if I can find any literature on these Onkilons. And I shall sound the ground at the Academy about fitting out another expedition to search for Toll. But I doubt very much if anything will come of it. Come and see me in any case."

A VANISHED PEOPLE

Shenk was an old bachelor and had travelled widely when he was younger; he had investigated the lower reaches of the Yenisei, the Transbaikal area, the Amur basin, and even Sakhalin Island, searching for the remains of the mammoth in the tundra and studying the geology and flora of these regions. In the capital, he was now busy working on the materials he had accumulated.

He lived alone and very frugally, using most of his academician's salary to help young scientists and to subsidize expeditions to places in Siberia that he was interested in and to polar regions. Quite a large portion of his income had been spent on the expedition headed by Toll, whom he valued highly as an explorer, and later on the search for him.

Returning home from the meeting, Shenk looked up what he could on the enigmatic Onkilon tribe.

A few centuries ago they had inhabited the whole of the Chukotsky Peninsula. Later, the Chukchis pushed them to the shores of the Arctic Ocean. The Onkilons were quite different from the Chukchis in their build, the clothes they wore, their language, and way of life, their nearest kin being the Aleuts on Kadyak Island.

During his voyage in the *Vega* along northern Siberia in the region of capes Irkaipi,* Shelag, and Yakan, Nordenskiöld found numerous abandoned Onkilon dwellings. They were a kind of mudhouses sunk half-way into the ground; the roofs were made from whale ribs and were covered with mud. Excavations had brought to light stone and bone weapons—axes, knives, spearheads, arrows, scrapers, and so forth. Some even had bone or wooden handles, which, together with the thongs holding the arrow- and spearheads and axes, were preserved through the centuries thanks to the frost-bound soil. The Onkilons did not know the use of iron or other metals and, strictly speaking, were people of the Stone Age.

From the Chukchis, Wrangel learnt that the Onkilons left the shores of the Arctic Ocean after bitter warfare started by a feud between their chief, Krehoi, and the chief of the nomad Chukchi herders. Fleeing from pursuit, Krehoi and the remnants of his tribe at first fortified themselves on the rocks of Cape Severny, then crossed to Shalaurov Island, and, finally, boarding fifteen canoes, made for the land whose mountains are to be seen in the distance from Cape Yakan (i. e., Wrangel Island).

"This is all very scanty and contradictory," Shenk thought, closing the last book. "Still, it would be interesting to know what became of them."

In the course of the next few days Shenk kept his prom-

---

* In Nordenskiöld's map, Cape Irkaipi corresponds with Cape Rirkaipi, or Cape Severny in Russian maps.—*Ed.*

ise "to sound the ground at the Academy" and spoke with some academicians who were keen on studying polar regions, but he did not succeed in enlisting their support for a plan to send another expedition to find Sannikov Land and Baron Toll. There was no scientist of note who could be entrusted with such a misson and they felt it would be imprudent to turn money over to some dreamer, adding that in any event it would be embarrassing to ask for this money.

In the end, Shenk had to fall back on his own resources, deciding that he could risk a few thousand rubles on the venture, although he did not think that that sum would be enough.

"Ah, well," he told himself, "I can get the equipment for the young man gratis from various ministerial departments and the expedition itself must not last more than a year. In that time he will either find this land and the situation will be quite different, or he will satisfy himself that no such land exists and set our minds at rest."

PREPARATIONS

The young man appeared on the appointed day and hour. Shenks was waiting for him.

"I have read everything there is about the Onkilons," he said, "and I found it all very inconsistent. Unquestionably, this people existed and fought the Chukchis, leaving behind dwellings and stone and bone weapons. But nobody knows where they went. We can only think that they either perished on one of the islands as a result of the stern conditions of life on them, or that they remained on the mainland and were wiped out long ago by some epidemic."

"If they perished on the islands their remains would have been found," the young man contended. "People do not vanish into thin air. If they had died out, legends about them would have been current among their new neighbours—the Yakuts, Tunguses, and Lamuts. No such legends are current."

"Then where can they be?" Shenk exclaimed. "They cannot have gone to the moon!"

"Obviously, they are in Sannikov Land, where the migratory birds fly. Probably, the birds were their guides."

"If people could fly I would have readily believed you. But the Onkilons could not fly and had to reach this land either by water or across the ice."

"They did not go by water because they took their herds with them and that is more than any canoes can carry."

"But they could not have gone across the ice. According to all available data, the Arctic Ocean does not freeze over its whole length and breadth. There is always a more or less broad stretch of open sea at a certain distance from the shore. That is why not a single Chukchi—and they are a brave people—has been on Wrangel Island, and not a single hunter—they are not cowards either!—has ever reached Bennett Island. The loss of Baron Toll likewise proves that the ice is impassable."

"All this is very true," the young man calmly pointed out to the excited academician. "But may I remind you that the climate varies. Periods of cold weather alternate with spells of warmth, depending on the sun spots...."

"Yes, yes, I know all that!" Shenk said.

"We know that the Onkilons moved to the New Siberian Islands for their mudhouses and artefacts have been discovered there as well."

"I'll grant you that!"

"They found that the place was unsuitable, game was scarce, and birds were hunted out of existence. The prospect of starvation must have driven them farther, while the birds flying northward in huge flocks showed them that in that direction there was land where game was more plentiful. Suppose that just at that time there was a cold period and that as a result of a few exceptionally cold winters the sea was frozen over. Early in the spring, when the days are longer, the Onkilons safely crossed to Sannikov Land."

"And died there from cold and hunger because I cannot assume there is land on the 80th parallel where man can live. Geese and ducks may find food in the thawing tundra, but man...."

"Man catches these birds as well as walruses, seals, polar bears, and fish, and lives in Greenland, on the islands north of America, on Spitsbergen, and on Novaya Zemlya. He lives in the polar regions, even likes them, and is homesick when he is away."

"I see that you are fully convinced of the existence of Sannikov Land and that the Onkilons live there."

"I'm certain about the first point, and the only possible explanation for the disappearance of the Onkilons is that they are living in Sannikov Land."

"Unfortunately, the Academy does not share this view. I have made inquiries. My colleagues believe there is no such land and that Toll is dead."

"That's a pity, because the only place where Toll could have found safety is Sannikov Land. I don't insist that he is there, but it's possible and there's nowhere else where a search could be made for him."

"After all that has already been done I doubt if anyone

would now undertake to look for this land and for Toll even if we found the money."

"I'd go willingly and I think I can get reliable companions from among the exiles in Yakutsk Province and the hunters living on the northern shore."

"If you had the money how would you organize the expedition?"

"The men I have in mind are two exiles who also live in Kazachye. We often went over the details of such an expedition, platonically, of course, because we have no money apart from the tiny allowance the tsarist government fitfully gives its prisoners. We live quite like the natives—by hunting and fishing. Both my friends are young and exile has not demoralized them; work helps us to keep ourselves in hand and we are physically fit. Besides, I would engage two experienced hunters who have been to the New Siberian Islands and have dogs and the necessary equipment."

"You are right, it is impossible to do without them. What would be your next step?"

"We would cross the ice to Kotelny Island early in the spring, set up our base and storehouse there, and immediately make an attempt to penetrate farther north while the ice held."

"What if the sea is not frozen, as is doubtlessly the case?"

"To meet that contingency we'll have two light canoes and try to cross the open water in them. It cannot be wide for there's always ice near the shore. After that we'll transfer to our sledges and proceed across the ice to the land, investigate it, and return by the same route at the end of the summer."

"But by that time the open sea will be very wide and

I don't think you'll be safe in your heavily loaded canoes. And you must not forget that the close of summer is the season of snow-storms."

"If we fail to cross the sea in canoes, we'll winter in Sannikov Land and return early next spring."

"Do you know how much food your dogs will need for a whole year? The load will be too much for you."

"Of course. But I'm not going to take such a store with me. I expect there'll be plenty of game in Sannikov Land. During the summer we'll stock up enough food for the winter and for the return journey to our base."

"But suppose you do not find any land?"

"In that case we'll turn back to Kotelny immediately, spend the summer there and make for the mainland in the autumn as soon as the sea freezes over. Even in that event, which I think is quite improbable, we'll need a storehouse on Kotelny Island, bearing in mind the possibility that we'll not find enough game during the summer."

"Have you estimated what such an expedition will cost?"

"Not much. The three of us are not out to earn anything. All we'll need is food. The two hunters will naturally have to be paid, but they are modest people. The chief expense items will be dogs, food for them, sledges, canoes, guns and ammunition, and clothes. I've already priced things here and in Kazachye and I think that two or two and a half thousand rubles will be enough."

"That is not a very big sum of money!"

"The sledges they make in the north are not very strong, because they don't use the right kind of wood, we'll need the best we can get so that no time is wasted on repairs. The same is true for the guns and ammunition; the ones on sale here are much better and cheaper. All the rest can be got on the spot."

"I like your plan," Shenk said, "and I think I shall be able to let you have two and a half thousand rubles. But my conditions are that you will bring back from Sannikov Land collections of rocks and plants and, if possible, small animals together with notes on the flora, fauna, and climate. And, of course, notes about the Onkilons, if you find them. Are you sure you and your companions will be able to do that?"

"I think so. Naturally, none of us are real explorers, but we've all had some training; one of us is something of a geologist, the second is a botanist, while personally I am more interested in zoology and anthropology."

"Splendid! I shall see that the Academy provides you with a barometer, thermometers, compasses, and other instruments for scientific observations. Of course, you realize the importance of determining the latitude and longitude of several points in this land—if you find it," Shenk smiled, "and of making at least a rough map and of charting the route to it."

"That goes without saying. I'll do the charting myself. But who'll determine the latitudes and longitudes? None of us know how to do that."

"Oh, but that is not very difficult. You can take a few lessons at the Central Physical Observatory. I will write a note to the director. That will not take more than two or three weeks. Do you have the time? When are you planning to leave the city?"

"Let me see, it's the end of November. I'll have to leave in a month in order to reach Kazachye by the end of February and set out for the islands in the middle of March."

"People usually go there in April."

"Yes, but we'll have to go earlier so that the beginning

of April, when the sea is still frozen over, will find us ready to start for Sannikov Land."

"But will a month be enough to prepare and buy all you need?"

"Yes. I've already inquired at the workshops. The sledges can be made in two weeks. That will give me time to buy everything and take the course at the observatory."

"You will finish your business here, but you will still have plenty to do in Kazachye."

"If we decide the matter here and now I'll send a cable to Olekminsk and it will be forwarded by mail to Kazachye, so that my comrades can begin buying the clothes, dogs, and the food for the dogs."

"But they haven't got the money."

"They'll be given credit until I arrive. The people in Kazachye know us."

"How much money do you need now to pay the deposits for your purchases?"

"About five hundred rubles will cover everything for the time being."

"I shall give you that sum out of my own money and get the rest together with the instruments in two or three weeks."

Shenk made out a cheque and wrote a letter of recommendation to the director of the observatory. Handing them to the young man, he said:

"Come and see me in a fortnight at the same hour to tell me how your preparations are progressing."

"Allow me to express my delight that the question has been settled so quickly!" the young man exclaimed with deep emotion. "As I was coming up to see you I very much doubted the feasibility of my plans. But here everything

23

turned out so simply. You are giving a big sum of money to a total stranger, taking him at his word."

"I haven't lost my faith in people in spite of my grey hair," Shenk replied kindly. "I have lent a hand in many scientific undertakings and my trust has been very rarely imposed upon. Besides, I can judge a man almost at first sight. But you have reminded me that I do not know your name or the names of your friends. That is essential for the pass I shall get for you. You will need it for the authorities in Siberia. Will you please tell me your name."

"Matvei Goryunov, former student of Petersburg University, exiled to Yakutsk Province by administrative order. My friends are Semyon Ordin and Pavel Kostyakov, also former students. The first of the University, the second went to the Polytechnical Institute. We were exiled for five years for the student disorders in 1899."

"What was the crime that got you exiled so far like dangerous criminals?"

"We presided at meetings and were marked out as ringleaders. They wanted to press us into the army—there was an order to that effect, remember—but we resisted. So they sent us to live with the polar bears."

"Will your exile be up soon?"

"Mine's up and that is why I was allowed to go home to Vologda Gubernia under police surveillance; I'm here in the capital without permission, of course. My comrades will be released next year."

"That means we shall have to apply to the Governor to give them permission to go to Yakutsk Province."

"I don't think there'll be trouble over that."

24

THE START

A month later, supplied with money and documents, Goryunov departed for the east, taking with him instruments and other equipment, including three sturdy sledges and a big folding canoe, which could be assembled in less than half an hour. It could hold four men, three loaded sledges, and ten dogs, thus enabling the entire expedition to cross a stretch of open sea in two trips.

From Irkutsk began the long and tedious journey on horse-drawn sleighs down the Lena through Kachuga. Right up to Yakutsk, the chief town in the stern territory to which people were exiled, the road lay through the interminable, snow-blanketed corridor formed by the high and frequently precipitous banks of the frozen river. Farther, the road led across the lower reaches of the Aldan, the wild ravines of the sombre Verkhoyansk Mountains, and the hills and plains of the great Yana River basin to the river's mouth, where, on the edge of the world, was situated the village of Kazachye, its houses standing up to their roofs in snow. By the time Goryunov left Yakutsk, there was hardly any sun during the day, while beyond the range of mountains the polar night was already supreme; only the stars, the moon, and the northern lights illuminated the way—when no snow-storm raged.

Goryunov reached Kazachye at the close of February. His friends had prepared everything for the expedition— thirty dogs, a stock of *yukola* (dried fish) for them, provisions for members of the expedition, warm clothes, and skis. Two experienced hunters, a Yakut, Nikita Gorokhov, whose brother was with the ill-fated Toll expedition, and a Cossack, Kapiton Nikiforov, agreed to go with the expedition. Both had been to the New Siberian Islands, their last visit there being with the expedition that looked for Toll, and they knew the entire coast. They believed in the existence of Sannikov Land, and declared that they had seen it on clear days from the mountains on Kotelny Island. That mysterious land attracted them as much as it did Goryunov and his friends and they were glad of this opportunity of being the first to go there.

The village of Kazachye lies along the northern fringe of a forest on the flat, elevated right bank of the Yana River just above its delta where it crosses the 71st parallel; distributed on the elevation in disorder were a few Cossack huts and traders' houses, some Yakut *yurtas*, and a little church. In winter, smoke curling from the chimneys. sparks flying out of the *chuvals* (fire-places) in the *yurtas*, and the snow-plastered belfry were the only signs that this was a human habitation. The unbroken tundra fans out boundlessly to the north, east and west; in winter it becomes a white plain with hard, flat snow-drifts piled up and packed by violent blizzards. To the south looms the dark outline of a sparse forest of stunted trees, while the round Kular Mountains, which cut the mouth of the Yana off from the rest of the world, as it were, can be seen on the horizon on a fine day.

All the final preparations were completed in two weeks and the expedition set out in the middle of March when the day is already eleven hours long. Travelling in three sledges, the members of the expedition were accompanied to the New Siberian Islands by five teamsters on sledges with reserve food for the dogs, provisions and various supplies intended for the storehouse on the islands and for use on the way there.

The route led north-eastward down one of the arms of the Yana delta, past the deserted site of the old settle-

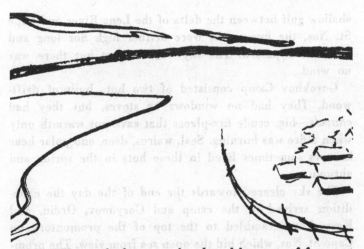

ment of Ustyansk that was abandoned because of frequent floods. The mouth of the river was reached in two days, thanks to the smooth road. Unnoticeably, the low-lying plain gave way to the surface of the sea, which likewise was white and even. Islands resembling flat knolls dominated the white expanse here and there, while to the right were capes jutting out far northward. The expedition moved in that direction, crossing bays and seeking to camp on the shore at least every other night in order to have the opportunity of building a fire with the drift-wood carried down from the south by the Yana and cast up by the sea.

In that way they passed Yarok Island, Cape Maniko on which stood a solitary *yurta*, the wide Selyakhsk Gulf, Cape Turuktak, Vankin Bay, and Cape Darichan. From there they followed the shore to Cape Churkin, crossed the Gulf of Abelyakhsk and stopped at Gorokhov Camp on the southern side of the long Cape St. Nos.

This journey of about two hundred kilometres from the mouth of the Yana took four days because the expedition moved unhurriedly so as not to tire the dogs. In the huge, shallow gulf between the delta of the Lena River and Cape St. Nos, the hummocks were neither high nor long and could be bypassed. The sky was overcast but there was no wind.

Gorokhov Camp consisted of two huts built of driftwood. They had no windows or stoves, but they had *chuvals*—big, crude fire-places that gave out warmth only when a fire was burning. Seal, walrus, deer, and polar bear hunters sometimes lived in these huts in the spring and autumn.

The sky cleared towards the end of the day the expedition arrived in the camp and Goryunov, Ordin, and Kostyakov scrambled to the top of the promontory on Cape St. Nos, which hid the open sea from view. The promontory consisted of precipitous black basalt, which, in this area, once gushed out of the earth's bosom in a fiery stream. They clambered up the rocks to the flat top and gazed at the frozen sea, which stretched before them as a dazzling-white plain criss-crossed by hummocks and thickly covered with snow.

Directly ahead they saw Bolshoi Lyakhov Island—a flat mound with four peaks—faintly outlined on the northern horizon; here and there black spots on the white background betrayed cliffs and precipices. This was the nearest of the New Siberian Islands and was famous among hunters for its abundance of mammoth tusks. As the crow flies, the island was nearly seventy kilometres away, and the route of our explorers lay across it.

The sun sank beyond the horizon. A cold wind began to blow from the ice-field and the travellers quickly returned to the camp, where in one of the huts a fire was burning, a kettle boiling, and the dinner ready. Plates were laid on a travelling chest; smaller chests served as chairs. Gorokhov and Nikiforov, pipes between their teeth, were impatiently awaiting the return of their companions so that they could have their dinner. They had finished tidying up the hut, unharnessed the dogs and prepared the sleeping-bags. The sound of conversation and laughter came from the second hut, where the five teamsters were quartered.

At sunrise on the following morning, a caravan of eight sledges pulled by eighty dogs left the mainland, skirting the cliffs at the tip of Cape St. Nos and heading north across the ice-bound sea. The teams made such rapid progress over the smooth stretches that the men had a hard time keeping up with them on their skis. But where the route was blocked by hummocks, the pace fell off considerably; at each hummock a passage was chosen, then the sledges had to be hauled separately, the men helping the dogs, some by pushing the sledge from behind, others guiding it at the sides and supporting it with their skiing sticks. When no convenient passage could be found, a way had to be cut with axes; the ice, stiffened by winter frosts of 30-40 degrees below zero, jingled like glass. While the men hacked at the ice, the dogs curled up as though by command, knowing full well that the ring of the axes meant there was a quarter of an hour's hard work ahead.

Now faster, now slower, averaging about seven kilometres an hour, the expedition covered half the distance to the island by midday. Without unharnessing the dogs, they stopped and ate a meal of cold meat, biscuits, and hot tea. They did not build a fire. Goryunov had brought thermos flasks from the capital so that during the stops no time would be lost on lighting a fire and boiling water. The teamsters were delighted with these remarkable bottles and with the tea that was hot without a fire, and they drank it with especial satisfaction, as though it were a sacred drink. They refused to believe that no witchcraft was involved when in a frost of 30 degrees scalding-hot tea was poured out of a vessel that was cold to the touch. During the expedition's first stop for lunch on the day it left Kazachye, Goryunov, with a twinkle in his eye, announced he would boil tea faster on the snow than the teamsters would over a fire. When they hung their kettle over the fire, he got out the thermos flasks, half buried them in the snow and five minutes later poured hot tea for the dumbfounded Yakuts. Gorokhov and Nikiforov, who had been initiated into the secret, rolled with laughter at the exclamations of the teamsters and at the expressions on their faces.

After breakfast they resumed their journey. They drew closer to the island, which towered above the ice-field and shut out the northern horizon; amid the gleaming snow they could make out some dark boulders and black spots on the low-lying, abrupt shore. At sunset, crossing the last hummock, they developed a headlong pace—the dogs knew that food and rest awaited them on land and when a hut, looking black at the base of a cliff, loomed into view, all eighty began to bark in a chorus and broke into a mad gallop.

But near the shore they had to slow down, for the storms which had raged here in the autumn when the sea froze over had heaped up an ice wall and the sledges had to be pulled over it one by one before the expedition finally got to the Maloye Zimovye Camp. This was a hut built by Sannikov, the famous hunter and companion and guide of Hedenström, who, at the beginning of the 19th century, brought back the first description of this island. The century-old hut had suffered practically no damage in this cold climate. The salt-saturated drift-wood logs had only turned black and were covered with lichens here and there, but inside they were in excellent condition. Many hunters had taken refuge in this hut on their way to and from the island, and each had contributed towards the repair of the door, which hung on leather hinges, and the roof, which needed additions of earth from time to time. Near the hut somebody had even left some drift-wood that could be used as fuel. This was very opportune for it obviated the need to look for fuel along the shore or digging it out of the snow.

A fire was soon blazing by the hut, its red flames lighting up the high wall of ice stretching far in both directions.

GRAVEYARD OF MAMMOTHS

Bolshoi Lyakhov Island, or Blizhny as it is sometimes called, is remarkable for its geological structure. Its four flat rugged eminences or rather groups of eminences are of granite, while the rest of the island consists of soft Quaternary deposits. The numerous rivulets and streams rushing down the elevated ground and cutting deep into the yielding soil had broken the island up into a multitude of almost completely barren hills and hillocks. During the short summer, the island appears as a moss-overgrown clayey waste with snow-drifts in the deeper ravines and valleys facing the north.

These soft deposits, extending down to the very shore, were broken by the surf into long or short sheer, even overhanging, cliffs with the valleys of rivulets and streams cutting through them. These layers of soil are frost-bound from top to bottom, the summer thaw affecting only a negligible depth; the thawed mass either slides into the sea or, washed by the waves at the base, collapses. In this fashion, the island is being gradually destroyed by the sea. Had it not been for the eternal frost which is considerably slowing down this process of erosion, the island, with the exception of its granite kernel, would have been obliterated long ago.

Great numbers of mammoths' tusks are found in this soil, while here and there are unearthed whole carcasses of these animals and of their contemporaries—the woolly rhinoceros, the primitive ox, the Canadian deer, and many others; the eternal frost has preserved these carcasses complete with fur, tusks or horns, and intestines. However, as a consequence of the summer thaw, which penetrates to a certain depth, the streams and rivulets wash the carcasses and separate bones and tusks out of the ground and carry them down to the sea. Similarly, as a result of the thaw and of erosion, the cliffs on the shore yield up the carcasses and the bones of extinct animals, which in the end are likewise swallowed up and given a second burial by the sea. Frequently, these carcasses are devoured by carrion-eating birds and beasts, which do not scorn meat that had lain frozen for thousands of years.

Every spring, Bolshoi Lyakhov Island attracted hunters from the mainland, who scoured the level shore and the mouths and valleys of the streams for mammoths' tusks released from the frozen ground in the course of the previous year and still sticking out of the thawing soil or thrown up on the shore. Splendidly preserved by the frost, these tusks are as valuable as the ivory tusks of elephants. The hunters sold them to the local traders or to merchants from the interior, who took them to the fair at Yakutsk from where they were sent on farther into Siberia and to

Russia and used in the manufacture of combs, cuff-links, caskets, billiard balls, and so forth.

The hunters had no use for the bones of other fossil animals; scientists studying the fauna of past ages were the only people interested in them. Brought to light here and there by the thaw, the carcasses of these animals sometimes attracted attention, but for the most part they perished because the hunters neither realized their value nor knew how to measure and make a record of the specimens or to preserve them against spoilage.

Goryunov and his two friends had been to the island once before with some tusk hunters and the large number of tusks had excited their curiosity. But they could not explain why there were so many of them and, quite naturally, in Kazachye they did not find any pertinent literature.

In the capital, Goryunov had used some of his time to read up on the subject and had brought one or two books with him. Now the travellers decided to spend a day on the island in order to examine the cliffs along the shore more closely and, at the same time, give their companions and dogs a rest.

Next morning, accompanied by Gorokhov, the three friends set out to investigate the shore. The summer's work of destruction by the sun and the sea had not yet commenced although the slanting rays of the low-hanging sun had already given the cliffs a foretaste of what was to come. The cliffs were from twenty to twenty-five metres high and festooned along their top with jagged masses of solidified snow that resembled the icicles left hanging from a roof after a fierce snow-storm. The only difference was that since storms were very frequent in winter, the "icicles" here were between four and six metres long, twenty to forty metres wide and one or two metres thick. Below them began the overhanging face of the precipice the top of which was composed of alternating layers of ice, sand and clay. Along the precipice masses of ice fashioned into walls of varying thickness stretched deep into the island. The gaps between these walls were filled in by narrow interchanging deposits of clay, fine sand, and ice. On the edge of the precipice, wherever the pendent snow broke off, the ice and the alluvium were covered with sand, clay or peat which ended at the ground surface with a layer of black tundra soil under yet another tier of packed snow.

The lower part of the precipice was covered with a hard, sloping blanket of snow that had piled up in the shelter of the shore during the winter. Eight to ten metres high, this slope afforded an approach to the precipice itself and showed that the upper layers of ice and the deposits of soil between them rested on solid ice which comprised the island's foundation and stood twelve to fifteen metres above sea level.

This investigation revealed that the fossil animals were not in the ice but in the deposits of soil between it. This was confirmed by Gorokhov, who had been to the island on many previous occasions and had come across a few whole carcasses; the latter had likewise been locked in the soil deposits.

After examining some ten kilometres of the shore and making sure that the composition of the ground was the same throughout, the travellers returned to Maloye Zimovye for dinner, bringing with them several bones, including the skull of a rhinoceros and a mammoth's tusk.

During dinner Goryunov told his friends how Toll accounted for the formation of this strange island and for the numerous carcasses of prehistoric animals on it. According to that scholar, the ice on the island, surviving until the

time of the great glaciation, was the remains of a vast glacier. Much reduced at the close of the period of glaciation, the surface of this glacier was furrowed by streams of melted ice which ran down from the more elevated parts.

the water depositing sand and silt in the resulting hollows and channels. Plant fossils found in those deposits showed that in those days the vegetable kingdom here was much richer than it is now, when it consists of nothing but lichens, moss, and dwarf flowering plants; formerly, in spite of the neighbouring ice, there were alder groves, the trees attaining a height of four to six metres, willows, and numerous cereal plants. The post-ice-age climate was, evidently, milder than it is today, because in our day these plants grow only on the mainland, a few degrees to the south. The food remains in the stomachs and teeth of mammoths indicate that these animals subsisted on cereal plants, while the position of the carcasses in the deposits of soil between the ice prove that the mammoth once lived on the island.

The reason Bolshoi Lyakhov Island became a favourite haunt of various mammals of the post-ice age is that at the beginning of the Quaternary period the mainland of Siberia extended considerably farther north than it does now and included the New Siberian Islands. At the end of the last glacial period, when the mammoth, the woolly rhinoceros, and the primitive ox still roamed in Siberia and primitive man had already made his appearance, great pieces of this northern perimeter of the mainland broke off and, in some parts, sank in the sea. By degrees, the elevated sections became free of ice and grew over with vegetation. Judging from the remains of flora found in the soil, the climate was warmer in those days. Driven by the advancing waters, the animals sought refuge in the highlands. Bolshoi Lyakhov Island, like the other islands of the New Sibirian Archipelago, was one of these highlands. A particularly large number of animals, instinctively moving southwards, collected on it because it was the southernmost place in the archipelago. But it was already cut off from the mainland by a broad sheet of water and the animals could go no farther. There were so many of them that there was not enough food for all and the island became their graveyard.

The number of tusks brought to the Yakutsk fair in former days was evidence that there had been great herds of mammoths on the island. Statistics tell us that sixteen to twenty-two tons of tusks, or an average of nineteen tons, were brought to the fair annually. A pair of tusks from a big mammoth weigh 80 kilograms. Consequently, the tusks of 240 mammoths were on sale at the fair every year. Most of them came from Bolshoi Lyakhov Island, where the sea washed the ice wall, releasing innumerable tusks from the grip of the ice and soil and leaving them exposed on the shore. That was where the hunters collected them for it was much easier to do that than to dig for them in the frozen ground.

Thus, at some time towards the close of the last glacial period, when this part of the mainland was already an island with a wide sound separating it from the continent, many hundreds of mammoths wandered about on it, gradually dying off from hunger. Some were caught in the mud streams that formed during the summer when the ice melted, others, lured on by the grass, floundered in the marshy soil, and still others fell into the cracks in the ice, on which they sought respite from annoying gnats and gadflies, and sand and silt covered their carcasses. These carcasses were preserved by the eternal frost that set in at the end of the ice age, while those that lay exposed on the ground were eaten by wild beasts and birds, the only remains being the bones, which crumbled into dust with time, and the more durable tusks. That was why the island became the principal depository of mammoths' tusks and attracted hunters from the entire northern coast of Siberia.

"I must say," Goryunov concluded, "that not all scholars share Toll's views on the origin of the fossil ice on Lyakhov Island. For example, Bunge, who studied the island at the same time Toll did, believes that it is not a remnant of a former glacier but a later formation and that similar ice is still forming in the whole of North Siberia through the freezing of the water that in spring finds its way into the deep crevices in the frozen soil, which appear in the autumn as a result of frost and become filled with snow in the winter. Accordingly, this fossil ice belongs to a younger age than the age when mammoths lived."

"How did they get into the ice in that case?" Kostyakov asked.

"The fact is that they are not in the ice but in the tundra soil between the ice. Toll noted and stressed this point."

"What you say means that the mammoths wandered into the tundra and got stuck in the marshy soil. Was it such a quagmire in their lifetime? So far as we know there were some pretty big trees and luxuriant grass growing in the tundra," Ordin remarked.

"If we accept Bunge's view, then what you say is right," Goryunov replied. "But I am inclined to accept Toll's hypothesis. In the cliffs we examined today, we saw that it is not the ice that packs the gaps in the tundra soil, but, on the contrary, that this soil fills in the hollows and crevices in the ice."

"Is there any other data, apart from what is known about Lyakhov Island, to show that North Siberia was an ice-field?" Ordin asked.

"The whole point is that there is. Toll found old moraines on the Taimyr Peninsula, along the Anabar River, and on Kotelny and the New Siberian Islands. Middendorf found so-called erratic masses of rock all over the Taimyr tundra."*

"I've read somewhere that there are other ways in which fossil ice forms," Ordin observed. "In the tundra, small lakes often freeze to the bottom and if in the spring the ice gets a covering of silt which prevents it from melting it becomes fossilized. A big snow-drift somewhere on the slope of a hill, at the foot of a precipice overhanging a river, or in a ravine may likewise be accidentally covered with sand and silt and slowly turn to ice which will hold until its protective crust is destroyed."

"Quite true," Goryunov said, "and I can tell you of yet another way. I mean the overlying ice on the banks of the Siberian rivers, which, sometimes, is extremely thick, long and wide. In springtime, this ice, too, may get a coat of silt and sand."

"The carcasses of animals that lived in the same age as the mammoth have been found in this fossil overlying ice, as well. But we must admit that the problem of fossil ice still has many dark sides that await further investigation. So far nobody has made this the subject of special and all-round research."

"I think that the problem of the conditions of life and of the extinction of the mammoth and its contemporaries has likewise been insufficiently explained and deserves further study," Ordin put in. "Take, for instance, the question of why they went on to the glaciers or climbed on to the overlying ice."

"That is easily explained. They were seeking salvation from gnats, gadflies and other insects, which, apparently,

* According to new data, the whole of North Siberia down to the 60th-62nd parallels was buried under a thick layer of ice.—*Ed.*

were already numerous. Even today you'll find the reindeer doing exactly the same in summer, finding relief on unmelted snow-drifts, overlying ice or in ice-fields along the sea-shore; after eating their fill, they stand for hours in these cold places, dozing or chewing the cud. Of course, apart from this, there is much we don't know about the mammoth. The extinction of these animals is believed to be due to a worsening of the climate. But that did not take place at once; the process extended over long ages. Consequently, extinction must be preceded by degeneration and diminution. That side of the problem has not been dealt with at all and in order to do so enormous collections of fossil bones are needed."

"It might be a good idea to take up these problems," Kostyakov said.

"Next year, when we return to Russia, we'll go back to the University and...."

AMIDST THE NEW SIBERIAN ISLANDS

At the first hint of daylight on the following morning, the travellers resumed their journey. For about five kilometres they moved westwards within sight of the southern shore of the island; in all respects, the ice cliffs there resembled the ones they had seen the day before. Farther on began the passage across the long western peninsula with the rocky Mount Kigilyakh, one of the four mountains of the peninsula, at its extreme end. This mountain's strange position far out at sea is best of all explained by the fact that with the exception of a long and narrow isthmus the part of the island on which it had once rested had been destroyed by the elements. The travellers had to cross this isthmus, for that shortened their journey by some thirty kilometres.

The mountain was named Kigilyakh because there were many tall, fantastically shaped pillars that had been hewn out of the granite by erosion. Local hunters imagined these pillars to be the figures of petrified people (*kigi*—man; *kigilyakh*—human) and stood in superstitious awe of the mountain.

They were extremely displeased when Bunge chipped samples of rock from the boulders and told him that that was blasphemy and would not go unpunished. They warned him that anyone climbing the mountain would be instantly enveloped in a thick fog and find his death at the bottom of a crevice. Indeed, sudden fogs are very frequent here and the prediction of superstitious people could very well come true. Bunge did not reach the summit and his companions offered up copper and silver coins as a sacrifice to the mountain.

The passage across the isthmus gave the travellers no end of trouble: the sledges had to be dragged up the side of a steep ravine cut into a cliff and, after a few kilometres of hilly terrain, lowered down the other side which was just as steep.

On the isthmus, the teamsters turned towards Mount Kigilyakh, bowed and prayed for a happy journey

and good hunting. They could not sacrifice coins to it since with its gloomy pillars, that were partially snowed under and resembled a gigantic ruin, the mountain was about twelve kilometres away and so they limited themselves to a pinch of tobacco, blowing it off their fingers in the mountain's direction. More worldly-wise than his ignorant kinsmen, Gorokhov did not share in the rite but gave Nikiforov a reproachful look when the latter said with a derisive smile:

"What a waste of tobacco, the superstitious beggars!"

After the sledges were lowered, the travellers proceeded across the ice in a north-easterly direction along the north-western shore of the island, which on a map resembles an irregular triangle with sides about a hundred kilometres long and the apex pointing to the north. The going was not hard for most of the hummocks ran parallel with the shore and the travellers could keep to the level ice between them, now and then crossing transversal ridges. The teamsters urged the dogs on to a faster pace, glancing frequently at the sky. The weather had been calm and sunny ever since they had left Kazachye, but now it was beginning to spoil; all day the sun had been shining through a film of light clouds while bursts of wind blew from the north-west. They had to hurry to avoid being caught in a snow-storm away from any suitable camping site. They had not taken any fuel with them, for they had expected to find drift-wood on the shore. But in the twenty-kilometre stretch from the isthmus the shore was lined with nothing but ice-coated cliffs. At one place, Gorokhov drew his companions' attention to a cliff with a hardly noticeable gully, which at one time had carried all the water from the fairly big Lake Chastny to the sea. The lake had been a favourite summer retreat of wild geese during the moulting period and had attracted many hunters who brought the geese down by the hundred with clubs. But when the lake disappeared, the geese found other summer homes and the hunters lost a source that had provided them and their dogs with food during the hunting season.

Beyond a stream called Bolshoye Zimovye, the shore of the island was flat, rising gently into the interior, where in the distance loomed the central Mount Khaptagai. From the mouth of this stream, the travellers should have turned gradually away from the shore and made for the southern tip of the next island in the north—Maly Lyakhov, the outlines of which could already be seen. But the teamsters, glancing at the western horizon, preferred to hug the shore and pressed the dogs on to an even greater effort.

"They want to reach Cape Vankin before the storm breaks out," Gorokhov explained after exchanging a few words with them. "We'll find better shelter against the storm on the lee side of the cape and there's plenty of drift-wood there."

After midday, when they were already past the little Bludnaya River, the gusts of west wind began to blow with increasing frequency, raising snow-dust off the hummocks. Gathering in clouds, it raced through the air or rushed with snake-like motions over the surface of the snow. By now the sun was almost completely hidden by this thin film of dust.

It grew colder. The dogs raced over the flat stretches and it was all the men on skis could do to keep up, recovering their wind only at the hummocks while helping to haul the sledges.

Soon, in the intervals when the wind abated and visibility was somewhat restored, they could see the dark silhouette of Cape Vankin. They sped past the mouth of the small Tirskaya River and began to skirt the long cape. They were just in time: in the west the sky had grown ominously leaden and the gusts of wind were becoming sharp; the snow lashed the men's faces, biting into their eyes; the dogs ran on, their heads lowered and turned to the right.

They began to breathe more easily when they reached the sheltered side of the cape: here there was practically no wind. A few metres overhead the sky was milky white from the clouds of rushing snow and the only flakes falling on the ground were those that accidentally were torn away from this stream.

It was still early but there could be no question of continuing the journey, for immediately beyond the cape began the white wall of the snow-storm. The big bay, which stretched to the east of the cape, was likewise enveloped in the white gloom: only a narrow strip was protected by the cape. There was no habitation and the travellers decided to pitch their tents against the side of a cliff on the flattest piece of ground they could find amidst the heaps of soil that had slid down the cliff during the summer. The teamsters chose differently: using their axes, they made a cave in the ice. Gorokhov advised the travellers to do the same because the wind was liable to change direction and no shelter would then be had from the cape. The snow-storm, he said, might last a day or two.

Not much time was needed to dig caves in the close-packed snow, which broke off in great blocks; a wall was made of these blocks at the entrances as protection in the event the wind changed direction. Drift-wood was found in the hummocks and snow-drifts along the shore. When that was done they unloaded the sledges and installed themselves in the two small but snug shelters. The dogs were already curled up among the loose lumps of soil behind the hummocks and sledges and resting in expectation of their dinner. To prevent the snow caves from melting, the fires were lit in the open, in the shelter of blocks of packed snow.

The snow-storm raged all night and lasted until noon of the following day.

They prepared to leave as soon as the wind showed signs of dropping. From Cape Vankin they headed north-westwards for the tip of Maly Lyakhov Island, which was about ten kilometres away. Much smaller than Bolshoi Lyakhov, this island is forty or fifty kilometres long from north to south and is very flat and low with only a few small hills scattered here and there. The travellers skirted it from the west, hugging the shore, and halted for the night still some way from the northern extremity. Here, the only shelter against inclement weather were the icy hummocks, but, fortunately, the night was calm.

The next lap of the journey was the most difficult one. It lay across the nearly seventy-kilometre gap between Maly and Kotelny islands. The difficulty was that an east-to-west current flowed through the gap, preventing the sea from freezing until late autumn. But even when the ice did form, storms frequently broke it. That caused the ice-field to move every now and then, as a consequence of which it was extremely hummocky.

The travellers took a supply of fuel to meet the very probable contingency of having to spend the night on the sea and moved on in a north-westerly direction towards Cape Medvezhy at the foot of Kotelny Island. The island could be seen on the horizon in the shape of a huge, flat, bulging mass that resembled an overturned cauldron, which accounted for the name (*kotel* is the Russian for "cauldron"). This "cauldron" is dominated by the slightly conical Mount Malakatyn, its highest point.

The first twenty kilometres were covered quite easily; the few hummocks in this stretch were small. But in the zone of the current, which in the autumn is full of unfrozen patches of water, they were formidable. Some of the ridges and ice heaps were more than twenty metres high. The road had to be cut with axes and the sledges dragged with plaited leather thongs for the dogs were too exhausted to pull them by themselves. Some of the hummocks held them up from half an hour to an hour.

Sundown found them only half-way across the gap, but the worst stretch was now behind. They stopped for the night before a huge hummock which they were too tired to climb, pitching their tents in the shelter of big blocks of ice. After a quick supper they soon fell fast asleep, for it had been a hard day.

Around midnight, Gorokhov was awakened by a loud clapping noise overhead.

"Can it be a storm again?" he muttered and was about to turn over on his other side when the tent was suddenly jerked so violently that he thought it would burst all its seams.

"Looks like trouble," he said to himself. He got out of his sleeping-bag and crawled to the entrance, struggled with the fastenings and looked out. There was a biting frost with crazily swirling snow. The tent quivered and shook as if about to take wing and fly away.

"Can't be helped! The others'll have to be wakened and the tent steadied," the hunter decided, "or there'll be hell to pay."

He shook his companions awake and all five crawled out

46

of the tent and drove the iron pegs holding the flaps deeper into the ice. Then, still crawling, they dragged up the loaded sledges, placing one on each of three sides of the tent, throwing ropes across the latter and tying it to the sledges. All this was done in the face of a stiff wind, which kept flinging them to the ground and made breathing difficult; the darkness was impenetrable and it was enough to take three steps to lose sight of each other. Above the howling and whistling of the wind, which groaned as it blew through the cracks in the hummocks, could be heard the ringing of axes; that sound came from the teamsters' tent some ten paces away and it meant that they, too, had awakened and were securing their tent.

After doing everything possible they returned to the tent but it took them some time to recover from the chill and go to sleep. Besides, snow had got into their sleeves and collars. When it began to grow light, Goryunov, who was the first to get up, looked out. The storm was still at its height, but the tent hardly quivered at all; held down by snow on the outside, the flaps bulged inwards like the stomach of a huge animal and threatened to burst under the weight. It was necessary to crawl out again and clear the snow away. Goryunov did not wake his friends and set about clearing away the snow by himself. The nearest heaps of ice could already be seen through the white gloom; the wind seemed to be weaker and the snow was coming down thicker and more gently.

A muffled scream, followed by a groan, made Goryunov turn towards the tent of the teamsters. A moment ago it had been possible to make it out, but now it could not be seen. Without wasting time, Goryunov ran to it, stumbling at every step over the dogs lying in the snow. Old and unreliable, the tent had given way under the weight of the snow; it tore along the ridge and collapsed on the sleeping teamsters, pinning them down under their blankets and muffling their groans; they were choking for want of air.

Goryunov ran to his tent, woke up his friends, grabbed a spade, hurried to the teamsters and began digging them out of their snowy grave. He was soon joined by Gorokhov and Ordin. They pulled away the tent flies together with the snow and freed the teamsters; one of them was unconscious.

It grew quite light while they were rescuing the teamsters; the snow-storm was evidently stopping: it was snowing lightly, the wind was blowing in bursts and the sun was peeping out in the east. They dug out the dogs and the sledges, had some hot tea and continued on their way. The new snow somewhat hampered their advance for it had smoothed out the rugged ground and the dogs and sledges frequently fell into deep cracks. Two of the men were obliged to go ahead on skis to pick a road for the teams.

The hump of Kotelny Island was already filling a quarter of the horizon. The travellers could distinguish the rows of flat-topped hills and the cliffs on the shore, along which boulders loomed black against the snow. To the right, on the far side of a narrow opening, was Faddeyevsky Island, indistinctly outlined on the horizon.

Towards sunset, after negotiating some very rough ground, they reached Cape Medvezhy and proceeded at a fast pace for another five kilometres to the hut on the south-eastern shore. Unlike Lyakhov Island, there were no ice barriers. The shore consisted of hard rock which either stood in a wall above the ice or, buried under snow-drifts, sloped towards the sea.

ALONG KOTELNY ISLAND

The hut on the shore was half ruined. Hunters rarely visited this island; it was difficult to reach and game was scarce. Restored only by scientific expeditions, the hut was left without care for years on end, with the result that the roof began to leak and cave in and the walls collapse. The travellers did not find it worth their while to repair the hut for the sake of a single night's lodging and since the weather was fine, they camped in the open.

At dawn they were all awakened by frantic barking.

"Must be bears!" Gorokhov exclaimed, rushing out of the tent half dressed and with a gun in his hand.

The others ran after him and an interesting scene met their eyes. Standing irresolutely about ten paces from the dogs were three polars bears; all the eighty dogs were straining at their leashes, getting up on their hind legs, barking, whining or howling. The din was terrific, enough to wake the dead. Evidently, the bears were singling out their victims, manoeuvring to safeguard their flanks and rear. They were already making for the dogs of the farthest team, which in their excitement had got entangled in their leashes and were lying in a helpless heap. At that moment shots rang out from both tents and one of the bears, struck by an explosive bullet from Ordin's gun, slumped to the ground; the other two took to their heels, leaving a scarlet trail behind them. The teamsters, Gorokhov and Goryunov, started off in pursuit and soon overtook one of them. Evidently, its wound was worse than its companion's. The third bear disappeared behind a hummock.

The travellers now found themselves in possession of plenty of fresh meat for themselves and their dogs and this allowed them to leave a greater supply of *yukola* in the storehouse they proposed to set up at the northern tip of the island.

The bears were soon flayed and cut up and the caravan resumed its northward advance. It took them another four days to reach the northern extremity of the island, for though the island itself was about a hundred and eighty kilometres long, the shore line extended for more than two hundred kilometres. Inland, it was a mountainous, rocky tundra.

When the travellers passed the mouth of the Reshetnikov River and were nearing the end of the last lap along the shore, the weather changed for the worse. The sky rapidly grew overcast, a fresh south-westerly wind rose and it began to snow. They pushed on through the snowstorm, for there was not much of a frost and the goal, the northern tip of Kotelny, was almost in sight.

This was a flat cape, close to which Toll's expedition had built a hut that was meant to serve as a storehouse in the event they would have to spend the winter on the island. Goryunov planned to use that hut as a base for the same purpose and as a store for the food his party would need for the return to the mainland.

The hut was in good repair and in it the travellers unexpectedly found provisions that had been left when the search for Toll was given up—quite a large quantity of *yukola*, some cases of canned food, a big tin of bear fat, a few boxes of biscuits and even the frozen carcass of a deer. During the summer, the islands in this archipelago are the grazing ground of big herds of wild deer which come from the mainland over the ice early in the spring and leave late in the autumn, when the sea freezes over. They make this long journey in spite of the danger that in the autumn the thin ice can easily be broken by the wind, because they feel freer on the islands and more secure against their chief enemy—man. Besides, there are no annoying insects, which on the mainland make life miserable for man and beast.

The deer had already begun their migration to the islands; there were tracks in the snow in various places near Maly Lyakhov, showing that the main herds could be expected soon. The teamsters had planned on hunting deer before returning to the mainland and, accordingly, after helping to unload the sledges they parted with our travellers and rode off along the eastern shore of Kotelny, intending to use the remaining daylight to find a spot which they could use conveniently as a base. Goryunov gave them a letter for Shenk, describing the course of the expedition. That was his last opportunity to send a letter and it was a sad thought that it would reach the capital only sometime towards autumn.

With heavy hearts the travellers said good-bye to the teamsters, following them with their eyes until they vanished behind a turning in the shore. That broke the last thread linking them with the rest of the world. Now they were alone, left to their own resources on the threshold of a land where they could not count on assistance from any quarter.

In order to distract their minds from these melancholy thoughts, they began to sort out and pack the provisions and equipment which they intended for the store so that on the following morning, weather permitting, they could hurry on northwards. March was almost over, the day was more than thirteen hours long, and in calm weather the sun was hot enough to spoil the ice. After the cases were sorted, marked and stowed away, there was still room enough in the hut for the travellers.

By midnight, the stillness that had reigned during the evening was broken by a screeching wind. The tempera ture fell to 40 degrees below zero and a snow-storm broke out. At dawn, Gorokhov and Nikiforov, who went outside to feed the dogs, returned chilled to the marrow and declared that it was impossible to go on. In such weather there was nothing to do except to stay under blankets for it was no pleasure at all to sit in the hut, which was dim and smoky from the fire in the *chuval*. The only need to get up was when food had to be prepared.

On the second day of this storm-enforced idleness, Niki-forov, who was lighting a fire in the *chuval*, found a strange billet among the firewood in the hut. It was flat, with a finely ribbed surface, slightly curved and had a sharp end. He turned it over in his hands and, doubting its worth as fuel, showed it to Gorokhov.

"That must be the claw of an *exekyu*," the Yakut said, looking closely at it.

"Claw! But it's only a little shorter than my arm," the Cossack exclaimed in surprise. "To have such huge claws your bird must be bigger than this hut. Where does it live?"

"The old men say that it lived on Kotelny Island. The first people to hunt there saw it. Do you think that's true, Matvei Ivanovich?"

Goryunov examined the find, laughed and passed it on to Ordin, saying:

"This is the horn of a fossil woolly rhinoceros, which was a contemporary of the mammoth. I saw horns like that in the Yakutsk Museum and in Petersburg, in the Museum of the Academy of Sciences."

"Then can you explain why people say it's the claw of a giant bird?"

"Because its form and ribbed surface make it look

more like a claw and because that is what the Yukagirs, Lamuts and Tunguses believe. Moreover, a hundred years ago that opinion was shared by certain scholars. Hedenström, who was the first to explore the New Siberian Islands, mentions these claws in his *Excerpts About Siberia* in the full conviction that they belonged to birds. On Kotelny Island, Toll visited Exekyu Hill near Dragotsennaya Stream, where, his guides assured him, this bird lived. They told him that it was so big that when it rose into the air it hid the sun. When the first hunters to reach Kotelny approached the hill, the bird screamed 'Mauk, mauk!' and flew away. On the hill they found an egg shell and some huge feathers. But the bird was never seen again."

"People say it had two heads," Gorokhov put in.

"Yes, I know. The most interesting part of it is that the Yukagirs think the double-headed eagle on our coins is the *exekyu*. Wrangel mentions some extraordinary legends that are current among those people. They say that a rhinoceros' skull, which is sometimes found with the horn, is the skull of an *exekyu*."

"In Siberia, the natives have quite a few fables about the mammoth as well," Ordin remarked.

That day the travellers whiled the time away by questioning Gorokhov and Nikiforov about the mammoth and other extinct animals and telling them what they themselves had read about these prehistoric animals.

ACROSS THE POLAR SEA

The storm, which held the travellers captive for three days, finally abated. The bright spring sun showed itself early in the morning and shed a dazzling light on the snow on the Polar Sea, which stretched to the north, east and west from the northern cape of Kotelny Island. Everybody had to put on snow-goggles to protect themselves against the painful blindness which in the extreme north afflicts many people in spring. At that time of the year the sun hangs low in the sky and the myriad of snow-flakes on the ice-field, especially after a fresh fall, reflect its rays as though they were millions of tiny mirrors. Eyes become inflamed from this brilliant light and blindness sets in for several days and is accompanied by shooting pains from which the sufferer knows no rest. The darkest glasses are frequently inadequate if the gap between the face and the glass is open. Instead of glasses, the natives wear a little board with a narrow slit to let through the minimum of light, but even that does not always help.

While Gorokhov and Nikiforov were clearing the snow off the sledges, putting the harnesses in order and distributing the load, our three friends went to the top of a hill at the back of the cape in order to examine the locality and choose the best route across the sea. Visibility was particularly good on that clear morning.

In places, the snow-covered plain of ice, where blizzards had roared unchecked in the winter, was broken by long lines of broad hummocks in the shape of white, uneven ridges with boulder-like pieces of ice sticking out here and there. This ice was bare of snow and glowed with a pale-green light. Some of it shone like a mirror, reflecting the rays of the sun. The snow was dotted with dark spots. These were not patches of ice-free water, but places where the ice had been swept clean of snow. Only in the distance, about forty kilometres away, did a line of low-hanging white mist betray the open sea stretching along the entire horizon so that it was impossible to by-pass it.

When the sky is overcast, the presence of ice-free water is recognized by dark spots reflected in the light-grey clouds.

A mist hid the snow lying beyond the ice-free water, but on the horizon itself, in the north, something dark loomed above the mist.

"That must be Bennett Island!" Ordin cried out excitedly. He was the first to see it.

Goryunov and Kostyakov looked round and the former at once took the dark spot's bearings by his compass.

"No, it's not," he said. "Bennett Island is more to the east and is too far to be seen from Kotelny. If it's not a mirage then we are looking at Sannikov Land, for it's exactly where Toll said it must be."

Two of the friends took out their field-glasses, while the third—an ancient spy-glass, a gift from Shenk "for the search for Sannikov Land." The dark masses now disappeared behind the mist over the ice-free water, now reappeared. Nevertheless, the friends made out that this was a range of dark, fairly sharp peaks, with snow lying between them. This range stretched for some distance in both directions before sloping abruptly out of sight. As the crow flies, it was at least a hundred and twenty or a hundred and thirty kilometres away.

"Obviously land!"

"Yes, and very high and mountainous!"

"Why isn't it all under snow?"

"Probably because the slopes are too steep."

"But if they are that steep I don't see how ducks and geese or the Onkilons can live there."

"There must be valleys."

"In any case, it's not a mirage. It's Sannikov Land," Goryunov declared. "It lies right where Toll and Sannikov saw it. No two people see the same mirage in one and the same spot. Mirages appear over ice-free water, and when that moves to another place the new mirages assume a different shape."

The spy-glass proved to be better than powerful field-glasses and Kostyakov, who had it, announced that he could see two chains of mountains: the first was almost completely white and lower than the second, which was black and craggy.

"I am sure there's a valley between those ranges and a very wide one, too."

"And there the Onkilons live in complete isolation," Ordin remarked.

"And here we are wanting to disturb their peaceful life," Kostyakov added. "It's hard to imagine a people who have been cut off from the world for whole centuries."

The yelping, howling, and barking of the dogs, which reached them from the foot of the hill, interrupted the conversation and reminded them that it was time to move on. When there is no snow-storm or a biting frost, huskies eagerly await the signal to start and express their joy in their own way when everything is ready. Goryunov rechecked the direction to the mysterious land with his compass and the three friends descended to the hut.

"Can land be seen today?" Gorokhov asked as they approached.

"Very well, and I'm sure it's the land we're looking for," Goryunov said.

"I must take a look. I'll go while you're having your tea. I saw it only once and very indistinctly at that."

Taking the field-glasses from the travellers, the two hunters climbed the hill. The dogs, seeing that some of the men went to the hut and others up the hill, grew silent and lay down on the snow in their harnesses.

Gorokhov and Nikiforov came down the hill and confirmed that Sannikov Land could be made out clearly and that it was exactly where they had seen it before.

Soon the small caravan descended from the cape to the frozen sea and headed almost due north. The dogs, refreshed by the three days' rest, kept up a vigorous pace in spite of the extra load in the shape of a week's supply of firewood. The crossing could be made in something like three days, but there was always the danger of a snowstorm breaking out again and holding them up. It would be very hard to spend a night in the bitter frost without an opportunity to boil some tea or have warm food.

They made rapid progress over the level places, slowing down at the hummocks. They covered about forty kilometres by nightfall and stopped in the middle of a wide strip of hummocky ice, choosing an even, sheltered place. They quickly pitched the tents, lit a fire, cooked a meal and then sat for an hour round the fire, which cast a red glow on the smooth ice. The sun was sinking in the west; in the south, the rising moon now showed itself through the light clouds, now disappeared; from the north came the glare of Aurora Borealis—yellowish arcs and pillars, which were quite distinct only when the moon hid behind the clouds.

Before going to sleep, Goryunov climbed to the top of a hummock and swept the horizon with his field-glasses. The moon showed in the sky and the snowy plain, hummocks and blocks of ice gleamed with a soft, bluish light. A cold wind was blowing from the south, while on the horizon there loomed black clouds against whose background the humped silhouette of Kotelny Island was faintly visible.

Next morning the weather was gloomy and the south wind blowing harder. Gorokhov and Nikiforov expected a snow-storm and egged on the dogs. But the ice was very rough. There was a broad belt of hummocks at almost every kilometre and much slower progress was made than on the previous day. All that day a dark strip, indicating a long, broad expanse of ice-free water, was clearly visible in the overcast sky ahead of them. By evening they drew close enough to hear the plashing of waves. At last, while negotiating a high hummock, they saw the open sea half a kilometre away covered with floes and foam-crested waves; it stretched to the north, to the very horizon, it seemed.

The travellers were determined to cross the sea on the following day if there was no snow-storm to stop them. Therefore, they decided to drive up to the edge of the ice where they would be able to lower their canoe without delay; the wind was blowing from the south and there was no danger of the sea breaking the ice on that side. They settled for the night amidst masses of broken ice on the last hummock, some hundred and fifty paces from the open water, selecting an even piece of ground which was just big enough to hold the sledges, the dogs, and the tent; on the south and west it was protected by masses of steep, inclining ice.

In the shelter of the hummock and with a little fire burning at the entrance it was cosy and warm in the tent. However, during the night the wind began to blow harder and a snow-storm broke out. In the light of the fire they could see streams of snow-flakes hurtling past them in the dark sky five or six metres above the tent. Pressed by the wind, the thick floes trembled and from time to time something like sharp gun reports could be heard above the whistling and wailing.

"What does it mean?" Kostyakov exclaimed with alarm when the first of these reports sounded.

"That another crack's formed in the ice," Goryunov replied.

"Yes, the ice is cracking," Gorokhov confirmed in a calm voice.

"But is our shelter safe?"

"As long as the wind doesn't change direction and blow from the north, because then the waves will hammer against the edge of our ice-field and raise and break it. But we'll be safe while there's a south wind."

"Still, it's gruesome here, Matvei Ivanovich," Nikiforov said, "whatever you say! To think that we're sitting here serenely, smoking our pipes and chatting, and there's only about two metres of ice holding us above a bottomless abyss! At any rate, it was much more cheerful there, between the islands: the sea wasn't deep and there was land hard by."

"What difference does it make whatever the depth

59

beneath us is, whether it's twenty or a hundred metres?"
Ordin laughed. "If the ice gives way it will be the end
of us in any case."

"All the same it's much more frightening here because
neither sea nor land is in sight."

"Then climb under that great fur coat of yours and
go to sleep. Perhaps you'll see what you want then,"
Gorokhov joked.

"There's something in that. Let's go to sleep and in the
morning, in the light, we'll feel better."

For all that, they spent an anxious night because with
their ears close to the ice they heard the cracking much
more distinctly. The dogs, too, contrary to their habit,
slept uneasily and every now and then one of them would
begin to howl or whine. Gorokhov got up several times
and peered out of the tent to make sure that the wind was
not changing direction. At dawn when everybody awoke
he calmed his companions, saying:

"I can't see a damned thing, but it's blowing as before
and you needn't get up."

They stayed in their sleeping-bags late into the morning, until hunger drove them out. A fire was lighted and
the kettle set to boil. Gorokhov and Nikiforov went to
feed the dogs who were huddling together between overhanging masses of ice, where there was practically no wind.
The character of the snow-storm began to change. For
five or ten minutes it would die away and the sky would
begin to clear, then it would start screaming again with
redoubled force. During one of these lulls Gorokhov clambered to the top of the hummock, looked around and gave
a drawn-out whistle:

"Hey, look! We're drifting! There's water everywhere!"

Alarmed, the others scrambled up after him and saw

that in the south from where they had come over the ice the previous day there was a sheet of water looking black in the white haze; a stretch of dark water loomed in the north, while to the east and west there were hummocks but they could not see where they ended. They were not given a chance to look long for a new burst of wind covered everything with snow and forced them down. They were compelled to return to their tent.

"The way I see it," Goryunov said, "is that our ice-field was stuck loosely to the rest of the plain and when the ice cracked the wind tore it away and took it out to sea."

"But where to?"

"To the north, apparently, in the direction it's blowing."

"But if there's a current in this part of the sea it might carry us far to the east or west!"

"That's very possible."

"Then what are we to do?"

"Nothing. In this weather it's dangerous to sail in a canoe. We'll have to wait until the storm stops."

"But what if the ice-field breaks some more?"

"Since it hasn't so far let's hope it'll hold, at least until it's thrown against another ice-field or the main ice."

"While we're waiting it wouldn't be a bad idea to get the canoe ready and stow all our things in it."

"That's what I think," Gorokhov declared.

After breakfast they unloaded the sledges and assembled the canoe. Then they arranged all their luggage and the sledges in it, leaving only the tent and their bedding, which could be packed at a moment's notice, at the first sign of danger. From time to time, when the wind calmed down, they climbed to the hummock, but saw no change; as before the sea stretched to the north and south and on both sides about a hundred metres of ice separated them from it.

It was an anxious day for the travellers. The storm raged on. After dinner they sat around the dying fire for a long time, tense with alarm. At times it seemed to them as though the ice beneath them was trembling. However, since morning there had been no further signs that the ice was cracking. Evidently, their ice-field was strong enough. At night, to be ready to meet any eventuality, they slept by turns. The wind began to drop and now and again the moon, lustreless and diffused, showed through the snowy haze.

Ordin, who had the last watch, began to doze at dawn and woke up from the glare of a sun-beam falling on his face. With amazement he saw that the sun had already risen and that there was a pale-blue sky overhead. The storm was over, there was a comparatively weak wind, which frequently stopped blowing altogether; the new snow sparkled blindingly.

Quickly climbing to the top of the hummock, he saw a blue sea extending southwards to the horizon with the sunlight playing on the ripples; westwards, the ice-field ended about half a kilometre away, while in the east it was even shorter. To the north, close beyond the strip of water, he could see the edge of a solid plain of ice. It was drawing slowly nearer. He hurried down to wake the others. The whole party assembled on the hummock.

"Had it not been for the rising sun which immediately gives us our bearings I would have thought that the sea was to the north of us as before," Kostyakov said enthusiastically.

"We've been amazingly lucky!" Goryunov declared.

"Instead of sailing in a canoe and worrying our heads

about how much it can carry, we slept peacefully in a tent while the storm gave us a lift across the sea."

"It's as though we've crossed a river in a pontoon," Gorokhov added.

"And at public expense, too," Nikiforov laughed. "It's those official permits of ours that were our tickets."

"Mother Snow-storm just gave us a scare as a warning to stay away from mischief," Kostyakov said.

"Do you think it'll take us alongside the shore or we'll have to lower the canoe after all?" Ordin asked.

"Let's hope it does. It isn't far now and there's a wind and our hummock is a fine sail."

"In the meantime, let's have our breakfast and get ready to go on," Goryunov suggested.

With only a light wind to drive it, the ice-field, which had served the expedition so well as a ferry, moved slowly. The travellers had their breakfast, took the canoe apart, reloaded the sledges and again climbed to the top of the hummock in order to wait for the moment when their ferry struck the edge of the motionless ice. About an hour went by before they felt the impact and saw the ice along the line of contact crush and rear to form a hummock. But the pressure was light; only a low ridge of broken ice appeared and the ferry stopped moving.

"We've made it!" Gorokhov cried.

Taking axes and spades with which to clear a road, the travellers drove the sledges to the point of contact and, choosing the smoothest place they could find, soon crossed to the stationary ice.

With mock seriousness, Nikiforov bowed to the ice-field and shouted:

"Thanks for the crossing, lad! In truth, that was a fine ride you gave us."

On the assumption that the ice ferry had not taken them far off their course, Goryunov led the expedition northwards, counting on seeing Sannikov Land from the top of one of the bigger hummocks and taking his bearings from it. At first the going was extremely rough, for where one hummock ended another began and by lunch-time they had advanced less than ten kilometres. The view was completely blocked by these hummocks. Finally, around midday, they reached a more level expanse of ice and through the thin mist saw the sharp peaks of the mysterious land silhouetted on the horizon. But they were still very far away.

"This is the third day that we're on the move and yet we don't seem to be able to see Sannikov Land any better," Gorokhov said in so strange a tone of voice that it caught the attention of Goryunov, who was standing near him.

"You sound as though something is oppressing you, Nikita," he said.

"You're quite right! I'm beginning to have my doubts. It's a bad omen that the ice-field carried us so wonderfully across the sea. And I'm thinking that what we saw was not land but a mirage. It'll always stay in front of us like a distant lighthouse and lure us on. We'll find ourselves so far away that we shan't be able to return."

"You certainly have an imagination!" Goryunov laughed. "You'll see, in a day or two we'll be within a stone's throw of that land."

"The way I think is that if we don't see it at all tomorrow we'd better turn back before it's too late."

Goryunov made no reply and checked the direction of the land. It proved to be to the north-east; evidently, the wind or the current had carried their ferry a good way to the west. There was nothing for it but to change the course. The more even ice allowed them to move faster and towards evening they had left another thirty kilometres behind them. Just before sundown the horizon completely cleared up and the travellers saw distinctly, without the aid of field-glasses, a chain of pointed black peaks rising above the arc formed by the ice. Even Gorokhov seemed appeased.

They kept to the same course for another two days, but low-hanging clouds prevented them from seeing land, evidently hiding it. At last, on the third day, soon after the stop for lunch, no further hummocks impeded their progress and the snow plain, covered with low drifts, began to rise perceptibly. The dogs at once slackened their pace.

"I wonder if there's land under us?" Ordin said.

"It's land, all right!" Nikiforov replied. "We're going uphill. That's clear from the way the dogs are behaving."

Just then the clouds in front of them dispersed for a minute and they saw what looked like a white wall a few kilometres away.

"So far we've seen nothing in this land except snow," Kostyakov grumbled. "The mountains have disappeared somewhere."

"There's impatience for you! We'll see the mountains once we're past that white wall. Meanwhile, there's something that's definitely not snow!" Goryunov said, pointing to the right, to something black lying about a hundred steps from him.

The three friends rushed to the spot indicated by Goryunov. Ordin drew a hammer out of his belt, getting ready for a struggle with the boulder because that was what was bulging out over the snow plain. Its surface had been polished flat and smooth by snow-flakes whipped into activity by storms. But a chisel inserted into a small crevice helped to chip off a piece of the rock. Ordin examined it carefully and announced:

"I think it's basalt."

"As I expected," Goryunov noted. "This volcanic rock is apparently widespread in the islands of the Arctic Ocean and shows that at one time tremendous quantities of lava were thrown up here."

"And I bet it was warm when that was happening. Nothing like what it's now," Kostyakov added in a tone of regret.

The piece of basalt was carried triumphantly to Gorokhov who had remained behind with Nikiforov by the sledges. There could be no better proof that there was land under them, the mysterious Sannikov Land, where, perhaps, no other men had ever set foot.

Moving slowly up the slope, in about two hours the caravan arrived at the foot of the white wall, which likewise proved to be a slope, only a much steeper one. Barrier-like, it stretched on both sides as far as the eye could see through the light, enveloping mist. Instead of rising in a straight line they pressed onwards diagonally. Pounded into place by storms, the snow was so hard that it scarcely gave way even under the runners of the heavy sledges.

ON THE THRESHOLD OF A PROMISED LAND

Inch by inch, cutting long zigzags, the caravan moved ever higher and there seemed to be no end to the ascent; the light mist clothing the slopes veiled the top, and the snow-bound incline was hidden in a greyish gloom a hundred paces away.

"What a tall mountain!" Gorokhov exclaimed at one of the turnings when they stopped to give the dogs a rest.

"Apparently, instead of stumbling upon a pass into the valley we've been so unfortunate as to find ourselves on the slopes of one of the bordering mountains," Ordin conjectured.

"It's very probable that the entire southern border is the same everywhere," Goryunov remarked. "If you remember, in front of the chain of rocky mountains we saw a high snow wall extending far into the distance. We're evidently climbing it now."

"A strange land!" Kostyakov said. "It hasn't got sheer precipices and rocky promontories such as fringe the New Siberian Islands and Bennett Island; there's nothing here except an endless, smooth slope."

"And there even aren't any glaciers creeping down from the top, only snow," Ordin added.

"Yes, it's strange! This slope faces the south and the snow on it ought to melt in the summer. But as we've seen, above it there's a range of taller mountains from which glaciers ought to be coming down to the sea by way of this slope. So far there's no sign of them."

"The only explanation for this extraordinary fact is that behind this snow wall there's a deep valley into which the glaciers descend," Ordin suggested, "and then drain into the sea somewhere in a huge icy stream as on Spitsbergen."

"Then where is the home of the birds that are supposed to fly here, to say nothing of the Onkilons, whose existence, by the way, I very much doubt?" Kostyakov demanded.

"Have a little patience, friends, the answer to the

riddle is almost at hand," Goryunov laughed. "Forward, and put more zest in your step!"

At the next stop the barometer showed that they were already nearly eight hundred metres above sea level. The mist seemed to be thicker, and Gorokhov announced:

"Do what you want, but I think we ought to turn back."

"Why?" Goryunov asked in surprise.

"Can't you see? We're climbing higher and higher as though we want to reach heaven. There can't be such a high mountain."

The three travellers burst out laughing and even Nikiforov joined in.

"But doesn't the mist mean anything to you? Remember Mount Kigilyakh, which covers itself with mist to stop people climbing up?"

"Well, Nikita, I see you've been steeped in superstition by the teamsters. It's quite usual for a high mountain to have an envelope of mist, especially in these places. Don't tell me that this is the first time we're seeing it."

"Do as you know best, but I've warned you. Later don't say that Gorokhov led you into trouble."

The caravan moved on. The mist became lighter and in half an hour the travellers finally saw several dark boulders amidst the snow. True, they were still a long way off, but everybody breathed a sigh of relief and pushed on with renewed energy. Here the snow was looser and although the slope had become gentler, the sledges kept floundering and the travellers had to lead the way for the dogs. That slowed down the ascent and they had to exert a great effort in the last half-kilometre.

The sun was already on the point of setting when the caravan reached almost the top of this long, interminable slope; the barometer showed the altitude to be nine hundred and seventy metres above sea level. Below, the white mist hid practically the entire slope and the foot-hill, but over it they had a good view of the pack ice on the frozen sea spreading to the very horizon.

Leaving the sledges at the foot of a flat, black boulder that rose a short way above the snow, the whole party climbed to the top of the mountain, stopping about two paces away from the edge of a huge precipice at which this snow-clad slope ended.

"Of all the wonders I've ever seen!" Nikiforov exclaimed, expressing the travellers' amazement at the scene unfolding before them.

Instead of snow and ice which was to be expected on the 79th or 80th parallel at a height of nearly a thousand metres above sea level, before them was a picture of awakening spring in spite of the fact that it was only the middle of April, when near Yakutsk, some 15 or 17 degrees to the south, melting snow was the only sign of the nearness of spring.

Sombre-looking black ledges with snow on them stretched from the edge of the precipice deep into a great valley extending to the horizon in the north. On the floor of the valley were big bright-green meadows separated by shrub thickets and forest, which were already donning a cloak of green leaves. Among the meadows sparkled the smooth surfaces of lakes interconnected by streams that wound in and out of the thick shrubbery like silver ribbons. A white mist, resembling smoke, hovered above the more distant lakes. A mountain range stood as a sheer wall to the west of this verdant valley. Its crest was cut up into pointed peaks which resembled the teeth of a gigantic saw; snow lay on them in strips and spots, although farther down, below the line of cliffs, there was hardly any snow to be seen. The sun was already sinking beyond this range, plunging the entire valley into the shadow of evening.

The mountains stretched northwards, dipping into the horizon and hiding in the mist shrouding the distant portion of the valley. In the same direction, as far as the eye could see, extended the ridge on whose top the travellers were standing and which was lower than the opposite range of mountains. In the south, the two mountain chains seemed to merge, completely closing the valley on that side.

The silent contemplation of the first few minutes gave way to an animated exchange of impressions.

"It's too remarkable for words, Matvei Ivanovich," Nikiforov uttered.

"A real promised land!" Ordin said.

"I simply can't account for all this greenery, this vegetation at this latitude," Kostyakov declared. "The valley is open in the north, in the direction of the Pole, as though it's getting its warmth from there."

"And no wonder that birds fly here from afar, disdaining our stern coast. It's quite possible that the Onkilons found a home here, too. But how are we going to go down these precipices with our sledges? We'll never make it even on empty sledges," Goryunov said.

"Yes, but animals seem to know a way!" Ordin exclaimed, pointing to some dark-brown animals which appeared on a ledge below them. They had enormous spiralling horns sticking out of the sides of their heads.

"They're mountain sheep! I wish I could bag a pair for dinner!" Gorokhov cried excitedly.

Apparently sensing the presence of human beings, the animals stopped and raised their heads in bewilderment.

For all that, they seemed to have seen human beings before, for after standing still for a minute, they sharply turned back and disappeared behind a protruding boulder.

In the meantime, Goryunov was scanning the crest on both sides of him with his field-glasses; in the north-east it continued to rise, but in the south-west it seemed to slant downwards, and there was the possibility that somewhere in that direction there might be a pass.

"That's the direction we'll take," he announced, pointing to the south-west. "If there's a pass at all, I'm sure it's there."

"We might have to go round the entire valley," Ordin remarked, "in order..."

"In order to convince ourselves that there's no pass for human beings and that only birds can get into the valley," Kostyakov broke in.

"In that case, we'll have to rest content with the discovery of a valley with rich vegetation amidst polar ice and immediately return to the continent."

Taking advantage of the remaining daylight, they went in a south-westerly direction, but there the crest proved to be uneven; where it was lower, the snow-field on the southern slope reached up to the very edge of the precipice, but on rising ground it was covered with boulders or sharp little spurs. At the sight of them Ordin remembered his hammer and chipped off a few samples.

These proved to consist of basalt, either solid or porous, while some were cindery, representing basalt lava.

"I'm beginning to think," he said to Goryunov, "that you were right when you told Academician Shenk you thought Sannikov Land is the remains of a volcano. This great valley with its surrounding ring of sheer precipices looks very much like the caldera of a mighty ancient volcano. The basalt rock that we saw on our way up and here bears that out."

71

"If what we ve just said about the origin of this valley is true then that explains why there's such luxuriant vegetation on this parallel," Goryunov added. "But let's not draw any premature conclusions. We'll see what follows."

The farther south-west they went, the more noticeably lower the crest became, but the side facing the valley remained as steep as ever. Dusk was gathering, but an almost full moon had already risen and was illuminating the way. Another hour passed.

Goryunov glanced at the barometer—it showed the altitude to be only five hundred metres above sea level.

"I think we'll have to spend the night here. There'll not be enough light from the moon to allow us to make a descent and, in any case, it's dangerous to follow an unexplored road in darkness."

"We'll stop as soon as we find a piece of level ground," Nikiforov agreed.

"But if a storm breaks out at night, it'll sweep us into the chasm below," Kostyakov said.

"There won't be a storm," Gorokhov declared. "The sky is clear, there's no wind, and the sunset wasn't red. The only worry is that shaitan might want to punish us..."

"Let's hope he won't," Goryunov laughed.

The spot they chose between two boulders was fairly even and wide. They pitched the tent, had their supper, but nobody wanted to go to sleep. The mysterious valley was too near and stirred their curiosity. The moon was already lighting up the part farthest away from them, leaving the immediate vicinity in shadow. Here and there, against the dark background of meadows and forests, the moon's silvery light was reflected in the lakes and meandering streams.

Sitting down close to the edge of the precipice, the

travellers gazed at the remarkable valley beneath them; in the moonlight, the cliffs along the opposite rim now seemed to be higher and steeper. Anywhere up to a thousand six hundred metres high, they looked impressive.

Suddenly, from the depths of the valley the stillness of the night was broken by a drawn-out lowing, which was followed by a deep bellow.

"Oh-ho, there are animals in the valley. They sound like cows!" exclaimed Nikiforov.

"What about the one that's bellowing? Think it's an elk?" Goryunov asked.

"No, and it's not a bull, either. It sounds as though it's blowing a huge trumpet. And I'm sure it's not a bear."

They hazarded a few guesses, but not one of the animals known to the hunters in the party made sounds like that and everybody was perplexed.

"But what's that?" asked Ordin, pointing to a star-like red light that began to glow intermittently somewhere in the centre of the valley.

"I should say it's a fire at the bottom of the crater of this volcano, which evidently hasn't completely gone out," Kostyakov laughed.

"You sure it's not a camp-fire?"

"Could be. That would mean people. Perhaps they are those lost Onkilons of ours," Goryunov suggested.

The travellers fell silent again, their gaze riveted on the new puzzle in this strange valley. Presently, faint sounds, like the beat of a drum, reached them from afar.

"It's a shaman's drum!" Gorokhov declared. "That means there are people in the valley and the fire is theirs."

"If there are people, there must be a pass," Goryunov remarked. "They couldn't have flown down through the air like birds."

"A landslip might have closed whatever pass there was!"

For half an hour nobody spoke. Fatigue was making them all drowsy, but just then something else caught their attention. In spite of the bright moon riding high in the sky, the farthest portion of the valley became obscure and soon disappeared in a mist. It crept southwards slowly until the entire valley resembled a vast lake of slightly heaving milk. It began to rise and wisps of it spread over the low-lying southern fringe, where the travellers were encamped.

A light wind, humid but warm, started blowing from the north and soon the crest, the boulders and the tent were enveloped by a thick fog, which all but blotted out the moon. "The show's ended, the curtain's rung down and it's time to go," Ordin said.

"I think we'd better go into the tent, out of harm's way," suggested Gorokhov. "Whatever you think, Matvei Ivanovich, but all this is only a mirage—the valley, the forests and the beasts. You'll see, when we wake up in the morning, there'll be nothing here except snow and we'll have to turn back as quickly as we can."

"All right, soothsayer, we'll see tomorrow," replied Goryunov.

The travellers turned in, but they slept uneasily because from time to time the dogs barked and howled, probably sensing the closeness of wild animals.

THE FIRST DAY IN SANNIKOV LAND

The mist did not disperse when day broke; it was so dense that five paces away the outline of a man was almost invisible in the milk-white gloom. Even in sight of the tent, the travellers had to feel their way with extreme caution for the edge of the precipice was only a few steps away.

There was nothing they could do but wait for an opportunity to continue the search for a pass. A fire was lit with the remaining wood brought from Kotelny. The dogs were fed and the travellers sat down to an unhurried breakfast.

Their watches showed them that the sun had risen an hour ago, but it was completely hidden by the mist, which seemed to flow over the crest like liquid jelly. It had filled the far-flung valley to the brim and was now streaming across the gap-toothed range of mountains.

"The smoke is from our volcano," Kostyakov ragged. "It's active at night; first a fire blazes up and then comes the smoke."

"Go ahead and laugh, Pavel," Ordin said. "For all that, this valley is a volcano and that discovery is as important as the finding of Sannikov Land."

"But can there be volcanoes amidst polar ice?" Kostyakov asked.

"Why not! In the Antarctic, there even are active volcanoes, Erebus and Terror, and some extinct ones. In the Arctic Ocean, we find volcanic rocks of different ages in Greenland, on Spitsbergen, in Franz Josef Land and even on Bennett Island, Sannikov Land's nearest neighbour."

"But they're all very old."

"Not all. What about Iceland with its prodigious volcanic activity?"

"Well, this volcano outdoes all the others in size," Goryunov noted. "That is what makes me doubt your hypothesis."

"You're right. It is very big. I should say it's twenty kilometres wide and between forty and fifty kilometres long."

"What's the size of the biggest craters known in the world?"

"So far as I can remember, Mauna Loa in Hawaii is nearly four kilometres and Hunung Tengger in Java is somewhat under six kilometres in diameter."

"There, you see! This one's place is on the moon and not on earth," put in Kostyakov.

"On the moon it would have been quite an ordinary one; the craters there are from sixty to over a hundred kilometres in diameter. For instance, Ptolemy Crater is a hundred and sixty-one kilometres in diameter, Langrenus is a hundred and fifty-eight kilometres, and there are more than a dozen with a diameter between seventy and ninety kilometres. Altogether, there are something like thirty thousand craters."

"It must have been a marvellous spectacle when all were active!"

While our travellers were talking about the craters on the moon, the sun did its work and the mist began rapidly to rarefy, rising and turning into thin films which gradually melted in the air. Soon the mist cleared sufficiently for the travellers to push on, but the valley still looked like a sea of milk with the surface heaving and pitching. They went in a westerly direction, following the curve of the crest, which continued to dip. At last, shortly before midday, they reached the lowest point; farther on the ground began to rise again.

"If there's no pass here, we'll have to look for one on the northern side," Goryunov declared.

"That would be very unfortunate," Ordin said, "because we have run out of firewood and there's only a three days' supply of food left for the dogs."

76

They went to the edge of the precipice to have a better look at it. The barometer showed they were only a hundred and twenty metres above sea level, and there was hope they might reach the bottom by lowering themselves from one ledge to another with ropes.

"Well, there is your pass!" Goryunov cried, pointing to the right.

His companions looked in that direction. Leading down from the crest was a long snow-covered slope, which actually was a huge snow-drift massed up by storms blowing from the sea and carrying the snow over the crest where it was lowest. The incline was fairly steep and looked like the side of a gable roof with a broad ridge resting on the very edge of the precipice; to the right and left there were other snow-drifts, but they fell short of the crest, so that it was possible to make the descent only along the one Goryunov had indicated. The snow was hard enough—underfoot it gave way no more than four or five centimetres.

As the angle of the slope was nearly forty degrees, the sledges could not be lowered with the teams harnessed to them. The dogs were therefore unharnessed. Four of the men tied themselves in pairs to each of two of the sledges and began the descent. While these two sledges were being lowered, Kostyakov remained behind with the third sledge and the dogs. When Gorokhov and Nikiforov returned, he led all the three teams down the slope; the dogs could not be allowed to go down by themselves for there was always the chance of some animal attracting them and leading them away on a chase. But it was no easy task to lead thirty dogs down a slope; when they caught sight of the sledges and the men at the bottom, they strained at the leash so much that Kostyakov lost his balance, fell prone on the snow and slid down on his stomach, raising a cloud of snow dust to the delight of the watchers below and above.

When the whole party was at last assembled at the bottom, they took stock of their surroundings. The ground in the immediate vicinity of the snow-drift was bare of vegetation. The sun reached this spot only at the height of summer from the northern side, i. e., at night, when it hung low and hardly any warmth came from it. Evidently, the snow took a long time to melt and vegetation could not grow. But some thirty steps from where the snow-drifts ended, amidst slabs and broken pieces of basalt there was green moss, and dwarf flowers were opening their first petals. As yet leafless creeper bushes stood a little farther off with more luxuriant shrubbery showing the first signs of greenery about half a kilometre behind them. Beyond that was a dark forest of short trees.

During lunch, which was really a snack with tea boiled on what firewood they could scrape together from the sledges, the travellers discussed the important question of what their next step should be. The canoe, the sledges and the dogs were no longer needed for there was no snow in the valley and the rivers were too small to be navigable.

Thirty dogs and the constant worry of having to feed them would hamper the expedition too much. Besides, the abundance of game was too great a temptation for the dogs, but to keep them leashed together would mean devoting all attention to them and occupying at least three members of the expedition with that task. To harness the dogs to the sledges and drive over the grass and through the forests would mean sacrificing the runners and rendering the sledges uselesss for the return journey over the ice, besides exhausting the dogs.

The only acceptable plan they could think of was to leave all the extra load and the dogs here, by the snow-drifts, in charge of one member of the expedition; it was cool and whoever was left could devote his time to hunting food for himself and the dogs. The others, carrying a light load, could tour Sannikov Land on foot and return to the base now and then to leave any collection they would make. Gorokhov, who knew the Chukchi and Lamut languages, was needed as an interpreter in case they came across the Onkilons and so Nikiforov had to stay behind and guard the equipment and the dogs. The latter was a little disconcerted by the unusual situation, but like all the hunters of the north, he was not afraid of spending a few days or weeks in solitude; the pack of dogs was adequate protection against wild beasts and, at the same time, would give him enough to do to keep him from being bored.

The travellers set their tent up between two snow-drifts and spent the rest of the day sorting their equipment. Having decided to explore the valley on foot, they could not burden themselves with heavy baggage; all they could take along were bare essentials—a change of clothes, an extra pair of boots, guns and ammunition, a pot and a kettle—counting on game for food and on sleeping in the open.

Towards evening the sky became overcast and a wet snow, that sometimes changed to rain, began to fall; they had to seek the shelter of the tent.

"From what we've seen of the weather here we must do something to prevent the things we're leaving behind, including the sledges and the canoe, from rotting and spoiling during the summer," Goryunov said.

"A hut built from stakes and bark will do," Ordin observed.

"No, that's no use and, besides, we would have to go a long way for the bark," Gorokhov declared.

"Why not use these snow-drifts? I'm sure they don't melt inside. We can make a cave in one of them and put all our things in it; it would be cool, dry and safe."

"Yes, and we can dig another cave for the dogs," Nikiforov added. "They don't like heat and I'll be able to shut them in for the night."

"Not only for the night! When you go hunting you won't need more than two or three of them; the rest can stay locked in. You can't have the whole lot around all the time. If you do you'll never shoot any game and will only frighten all the animals away," Gorokhov commented.

"Quite right! A splendid idea," Goryunov said. "We'll start on the caves first thing in the morning."

That evening it was cold and uncomfortable in the tent; there was no fuel and the dinner was cooked on a fire that the travellers managed to build with twigs and branches they gathered near the shrubs. The different sounds—lowing, bleating, and bellowing—reaching them from the valley, frequently alarmed the dogs, whose barking and howling gave the travellers very little sleep.

"I don't envy Kapiton, who'll have to sleep near those howlers," grumbled Kostyakov during one of the concerts.

"They'll be quieter in a cave," replied Goryunov, turning over on his other side.

In the morning, they set to work, using their axes to cut a deep gallery in the snow-drift close to where it abutted on a basalt cliff. Below a layer of snow, they struck solid ice, which must have been there for centuries, so there was no danger of its melting during the summer. In the cave they stored all the extra equipment, the canoe and two of the sledges, after which they sealed the entrance with lumps of ice, making it air-tight and safe against any wild beast that might find the gallery in Nikiforov's absence. Close by they made three smaller caves, one for each of the teams.

The third sledge was left for Nikiforov's use, so that he could transport firewood and game from the forest. The Cossack was very pleased with the caves and planned to make two more: one as a storehouse for meat and the second for the tent where he would feel safe against any attack. An uninvited guest could approach the cave only from one and not from any side he chose as with a tent in the open and it would be enough to have two dogs at the entrance to feel absolutely secure.

This work took up almost the whole day; all they had time for was a trip to the edge of the nearest forest to chop some firewood for the night.

STRANGE ANIMALS

Though the morning was gloomy, there was no rain or mist and that allowed the travellers to begin their explorations. With knapsacks on their backs and guns slung over their shoulders, they started off northwards, taking along two dogs, the brightest in the pack and team-leaders; one was black and the other almost white; the first was called Krot and the second—Belukha. Nikiforov and Pestrushka, the leader of the third team, accompanied the travellers part of the way; the hunter wanted to lay in a few days' supply of meat for himself and the dogs.

Away from the snow-drifts, the vegetation became more and more plentiful: moss gave way to grass and soon they came across overgrowths of polar creeper birch, willow, and alder. Here the soil was warmed by the noon sun for a few hours every day and the vegetation was coming to life. Deeper in the valley, the shrubbery was taller and was replaced by representatives of a more moderate zone—larch, white birch, alder—while here and there bright flowers peeped out through the grass. The trees were three or four metres high and grew in little woods, which alternated with meadows.

In one of these woods, the dogs, which were led on a leash, showed signs of nervousness, and began to pull and growl. The travellers unslung their guns and cautiously approached the edge of the woods, where, in a meadow, they saw a big herd of grazing animals. Their backs were black and they had fairly big humps and short tails that looked like thick brushes. When one of them raised its head, the travellers saw that it bore a resemblance to an ox's, only it was shorter, blunter and was crowned with long horns that curved forward and up. The animal had already sensed danger and gave a booming bellow, which alarmed the entire herd.

There was no time to be lost. Goryunov fired his Winchester at the nearest ox. It leapt into the air and fell to its knees. The other animals shied in confusion but did not run away. The horns of some were shorter and thinner; calves of different ages could be seen.

The travellers unleashed the dogs and ran to the wounded ox. At the sight of human beings, the herd took to its heels, but the dogs managed to stop a calf, which Nikiforov brought down. When the wounded ox saw the travellers approaching, it struggled up to its feet and charged with a fierce bellow, its head lowered, its huge horns thrust forward, and leaving a trail of blood as it ran. But the dogs, which had rushed up from the flank,

distracted its attention; it veered sharply and, struck by two more bullets, sagged to the ground.

The travellers ran up to their quarry and gazed at it with wonder.

"It's definitely not a musk-ox as one might have thought," Kostyakov declared. "It's got shorter wool and its head and horns are not the same."

"Yes, it looks more like a wild Tibetan yak, which I saw in a zoo," Goryunov said.

"But in the north the only representative of that family is the musk-ox or *Ovibos moschatus*, to use the scientific name," Ordin observed. "And it lives in North America and not in Asia."

"You're right, and I'm certain that this animal is not a musk-ox."

"But how did a Tibetan yak get so far from its homeland, which is at least ten thousand kilometres away?"

"That is another of the riddles Sannikov Land is posing us with," Kostyakov said. "Perhaps the Onkilons drove them here and we're encroaching on their property rights?"

"No! These animals are wild," Gorokhov said. "I've never seen their like in our country."

"To solve the riddle, we shall have to preserve and take away with us at least its skull and horns," Goryunov said. "If I'm not mistaken, the horns of a yak are more curved at the ends and are thinner, while the tail is shorter and thicker."

In the meantime, Nikiforov appeared with the calf he had shot. It was only two or three weeks old.

"It'll make a fine roast," he said. "I haven't had veal for many a year."

"Go back to camp, Kapiton," Goryunov ordered, "and bring the sledge. We'll skin the animals while you're gone."

Nikiforov, with Pestrushka at his heels, strode off, taking his bearings by the snow-drifts that could be seen against a black precipice showing above the forest of short trees.

While the ox and the calf were being skinned, Goryunov measured them and made a few notes. Some big birds, vultures to all appearances, were already circling above the meadow in the hope the hunters would leave something for them. But they were disappointed, because Nikiforov was shrewd enough to bring all the dogs in order to feed them on the spot and thus lighten the load he would have to take back to camp. Before leaving, the travellers instructed Nikiforov to preserve the skulls and skins of the animals he would shoot, by storing them in the cave.

Farther from the edge of the valley the scenery was different; the trees were taller and the grass more luxuriant; poplars, aspens, bird-cherry trees, honeysuckle, sweet brier, and other trees and shrubs appeared; some had already burst into leaf, others were blossoming. The vegetation fascinated Gorokhov; he had never seen anything like it around Kazachye or along the entire coast, and all his trips south had been made in winter. The others, too, were amazed to see thriving here, at the 80th parallel, trees and shrubs that in Siberia never grow within the Arctic Circle.

As before, meadows alternated with woods, only the latter were now denser; oxen were grazing in two of the meadows and the travellers gazed at them with interest. However, when the party tried to get a closer look, the oxen fled, proving that there were people in the valley who hunted them but did not have firearms, because the report of a gun did not frighten the animals. In a meadow about eight kilometres from the edge of the valley, the travellers noticed that in addition to the black oxen there were some brown ani-

mals of the same height. When one of them raised its head, Gorokhov cried:

"Matvei Ivanovich, it's a horse!"

"Looks like it! Do you think it's tame?"

"Very unlikely; they're all alike in colour— brown, with a black stripe running down the spine—and then the tails and manes are thinner and the ears are longer," Ordin announced, examining the animals through field-glasses.

"They resemble the wild horse Przhevalsky discovered in the heart of Central Asia," Goryunov said.

"But here, in the Arctic? That's another riddle of this strange land!" exclaimed Kostyakov.

"Let's try and get nearer."

Making a circuit round the meadow, the travellers managed to get closer to the horses. They were grazing separately from the oxen. One of them, evidently an old stallion and the leader of the herd, kept raising its head, surveying the glade and, with distended nostrils, sniffing at the air. Suddenly, noticing human beings, it uttered an alarmed neigh, that sounded rather like the cry of an ass, and the whole herd, about twenty adult animals and ten foals, bolted, their heads held high and their tails arched.

"Hell, the game's slipped away!" Gorokhov said. "I wish we had brought down a foal. Their meat's tender."

"What for? We've got enough meat for today and there's no sense loading ourselves. And then why kill for the sake of killing?"

"What about the collection?" Ordin asked. "Isn't a wild horse a rarity and possibly these are a special species."

"Simply horses run wild," Kostyakov offered.

"Not on your life! The horses we have are white, with a rare grey or dapple-grey among them," Gorokhov said.

"And their points are different," added Goryunov. "Evidently, due to some conditions existing here, which we can't explain so far, prehistoric animals, which died out in other countries, have survived in Sannikov Land."

"Much in the same way as marsupial animals, including the kangaroo along with other living fossils, as they are called, have survived in Australia," Ordin explained.

"You'll be telling me next that the mammoth, the woolly rhinoceros, the cave-bear and other contemporaries of prehistoric man live here," Kostyakov laughed.

"It's quite possible, if man hasn't exterminated them," Goryunov replied.

"And the interest that Sannikov Land will arouse in the world because of its position and shape will be all the greater because of its living fossils," Ordin added.

"See that lake, there in the middle of the meadow? How about going there?" suggested Kostyakov. "The way we're discovering things we might find a hippopotamus in it."

"A hippo is not a living fossil," corrected Goryunov, "and lives in great numbers in the rivers of Africa. I'm sure there aren't any here."

But the soil was too marshy and closer to the lake there was an impassable quagmire with an overgrowth of swamp plants. This lake had once been much larger but had gradually been reduced by the vegetation advancing from its banks. The travellers had to turn back without tasting the water or learning whether there were any fish. Naturally, there could be no question of a hippopotamus living in the lake: the quagmire would have engulfed its massive bulk.

In the forest beyond this meadow the trees and under-brush grew so thickly that if it had not been for the paths worn by animals, the travellers would have had an extremely difficult time making any headway at all.

On one of those paths they heard the musical spring trilling of various birds, and the cooing of turtle-doves; even the call of a cuckoo reached them faintly from afar. They saw jays, magpies, jackdaws, and a pair of eagles. The latter were soaring high in the air, looking for prey in the meadows.

"This is truly amazing!" Goryunov exclaimed. "One might think we're somewhere in the south and not ten degrees from the North Pole."

"Yes, and the low position of the sun, in spite of its being noon, is the only indication that we are in the extreme north," Ordin pointed out.

"The black, snow-striped peaks of the mountains encircling this valley remind me of my native Irkut Valley with the Tunkin Alps stretching along it," Kostyakov said, "while the vegetation and the birds heighten the illusion."

In the next meadow, which also had a lake in its centre, there were some oxen and horses. The travellers stopped on the fringe, deciding to watch the animals and, at the same time, to cook their dinner. Fresh water was obtained from a little stream flowing across the meadow. Stopping on the path where it wound through the bushes into the meadow, they quickly made a fire, hung the kettle and soup pot over it on a tripod, and cutting the veal into pieces, they strung them on twigs, and set to roast. Then they hid in the shrubbery near the path and observed the grazing animals.

Suddenly, from the depths of the forest came the sound of heavy, rapidly approaching footfalls. The consternated travellers just managed to lie back in the bushes when a huge, dark-brown animal rushed past them with a deep-toned bellow.

"What was that? What was that monster?" Gorokhov said in a frightened whisper.

"Did you see the huge horn on its snout?" asked the no less astonished Goryunov.

"And the curly little tail like a pig's?"

"Here is its footprint," Ordin said, pointing to an imprint on the trail where they had spilled some water; the imprint was nearly eighteen centimetres in diameter and ended with grooves left by several hoofs.

"Well, we've just seen another living fossil—a woolly rhinoceros!" said Ordin.

"Damn its fossilized hide!" cried Kostyakov. "It's gone and spoilt our whole dinner."

Indeed, the rhinoceros had made a mess of things when it rushed down the path like a hurricane: the pot with the soup was lying in the bushes without its contents, the meat was in the grass, the twigs with the roasting pieces of veal had been trampled, and the kettle was on its side.

"Begin from the beginning, cook," Gorokhov said with a wry smile, picking up the pot and the kettle to go to fetch more water.

"What a clumsy beast!" grumbled Kostyakov, collecting the pieces of meat. "As though there was not enough room for it on the path."

"Next time," laughed Goryunov, "we'll know better than to camp on an animal trail."

"There's another animal coming this way," Ordin shouted, jumping into the shrubbery; the others followed him.

A few seconds later, three rhinos, following one another in a line, ran past with deep bellows. The travellers had a better look this time. Leading the trio was a male rhinoceros with a huge horn on its snout and a much smaller one in the centre of its head. The second was a female animal with one small horn. The rear was brought up by a hornless baby rhino, which was straining hard to keep up with its parents on its short legs. All had thin, but fairly long brown fur.

"Keep your eyes peeled, chaps!" warned Goryunov. "As likely as not, they're running away from some animal. Have your guns ready!"

No sooner had Goryunov warned his friends than a beast of prey appeared on the trail. Though it was huge, it was easily identified as a bear; it ran with a rolling gait, its nose close to the ground as if sniffing at it. Noticing the fire smouldering by the trail, it stopped, raised its head, and opened its mouth, revealing enormous fangs and a red tongue. Just then the dogs attacked it from behind. It turned sharply and ran back into the thicket with a displeased growl.

"Come, comrades," Goryunov said in a loud voice. "Let's move to the meadow. If we stay here, animals will not only prevent us from cooking our dinner, but also eating it in peace."

"A real grizzly! I never saw such a big one in my life," Gorokhov said, crawling out of the shrubbery.

"It's big all right, but not very brave if the dogs could frighten it off!" Ordin laughed. "Do you know, I'm sure it is not simply a very big brown bear, but a fossil cave-bear, a contemporary of the woolly rhino and the mammoth. Did you notice the jaws?"

"Another of your living fossils," Kostyakov said. "Our collection is growing fast and is too good to be true."

"Yes, we'll have to photograph all these fossil animals right in nature's bosom, otherwise nobody will believe us," Goryunov observed. "Pity we took so few plates with us. But who could have foreseen that Sannikov Land was a zoo or, more correctly, a palaeontological gardens."

"Nikita, now you'll be able to tell your teamster-friends that on the snout of a rhino you saw for yourself the horn that they think is the claw of an *exekyu*."

"I saw a creature like that before."

"When? Last night, or what?"

"No, long ago. On the Achada River, the one that flows into the Yana from the right. The carcass of an animal like it tumbled out of the bank in the spring and lay near the water. Polar foxes had already picked its face and stomach clean by the time I saw it. Our district constable informed the governor and he sent an official to fetch the animal. But when that official arrived there was nothing to fetch; all the meat had been eaten by polar foxes and the river had buried the bones."

"That is what always happens to these finds," Goryunov said. "By the time somebody accidentally discovers them and informs some official and that official sends a report to the Academy in St. Petersburg and the Academy sends a scientific expedition to investigate—many months pass. Meanwhile, birds and animals and the rivers do their work. Countless rare finds are lost that way."

"Well, we shall bring back something much better," Ordin said. "Skins, skulls, and photographs not of dead but of living fossil animals."

"Photographs, maybe, but we shall have to select as few skulls and skins as possible for we only have three sledges," Kostyakov reminded him.

"You'll not take away the skull and skin of a mammoth with the means of transportation that we've got!" Goryunov laughed.

"You're reckoning on us seeing a live mammoth, I suppose," Kostyakov said with a note of derision in his voice.

"Why not? If the rhinoceros thrives and multiplies here, as we saw by that baby rhino, there's no reason why the mammoth shouldn't."

"Well, I should say that if there were any, your Onkilons pushed it out of existence long ago."

"Why should they? They don't need the tusks; there's nobody to sell them to. Then there's plenty of other game and you must remember that it is not easy to bring a hulk like that down without firearms."

"The stone-age man hunted the mammoth with the most primitive of weapons."

"It's my guess, Matvei Ivanovich," Gorokhov broke into the conversation, "that if this mammoth you're talking about lives here, the people of this valley worship it as a god, like the *exekyu*."

"There's something in that, Nikita. It's the very reason I hope we see this animal."

Collecting their kit together, they moved to the edge of the meadow near the stream and again lit a fire. The meadow was deserted; with their stamping and bellowing, the rhinos had probably frightened away the oxen and the horses.

"They've spoilt things for us here as well!" Ordin said. "And I was hoping to steal up to the horses and oxen and take a few photographs while our dinner was cooking."

"All that's left are birds that are only good for the oven," Kostyakov said, pointing to a flock of ducks flying over the lake.

BUBBLING LAKES

They dined and rested without further incident and moved on, following the bank of the stream. Soon they came upon a sheet of water about half a kilometre in diameter and bordered with green reeds; the leaves of large water lilies floated on the surface together with the tiny leaves of the water chestnut or *Trapa natans,* a plant that has almost died out in the world but which grew profusely here. The lake deepened gradually and water beetles and shoals of tiny fish darted in and out of the aquatic overgrowth. Piercing through the clouds, the slanting rays of the midday sun lit up this peaceful picture of abundant life, so inconceivable at this latitude.

"The stream is not emptying into the lake but is flowing out of it," Goryunov noted.

"What conclusion must we draw from that?"

"That the waters of this valley must have an outlet to the sea. In other words, that there is a pass somewhere in the ring of mountains."

"Let's suppose that that is so."

"We must find out if it is, because the snow-drifts down which we descended into this valley will lose much of their height in the course of the summer and we'll be unable to get out. Consequently, only a pass in the mountains will allow us to leave the valley."

"But there may be no pass at all," Ordin said. "The water may be draining into an underground channel. You frequently get such channels in layers of lava. Remember the Dolphins of the Hawaiian Islands from your geology course?"

"What are they?" Kostyakov asked.

"They are long tunnels in the lava which stretch deep inland from the sea. When the tide is in, they are filled with water which spurts out of cracks like a fountain. Hence the name."

"Not a very apt one, I must say, because dolphins do not spout water but only raise a splash when they play," Goryunov remarked. "But it will be very unfortunate if there is no pass. It will mean having to wait until the close of winter, when the snow-drifts will be high enough again."

"It doesn't matter. We planned to spend the winter in Sannikov Land if that proved to be possible. From what we've seen it's quite obvious that it is possible."

At this juncture, Gorokhov, who was looking intently at the lake, interrupted the conversation, exclaiming:

"Look, look what's happening over there. Some monster's climbing out of the water!"

In the middle of the lake, the water was rising, taking the shape of a protuberance or bubble. Suddenly, the bubble burst, releasing a cloud of white vapour, which quickly melted in the air. Ringlets, forming where the bubble had burst, spread out in all directions, rocking the water-fowl swimming in the lake.

"There might be a whale or some other big animal on the bottom," Gorokhov suggested.

"Whales do not live in fresh water," Goryunov commented. "But I wonder what caused the bubble?"

Ordin, meanwhile, took a thermometer out of its case and dipped it in the water. Gorokhov laughed, so absurd did this method of finding out what lived in the lake seem to him.

"Imagine, 25°C!" Ordin ejaculated.

"Early in the spring so far north and 25 degrees! Incredible!" Kostyakov said. "Are you sure you're not erring by 20 degrees or thereabouts?"

"Look for yourself if you don't believe me."

"But what's the explanation?"

"Judging by what's just happened, this lake apparently has an underground source of hot water or, what is more probable, steam. That conforms with my hypothesis that this valley is the crater of an old volcano which at intervals still liberates heat through fissures."

"We must wait and see if another bubble rises," Goryunov said.

"Yes. And if there are many of these lakes here in the valley, then we have discovered one of the reasons for the warm climate in Sannikov Land."

The ringlets subsided and the surface of the lake again became as smooth as a mirror. The travellers waited eagerly. Goryunov held a watch in his hand.

Thirty-two minutes after the first swelling, the water again rose in a bubble, which attained a height of approximately two metres before bursting and releasing vapour.

"I think your explanation is correct," Goryunov said, turning to Ordin. "What we are observing is a periodic discharge of steam or hot air from the bowels of the earth, which directly or through the water of the lake warms the valley."

"Yes, and we saw quite a few of these lakes from our perch on the precipice."

"I still think it's a fountain from a whale," declared

Gorokhov, who was unable to make head or tail of what his companions said.

"How could a whale get into the lake, Nikita? Surely, it did not climb over these mountains."

"How did the rhinos, the oxen and the horses, which cannot climb precipices either, get here?" demanded Kostyakov.

"You don't seem to know the geological history of the New Siberian Islands," Ordin protested. "At the beginning of the Quaternary period they were still part of the mainland of Siberia and this volcano, which, evidently, was extinct by that time, attracted animals; later there were upheavals as a result of which a considerable area sank to the bottom of the sea and the rest broke up into islands. The animals were cut off from the mainland and when the climate deteriorated they died off and the only island where they survived was Sannikov Land, thanks to the warm soil."

"But that doesn't explain how big animals descended into this hole!"

"First, in those days the walls of this crater probably had deeper clefts, which were blocked up at a later period. Secondly, we've only seen a small part of the surrounding mountains and somewhere in the north there may be a more or less convenient pass."

"Now I have no doubts that we shall make many more unexpected and interesting discoveries," Goryunov said. "And I am very happy that the money the old academician gave us so trustfully has not been spent in vain and science will receive a valuable gift—a breeding ground of extinct animals."

"And, perhaps, of people," Ordin added.

"The only pity is that our expedition is so poorly fitted

for scientific observations. We cannot substitute for experienced investigators and are likely to miss a lot."

"It can't be helped. We discovered this wonderful land and the way to it. The Academy will, of course, organize a big scientific expedition and we shall be its guides."

While the travellers were talking, another bubble rose on the surface of the lake and the phenomenon repeated itself with precision.

"This time I kept my eyes on my watch," Ordin said. "The interval was exactly thirty-three minutes."

"But how do birds and fish live in hot water?" Gorokhov inquired.

"Did you notice that none of the birds are swimming in the middle of the lake? Apparently, where those bubbles form the water is too hot for them and they avoid it."

"Fish keep away, too. But then there's enough room for them along the sides."

Finishing their observations, the travellers went on, skirting the meadow as close to the edge of the forest as they could. They came across the same family of rhinos that had rushed past their camp: the two adult animals, their heads thrown back, were feeding on green shoots off the bushes, showing their enjoyment by wagging their little tails, while the baby rhino now nibbled at the grass, now gambolled so clumsily that it was impossible to watch it without laughing; it looked as though a large barrel with four thick little columns stuck to it was skipping and leaping for fun. Concealing themselves in the shrubbery, the travellers looked at this family idyll for a long time and perpetuated it on a photographic plate. Only Gorokhov watched the animals with more prosaic eyes, although he, too, laughed at the capers cut by the baby rhino; he was calculating the quantity of fat that could be obtained from this barrel and how many strong sledge thongs could be cut from its hide.

His gun was already aimed when Gorokhov stopped him, whispering:

"You're out of your mind, Nikita! The parents will trample us to death if we touch their offspring! These animals are nasty customers."

Carefully bypassing the rhinos, they found themselves on a path running across the next woods, which was really a forest; here the trees were almost ten metres high and the dense underbrush made further progress difficult and noisy. There was the danger of meeting some big animal on the trail and, taught by experience, the travellers kept their guns in readiness and let Krot lead the way. Accustomed to the bare tundra of North Siberia, the dog was afraid to plunge into the thickets and lose sight of its masters.

The forest teemed with life. In addition to numerous small birds, the travellers saw hazel-grouse whistling on the boughs of the trees, particoloured jays calling to each other, magpies flying from tree to tree and chattering without stop; they heard the warble of thrushes and other singing birds. Rustlings in the bushes betrayed the presence of small mammals. Coming out on a straight stretch, after rounding a bend, they saw the dark shape of what looked like a bear. It was moving in their direction, sniffing at the earth. Noticing human beings, it sharply turned off the path and vanished in the thicket.

"There seem to be quite a few of these Bruins hanging around here," Gorokhov said.

"Only they all look timid to me," Kostyakov said.

"It all depends. If they're hungry they'll attack people as well."

"We must make it a rule to keep two of our guns loaded with explosive bullets so as to be prepared for any eventuality," Goryunov declared.

This time the forest stretched uninterruptedly for about two kilometres; beyond it was another meadow with a stream fringed with tall poplars, willows, bird-cherry bushes, hawthorns and sweet briers, from which a many-voiced bird chorus could be heard. The travellers followed the stream to a lake, which was bigger than the one they had already seen and did not have swampy banks.

"I wonder if this lake bubbles, too?" Ordin said.

"Let's rest here for a while and see."

The travellers stayed on the shore of the lake for a quarter of an hour, observing the birds; frequent splashes indicated an abundance of fish.

"It's a regular paradise, that's what it is," Gorokhov was entranced. "Game of every kind, fish—as much as you want, not like in our poor tundra."

"I can understand now why migratory birds seek this land out, braving the ice and snow of the ocean; they live a life of plenty here," Goryunov said.

"It's strange that with a wonderful place like this to fly to large numbers of them go no farther than the northern tundra."

"When birds migrate they are guided by an instinct which one generation inherits from another," Goryunov explained. "The only birds that come here are the ones that are hatched in this place. Birds reared in the tundra stop there and do not fly any farther north even though they see others doing it."

"Yes, if birds were cleverer we'd have a terrible time in the tundra. Migratory birds and moulting geese frequently save us from starvation when fishing or hunting brings nothing," Gorokhov said.

"It has been noted that sometimes birds do not fly in a straight line but make a big detour only because that is how their forebears flew, skirting localities where once they could not stop for a rest, for instance, glaciers, which disappeared long ago, or dense forests, which had been cut down."

Just then the water in the middle of the lake began to rise not in one but in two places. Each bubble released a cloud of vapour and subsided.

"We ought to wait for the next eruption in order to time the interval," Ordin suggested.

"That's a good idea and while we're at it let's make some tea."

They lit a fire in a convenient spot and hung the kettle up. Gorokhov, taking his double-barrelled gun, crept up to some ducks swimming near the lakeside. Soon a shot was heard and the ducks rose into the air, leaving two of their number behind. There was  another report and immediately after it Gorokhov was heard shouting:

"Quick, help!"

His three friends seized their guns and hurried in the direction of his voice; but the reeds and bushes held them up and when they got to Gorokhov they found him

stretched out on his stomach near the water, the surface of which was disturbed, showing that something heavy had immersed in it.

"What's the matter? What happened?"

"You're too late," Gorokhov said disappointedly. "It slipped away."

"What slipped away? A fish?"

"No, a seal, a real seal," the hunter replied with a sigh.

"I don't believe you," Kostyakov declared. "You don't get seals in fresh water. Most likely it was an otter."

"Well, I like that!" the Yakut said, touched to the quick. "I've seen enough seals to recognize one when I see it."

"Where was it?"

"Right here, between those mounds. When I let fly at the ducks it raised its head out of the grass and stared at me as though it had gone crazy. I could not resist and let it have the duck shot. It began to twist. I fell on it and yelled. But by the time you got here it wriggled out of my hands. There was no way I could hold on to the slippery beast. And that was the last I saw of it."

"Was it big?"

"No, smaller than ours; it could have been a young one."

"Can anyone tell me how it came to be in this lake?" Kostyakov was nonplussed. "Somehow I don't believe it."

"I can't see why you don't, Pavel," Ordin said. "Remember that a special species of seal called *Phoca sibirica* lives in Lake Baikal, which is a fresh-water lake, too. I've heard people say that it also lives in Lake Oron, which lies on the Vitim River where it widens between two gorges. Its presence here is all the more understandable because of the proximity of the Arctic Ocean."

"But how did it get into this comparatively small lake?"

"This only proves that the lakes in Sannikov Land were once bigger and accessible from the sea. That was when the seals got here; it's possible that this whole area was a salt-water gulf, which gradually became a fresh-water lake so that in the course of many centuries the seals slowly adapted themselves to a new home."

Returning to the fire, over which the kettle was already boiling, the travellers soon witnessed another eruption of vapour in the centre of the lake. The interval had lasted forty minutes.

After tea, the travellers walked round the lake and found that what Gorokhov had told them was true.

A small seal stuck its head out of the water and gazed at the travellers with round velvety eyes. The dogs, recognizing a tasty morsel in the familiar animal, rushed to the side of the lake, barking, and the seal, snorting disdainfully, disappeared.

"You were right, Nikita. It is a seal," Kostyakov admitted.

FIRST SIGNS OF MAN

Finding themselves in another forest, the travellers again followed an animal trail, letting Krot and Belukha go in front of them.

Suddenly they heard the dogs barking. Approaching with their fingers on the triggers of their guns, they saw that the dogs had stopped a herd of horses that apparently had been heading for the lake. Their tails between their legs, Krot and Belukha were barking and yelping while the horses looked with amazement at these audacious dwarfs who were barring their way.

They stamped their hoofs, snorted, but could not make up their minds to advance.

"What are we to do?" Kostyakov said in confusion. "We can't go on."

"How about firing at them?" Gorokhov suggested.

"Only not with bullets!" Goryunov said. "We have enough meat and, besides, they're standing inconveniently and if we wound the leader he will charge at us and the rest will follow. Use duck shot. It will sting the nearest horses and scare them away."

The thunder of the guns resounded in the narrow green corridor of the trail and the small shot showered on the horses in front, causing an astonishing commotion.

A frantic neighing filled the air and the horses reared and turned in the narrow path, knocking each other over and breaking the bushes and young trees growing on either side. Finally, the entire herd turned and made off in the opposite direction.

"Now we can proceed without fear of meeting any other animal," Ordin said.

Indeed, the wild stampede had frightened not only animals but also birds, which grew silent for some time. Without further hindrance, the travellers reached the next meadow, where their attention was immediately arrested by a snow-white hill towering in the centre and standing out sharply against the green vegetation.

"Of all things, what a big snow-drift!" Gorokhov exclaimed.

"I should say it's an ice-cap which didn't melt," Goryunov corrected him.

"But are they usually so tall?" Kostyakov asked.

"No! Unless it's an ice-cap which had formed at the mouth of a very powerful spring."

"Then what is it?"

Crossing the meadow, the travellers saw that the hill was in the centre of a small lake, thus upsetting the presumption that it was an ice-cap or a snow-drift. From where the travellers now stood, they could see that the hill consisted of ledges rising one above the other and through field-glasses they discerned streams of water flowing down its sides.

Perplexed, they examined this strange hill until suddenly, whistling and hissing, a fountain of water, accompanied by clouds of steam gushed out of its top to a height of about ten metres and then rained down on the ledges. This interesting spectacle lasted no more than a minute after which the hill resumed its former appearance, with only a light vapour rising from it.

"That explains everything! It's a geyser, an intermittent hot spring which is quite common in volcanic regions," Ordin said.

"You're right, and the hill is a deposit of calcareous tufa, which is precipitated by the water as it flows down the sides."

They took the temperature of the water in the lake. It was 35°C but seemed hotter.

"That is why there are no birds on the lake," Kostyakov observed.

"Possibly there are no fish, either. I don't see any splashes," Ordin added.

But the lake was not totally devoid of life. On the bottom were strange reddish weeds among which scurried masses of small crustacea that seemed to feel very much in their element in the warm water. But it was not to the taste of higher animals and birds—a few ducks, which had alighted on the lake, rose into the air again with frightened quacks.

"Isn't it time we thought of where to spend the night?" Goryunov said.

"Yes. The sun's already sinking and we've had enough impressions for one day," Ordin agreed.

"We must choose some place where we'll be safe from animals," Kostyakov said.

"That would be a tree where we could sleep on the boughs like birds, but I don't think we'll like it."

"My suggestion is that we camp not in the forest but in a clearing and watch by turns," Gorokhov said.

"A very good idea. And the chap on duty will keep the fire going so that we're not molested by wild beasts," Goryunov said.

Inasmuch as there was no firewood to be had around the lake, they followed a stream flowing out of it until they came to a forest, where they made themselves comfortable beneath a solitary poplar. Before it grew dark, they cut enough fuel for the night and lit two fires; after supper, they lay down in the space between the fires, detailing to each a two-hour spell of duty. The night passed not very peacefully; ever and anon, now close by, now from afar, came different sounds—the bellowing of oxen, the neighing of horses, the roaring of rhinos, and the hooting of owls, to which the dogs replied with growls and barks. At midnight, a mist began to settle on the meadow, shutting out the waning moon almost completely; the mist crept southwards, breaking every now and then to let the moon illumine the meadow for a few minutes and the white hill in the middle of the lake would seem to be floating on a sea of milk. The eruptions repeated themselves every twenty minutes and likewise disturbed the hush with a soft whistle and the splashing of falling water.

A strong north wind arose at daybreak, quickly dispersing the mist. The sun, emerging in the east from behind the black range of sharp-toothed mountains with snow lining the ledges and recesses, found the travellers ready to resume their explorations. That day they decided to go eastwards to the edge of the valley and to proceed along it back to their base at the snow-drifts in order

to see how Niki-
forov was getting
along, to tell him of
the big bears and
rhinos they had
seen, and to warn
him to refrain from
hunting them.

A narrow path
led from the mead-
ow to the east
through a forest,
which stretched for several kilometres and where the trees
gradually diminished in size. They bagged a few hazel-hens
and a big wood-grouse, which the dogs drove to a tree
from where it gazed with wonder at these strange animals
until a bullet brought it down. The meadow on the far
side of the forest proved to be very soggy; in its centre
was a moss-grown swamp, which evidently was once
a lake.

The travellers had to keep to the edge of the forest,
where the dogs soon brought a magnificent deer to bay.

"As I thought, it's an elk," Gorokhov exclaimed.

However, it was not an elk, but a deer of the same size,
with a proudly raised beautiful head crowned with huge
antlers that combined the peculiarities of the antlers of
an elk and a Manchurian deer; they resembled the latter
by their size and the former—by ending in a broad, jagged
spade. This splendid animal excited the travellers and,
stopped by the dogs, it fell a victim to an explosive bullet.

"It looks like an elk and yet isn't one," Gorokhov announced. "Do you know what it is, Matvei Ivanovich?"

"I think," Goryunov replied after examining the animal,

"that is a giant fossil deer called *Cervus euryceros*, a contemporary of the mammoth."

"But it's not a big one; probably a young specimen," Ordin added.

"No, this deer is old," Gorokhov declared. "Count the branches on the antlers. I should say it's fifteen years old."

"Apparently a degenerating species," Kostyakov suggested.

"And rare. We've seen quite a few other living fossils, but this is the first deer."

"Consequently, we must measure it and take along its skull and antlers," Goryunov said.

"The antlers are too heavy and, moreover, they can't be preserved—look, they are spring antlers, soft and filled with blood," Kostyakov observed.

"Pity! Well, at least we'll have a picture. I managed to take a photograph when it was warding off the dogs," Ordin said.

Without losing time, they took the measurements, carved out the choice meat, fed the dogs, chopped off the antlers and carried away the head, intending to take it to their base.

"The brains and the tongue for dinner! It'll be a dainty dish," Gorokhov exulted, also cutting the skin off the back for any repairs that their boots might need.

At the end of the meadow there was another forest, which extended almost to the foot of the fringing precipice, gradually becoming sparser and lower. Running parallel with the forest for about five hundred metres was a piece of ground richly overgrown with moss; green liverwort and whitish reindeer moss made a thick blanket on the uneven ground, hiding the rocks that fell from the precipice.

"What a marvellous place for deer! If only they could be driven here for the summer," Gorokhov sighed.

"Have you noticed that in spite of the many lakes and marshy meadows there are practically no parasitical insects?" asked Goryunov.

"Yes. No horseflies, gadflies or midges and very few gnats," Ordin corroborated.

"In a nutshell, a heaven on earth! Not like in our country, where in the summer these insects make life a misery," Gorokhov added.

"Remember, Nikita, what you said not so long ago about mirages and shaitans?" Goryunov laughed.

"Do you think we're imagining all that we see?" Kostyakov asked.

Gorokhov gave an embarrassed smile and shook his head. Everything he had seen during the past two days was unusual but it certainly was not the work of his imagination.

"I'll give you my opinion when we're safely back in Kazachye," the Yakut parried.

They noticed some reindeer grazing in a moss field close by. The animals disappeared in the undergrowth as soon as they sighted human beings.

Closer to the foot of the precipice, there was a flock of mountain sheep, which had been concealed by a huge boulder that had fallen from above. At first, the sheep ran along the precipice and then with astonishing agility climbed a narrow ledge, leaping across the wide gaps dismembering it. Reaching an elevation of about a hundred metres, they vanished on a broader ledge.

The precipice, in the form of gloomy black walls with brownish-red lichens growing in patches and spots, had high ledges stretching upwards; it consisted of basalt, of which the entire rim of this remarkable valley was made up. No vegetation grew at its foot; broken pieces of rock, covered with lichens, were strewn about chaotically; here and there, in the spaces between them, snow could be seen. The highest cliff sheltered a platform of several square metres, which was free of broken rock but was trampled and befouled by mountain sheep. In its depths there was something not unlike a natural niche on the wall of which Gorokhov's keen eye discerned a thin coating of soot.

"Ho, people have been there!" he cried.

"Those who herded the mountain sheep?" Kostyakov laughed.

The travellers gathered round the niche; in it were brands, coals, ashes, and charred bones. Carefully examining the platform, the travellers found some very crudely made flint weapons and pieces of flint.

"People of the stone age!" Ordin announced. "And not even of the neolithic but of the palaeolithic period, judging by the primitive finish."

"But when did they live here? A thousand years ago?" Kostyakov demanded.

"No, the fireplace is quite fresh. It's on the very surface and is covered not with pieces of rock but only with dust, which was probably raised by the sheep."

"Does this mean that somewhere in Sannikov Land we shall run across stone-age savages, who might even turn out to be cannibals?" Kostyakov asked.

"The charred bones seem to be human," Ordin commented.

"Is it possible that they are our Onkilons?" Kostyakov said to Goryunov in a voice pregnant with reproach.

"The Onkilons left Siberia a few centuries ago. At that time the peoples of the north were no longer of the stone age. They knew the uses of iron."

"Yes, our forefathers were already digging ore and forging iron knives, stirrups, rings, and hooks," Gorokhov put in.

"In addition, they widely used articles made from horn, bone, and stone, which are still in use among all the small peoples living in places cut off from modern culture and where iron goods penetrate with difficulty. But the finish of these artefacts shows that they belong to the neolithic and definitely not the palaeolithic period," Goryunov explained.

"Are we to take it that this is not an Onkilon fire-place?"

"Certainly. Evidently, in Sannikov Land there are survivors of stone-age people, who lived at the same time as the mammoth, the cave-bear, and other animals of the end of the glacial period."

"And if these animals have survived, as we have already seen for ourselves, there is no reason why people did not survive as well," Ordin added.

"If the Onkilons, who had a much higher culture than these savages, did not annihilate them," Goryunov said.

"The fire-place shows that they either still exist or existed very recently, possibly a handful," Ordin remarked.

"It would be extremely interesting to see stone-age savages," Kostyakov said. "They probably live in caves on the outskirts of the valley, and we must warn Nikiforov because if they really are cannibals I doubt that a meeting with them would be safe."

Returning to the shrubbery, the travellers headed southwestwards and came within sight of their base towards evening.

When the snow-drifts were already near, Gorokhov could not resist firing at a mountain sheep that was making a fine target on a ledge.

In reply, a shot rang out from the base and presently

Nikiforov appeared accompanied by Pestrushka, who, with its tail wagging merrily, ran to sniff at Krot and Belukha, who responded in a like manner.

The day before, Nikiforov had brought the carcass of the ox to the base, while on the day his friends returned he had shot a mountain sheep and cut a supply of firewood. He had already made a cave for the tent, blocked the exit with lumps of ice, and with Pestrushka to keep him company felt perfectly safe.

ONKILONS

The calm weather of the next day held the travellers up at the base until noon, for only then did the air become clear of a dense mist, which as they now realized was a characteristic feature of the climate in Sannikov Land, in spring at any rate. That was not surprising: the numerous warm lakes and streams filled the air with moisture, while the extensive area of snow and ice around Sannikov Land caused this moisture to condense into mist after sunset. The humid climate was also the reason for the abundance of moss and lichens in the forests; the trunks of all the trees were overgrown with moss while grey lichens formed countless shaggy locks that drooped from the branches.

The mist was the reason why Sannikov Land, despite the altitude of its mountains, was so rarely seen from Kotelny; in spring, mists probably hung over it almost continually, while later, when the sea was free of ice, the mists over the latter formed a thick curtain around the land.

The second expedition into the valley was made in a north-westerly direction. There, too, forests alternated with more or less extensive meadows; these had many lakes; the southernmost lakes were already growing over with rushes and becoming swamps, a fate that was not yet threatening those farthest away, but eruptions of vapour, which were very weak here, were noticed only in a few lakes. Obviously, here the volcanic activity of the valley was already stopping. In the meadows there were oxen and horses, but they were fewer in number and much more careful, evidently aware of the danger that the nearness of man spelt for them. Rhinos were seen only once, in the distance. But there were many wild boars in the rushes around the lakes and one of them was shot for dinner.

That night the travellers chose to encamp on the border of a large meadow. Leaving their knapsacks and guns behind, they went into the forest to chop wood for the fires. But they had not been gone long when Krot and Belukha, who had been left in the meadow, filled the air with a frantic barking. Gorokhov and Ordin were closest to the spot. They rushed back and saw an enormous bear sniffing at their knapsacks; the smell of fresh meat had apparently stirred its appetite. Barking and squealing, the dogs were trying to bite its hind legs, but it nimbly evaded their teeth and growled angrily.

What was to be done? The guns lay beside the knapsacks, which were in danger of being torn to shreds in spite of the zeal of the dogs. Ordin, who had an axe with him, whispered to Gorokhov:

"I'll tackle it from behind with my axe. When it turns on me grab a gun and shoot."

With its claws the bear tore open one of the knapsacks and stuck its nose into it. At that moment, Ordin sprang up from behind and, swinging the axe with all his strength, drove it to its very butt into the bear's sacrum and quickly stepped away. A terrible roar rent the air; the bear rose on its hind legs and then fell on its back, almost crushing Krot. Its spine was broken and it rolled on the grass bellowing and waving its front paws. The dogs clung to its motionless hind legs, while Gorokhov, seizing a gun, fired an explosive bullet into its left side. A few moments later, the huge animal grew still, its blood staining the grass.

Goryunov and Kostyakov, carrying armfuls of firewood, joined their friends and together they stood round the bear, marvelling at its size; it was half as big again as the familiar brown bear, while its fangs were more than ten centimetres long.

"This time we got off cheap," Goryunov said.

"One torn knapsack and a wounded dog, but it could have been worse."

In point of fact, in its agony the bear had grazed Belukha's side with its paw, tearing the skin. The dog was already licking its wound, which, luckily, was not deep.

"It will be a lesson for the future. One of us must always stay to guard our things," Ordin said. "We shan't have many chances to stick an axe into the back of such a big animal."

"Yes, if a beast like this lays its paws on you—you can say good-bye," Gorokhov remarked, getting down to skin the bear. Ordin measured it, but it was too late to take a photograph; twilight was already setting in.

They had to move their camp to another place because of the unpleasant odour coming from the carcass, but that did not prevent the dogs from eating their fill of bear meat. The travellers spent a restless night. The dogs growled incessantly but whatever caused them to be uneasy was hidden by a dense mist that settled on the meadow at midnight. Near the bear's carcass, which lay about a hundred paces away, there was an uproar in which the sound of champing and the crunching of bones could be distinguished; some nocturnal beasts were feasting on the remains. At daybreak, Gorokhov found only the skeleton, which had been picked clean, and caught a glimpse of two wolves that fled at his approach.

That day, thanks to a wind, the mist dispersed earlier than usual and the travellers continued their journey to the north-west. Gorokhov stretched the bear's skin between two trees in the meadow, intending to retieve it on the way back. They passed two more meadows with lakes; in the second lake there was a white tufa hill, but evidently there had been no eruptions for a long time, for the tufa was covered with lichens.

As they emerged from the forest and stepped into the third meadow, the sound of human voices reached them from the opposite fringe. But the dogs began to bark and the voices at once fell silent. A well-beaten path led across the meadow, skirting a small lake near which the imprints left by human feet shod in soft fur boots could be easily recognized in the moist soil.

"These are not people of the stone age!" Goryunov exclaimed. "If they were their feet would have been bare."

"And since they have the same footwear as our northern peoples they must be related to them and we have nothing to fear," Ordin added.

When they had circumvented the lake, the rushes of which prevented them from seeing the opposite side of the meadow, they found themselves in front of a green hill with smoke curling out of its top. Beside the hill was a knot of people; one man was standing on the hill and apparently scanning the meadow. Noticing the travellers when they appeared from behind the lake, he informed the others, causing a commotion among them. About thirty warriors formed a chain across the meadow and advanced towards the travellers. When they came closer it could be seen that all were armed; each had a long spear in his right hand and a bow in his left; feathered arrows peeped over their shoulders.

The warriors stopped when they were about a hundred paces away and one of them, evidently the chief, raised his arm and shouted something.

"What is he saying? In what language?" Goryunov asked Gorokhov.

"Sounds very much like Chukchi," Nikita replied. "He's ordering us to raise both hands to show that we come in peace."

They raised their arms. Slowly, the warriors renewed their advance, but when the distance was reduced to some thirty paces, they again halted at a sign from the chief, who now asked:

"Who are you, where from, and why have you come to our land?"

"Tell him that we are white men and have come from the south, from a big country, in order to see this small land amidst the ice," Goryunov ordered.

Gorokhov interpreted what Goryunov said.

"Approach, white men, but know that we are many and that all are armed," the chief said.

The travellers approached with thirty pairs of eyes vigilantly following every movement they made; Goryunov stepped forward and stretched his hand out to the chief. Before shaking hands with the stranger, the chief brought his right hand up to his forehead and then touched his chest over his heart. He repeated the gesture with the others.

Meanwhile, the warriors coming up from the flanks closed the ring round the travellers, standing shoulder to shoulder, their weapons grasped firmly in their hands and exchanging impressions about the strangers' clothes, footwear, knapsacks, the axes tucked in their belts, and the shining sticks on their backs.

All were bared to the waist and wore skin trousers and boots. Wavy lines, circles, and dots were tattooed on their faces, chests, and forearms. Each had a necklace of what looked like wolves' teeth, with one, two or three big bear's fangs in front. Their black, straight hair was twisted on the crown of their heads in a knot in which were stuck one, two or three eagle's feathers. They had muscular bodies, swarthy faces, and flattened cheek-bones, black eyes and straight noses. The two upper middle cutting teeth were painted red, which gave them a queer look when they smiled—the mouths seemed to divide into two round holes. The chief was more powerfully built and taller than the rest, wore a necklace of bear's fangs and had a red line painted across his forehead; there were red feathers in his hair. Evidently, this was a warlike tribe and the warriors were formidable foes in spite of their primitive weapons: the spearheads were made of a transparent stone, the arrow-heads were of bone, while stuck in the belt of many of the warriors was a stone hatchet with a wooden handle. In addition to a quiver full of arrows, each had a small shield on his back.

"Who are your people and what is this land called?" Gorokhov asked, interpreting Goryunov's question.

"We are Onkilons and this is our land, conquered by our forefathers. I am Amnundak, the chief of the Onkilons. What is your name and what is your land called?"

Receiving a reply to these and some other questions aimed at learning why and how the white men came to them, the chief declared:

"You have come from afar and you are few. Be our guests. Come to my dwelling."

He turned and went up the path, the travellers following him with the warriors marching on either side and bringing up the rear. They questioned Gorokhov about the travellers' clothes and weapons, their journey across the ice, and the great country in the south about which they knew something from legends. Gorokhov had a difficult time answering all these questions, especially as the Onkilons spoke in a tongue that differed greatly from the Chukchi language and the parties in the conversation did not always understand each other.

The green hill proved to be a big mudhouse—the dwelling of the Onkilons. The chief stopped at the entrance, raised the skins that served as a door, and, with a gesture, invited the travellers to go in. Everybody had to stoop because the entrance was low. A fire was burning in the middle and a few pieces of meat strung on a cross-piece as on a spit were roasting over it. About six metres square, this central part was marked off by four thick columns;

to these columns were tied thick cross-beams that supported the roof which had a hole that was at once a window
and an outlet for the smoke. A long log sloped from each
cross-beam, its bottom end resting on the ground. On the
sides, each slope was secured with shorter and thinner logs,
likewise set obliquely. That resulted in a cross-shaped
dwelling with rounded re-entrant angles. Three branches
of the cross served as bedrooms; in the fourth was a door
and a store-room. The central square was the kitchen, din-
ing-room, and reception hall. On the surface, the whole

frame was covered with a thick layer of earth, which over-grew with grass. Altogether, though the dwelling was dark, it was spacious and warm.

The chief entered and led his guests into the square, squatting on a bear skin and motioning to the travellers to sit on either side of him. The warriors arranged them-selves along the other sides of the square around the fire. When the travellers grew accustomed to the semi-darkness, they noticed that the space beneath the sloping logs was crowded with women and children, who were staring at them with curiosity and gradually edging towards the sit-ting warriors. The women were almost naked; only a piece of dark leather no wider than the palm of a hand and scarcely differing from the dusky skins in colour was wound round the hips and the lower part of the stomach. The loin-cloth worn by the young women was ornamented with black, yellow, and red straps. In addition to a loin-cloth, they wore necklaces made of small white, grey, green, and reddish stones and matching bracelets on their forearms and wrists. Their nakedness was somewhat offset by the fantastic flowers and leaves, wavy lines and circles tattooed on their breasts, stomachs, backs, arms, legs, and faces. Par-ticular attention was drawn by the chief's wife, whose tattooing represented two snakes curling round her legs in rings, then winding up her stomach and sides and ending with heads facing one another between her breasts and collar-bones; two smaller snakes were tattooed on her arms, their heads meeting at her shoulder blades. On the dusky skin, these bluish-black snakes made an uncanny picture.

The lines of the women's faces were softer than the men's and some of them were quite pretty; they were slen-der and well-proportioned.

The children had no clothes at all, but the juveniles of both sexes wore the same kind of loin-cloth as the women, only those of the girls were embroidered. The girls' hair was woven into little plaits, while the boys had theirs twisted into a knot on the crown of their heads. The women wore their hair in two braids that fell on their breasts and were adorned with little stones. Girls of marriageable age had four braids: two on the sides of the head and falling on the breast and two at the back of the head and coming down the back.

At a sign from Amnundak, the woman with the snakes fetched some small wooden cups from a leather-covered chest, filled them with milk from a leathern pitcher hanging on one of the columns, and gave them to the chief, who passed them on to his guests. Leaving the last cup for himself, he raised it to his lips and, with a graceful gesture, invited the travellers to follow his example. The cups contained thick deer's milk; it was a little sour but very pleasant, or so it seemed to the travellers, who had not tasted it for a long time. The cups were refilled, after which the woman took down the roasted meat, cut it into thick slices with a bone knife and brought it to the chief on a wooden tray. The chief gave a slice to each of his guests. While they were eating the meat and washing it down with milk, Amnundak spoke to his people. The words followed one another too rapidly for Gorokhov to catch their meaning and Goryunov asked the chief to repeat what he said. Speaking slowly, so that Gorokhov could interpret every word, Amnundak said:

"Many years ago, our people, the Onkilons, exhausted by unending wars with the Chukchis over deer pastures, decided to find another home for themselves. At first they crossed the ice to the nearest islands, built mudhouses and

settled down to a peaceful life. But they did not like the land: there were mists in the summer, mists in the winter, mists in the spring, mists the whole year round. The people began to die off and so did the deer. It was seen that in spring birds flew farther north and returned fat in autumn. So the people made up their minds to go where the birds flew. The first time they tried, the sea stopped them, the second time the ice was thin, a storm arose and broke the ice, and many people and deer perished. They waited for the coldest winter and sent out scouts. The ice was strong. Everybody went and this land was found. Only a few reached it; I cannot tell if there were more than fifty of them.

"At that time the chief was a great shaman, who cured all illnesses; he showed the people the way to this land. Before he died, he said that the Onkilons would live peacefully until the appearance of white men from the great land in the south. And he said that in their hands, like the rulers of heaven, the white men would have thunder and lightning, which would kill at a distance.

"When we saw you, the first white men to come to us from the big land, we recalled the words of the old shaman."

"Tell the chief," Goryunov said to Nikita, "that we are peaceful men and mean no harm. We, too, were brought here by the birds flying north. All we wanted was to see where the birds spend the summer. We shall take a look and go back from where we came."

Gorokhov interpreted these words.

"And do you have thunder and lightning that strike from afar?" Amnundak inquired.

Everybody watched the strangers anxiously. Gorokhov turned to Goryunov with a confused look, but the latter said:

"Aren't our guns the thunder and lightning he means? One way or another, the Onkilons are bound to find out. So let us take advantage of this opportunity and surround ourselves with still greater respect and safety by making them think we are messengers of the gods."

"Yes, we have thunder and lightning!" Gorokhov informed the chief.

An alarmed whispering filled the dwelling. Those who were sitting closest to the travellers involuntarily backed away. The chief said:

"Show them to us so that we should know that you really are sent from heaven. But I ask you not to kill Onkilons."

"Let us go outside so that our lightning does not harm anyone," Goryunov said.

The chief solemnly rose to his feet and made for the exit, followed by the travellers and the Onkilons, who now kept away at a respectful distance.

"Bring a sacrificial deer," Amnundak ordered, "and let the white men kill it as a sacrifice to the gods."

Several warriors ran to the woods behind the dwelling and soon returned leading a big, almost white reindeer, which, as though sensing the fate awaiting it, bellowed and struggled to free itself. Directed by Gorokhov, the warriors tied the animal to a stake some two hundred steps from the dwelling. The travellers replaced the explosive bullets in their guns with ordinary ones and fired a volley. The deer dropped heavily to the ground. All the Onkilons fell to their knees when they heard the thunder of the guns and bowed to the mighty strangers.

Rising, Amnundak said in a loud voice so that all might hear:

"Now we know that you are the messengers of heaven the great shaman spoke of. You shall be our guests; everything we have, our dwelling, food, clothes, and deer are yours to dispose of as you wish! Tonight, our shaman will appeal to the gods to spare the Onkilons, who were happy to welcome the messengers from heaven."

When Amnundak finished speaking, he raised his hand to his forehead and heart and bowed low to the travellers; all the Onkilons followed his example. The carcass of the deer was dragged to the feet of the chief, who pointed to the four wounds in the animal's side and said:

"All four lightnings struck the sacrificial deer. Women, prepare the meat for the evening rites. Warriors, ask the shaman to come to our dwelling."

Back in the dwelling, the travellers were again given milk and roasted deer meat, which this time was served with baked martagon bulbs and pancakes made of ground water chestnuts. The Onkilons had neither bread, nor tea, nor tobacco, and the few biscuits and pieces of sugar that the travellers took from their knapsacks were handed round, examined, sniffed at, and tasted with immense interest. Still greater attention was drawn by the pipes, which Gorokhov and Ordin lit after finishing the meal. The Onkilons looked on with trepidation as the white men swallowed the smoke, which made the warriors sitting near them cough and sneeze. The copper kettle that was hung over the fire won everybody's admiration; the Onkilons only had wooden and clay utensils in which they cooked meat; water was heated with hot stones. But tea without sugar, of which the travellers had too small a supply to treat everybody, found no favour. Amnundak forced himself to drink the cup of tea he was offered but declared that the beverage of the Onkilons—he pointed to the leathern pitcher with milk—was better.

The axes and knives likewise caused great excitement; they were touched, stroked, and tested and their shine, strength, and efficiency delighted the warriors. Amnundak made a sign to his wife, who went to the chest and brought a rusty, crude iron knife that was kept as a relic. Showing it to the travellers, the chief said:

"Our forefathers had such knives, axes, and spear- and arrow-heads, which they obtained from the Yakuts but did not know how to make themselves. And when they came here, these weapons gradually became useless, broke or were lost and the Onkilons again began to make weapons from stone and bone."

Krot and Belukha, who lay at the feet of their masters, at first instilled some fear into the Onkilons, who had no dogs. When Gorokhov asked why they had no dogs, Amnundak said:

"The war with the Chukchis was started because of these vicious animals. Our forefathers were deer-herders and kept no dogs because they attack deer. Our forefathers lived on the sea-shore, herding deer, fishing, and hunting walruses and seals; they built dwellings with driftwood. One day the Chukchis came; they had many dogs but no deer.

They began to chase our forefathers out of their fishing and hunting grounds; when there was not enough fish for their dogs, they took our people's deer. War broke out because of that. The Chukchis were many and our forefathers were few. There was nothing they could do but leave and come here."

"How many Onkilons live here?" Goryunov asked. "Is this all there is of your people?" he swept his arm in a semicircle.

Amnundak laughed.

"There are twenty such dwellings with a clan of twenty to thirty people living in each."

"Where are the other dwellings?"

"In different places. The deer need moss. We cannot live near each other. If we did there would not be enough room for people and for deer."

"Is there a chief like you in every dwelling?"

"No. I am the chief of all the Onkilons," Amnundak said proudly. "My clan is the biggest. But in each dwelling there is a headman, the head of the clan."

Counting the women and children, there were nearly sixty people in the dwelling. Goryunov calculated that if an average of twenty-five people lived in every dwelling, there should be about five hundred and thirty Onkilons in Sannikov Land.

The travellers and their hosts conversed till evening. Towards sunset, a herd of deer was driven to the meadow where the dwelling stood and the travellers watched the animals being milked. All the women and girls shared in this work, swiftly moving from one deer to another with wooden pails. There were over two hundred animals in the herd, which stayed in the meadow for the night, guarded against wild beasts by warriors.

When twilight set in and everybody had returned to the dwelling, the shaman, who lived a few kilometres away, appeared. He was a tall, spare old man with hollow cheeks and piercing eyes set deep beneath bushy eyebrows. In spite of the comparatively warm weather, he was in a long, shaggy fur coat. On straps hanging from his collar and belt were strangely shaped copper and iron plates and rods. They were time-worn and had obviously been brought from the mainland and inherited from his predecessors. He carried a small flat drum decorated with red and black bits of leather and rattles. A tattered, peaked hat sat on his head. After making a dignified bow to the chief and scrutinizing the travellers and their dogs, which growled throatily at the sight of this grotesquely dressed man, the shaman seated himself apart from the others at the brightly burning fire, put his drum on the ground and stretched his bony hands out to the flames, mumbling something. At a sign from the chief, the women gave the shaman a cup of milk, which he drank after sprinkling a few drops on the fire.

Small pieces of deer meat, strung on long sticks, were roasting over the fire. Near by, women were cooking soup or, to be more exact, a gravy of deer meat and martagon bulbs in a cylindrical wooden vessel, in which the water was kept boiling with small white-hot stones taken from the fire. Now and then one of the women, using two sticks with flat stones fixed to their ends, took a heated stone and dropped it into the soup vessel, extracting the cooled stone and putting it back in the fire.

When the meat was ready, it was served to the chief, the shaman and the travellers in a cup of soup and each was given quite a gracefully shaped wooden fork. The travellers tasted the soup and found that it was not salted at all. Like the Chukchis, the Onkilons did not use it in their food.

Salt had to be taken from the knapsacks for the soup. It, too, was handed round for inspection; the warriors tasted it, expecting it to be sweet like the sugar the travellers had given them, but they were disappointed and spat it out with disgust, wondering why the white men spoilt such delicious soup and meat with this bitter powder.

The soup was followed by roast meat and water chestnut cakes; the dinner was rounded off with a cup of milk. When the utensils were taken away, the remains of the fire were moved far to one side in order to clear the central part for the rites. A gloom descended on the dwelling, the only illumination coming from the red light of the smouldering coals.

During the meal, Amnundak had told the shaman how the white men appeared in the land of the Onkilons, who they were, what they did, and how they slew the deer. The shaman had listened in silence, nodding his head and asking a question now and again. After dinner, before starting the rites, he demanded that the dogs be taken out of the dwelling. When that was done, he sat in the middle of the square, surrounded by a ring of spectators, took a pinch of whitish powder from a skin pouch tied to his belt, sprinkled it on the palm of his hand and licked it with his tongue. Gorokhov informed the travellers that this powder was made from fried amanita, which the Kamchadals, Koryaks, and some other peoples used as a drug to bring on a peculiar drunkeness.

Sitting in silence for some time, his eyes fixed on the glowing coals, the shaman picked up his drum and passed his hand across it, his fingers drawing a hardly audible sound from the taut skin. To the accompaniment of this drumming, which gradually grew louder, he sang softly in a guttural voice, slowly at first and then quickening the rhythm until the singing and the drumming mingled in a continuous rumble, in which separate words, sounding like wails, could be distinguished. In the beginning, the shaman rocked to and fro without taking his gaze off the coals, but later, working himself into a frenzy, he sprang to his feet and began to spin on one spot, going faster and faster and continuing to beat his drum and to wail. His long coat and the straps with the plates and rods made a hoop as he spun round until finally they formed three cones, one on top of the other and crowned with the conical hat. The hands holding the drum were held above the hat and were in constant motion; the drum twisted, swayed, and danced, giving forth a loud rumble.

Suddenly, the singing stopped with a wild cry, and the shaman sank to the ground, his arms outspread and dropping the drum as though he were in a swoon, which nobody dared to disturb. A thin stream of foam trickled out of the corner of his mouth and flowed down his sunken cheek. All the onlookers kept still and there was a deathly hush in the dwelling, which only a moment before had been filled with a chaos of sounds. Even the dogs tied outside, whose barking had burst into the shaman's singing from time to time, fell silent.

When something like five minutes had elapsed, the shaman rose to his feet, drank a cup of milk and said a few words in a low voice, giving rise to agitation and whispering among his hearers. The chief repeated the words loudly and Gorokhov interpreted them:

"The spirits told the shaman that great misfortunes are in store for the Onkilons."

Amnundak raised his arms heavenwards, but the shaman stopped him with a gesture and said a few more words. A happy whisper ran down the rows of spectators and the chief, lowering his arms, declared:

"The shaman says the misfortunes will not begin while the strangers live in the land of the Onkilons. Such has been the revelation."

The shaman got up slowly, bowed in a general way to the chief and the travellers, and went out, accompanied by two armed warriors. A lively discussion started after his departure. The travellers likewise whispered among themselves. The results of the divination were totally unexpected. Though they were safe and could count on the Onkilons helping them in every way, they knew that now they were tied to these people for a long time as a unique insurance against misfortune. Their plan had been to spend the winter in Sannikov Land and to stay no longer than the beginning of next spring. Would the Onkilons let them leave by then?

"It isn't hard to guess," said Goryunov, "why that wily shaman thought up this amendment to his prophecy, which is a variant of the legend the chief told us. The old man realized that men commanding thunder and lightning would be extremely useful to the Onkilons as friends and very dangerous as enemies."

"And if permitted to leave," Ordin added, "they will, knowing the way to this wonderful land, return in great numbers and drive them out as the Chukchis once did."

"You're absolutely right," Kostyakov noted. "For, having been cut off from the world for centuries, these people have no idea of what is happening today and live only with memories of the past."

"In any case, for the time being we mustn't tell them of our intention to leave," Goryunov said.

"Yes, if we do, they might lock us up and make prisoners of us," Ordin added.

"Or, at best, keep us under surveillance and restrict our movements," Kostyakov pointed out.

"We'll live here for a while, get to know them better and, by degrees, convince them that this prophecy is all nonsense and that nothing is threatening them."

The chief listened to the conversation among the strangers and at last got up and spoke in a loud voice. Instantly, the Onkilons fell silent.

"Onkilons, warriors and women! You have heard what the divine spirits have revealed to our shaman. While the strangers live with us there will be no misfortunes. So let us ask them to stay!"

"Yes, yes!" the Onkilons cried.

The chief turned to the travellers and, with bowed head, said:

"White men, messengers of the gods, the Onkilons beg you to live with them. You shall save us from misfortune. We shall give you everything you wish—the best dwelling, food in abundance, warm clothes when winter comes, and the most beautiful women—so that you should not be in want of anything. You shall live as our chiefs."

"Take anything you want, only stay with us!" cried a chorus of male and female voices and from all sides hands were stretched out to the guests in pleading gestures.

Goryunov rose and replied:

"All right, we agree to stay with you as your guests until you yourselves will let us go. But we want to see all your land and you must show it to us."

Gorokhov interpreted these words and happy shouts filled the dwelling; the chief bowed to the guests again and shook hands with them, first touching his forehead

9*

and head, which, as the travellers later learnt, meant "from the bottom of my heart and without evil intentions." Then he said:

"Soon we shall hold our spring festival at which all the young women and maidens of the tribe will gather, and you shall, if you wish, choose wives. Your wives are far away," he pointed to the south, "and a man feels lonely without a wife."

"Well, now we are bridegrooms," Gorokhov laughed.

"But it will hamper our freedom," Goryunov said.

"Oh well, we'll see what we'll see," Ordin concluded philosophically.

THE SACRED STONE

When the Onkilons, who were noisily expressing their delight at the strangers' consent to live with them, had somewhat calmed down and the women relit the fire, Amnundak turned to Goryunov and his friends:

"You said that you want to see all our land. But do you know that that is dangerous? The forests are full of wild animals."

"We are not afraid of them. Our lightnings will kill any beast before it can attack us," he was told.

"In addition to wild animals, there are savage men, who are much more dangerous than the animals."

"That's interesting," Ordin said to his friends, while Goryunov asked:

"What, are they Onkilons, too? Why are they dangerous?"

"No, they are not Onkilons. They are wild men and we are constantly at war with them. They are very strong and we cannot fight them singly. We call them Wampus, which means 'naked men.' "

"Where do they live?"

"Farther east. They hide in the forests and sometimes attack our dwellings when the warriors are away hunting. They kill the old people and the children and take the women. We are very much afraid of them. Even you will not be able to cope with them if they waylay you and attack you with clubs, spears, and knives."

"Are there so many of them?"

"We don't know how many there are. When our forefathers came here this whole land was populated with these savages. They fought them for a long time, finally driving them to the east."

"Do they live in dwellings like you?"

"No. They live in caves in winter, and in summer they build nests on trees like birds."

"That's whose footprints we found when we went inland the first time!" Goryunov said.

"They worship live gods, who are huge and very illtempered," Amnundak continued. "They offer sacrifices to them."

"What are these gods?"

"Did you see a big animal with horns on its snout?"

"Ah, a rhinoceros! Yes."

"Well, their gods are much bigger. But instead of horns they have a long, supple fifth leg or arm on their heads. The animal breaks trees, seizes people, and throws them on the ground with that leg and tramples them to death with its other legs."

"What an animal!" Gorokhov exclaimed in wonder.

"It has two big white teeth, like the fangs of a bear,

133

sticking out of its mouth, only they are much longer and thicker."

"Sounds like it is an elephant," Goryunov said.

"Possibly a mammoth," Ordin suggested. "There are no elephants in the north. Has it got any fur?" he asked the chief through Gorokhov.

"Yes, a shaggy, red fur."

"Did mammoths have red fur?" Kostyakov looked puzzled. "From the pictures I've seen I thought their fur was black."

"Well, you were wrong," Ordin said. "On the carcasses that were found in Siberia the fur was reddish-brown or ginger. But I wonder if all this means that it's been domesticated by the Wampus?"

"With these teeth," the chief continued, "the animal digs for roots, which it eats, while in the winter it clears away snow to find grass. The teeth are of great use to us; we make our best knives, spears, and arrows from them. But we rarely get a chance to kill one of these animals for the savages vigilantly guard their gods."

"That makes it even more interesting to make the acquaintance of the Wampus and their tame mammoths!" Goryunov exclaimed.

"I have told you everything," Amnundak concluded. "Now you know that you cannot go to the savages alone. They will kill and eat you and misfortunes will come down on the Onkilons. We shall protect you; all our warriors will go to the savages with you. We shall start a big war and destroy them. Your lightnings will help us to kill the Wampus and their gods."

"A punitive expedition," Ordin laughed, "and us in the role of hangmen. Not very flattering, I should say."

But the warriors were pleased with what the chief said.

They evidently had good reason to hate the Wampus. Fierce neighbours such as these were not likely to be welcomed by an inherently peaceable tribe, which had quitted the mainland because of wars.

When the subject of the Wampus was exhausted, Amnundak declared that it was time to prepare a place where the travellers could sleep. In the slanting part of the dwelling opposite the door, where the chief and his family lived, the women cleared a space and spread deer and bear skins on the ground, bringing out even pillows—cylindrical skin bags stuffed with deer wool. This space was partitioned off with a line of little chests containing household utensils, and Amnundak invited the guests to occupy it for the night. Along the other sides of the dwelling, the Onkilons were already preparing for the night; the men undressed completely and folded their clothes, which they used as pillows, and placed their weapons within reach. One warrior remained on guard at the entrance and three others lay down in their clothes by the fire and in the passage in order to relieve him by turns. The guard fed the fire, now and then going outside to fetch wood. The warriors guarding the herd of deer in the meadow also had reliefs and could be heard calling to each other.

The night passed peacefully. The Onkilons began to wake up at dawn, the women getting up first. Some added wood to the fire and began to roast meat and to heat stones with which to cook soup, others ran to milk the deer, putting on clothes for it was cold outside. These were unique skin garments, the trousers of which were sewn to the jacket which had a wide cut at the breast; first the women slipped on the trousers and then quickly drew the rest of the garment over their bodies, thrusting their arms into the short sleeves. Returning to the dwelling, they threw the jacket off their shoulders with a light movement and the entire garment slid to their feet.

From where they lay under the skins, the travellers curiously watched how quickly and easily the women dressed and undressed and how, almost naked, they fussed round the fire, which threw a bright light on their dark bodies; they were not in the least embarrassed by the gaze of numerous men's eyes.

The travellers noticed that the young women and girls, who could be easily distinguished from the latter by their four braids, were casting frequent glances in their direction, whispering among themselves and giggling. They were wondering which of them were destined to be chosen by the mighty strangers as their wives.

Gorokhov overheard them saying that the thick moustaches, beards, and light skins of his comrades intrigued them most of all.

The Onkilons had practically no growth on their faces and only the old men had sparse moustaches and little scraggy beards. Being a Yakut, Gorokhov somewhat resembled the Onkilons in that respect and had a similarly dark skin. He did not attract the girls.

While the women were bustling about, the men dressed unhurriedly and then inspected their weapons. The voices of children and sometimes the crying of a baby came from various parts of the dwelling and one or another of the women responded to the sound and hastened to feed it.

Soon the entire clan was up and sat down to breakfast. The bill of fare was unvaried—roasted and cooked meat; only instead of cold milk from the leathern pitcher they were given a kind of light milk soup with water chestnut flour mixed into it and with little pieces of fried fat floating on the surface. The soup proved to be quite good.

During breakfast, the travellers asked the chief how long the Onkilons had been living in Sannikov Land. They already knew that this people did not have a written language and that everything concerning the lives of their forefathers was passed on from one generation to another with slight distortions. However, it turned out that there was a primitive chronicle.

"More than four hundred years," Amnundak replied after some reflection. "If you want to know exactly, we can go to the shaman; near his dwelling there is a stone on which every year is marked."

After breakfast, accompanied by the chief and ten warriors, the travellers set out along a wide path leading westwards through the forest. On the way, Amnundak showed them a skilfully concealed trap; it was a square hole more than two metres deep dug in the path and covered with thin poles, branches, and fallen leaves. Occasionally, oxen, horses, and even rhinos, which the Onkilons finished off with spears and arrows, fell into traps like this.

"We have quite a few of these traps along animal trails and you may be caught in them if you go about without a guide," the chief warned.

"We always have a dog running in front of us," Goryunov said. "It's cleverer than a rhinoceros or an ox. It will stop in front of a trap and let us know about it."

"Dogs would be very useful to the Onkilons," Ordin observed, "for hunting, for guarding their dwellings, and in the wars with the savages."

"Your dogs will multiply and in a few years we shall have guards," Amnundak said with such confidence that there was nothing left for the travellers to do but to exchange quick smiles.

Presently they turned off the path and found them-

selves in a small glade where the dwelling of the shaman
stood; it resembled the dwelling of the chief, but it was
much smaller as the shaman lived only with one pupil
and an old woman, who did the cooking.

The shaman, who, apparently, had been apprised of the visit, was waiting at the threshold of the dwelling and led the guests to the place of honour opposite the door. Inside, the dwelling looked like an anatomical museum; on four posts, on the cross-beams and beneath the slanting walls lay the whitened skulls of sacrificial deer, oxen, and horses, while over the place of honour hung the skull of a rhinoceros with an enormous horn.

As soon as the guests were seated, the old woman brought refreshments, which consisted of the cooked brains, tongue, and lips of the sacrificial deer the travellers had shot the day before. As the minister of the gods the shaman claimed these dainty parts of sacrificial animals.

Learning from Amnundak of the guests' desire to see the stone on which was kept a record of the years spent by the Onkilons in Sannikov Land, the shaman, when the repast was finished, led them farther to the west. The path soon brought them to the outskirts of the valley. Here, too, was a high, inaccessible wall of black basalt, the top of which was hidden in the low-hanging clouds. Lichen-covered rocks and boulders, that had fallen from above, were scattered about the foot of the precipice as in other places. Among them towered an immense boulder weighing a few hundred tons. The ground around it was cleared of stones and levelled to form a wide circle. This was where the Onkilons gathered for religious rites and made their sacrifices to their gods. The bones of sacrificial animals lay in a chain girthing the foot of the black boulder and making a sinister-looking line.

"This stone," Amnundak explained, "fell from the sky the same year our forefathers came to this land. Therefore, we revere it as a gift from the gods. Every year, when the sun shows itself for the first time after the winter night, we come here for a great ceremony and offer a sacrifice. The shaman records that event with a mark on the stone. By counting these marks you will find out how many years my people have been living here."

He took the travellers to the southern side of the boulder, where it was very smooth and had small vertical lines carved on it with a hard tool; every tenth line was a little longer than the rest and that made it easy to count them. The travellers found that the Onkilons had been living in Sannikov Land for four hundred and twenty-four years.

"When Amnundak told us that this boulder fell from the sky," Ordin remarked in a low voice, "I thought it was a huge meteorite and was very interested. Now I can see that it is simply a basalt rock and that, of course, it dropped from this precipice."

"What is he saying?" the shaman asked.

Gorokhov said that the white man thought the boulder fell from the mountain and not from the sky.

The shaman shook his head reproachfully and said:

"The great shaman, who led our forefathers to this land, saw this stone fall from the sky and was the first to bow to it."

"Only small stones drop from the mountains," Amnundak added, "while this one is bigger than our dwellings. Under it lie five deer, which it crushed as the first offering from the newcomers to this land. Since then we have been offering sacrifices here. It was a sign from heaven."

While this conversation was taking place at the foot of the sacred stone, Kostyakov moved away and unnoticeably took a photograph of it together with the men standing close by.

Amnundak led the travellers to the edge of a crag and

showed them a big cave in which the Wampus had lived. Just before the appearance of the sacred stone, there was a fierce battle at the foot of the precipice. There the Onkilons won their first victory over the Wampus and forced them to retreat to the east. That event was also linked with the stone.

Still strewn about the cave were rotting clubs, broken spears with flint points, and mildewed remains of animal skins; a fire-place and a heap of charred and broken bones could be seen.

On the whole, this cave with the bones, the dismal black wall rising into the clouds, and the huge black boulder surrounded by heaps of bones amidst scattered rocks and stones made a horrible picture and the travellers were glad to return to the green forest.

In the meadow before Amnundak's dwelling, they found the Onkilons busily building a house for them. Warriors and women shared in the work; some were digging holes for the four posts of the frame, others were cutting and squaring logs, and still others were carrying logs from the forest, where the thud of axes could be heard; the women were cutting turf for the roof. But in spite of the zeal displayed by the builders, the work progressed slowly because the stone axes, the bone knives, and the flint scrapers were inadequate for the task.

Seeing what a long time was spent to cut a thick log into posts, Goryunov suggested to this friends:

"Come, let us show them what we can do."

"Yes, let's," Gorokhov agreed.

The four men fetched their axes and set to work; chips began to fly and with each blow the axes bit deeper into the wood and what took the Onkilons half a day to do with a stone axe, a steel axe did in a quarter of an hour.

When the axes of the white men began to ring on the logs, the Onkilons stopped working and crowded round them, their eyes filled with admiration; they smacked their lips and expressed their astonishment with cries. By the time the women had hollowed out four shallow holes, digging the ground, which, happily, was soft, with knives and scooping it out with their hands, the four posts and the cross-beams were ready.

"What a pity we haven't got a drill with which to make a hole for a good bracing wedge," Gorokhov complained.

"Or a chisel to make a joint on the post for the cross-beams," Goryunov added.

"Yes, that would have been just the thing, because if ever we get even a light earthquake, the whole structure might come loose and pin us down as in a trap," Ordin said.

"Do you think there might be an earthquake?" Kostyakov asked.

"I certainly do. Don't forget we're in the crater of an old volcano which is not quite extinct as the hot springs in the lakes show. Anyway, to keep on the safe side, let's tie an extra cross-beam."

By midday, the four posts were in position and secured with cross-beams. After lunch, the travellers went into the forest with the Onkilons to cut thin trees for the joist, because that work, too, progressed slowly; a tree with a diameter of ten to twelve centimetres resisted the efforts of an Onkilon for over an hour, while with a steel axe no more than five minutes were needed to fell it. Towards evening enough timber had been felled and carried to the meadow.

That day detailed news of the appearance of white men spread to all the Onkilon camps and by sunset groups of warriors began to arrive. They wanted to see the strangers, who were tired after the day's work and resting in the dwelling, which soon became crowded. But the newcomers bore themselves with dignity, questioning the inhabitants of the dwelling, gazing upon the travellers, and exchanging impressions. At Amnundak's request, the axes and the knives were passed round for inspection because everybody mentioned the fast work of the strangers, thanks to whom a dwelling which ordinarily took a week to build was almost finished in a day.

The newcomers stayed in the dwelling until after dinner, when they finally settled down for the night round fires in the meadow.

Amnundak decided to take advantage of the presence of most of the Onkilon warriors and arrange for a rhinoceros hunt for the next day, banking on the guns of the white men. These animals rarely fell into the pits and when they did the spears and arrows of the Onkilons broke against their thick skins, which were valued highly as the best material for shields to ward off blows from the clubs of the Wampus.

THE RHINOCEROS HUNT

Next morning, with the help of the numerous warriors from other camps, the dwelling was finished in a quarter of an hour.

Leaving the women to roof it with turf and to arrange the interior, all the warriors with Amnundak and the travellers at their head set out eastwards, where a few kilometres away a family of rhinos had been spotted on the previous day. The warriors, numbering more than a hun-

143

dred, rapidly picked their way along the fringe of the forest without making a sound and surrounded the glade in which the animals were grazing. The chief and the travellers stood near the trail along which the rhinos were to be driven.

When all were in their places, Amnundak gave the signal and the warriors began to beat the trunks of the trees with clubs and to fill the air with war cries. Caught unawares, the rhinos rushed about the glade seeking to escape, but were stopped everywhere by a terrible din raised by enemies they could not see. At last they found themselves close to where the hunters were stationed; four shots rang out. The male rhinoceros slumped to its knees, sprang up, ran to the edge of the forest and dropped to the ground. The female animal with the baby rhino running after it made off in the opposite direction and came up against the chain formed by the Onkilons, who had emerged from the forest at the sound of the firing. Now it saw its enemies and, paying no attention to the cries or to the shower of spears and arrows, it broke through the chain, throwing a warrior into the air with its head, and disappeared in the forest. The baby rhinoceros, which, evidently, was only a few weeks old, was unable to keep pace with its mother and was stopped by the dogs, who sank their fangs into the folds of the skin on its sides. They would probably have come off badly if the Onkilons, who ran up, had not dispatched the young animal with spears.

The entire hunt lasted fifteen minutes, but there was one casualty. The warrior who had been thrown by the female rhinoceros had broken his leg in the fall. However, that did not dampen the joy of the hunters. The wounded man was put on a stretcher that was quickly made from the skin of the baby rhino and two poles and taken to the

shaman who was also the Onkilons' medicine man. The
men who remained got down to skinning the old rhinoceros and in half an hour there was nothing left except
the skeleton and the contents of the stomach and intestines; all the rest was cut up and carried away to the camp.

When the travellers returned for lunch, they found
their dwelling ready for tenancy; the only omissions were
skins for bedding and housewives. The former were given
by Amnundak out of his stores, but the latter had to be
chosen at the spring festival, which would be held in three
days. The travellers decided to use the intervening time
for a visit to their base in order to see Nikiforov and to
collect a few things.

Protracted negotiations were required to convince Amnundak that two warriors was all the convoy they needed.

Next morning, the travellers started out, choosing a
route along the western outskirts of the valley in order
to make a closer study of it. They proceeded along the
edge of a grove of polar birches and saw numerous deer
trails. Here they found the herd of Amnundak's clan watched
by herders and grazing in fields of moss stretching in a
strip between rocks and the underbrush.

Reindeer were the Onkilons' only domestic animals; they provided them with milk, meat, and hides. Game and fish supplemented the products yielded by the herd, while water chestnuts and martagon bulbs gathered by the women formed the vegetable food of this essentially peaceful tribe, which only the Wampus living in the vicinity made warlike. Hunting was the sole occupation of the Wampus and, unlike the Onkilons, they exterminated many wild animals; for that reason the animals kept mostly to the southern part of the valley, where they were hunted less, while the Wampus raided the lands of the Onkilons, killing the domesticated deer as well. That was the principal reason for the hostility between the Onkilons and the Wampus, which forced them to develop a warlike way of life. In addition, whenever they had the opportunity, the Wampus abducted maidens, who, if they failed to escape, soon died from rough treatment and the difficult conditions of primitive life. Naturally, that circumstance did not tend to promote peace between the Onkilons and the Wampus, and the strife between them never ceased.

On this side, too, the valley's perimeter consisted of tall, impassable basalt cliffs. Porous or even ashy layers of basalt alternated with solid rock shaped in what looked like hexahedral pillars of varying thickness and length; here and there gaped the black mouths of caves or niches whose shelter was sought by mountain sheep. Apparently, the gigantic volcano that had once occupied Sannikov Land had been active for very long, throwing out streams of lava in all directions before its centre caved in and formed a vast hollow with hot springs—the last signs of volcanic activity. Some of the deposits of lava contained large amounts of chalcedony, agate, sard, and semi-opal and the warriors accompanying the travellers said that from these deposits their people obtained coloured stones for women's ornaments and used the bigger pieces of chalcedony to make heads for arrows and spears although they preferred bone which was easier to fashion.

After a tiring march and only thanks to the fact that at this time of the year the day was already very long, the travellers reached their base, where they found Nikiforov roasting meat over a fire. The Cossack gazed with surprise at the two warriors, who had come with his friends, and in their turn, the Onkilons regarded with wonder the tent set in the snow cave and were astonished that anybody should elect to live in the snow instead of in a forest. They also took an interest in the caves for the dogs, but were not shown the sledges and the canoe. The travellers were unwilling to reveal their means of transportation across the ice and the Onkilons were convinced that white men lived in a land of snow and that dogs were their beasts of burden.

The warriors retired for the night to the belt of forest, as far from the snow as possible, while the travellers made themselves comfortable in the tent. Just before daybreak, the dogs sleeping at the entrance broke the stillness with furious barks. Nikiforov looked out of the tent and saw the outlines of an enormous bear. With its hind legs it was trying to drive away the three dogs that were annoying it, and with its paws it was scattering the blocks of ice piled up at the entrance to the store-room, where the skins, skulls, and stocks of meat were kept. The Cossack woke his friends and ran out with his gun. The usual thick mist was enshrouding the valley and the travellers had to call the dogs off to avoid hitting them. Hearing human voices, the bear got up on its hind legs and advanced in their direction. In the gloom of the night and the fog it looked huge, considerably taller than a man. Only two or three steps separated it from the tent when two bullets struck it in the breast. The bear swayed, let out a roar and fell into the entrance of the cave. Nikiforov just managed to hop out of the way, while Goryunov backed away into the tent, where Gorokhov and Ordin were groping for their guns in the darkness. Flinging its paws about in its agony, the bear loosened and let fly chunks of ice, the dogs howled and from the caves nearly thirty throats howled in reply. The situation in the tent was growing critical. The bear had moved up a little and the men huddled in the tent were within reach of its paws. There was nowhere they could go. Luckily, Nikiforov remaind cool; loading an explosive bullet into his gun, he seized a favourable opportunity and fired at almost point-blank range. The bear made a few more convulsive movements and lay still.

In the meantime, the noise and the shots attracted the Onkilons and they came running with flaming brands in their hands. Together, the seven men dragged the bear out of the entrance. It was so big that even the warriors were astonished. Before hunting bears, the Onkilons assembled in large numbers and it was a rare hunt when no warriors were killed or seriously injured. For that reason they prized bears' fangs very highly and wore them in their necklaces.

It was already growing light and since there could no longer be any question of sleep, everybody joined in skinning the bear and cutting up the carcass. Nikiforov received a big supply of meat for the dogs and as for the skin the travellers decided to adorn their new dwelling with it. They persuaded the warriors to take it to the chief's camp, promising to follow. With this manoeuvre they aimed to rid themselves of their escort for the day, planning to make an attempt to penetrate Wampus territory and get a glimpse of the savages before joining the Onkilons on their war-path as Amnundak wanted.

WAMPUS

Leaving Nikiforov to clean and store the bear's skull, the travellers started out in a north-easterly direction along the circumference of the valley. After midday, passing places they had already traversed on their first expedition, they reached a meadow where in the moist ground by a lake they noticed the imprints of bare human feet mingled with tracks left by oxen and horses. They could not be the footprints of Onkilons since the latter wore boots. Moreover, in the imprint the travellers' attention was drawn by the size of the strongly developed toes and the abnormally large space between the big and the second toes and the length of the latter.

Getting the dogs on the scent, which took them north-eastwards, the travellers crossed two more meadows and were approaching the third when they heard the drone of voices. The dogs were leashed and the travellers cautiously stole up to the edge of the forest, from where they caught sight of Wampus. Eight men were dancing round something dark on the ground—clearly a big animal they had stalked. The Wampus were stark naked and had very dark, hairy bodies. Their tangled hair came down to their shoulders and their faces were framed in scanty beards. With a short spear in one hand and a club in the other, they danced, now hopping on one spot now stepping back and forth and swinging their arms. In time with their movements, they repeatedly shouted "Oi-go-go," and "Ai-du-du."

The dance lasted about ten minutes after which the Wampus crowded round the animal and began to skin it. Then the feast began: the Wampus sliced off pieces of warm meat and stuffed them into their mouths. When their hunger was appeased, they carved out bigger parts of the carcass. Seven of them picked up the meat and the skin and made off eastwards across the meadow, leaving the eighth man to guard the rest of the carcass against eagles, four of which were already circling directly overhead. The Wampu squatted on the ground and went on eating. He was so engrossed in this task that he did not notice four men and two dogs silently coming up behind him. Krot growled and that made the savage look round. He wanted to spring to his feet but was so bewildered by the sight of men whom he could not identify as Onkilons aiming shining sticks at him and followed by two animals resembling wolves that he remained sitting, shaking with fear and gripping a piece of meat.

Over his small, deep-seated eyes, his low forehead protruded in two massive lumps; his mouth was open, revealing big, white teeth and fairly prominent fangs, while the extremely short chin gave him a ferocious look. The nose was flat with broad nostrils that were half-concealed by a long, white stick; the ears were large and round pieces of white bone fixed into the lobes stretched them almost to the shoulders. Around his neck he wore a necklace of boar's and bear's fangs. His body was covered with thick, black hair, which thinned out on his shoulders and chest, exposing a dark skin.

For a few moments the Wampu and the travellers gazed at each other in silence.

Then, with a swift movement, the Wampu pushed himself off the ground with his feet, vaulted over the carcass where his escape was not blocked by his enemies and, bending his body sharply forward, raced across the meadow.

"That's that," Kostyakov lamented. "We should have tied his hands and taken him with us."

"I can just picture him letting us do it," Goryunov laughed. "I suppose you saw his muscles and teeth? The four of us would have been no match for him. He would have wrung our necks or bitten through our throats."

"And what would we have done with him?" Ordin asked.

"Held him captive, studied him and tried to learn something of his language and psychology; the psychology and language of a prehistoric man—I can't think of anything more interesting. Look at his weapons."

The Wampu had left his spear and club on the grass. The spear was nearly a metre long and was made from the trunk of a straight, young birch; its tip was split a little way with a long fragment of roughly fashioned flint wedged into it and held fast by a thin raw hide strap. The club was made from the trunk of a thicker tree with part of the roots forming a cap the size of a fist. It was about seventy centimetres long and, wielded by a muscular arm, was a formidable weapon for close fighting: with such a club it was easy to crack a human skull or to stun a horse or an ox. Another club, left behind by one of the other Wampus had a sharp piece of flint fixed to its thicker end, which enabled the wielder to fell a large animal with a single blow.

Half of the ox's carcass was bare of meat. The side lying on the ground and the head were intact and the Wampus were sure to return to their prize.

"I think they will not come back. The chap we scared off will frighten them with his story," Goryunov surmised.

"They might return if only to take a look at us or even to hunt us," Kostyakov pointed out.

"Let's hide and wait and later follow them to their camp," Ordin suggested.

"But what if they should track us down. I should imagine they are good pathfinders," Goryunov said.

"What we should do is to go due west so as to leave

tracks and then turn into the forest and come back to this meadow by a roundabout route."

Leaving the carcass and the weapons untouched, the travellers followed this advice and when they returned they hid on the northern side of the meadow. Apparently, the Wampus lived close by, for soon the observers noticed a movement in the bushes along the eastern edge of the meadow and then saw the shaggy head of a scout stealthily showing itself. Two eagles were already perched on the carcass and picking at the meat, while a little way off two other eagles were busy with the entrails. That instantly told the Wampus that there was nobody in the meadow and a whole horde of them, about twenty men and ten women, poured out of the underbrush and swiftly walked to the carcass. The eagles rose into the air and began to circle overhead.

The Wampus surrounded the carcass and evidently began to laugh at their informant, pointing at the untouched meat and weapons. They were probably saying that he had imagined it all because it was unlike the Onkilons to leave any meat or to allow a Wampu to escape. The erstwhile guard tried to convince his fellows by showing them where the strange men had stood. He indicated the size of the dogs with his hands and imitated their bark. When he finished, some of the men examined the ground near the carcass and apparently found the tracks left by the travellers for they started out in pursuit. In the meantime, the others again turned their attention to the carcass, cut up the rest of the meat and broke off the marrowbones, flinging away the stomach. The women returned to the camp heavily loaded, while the men rushed off to join the trackers in order to overtake the strangers who had frightened their comrade. Nothing was left of the carcass except the spine with the ribs, the shoulder-blades and the hip bones and these were picked so clean that there was hardly anything for the eagles.

"That's splendid," Kostyakov exclaimed. "The men have gone away and we shall pay a visit to their camp."

"And take the risk that the men will soon return and bash our heads for our pains?" Goryunov asked.

"Anyway we can't go on for they are now between us and the Onkilons. We're bound to run across them. So I think our best plan is to take a look at their camp and then make a detour to the south."

The desire to see the life of the camp overcame any misgivings they had and they took the trail to the east; drops of blood on the ground showed the path taken by the women. Presently, ahead of them they heard shouts and laughter and, picking their way with still greater care, they approached to within sight of the camp, which was situated in a little glade. It was a temporary or summer camp at the foot of a tall, solitary poplar. A fire was burning with women and children of various ages sitting or standing round it. The women were a little shorter than the men, somewhat slimmer and less hairy, especially in front; though the hair on their heads was longer it was similarly dishevelled and matted; their faces would have looked less savage if it had not been for the sticks in their nostrils and the white bones fixed to their lower lips, which made them protrude, and similar pieces of bone in their ears; on their dark necks they wore white necklaces; there was no trace of clothing. The children were not so shaggy and hairy as the adults.

Spearing up pieces of meat with sticks, the Wampus roasted them for a few moments over the fire and then ate them. Nearby was a rock on which some women, using stones, were cracking marrowbones and noisily sucking out the marrow. They laughed and shouted—the horde was taking delight in its food.

When they could eat no more, the women hung what was left of the meat on boughs, while two of their number spread the skin on the ground and began to scrape away the bloodstains and fat with sharp pieces of flint. The others stretched themselves out on the grass near the fire, satisfied and drowsy. The children began to play, chasing one another; some rolled on the ground and squealed; a few climbed the poplar with the agility of monkeys and their merry voices could be heard in the foliage.

"What if we show ourselves?" Kostyakov said. "They'd probably run away in fright and that would give us an opportunity of taking a closer look at the camp and making a collection of weapons and utensils."

"And what if they don't run away and begin to defend themselves? There are more than twenty adult women and any one of them is stronger than we are," Goryunov objected.

"We could scare them away by firing in the air."

The idea was very attractive and the travellers, their fingers on the triggers of their guns, stepped out of the bushes and strode towards the camp, while the dogs, barking for all they were worth, rushed towards the children who were crawling on all fours, taking them for a special species of game. They frightened the Wampus out of their wits. The women leapt to their feet and huddled round the fire and the tree, staring open-mouthed at the approaching strangers, about whom they had heard from their fellow clansman. The children fled from the dogs, hiding behind the women and whimpering with fear. But the women soon recovered, seizing spears and clubs. One of them ran to help a child, which lay shrieking on the ground between the growling dogs. Goryunov called the dogs off before the woman could swing her spear at them.

"As you see, they're in no mood to run away and are already raising their spears to fling them at us," Ordin warned his friends.

"We'll have to fire before it's too late. If we turn back now they will think we are afraid and attack us from behind," Kostyakov declared.

"Now that we've started this game we'll have to go ahead with it," Goryunov said. "Fire two shots over the women's heads and keep two shots in reserve."

Kostyakov and Ordin fired. The travellers were totally unprepared for what followed. The flame, smoke, and thunder from the shining sticks and the whine of the bullets paralyzed the women with fear; they fell to their knees, dropping the spears and clubs, stretching their arms out in an imploring fashion and bowing to the ground with wails of terror; the children bawled at the top of their voices.

"I never thought anything like this would happen," Kostyakov exclaimed. "I thought they'd run away and leave us a clear field."

"There's nothing for it but to go up to them calmly and humour their belief that we are gods," Ordin said.

"Who steal clubs and spears? But first let's load our guns."

When that was done, the travellers walked serenely towards the kneeling women, but when they had only a few more steps to go, the children lost all control of themselves and sped across the meadow into the forest. They were followed by all the women except one, who lay with her face to the ground, her whole body shaking.

The travellers went up to her. Her back was covered with short, sparsely growing hair, the soles of her feet and the palms of her hands were bare; on the soles the skin seemed to be as hard as horn; the big toe was isolated from the rest; the hair on her arms and legs was thicker than on her back. In front she proved to be less hairy, while her breasts and face had no growth at all; but, because she had no beard, the shortness of her chin was more accentuated than that of the men; on the other hand, the bumps above her eyebrows protruded less. Broad cheek-bones, small, sunken eyes, a flat nose with a stick through the nostrils and a drawn-out lower lip with a round piece of bone in it certainly did not make her face beautiful. The hair, which had never been washed or combed, was tangled and had bits of grass, leaves, and other rubbish in it. But the well-developed muscles of her body showed that she was very strong.

At last, the poor woman was left in peace. A thong held one of her legs to a stake driven into the ground. That explained why she had not fled with the others; she was being punished for something.

Selecting a pair of representative clubs with and without flint heads, a pair of spears, scrapers, and a rough wooden cup that was glossy with fat and coloured brown from blood, and taking off the woman's necklace, the travellers turned to go when Goryunov said:

"I suppose you realize that this is called robbery. We frightened the women to death and then took some of their wretched belongings."

"But it was all done in the name of science and not from mercenary motives," Kostyakov protested.

"It's vile, nonetheless! We must leave them something in exchange."

They rummaged in their knapsacks and found a small mirror, a string of glass beads, a broken penknife, and a capsule tin, added two empty copper cartridges to this little store and placed it within reach of the prostrated woman, who kept her eyes shut. Then they left quietly. Back in the forest they hid in the bushes and waited to see what would follow.

For a while nothing happened. Then the woman raised her head. The strange men were gone and had not harmed her. She sat up, looked round and, putting two fingers in her mouth, gave a piercing whistle. In response, whistles and voices came from the forest and soon the women and children began to appear. While they were coming up, the woman caught sight of the shining knick-knacks on the ground. At first, she could not make up her mind to touch them, now stretching out her hand, now withdrawing it as though she were afraid they would scorch or bite her. Eventually, curiosity got the better of fear and she picked them up by turn, examining and sniffing at them and uttering cries of wonder. The other women ran up and the knick-knacks were passed round, giving rise to ejaculations and arguments. The woman tied to the stake was about to put the string of beads round her neck to replace her necklace when two other women clutched at it; the string snapped and the beads scattered about the ground. All the women rushed for them, picking them up and hiding them in their mouths.

"Our presents will cause nothing but mischief. They'll fight over them," Goryunov laughed.

The travellers did not wait for the end of the quarrel but proceeded in a south-easterly direction to avoid meeting the Wampus. They had to spend the night in a meadow and arrived in Amnundak's camp only towards noon on

the following day. There they learnt that Amnundak had
sent out search parties early in the morning, fearing that
the white men had lost their way or gone back on their
word and disappeared. Seeing the Wampu clubs and spears
in the hands of his guests and told where they had been,
he reproved them for their recklessness and declared that
no four Onkilons would have ventured into Wampu territory alone.

Although their new home had been finished in their absence, Goryunov and his friends stayed one more night
in the chief's dwelling. From their base they had brought
a change of clothes, tea, sugar, plates and dishes, counting
on settling down a little more comfortably and living not
quite so primitively as the Onkilons.

THE SPRING FESTIVAL

The next day was set aside for the spring festival to
mark the advent of the vernal season, the arrival of migratory birds and the calving of the reindeer. Parties of Onkilons from all camps began to arrive in the meadow at sunrise, leaving behind only old men and women, children
and the herders. Each clan cleared a space for itself and
lit fires. The women cooked the midday meal while the
men looked to their weapons in preparation for the com-
petitions or went from one camp-fire to another exchanging
news.

Groups of warriors went into Amnundak's dwelling to
take a look at the strangers, who commanded thunder and
lightning and who had consented to live with the Onkilons
and thus avert the misfortunes foretold by the shaman.
The conversation flowed more freely than during the first

days, for Gorokhov had refreshed his knowledge of the Chukchi language and spent some time practising, while the others had picked up quite a few words. The dwelling was cleared of its inhabitants so that it could accommodate an entire clan led by its headman. The warriors seated themselves along three sides of the square, the women taking their places behind them. The headman of each clan brought Amnundak, the shaman, and the strangers, who occupied the places of honour facing the door, a present—the skin of a fox or a marten, the teeth of a boar or a bear, a piece of agate, cornelian or chalcedony, or a stone hatchet—and in return received an eagle's feather, which then and there he stuck into his head-dress. The length of time each headman had held his office could be told by the number of feathers he wore. The hair of some of the headmen was already grey but they were still in their prime and their head-dresses contained from twenty to twenty-five feathers fashioned into a fan.

The travellers were told that the title of headman was not hereditary; every clan elected a headman from among its warriors for his courage, hunting skill, and prowess in war and he kept that title for life or until old age incapacitated him. A senile headman relinquished his authority himself and ordered new elections to be held, remaining a respected member of the community without any particular duties. In the event a headman died, the clan concerned at once elected someone to take his place. The title of chief of the Onkilons was not hereditary either; the headmen elected him from among their number. As a matter of fact, that title was more honorary than anything else; the chief, like the other headmen, directed the affairs of his own clan and only settled interclanal disputes, arranged for hunts in which all the clans participated or declared war on the savages; disputes were few and far between and those that arose concerned deer pastures or abductions of maidens.

Each clan occupied a single dwelling and was a small community sharing the common property—the dwelling, the deer, and the household utensils. The women jointly cooked the food, dressed skins, sewed clothes, and gathered mushrooms, berries, and roots; the men herded and guarded the deer, made weapons, cut firewood, hunted, and fished, and fought the savages.

After the travellers had been introduced to all the nineteen clans, they followed Amnundak to the meadow where with a beat on his drum the shaman opened the festival. The women, maidens, juveniles, and a few old men from nearby camps sat down on either side of the dwelling. The men lined up by clans. Amnundak, the travellers, and the shaman sat at the entrance of the dwelling. At the second signal, the clans marched past the chief, performing a war-dance, carrying spears, shields, and bows in their hands and quivers of arrows on their backs. The warriors leaped into the air, tossed their spears, and bent their bows; the movements in all the groups were co-ordinated, presenting a very picturesque scene.

The martial music was supplied on a big war-drum made from a two-metre-long hollowed out stump of a thick poplar with pieces of rhinoceros hide stretched on both sides; it rested on trestles and had a number of holes. The travellers were told that every clan had such a drum and used it to communicate important news to the whole tribe. Its resounding beat could be heard for a few kilometres around.

While the war-dance was being performed, the travellers estimated that the Onkilons could muster a force of four hundred to four hundred and fifty men since each clan was represented by twenty to thirty warriors. Together with the herders left in charge of the deer, the old men and women and the children the strength of the tribe stood at twelve to fifteen hundred persons, which was considerably more than the travellers had thought at first, when Amnundak told them that there were twenty to thirty people in every clan; it turned out that he had meant only warriors and could not give even an approximate figure for the whole tribe.

The dance was followed by spear-throwing and bowmanship contests. A long leather thong was stretched between two stakes and the clans lined up in rotation about forty paces away. The warriors were allowed only one try and did their best to hurl their spears over the thong. The judges, comprising the headmen of three clans, kept a count of the throws. The clan with the greatest number of successful throws was declared the winner. For the bowmanship contest, the Onkilons hung the skin of a wild horse on spears; the dark stripe along the back was the target. The bowmen of each clan stood fifty paces from the target and every warrior let fly one arrow. Only those that hit the stripe were counted and the clan scoring the most hits was named the victor amid a rapid succession of drumbeats and the cries of the spectators.

The next event was a wrestling match. Alternately, two clans faced each other, picking an equal number of wrestlers, the strongest, of course, who came to grips and tried to throw each other to the ground in the course of a set space of time, determined by fifty measured beats on the drum. Again, the clan winning the greatest number of bouts was declared the victor.

When the wrestling was over, the judges gave Amnundak

the names of the winners of each contest and together with him and the other headmen drew up a list of the clans in accordance with the successes achieved. After that the clans arranged themselves in a circle and Amnundak went to the centre and announced the results; the clans occupying the first ten places greeted the announcement with boisterous cries, the others, in humiliation, were silent. When the chief returned to his seat, the clans repeated the war-dance, re-arranging themselves in accordance with the list—the victors in front and the losers in the rear. The spectators applauded the victors. The losers could have their revenge only next spring and these contests forced the warriors to keep physically fit and developed a martial spirit in them.

After the dance, the Onkilons sat down to eat in the shade of the trees; the women had already prepared roast meat, soup, and cakes. The headmen of the clans assembled in Amnundak's dwelling as his guests and the conversation during the meal was about the results of the contests; the losers tried to explain away their failures. The travellers were asked to demonstrate their thunder and lightnings after the meal.

Two hours later the drum sounded again, this time calling young unmarried warriors to a contest to decide who would choose wives first. There were two or three such warriors in every clan and they competed not by clans but all together. First they vied in spear-throwing, each warrior getting three tries; then they showed their skill with the bow, each shooting three arrows. The judges were strict about the rules, marking every successful shot, after which they determined the place won by every competitor; in all cases where the same place was won by two or more competitors, the question was settled by a fresh contest between them. In the end, the list was drawn up and the warriors lined up in the corresponding order. There were forty-seven of them.

Then, at a signal given on the drum, all the girls who had reached maturity and wished to have a husband sprang up from the rows of spectators. Like the women, they had come to the festival not in the minimum costume they wore in the dwellings, but in light leather pantaloons, jackets, and fur boots beautifully embroidered with narrow red and black thongs. They wore flowers in their hair and garlands on their heads. But now, appearing for the bride-show, they threw off their garments, remaining only in a loin-cloth, in order to show the young warriors the beauty of the markings on their skins and, undoubtedly, their own comeliness. They stood in a line facing the chief's dwelling, in front of which the headmen of the clans also took their places. Amnundak rose and, addressing them, said:

"Maidens! You have heard that among us we have white men, messengers of the gods, who command thunder and lightning. They have consented to live with us to protect us against the misfortunes the shaman predicted would befall the Onkilons. We must give them a dwelling, food, and wives so that they should not lack anything. They will choose wives from among you and each maiden thus chosen must rest content. I have spoken."

These words did not dismay the girls for the news of that prospect had already spread to all the camps and now they gazed with curiosity at the strangers, whose wives four of them were destined to be. Some already had lovers among the young warriors and were grieved, but they hoped that the choice would not fall on them. Therefore, in response to Amnundak's speech, the girls cried:

"Let them choose. We are ready!"

"An unexpected complication to our stay on this island!" Ordin exclaimed. "They want to make sure of us by giving us wives. What are we to do?"

"I think we should give in," Goryunov said. "That will please the Onkilons and make them even friendlier than they are now."

"Do you mean that we should actually choose wives for ourselves?" Kostyakov demanded.

"I'll tell you what we'll do," Goryunov said. "We'll tell them that in our country the man who wants to get married and the girl who gives her consent must get to know each other better so that there is no mistake; for that reason they live in the same house for, say, six months or a year, study one another and if at the end of that period they still like each other they can get married."

"Wonderful! That's a good way out!" Ordin declared. "We'll suggest it to the chief and say that we'll choose wives in accordance with the customs of our country."

Gorokhov told Amnundak what the travellers had decided and the latter expressed his agreement with the words:

"White men, choose any girls you like as your future wives."

The travellers rose and their embarrassment was understandable; in front of them were fifty graceful girls, most of whom were very pretty, and it was difficult to make a choice. Accompanied by Amnundak, they went down the line, hesitating before almost each of the lovelier maidens; Gorokhov alone quickly made up his mind, fixing upon a petite maiden when he was still some distance away. Coming up to her, he said, stretching out his hand:

"This one!"

Covering her face with her hand and giggling, the girl stepped out of line and stood near Gorokhov. She was the first bride to be chosen and was greeted with a thunderous roll on the drum.

The others walked to the end of the line without any result. Surprised, Amnundak asked:

"Are our women so ugly that only one has pleased you, white men?"

"On the contrary," Goryunov protested, "too many of them are lovely and it is hard to choose. And, besides, we are afraid that the ones we'll choose will become our wives against their will and only because you have ordered them. In our country, the man always gets the consent of the girl he wishes to marry."

"I see. So you want the girls to choose you? All right. I shall call out those who agree to marry you. Maidens," the chief said, addressing the girls, "the white men cannot decide; all of you are too beautiful. Let those who wish to marry a white man step forward."

The girls smiled and tittered, some shifted from one foot to the other, hesitating to be the first.

"Well!" exclaimed Amnundak. "Surely there must be some amongst you who would like to marry our guests. Do you want them to get angry and leave us? If they do that there will be many misfortunes."

These words acted like a tonic and more than half of the girls took a step forward.

But the travellers had made their choice. Goryunov and Ordin indicated maidens from the chief's clan, whom they had had the opportunity of observing in the dwelling, while Kostyakov chose a pretty girl who was making eyes at him.

"The choice has been made," Amnundak announced. "Now let the warriors of the Onkilons choose."

Together with the travellers, who were followed by their brides, the chief returned to his place of honour; the girls asked for permission to dress and ran to where their respective clans were seated, saluted by cries from the women. They quickly returned and sat down beside the travellers.

The maidens waiting for husbands closed ranks. The drum sounded again and the Onkilon who won first place in the individual contests stepped out of the line of young warriors. He approached the girls and slowly began to walk down the line. He was greeted with jests and titters and almost every girl said: "Choose me, choose me!" because it was flattering to be the wife of this splendid young warrior and they frankly sought to attract him. But the youth replied with jests, quickly making up excuses such as: "You're too beautiful" (to a homely girl), "You're hunchbacked" (to a girl who was as straight as an arrow), "You're cross-eyed," "You have no teeth," and so forth, provoking protests and laughter.

Passing almost to the end of the line, he stopped in front of a girl who was not offering herself but standing with her eyes modestly lowered. He struck her on her shoulder and cried: "You please me!" The girl started, sprang out of line, and dashed across the meadow, the youth racing after her.

"What does it mean?" Ordin asked Amnundak. "Why is she running away from him? Doesn't she want to marry him?"

"Such is our custom. A warrior who chooses a maiden gets her for his bride only if he catches her."

"Another contest!" Ordin said.

"It is a very wise custom," the chief explained. "The maidens wear only a loin-cloth and it is easy for them to run; the young warriors run clothed and carry a spear in their hands. Few can overtake a maiden if she doesn't let them. If she dislikes the warrior who chooses her or loves another she will not let herself be caught."

"What a splendid custom," Ordin remarked to his friends and, turning to the chief, said: "What about the warrior who doesn't catch his girl? Does he remain without a wife?"

"No. He can go on choosing until he catches a maiden."

"How long does the girl have to run? All day?"

"No. Only once round the circle of the war-dance. Look, he has caught her!"

Indeed, the warrior was leading the girl by her braids; for appearance' sake, she was pulling in the opposite direction and slapping his hand. The women and the other maidens gibed at her. When they reached the line of prospective brides, the girl stopped struggling and went to one side with her bridegroom where they stood next to each other.

The drum rolled again and the second youth approached the girls. Many of them were eager to marry him, for he had been second in the contests; he was accorded the same favour as the first youth. But he maintained a dogged silence, moving slowly down the line, reaching the end and turning back. That gave rise to cries of indignation from the girls.

"How much time is he allowed?" Kostyakov asked.

"He can pass the girls three times, no more," Amnundak replied. "He is a very brave hunter and wants to worry the girls. Look how angry they are."

The young warrior went down the line a second time

without choosing anybody. The girls boiled with resentment and no longer tried to attract him. They made faces at him and shouted: "You can go away altogether! Go to the Wampus and choose a hairy wife for yourself! Girls like us don't please you!" The youth started down the line again, still saying nothing. Suddenly, he stopped and tapped one of the last girls in the line on her shoulder. She was so startled that when she broke into a run she could not at once develop enough speed and the warrior caught her after she had only made about twenty steps.

"What a crafty fellow," Gorokhov said. "He wore them out so that they could not run far."

"There's how your custom works," Kostyakov laughed. "In this way you can override any girl's wishes."

"That's how it was this time," Ordin said. "Look, she's not struggling like the first girl did to keep up appearances, but she isn't happy either."

The girl was following the warrior with bowed head and made no reply to the taunts of the others.

"She can blame herself—she should have kept her eyes open," Gorokhov said.

The third warrior quickly chose one of the first girls in the line but she was a fast runner and outstripped him. However, when she was near the end of the circle she stumbled and fell on the grass to the delight of all the spectators; before she could regain her feet, her braid was in the grip of the youth, who triumphantly led her after him. Obviously, the girl had tripped on purpose—it was one of the ways of consenting.

The fourth warrior walked rapidly past the girls three times without making a choice, then went up to the chief and lowered his head in silence.

"Don't you want a wife?" Amnundak asked in amazement.

"I do, great chief! In the camp next to ours lives a widow. I love her and want your permission to marry her. I have her consent."

The headman of the clan concerned confirmed what the youth said and Amnundak gave his approval.

The fifth warrior had to run twice, because the girl he chose first did not let him catch her; the second girl made him run a full circle to punish him for not choosing her first and surrendered a step away from the end, pretending to be tired. The sixth youth chose the girl who had evaded the fifth warrior and she let herself be caught half-way round the circle. When he led her past the girls, they shouted: "How quickly you lost your wind, sly boots."

With variations, the warriors went on choosing their brides, and the line of maidens kept growing shorter. This game, which lasted for hours, bored neither them nor the spectators. In spite of having to stand for a long time, the girls ran nimbly and only a few gave up quickly. Some of the warriors were compelled to run twice, while one ran even three times. Towards the end, when only a few girls were left, the game speeded up.

The last girl, who had already shown her heels to three warriors, ran away from the last youth as well, to everybody's astonishment. She was called to the chief, who said to her:

"Why don't you want a husband? Every maiden must marry to bear the tribe new warriors. You have rejected four suitors! What does it mean?"

"Good warriors ignored me and I am not going to be the wife of a bad one," the girl replied proudly.

"What will you do? Wait for next spring?"

"No. I should like to be the wife of that white man!" she said unexpectedly, pointing to the dumbfounded Ordin.

"But he already has a wife," Amnundak remonstrated.

"He is a big chief and can have two wives," the girl insisted. "I chose him at your command, but he took another. I shall be his second wife."

The girl's preserverance and proud bearing pleased Ordin and with great embarrassment he acquiesced. The girl ran for her clothes and sat down beside him.

In the meantime, marching to the beat of the drum, the young couples filed past Amnundak and the clan headmen; the girls had already rewoven their four braids into two to show that they were married. The warrior who was left without a wife hid himself among the spectators; he had to wait for the next festival.

It was now the travellers' turn to show the Onkilons their thunder and lightning sticks. For want of a better target, the Onkilons again hung the skin of a wild horse. To everybody's surprise, the travellers took up their positions about two hundred paces away, which was more than four times the distance set in the competition with bows and arrows. The spectators stood in a semicircle stretching almost up to the target itself and tensely watched the strangers do something to their sticks and bring them up to their cheeks. Puffs of smoke and deafening reports sent a shudder through the rows of spectators, but the next minute there was a general rush for the target and people jostled each other for an opportunity to poke their fingers in the holes made by the bullets. Many wanted to know where the lightning got to after piercing the skin and looked for it in the grass. Goryunov filled them with still greater wonder when he threw his cap up in the air and sent a bullet through it. Just then, Ordin noticed a flock of geese flying over the forest from south to north; swiftly changing the cartridge in his gun, he fired before the Onkilons could ask where he intended sending his lightning and a goose flopped down on the heads of the spectators, delighting them immensely. Finally, Amnundak ordered the warriors to bring a deer, which instead of being tied was set loose. The frightened animal turned back into the forest, but a bullet from Gorokhov's gun caught it before it ran twenty steps.

With that the strangers ended the demonstration of their power. The whole tribe escorted them as far as Amnundak's dwelling, which they now entered with their brides, who were extremely proud of their intimacy with the travellers. Fires were lit all over the meadow and while dinner was being prepared the young men and women danced round them.

After dinner, the chief told the travellers that they could take possession of their new dwelling.

"Now you have wives and there it is roomier and more comfortable than here, where we barely have space for all."

The women ran ahead to light a fire. The travellers, attended by the chief, tarried a while in the meadow, where the Onkilons had already posted sentries and were going to sleep round the fires, each clan separately, lying down on skins spread on the grass. Amnundak saw his guests to their dwelling.

Inside it was clean and cosy, a bright fire was burning and there was a smell of tar from the fir trunks, of which the walls were made. All the five girls were sitting round the fire in their indoor dresses, i. e., loin-cloths. They were engaged in a lively conversation but fell silent when their bridegrooms entered, got up, and moved to one of the

172

walls. The mudhouse already had a lived-in look; on one of the posts hung a leathern pitcher of milk, a kettle and a pot; mugs and wooden cups stood on a little shelf; on the ground were two wooden soup pots, a heap of stones, and sticks for roasting meat. On three sides, beneath the sloping walls, there were beds of dry leaves and fresh twigs with soft deer and bear skins, skin pillows stuffed with deer wool, and deer skin blankets. Next to the door was a pile of chopped firewood and a vessel with water.

After Amnundak's crowded and sooty dwelling, the travellers found this cleanliness and spaciousness a luxury and they felt like sitting by the fire a little longer and smoking a pipe before turning in. Sitting down, they called the girls and told them to do the same. The few words they had picked up were not enough for an animated conversation and most of the time they had to resort to gestures and mimicry. First, each asked his bride for her name; Goryunov's bride was called Matu, Kostyakov's—Papu, Gorokhov's—Raku. But Ordin found himself with a problem. Both his brides were called Annu.

"There's a how d'you do!" he exclaimed in confusion. "They forced two girls on me and to make matters worse they have one and the same name. How am I going to make them understand who I mean when I call them?"

"Call them Annu the first and Annu the second," Gorokhov suggested.

"What will that be in their language?"

"Annu-*ennen* and Annu-*ngirek*," Gorokhov told him, and both girls nodded.

"But those names are too long. Can't they be shortened? I'll call her Annuen," Ordin pointed to the first girl, who lowered her head, "and her Annuir," he took the second girl's hand and she likewise assented.

"You can simply call them first and second. They will understand," Goryunov said.

"Why should I? Annu is a nice name, but *ngirek* is too much of a tongue-twister."

Gorokhov interpreted these words and the Annus were flattered that Ordin liked their name. They listened attentively when the travellers spoke to each other and it could be seen that they already understood a few Russian words and guessed the meaning of others. Through constant intercourse, the travellers told themselves, complete mutual understanding would be reached in a few weeks.

Presently, they rose and took up the question of where they were going to sleep. The space beneath the sloping roof opposite the door was wider than along the side walls and was divided by a partition of stakes; this was occupied by the men. The space along the walls on the left and right was curtained off with skins and placed at the disposal of the women. Krot and Belukha, who had moved in with their masters, curled up near the door. The women threw some wood on the fire and everybody went to sleep.

Silence descended upon the dwelling.

THE BATTLE WITH THE WAMPUS

Early next morning the travellers were awakened by a loud noise raised by the Onkilons. Annuir anxiously went to the door, poked out her head, listened, and cried plaintively:

"Last night the Wampus attacked the dwelling of my clan. The chief will lead the warriors against them."

"Well, friends," Goryunov said, reaching out for his

clothes, "this is it! We've got to dress. I can't see our way out of this business."

"From the betrothal to the wars!" Kostyakov laughed. "Papu, bring me my shield and helmet, get my chain mail and don't forget my spear and my trusty sword! I am off to the wars like a young knight of old."

Of course, Papu understood nothing of this tirade and stared sleepily at her betrothed in confusion. But seeing him chuckling, she laughed and asked in broken Russian:

"Make fire, cook food?"

"Quite right," Ordin said with a burst of laughter, showing himself from under his blanket. "She knows that a man must be properly fed before he goes to war. Annuen, Annuir! Fire! Meat! Milk!"

Annuir was sitting on the threshold and weeping, her face in her hands. Hearing Ordin's voice, she roused herself and, realizing what was wanted, began to stir the ashes of the fire that had gone out during the night and salvage hot coals; the other women got up, put on their loin-cloths and helped her to start the fire.

There was a cheerful blaze, the meat was roasting and the travellers were completing their toilet when Amnundak entered, greeted them, sat down by the fire and said:

"White men! The first misfortune has befallen us. Last night the Wampus raided our most remote dwelling, killed the old folks and the herders, took the children with them and drove away the deer."

Annuir began to wail when she heard these words. She was from that camp and what the chief said meant that the Wampus had killed her parents and carried away her brothers and sisters.

"How did you get the news so quickly?" Goryunov asked.

"By the war-drum. One of the herders escaped and sent the news to us. I have called upon the Onkilons to take the war-path against the Wampus. All the warriors are here and we shall punish them without mercy. The warriors want the possessors of thunder and lightning to go with them to punish their enemies."

"Of course, we'll go," Goryunov hastened to assure the chief. "We'll join you as soon as we've had a quick breakfast."

Amnundak's face brightened as he rose and, leaving, he said:

"I shall tell the warriors that the white men will go with them; they will be pleased."

In a few minutes the news was passed on to the Onkilons and they filled the meadow with loud, jubilant cries. The women, too, looked pleased. Annuir stopped weeping, wiped away her tears with her hand and said to Ordin:

"I shall go with you."

While the meat was roasting, the travellers cleaned their guns, filled their cartridge-boxes, and packed their travelling kit in their knapsacks in case the campaign lasted for several days. The women raptly watched every movement they made with the result that several pieces of meat were burnt, for which Raku was instantly reprimanded by Gorokhov.

At last, all the preparations were completed, the breakfast was eaten, a supply of cakes and roast meat was put into the knapsacks and the travellers emerged from the mudhouse and walked into the heavy mist that always clothed the valley at this hour. Camp-fires loomed dimly through the mist and the silhouettes of men walking to and fro could be made out. From a distance came the hollow beat of a drum, which continued sending out details of the Wampu raid. Amnundak, fully armed, was standing at the entrance of his dwelling, and when he saw that the white men were ready he waved his arm. Instantly, a resounding tattoo was beaten out on the war-drum, announcing the start of the campaign and sending the news to the neighbouring camps. There was a stir round the camp-fires as each clan lined up and assembled in a column, the warriors in front, followed by women and juveniles who were returning to their camps. The women of Amnundak's clan, naturally, stayed behind; all of them and the children came out of the dwelling to look, perhaps for the last time, at their husbands and sons. The leave-taking was short; the women did not weep but embraced the men and rubbed cheeks with them, which among the Onkilons was a kiss. Drumbeats were heard again and the column moved off. At its head marched Amnundak and the travellers, who had brought along Krot and Belukha with the intention of using them to track down the Wampus. A quick pace was set in the direction of the plundered camp, which was about twenty-five kilometres away. Forests alternated with meadows and from time to time a group of women detached themselves from the column and turned off the path towards their own camp. The mist dispersed gradually, the sun broke through, and it began to grow hot.

Reaching their destination long before midday, they found the camp in a pitiful state. The dwelling, which had been set on fire by the savages, had caved in and the interior was reduced to ashes; smoke and little tongues of flame were still escaping here and there from beneath the turf, which had turned brown. In the meadow, the grass had been trampled and there were blood-stains. The beheaded corpses of some old men and women, whom the

Wampus did not care to carry away with them, lay about the meadow; the heads had been taken as trophies. On the ground were scattered broken spears and arrows, bits of torn clothing, and smashed utensils.

As the picture of this destruction unfolded before them, the women of this clan rent the air with their weeping and sobbing—while they had been at the festival their children had been abducted and their near ones killed. The warriors made no sound but their grim faces and glittering eyes showed that they would be ruthless avengers. Amnundak ordered them to take a short rest. The surviving herder, his head bandaged, appeared out of the forest and described what had happened.

The Wampus, apparently learning that most of the men were away at the festival, surrounded the meadow at around midnight and fifty or sixty of them surprised the herders, killing two and stunning the third. When the man regained consciousness everything was over: the dwelling was in flames, the deer were gone, and only corpses lay in the meadow. In the morning, he found the path taken by the marauders. He had escaped because he had been standing near some bushes and had fallen into them when the Wampus attacked: they could not find him in the darkness and mist.

Leaving the women of the unfortunate clan amid the ruins, the column moved on, this time heading north-eastwards in the tracks left by the savages and the deer. The dogs were sent ahead. That allowed the war party to make rapid progress for they knew that any ambush would be instantly discovered by the clever animals. Now that there were no women in the tail of the column, the warriors marched swiftly, often breaking into a trot; the only sounds were the light patter of soft boots and the breath-

178

ing of the men. The column moved in this fashion for about two hours, when suddenly the dogs stopped before a huge poplar growing on the fringe of a meadow and barked with uplifted heads.

"There is an ambush in the tree," Amnundak said and, in a whisper, ordered his warriors to surround the meadow.

Just then a stone shot from a sling hit Belukha and the dog let out a whimper. The travellers detected a movement in the foliage and immediately fired, while the Onkilons sent a hail of arrows into the poplar. An ear-splitting roar was heard and two dark figures, breaking branches as they slid down the tree, crashed to the ground.

"Only two?" Goryunov asked, reloading his gun.

"No," Amnundak replied, "at least five lie in their ambushes, as you shall soon see."

He gave an order and a few warriors ran into the underbrush. No sound came from the tree. The Wampus realized that the slightest rustle would betray them to the enemy. Therefore, though the Onkilons continued sending arrows into the crown of the tree, nothing moved; the Wampus were shielded by the trunk and the thick boughs. Before long a small group of Onkilon warriors came out of the nearby forest with armfuls of brushwood; using the brushwood as shields they ran to the tree, put the brushwood round its trunk and sprang away; a fire had already been lit in the wood for smoke began to rise from it. The attention of the Wampus hiding in the foliage was held by the warriors shooting arrows at them and they did not notice the men with the brushwood. But when a thick smoke rose, curling in the foliage in dense clouds, they roared with anger and threw a few spears into the fire. That only made matter worse—the disturbed brushwood caught alight and the position in the tree became untenable. The Wampus climbed to the very crown, but there the foliage was rarer and gave them away. A second volley brought down two more savages; one fell on the ground and the other slumped over a bough in full sight, his head drooping; a minute later at least ten arrows were sticking out of his body. The fifth Wampu climbed to the opposite side of the tree, crawled along a bough and, swinging from it, leapt to the ground from a height of four metres; he raced across the meadow, but the Onkilon warriors had already surrounded it and met him with a shower of arrows. He fell before reaching the forest.

Amnundak blew on a horn and from all directions warriors rushed out of the forest and gathered round the tree where a party of men, including the chief and the travellers, were already assembled. The three Wampus who had fallen on the ground lay motionless; they had bullet wounds, but to make sure they were dead the Onkilons stabbed them with spears. All resembled the savage the travellers saw during their expedition into Wampu country; they were hairy and muscular and had bestial faces; their hair was matted. But, perhaps because they were on the war-path, their faces were painted with ruddle which made them look even more repulsive. One Onkilon climbed the tree to assure himself that there was nobody on it. Collecting the clubs and spears of the Wampus, he threw them into the smouldering fire.

The Onkilons had won the first battle without suffering any casualties and they pushed on, following the tracks of the Wampus, which now led directly eastwards to the outskirts of the valley, where, apparently, their camp was situated. They did not come across any other ambush. The first had most likely been only an observation post, which was to have brought the camp news of the enemy's approach, but that purpose had been foiled by the dogs.

A few more kilometres were covered very quickly: the stunted trees indicated that the outskirts were close by. When the column entered the belt of shrubbery they stopped and listened; shouts and thumps could be heard. The scouts sent ahead reported that the Wampu camp was in a cave opposite the trail and that the savages were reinforcing it by piling up rocks at the entrance. Acting on this information, Amnundak divided his force into three groups: the first, headed by Ordin, went to the north through the shrubbery, the second, with Kostyakov in command, moved to the south; about a kilometre from each other these groups were to cross the woodless strip as quickly as they could and converge on the camp along the foot of the precipice. The third group advanced along the trail to the edge of the shrubbery where it hid and waited for the appearance of the flanking parties in order to fall upon the camp from three directions. The Wampus were working zealously, building a stone wall around the entrance to their cave; relying on their forward ambush, they had not posted sentries and now they failed to notice the movements of the enemy. They must have been busy building the wall since morning, for it was already breast-high. About twenty men were selecting suitable flat stones from the bare, rock-strewn ground and carrying them to the wall where others put them in position. These carriers suddenly caught sight of one of the flanking parties as it was crossing the woodless strip of country. With cries of alarm, they hurried to the wall with their burdens.

"We must fire while we can still see them," Goryunov said. "That will cause a panic and there will be less resistance during the attack."

From the shrubbery it was about four hundred paces to the wall. Goryunov and Gorokhov fired. The savages stopped short in bewilderment. They heard the reports but could not see the enemy; they looked around them and exchanged shouts with the Wampus behind the wall. A few were terrified, threw down the stones they were carrying and scattered in different directions; some ran to the cave, others headed for the shrubbery. Cries of terror rose from behind the wall. The Wampus who ran towards the shrubbery came within range of the Onkilons' bows; some fell, others turned and dashed off with the Onkilons in hot pursuit.

No Wampus showed themselves from behind the wall and Amnundak, seeing that the flanking parties were already near, gave the signal for the assault; his group, excluding the warriors chasing the stone-carriers, made a rush for the camp. When only some forty paces remained to be covered, the heads and shoulders of the Wampus appeared from behind the wall and spears and stones rained down on the attackers; a few Onkilons fell, but two shots fired at close range again sowed terror among the savages and they hid in confusion. In the meantime, the two other groups burst through the passages left in the wall at the foot of the precipice and hand-to-hand fighting started; Amnundak's group scaled the wall and joined the battle. The Wampus put up a feeble defence because Ordin's revolver kept renewing their panic.

It was all over in a few minutes; the ground was strewn with the dead and the wounded; about ten Wampus, who had leapt over the wall and sought safety in flight, were stopped with arrows. The women who defended the cave shoulder to shoulder with the men were also cut down.

In a corner of the cave, the travellers saw a few old

Wampu women and about thirty children huddled together and shivering with fear. The children were screaming. The Onkilons pushed them aside, looking for their abducted children, who could be easily distinguished by their faces, hairless bodies and lighter skins; out of this mass of rolling and squealing humanity, the children were pulled out one after another. The young Wampu resisted with tooth and nail. The abducted children were found in the very centre of the knot and all were in a terrible state—their "hospitable" hosts had marked them with bruises and bites. Of the thirteen carried away, only seven girls and two boys were found—four boys were missing. The infuriated Onkilons led all the Wampu boys out of the cave and put them to death. They wanted to do the same with the old women and the girls, but the travellers prevailed upon Amnundak to stop the massacre.

Under a pile of skins in the darkest corner of the cave they found a woman with tied hands and feet. Dragged into the light she proved to be an Onkilon woman who had been abducted at the beginning of spring. The unhappy woman had almost suffocated under the skins; her body was covered with bruises left by thongs and sticks. When she finally realized that she was safe, she told her rescuers that she had been constantly beaten and tortured, particularly by the women, who made fun of her hairless body, likening it to that of a frog. When the attack began, the old women had tied her up and piled skins on her.

Weapons, utensils, clothing, and bedding that had been stolen from the Onkilons were also recovered. The old women and girls were driven out of the cave in which the warriors made a heap of the Wampu clubs and spears gathered up from the battle-field and set fire to them. The scouts sent to scour the surrounding area discovered the herd of stolen deer among the bushes in the neighbourhood of the cave; not being herders and unable to eat them all at once, the Wampus had tied the animals to the bushes. Only a few, which had either strayed en route or had been eaten, were missing.

Towards sunset, the Onkilons withrew from the punished camp, leaving the dead Wampus lying where they had fallen; all the wounded had been dispatched as soon as the camp was taken.

Carrying the five dead and six wounded warriors, the Onkilons headed for home; the lightly wounded, including Ordin, who had been struck in the shoulder with a spear, walked unaided in the centre of the column, behind the deer and the warriors carrying the rescued children, the recovered property, the dead, and the seriously wounded. They made slow progress and reached the looted Onkilon camp only by nightfall. The women met the children with happy cries, but the happiness of some was clouded. Annuir ran to Ordin with tears in her eyes when she saw his bandaged shoulder and embraced him. Another of the new brides from this camp found her husband dead on a stretcher.

CEMETERY OF THE ONKILONS

The warriors sat down round fires and shared their impressions of the march and the battle, discussed individual episodes and praised the thunder and lightnings of the white men for it was with their help that they had destroyed a Wampu camp with such small losses—one Onkilon for every ten Wampus—and recovered almost everything that had been stolen. In previous battles, the ratio had been different—one Onkilon to two or, at best, three Wampus. This time the Wampus had been taught a lesson they would long remember.

The travellers, together with Amnundak, Annuir, and

the rescued woman, sat round a fire by themselves. Gorokhov gave Annuir a description of the battle.

Goryunov questioned the woman, who, during her captivity, had learned a little of the Wampu language and about the life of the savages. She said the Wampus lived as one family and that no enduring relations existed between individual men and women; all the women belonged to all the men and the children were considered common. Sometimes a man ran away with a woman and lived separately with her in the forest; the others never reconciled themselves to such a situation and the matter always ended with the man being killed and the woman returned to the cave. The life of the men was spent in hunting, eating, and making weapons and implements—clubs, spears, scrapers; the women gathered firewood, scraped skins, made thongs, but they too had plenty of time to spare; for hours they lolled around a fire or basked in the sun and dozed. Ordinarily, meat was eaten raw or slightly roasted and after a successful hunt they ate all they could; when no meat was to be had they went hungry for days on end or dug roots and caught snails, a species of big beetle, and frogs. They slept side by side with their feet to a fire, on skins or simply on the ground with a stone for a pillow. After a fortunate hunt and a copious feast they danced round a fire until they dropped from exhaustion or until a fight broke out over some trifle. They believed there were stone, forest, and water spirits and were afraid of them, never venturing out of their cave alone at night. Their gods were the boar and a big animal with a fifth leg on its head and enormous teeth for which the women gathered mushrooms and roots.

After dinner the warriors went to sleep and the women began the funeral rites for the dead, who were placed in a row near a fire with a spear and a bow in their hands and a shield across their knees. The women undid their braids, took off their necklaces and bracelets, and, covering their faces with their hands, sang mournfully about the valorous deeds of the fallen warriors; as they sang, they rocked to and fro, sitting at the heads of the dead men. Krot and Belukha joined in with howls much to the amazement of the women, who thought the clever animals were expressing their sympathy. Quieting the dogs, the travellers fell asleep with the dirge sounding in their ears.

As always, the day began with a dense mist, through which the fires glowed dimly. The women had finished lamenting the dead and were cooking breakfast; ten deer had to be slaughtered to feed the numerous host. When the mist began to lift and the sun peeped through, the shaman and his pupil arrived. The dead were put on stretchers and the entire war party silently filed westwards through the forest and only the beat of a drum followed the procession, communicating the news of the burial to all the other camps. No women or children were in the procession.

The main cemetery of the Onkilons was situated on the western outskirts of the valley, about ten kilometres from the camp; in it were numerous little burial mounds built up of stones; stuck in each mound was a spear with its head pointing skywards. The older mounds had already settled on the decayed corpses and the spears had either tilted or fallen; over the oldest graves even that sign was gone and the stones were covered with lichens.

The dead were put on the ground and the warriors began to prepare the graves, digging rectangular holes about a metre deep. When the graves were ready, a dead warrior was lowered into each with his legs pointing to the south, his arms stretched down his sides, his bow on one side and his quiver of arrows on the other; his face was covered with a skin, his spear was put at his head and the grave was filled with stones. The children's skulls and bones, brought from the cave of the Wampus, were put in one grave.

While this was being done, the shaman climbed to the top of a big boulder in the centre of the cemetery, beat his drum and tonelessly droned incantations which were meant to drive evil spirits away from the fresh graves so that they would not disturb the peace of the dead. The warriors not engaged in digging the graves stood in a circle and watched, leaning on their spears. When the graves were filled, all the warriors, as one man, raised their hands, lowered them, covering their faces, and uttered a drawn-out wail, which the travellers were already familiar with; but here, coming from five hundred throats and echoed by the cliffs, it made a deep impression. This was repeated three times, after which the warriors left the cemetery and sat down to rest.

Goryunov and his friends took this opportunity to examine the margin of the valley. The mist had dispersed and the morning sun was shedding a bright light on the black cliffs and ledges rising to a dizzy height; the travellers could see sharp-pointed peaks with snow gleaming white between them; there were a few small waterfalls running down the ledges. Now and again a lump of melting snow broke away, slipping down the precipices and scattering on the ground. A pair of eagles were sailing in the blue sky, scanning the ledges for a careless lamb or looking for a deer calf that had strayed from its mother. A deep stillness reigned in the air, and the numerous grave mounds amidst stones covered with green, yellow or red lichens, on the border between a gigantic black wall with white teeth and a strip of forest beneath a cloudless sky, engendered a solemn mood. The dead had left the verdant woods and meadows, where they had lived, loved, and fought, to lie in this shelter beneath the canopy formed by these black cliffs on which fantasy involuntarily drew an inscription in fiery lettering, which read: "Here is the kingdom of eternal peace."

At the foot of the cliff facing the cemetery the travellers saw a large cave, whose entrance was protected by a stone wall. Amnundak told them that it was once the home of a big horde of Wampus and that a fierce battle in which many Onkilons were killed was fought there. The horde was annihilated down to the last man, but the battle-field became a burial ground because the surviving Onkilons could carry away only the wounded. Since then all warriors who fell in battle against the Wampus were buried in this cemetery.

"You see, white men," Amnundak concluded, pointing to the numerous grave mounds, "how many of our brave warriors found their death at the hands of the Wampus. You can understand now why we hate them so. We cannot live peacefully while there is a single Wampu in our land."

The cave was littered with half-rotted human bones and skulls; bears, wolves, and eagles had had a great feast when the victorious Onkilons withdrew, leaving the dead Wampus in the cave. Judging from the condition of the bones, the battle must have taken place a few centuries before; many of the bones turned to dust when the travellers touched them. But the flint spearheads, scrapers, and knives lying everywhere were well preserved, and the travellers made a collection of these primitive artefacts. Thus, this cave was another graveyard, a dismal one, in humid

semi-darkness beneath overhanging arches covered with the soot of fires that had burned for many a long year.

Looking round the cave, the travellers could not help thinking how gloomy was the life of these prehistoric half-humans-half-beasts, who fought for their existence with primitive weapons, now starving, now gorging themselves like animals; they hid from the cold in cheerless shelters, wresting them from a ferocious bear or a cave hyena; throughout the long arctic night they shivered in hard, crudely made skins and whiled away the time by eating, sleeping or fashioning flints for their weapons. It was striking how much happier was the life of the Onkilons, who likewise were people of the stone age; they had clothes, utensils, clan rites, and festivals; they lived in forests and meadows and had brighter and warmer shelters; they knew how to vary their food, shape bones, and dress skins; they already had herds of domestic reindeer.

Like the remnants of the animals which had died out or had been exterminated everywhere else, primitive man survived in Sannikov Land because it was cut off from the rest of the world by a barrier of ice and it was due to that isolation that his development had stopped at a very low level. The Wampus lived like their ancestors did in the remote age when this land was divorced from the mainland and was surrounded by ice; the climate had not changed, there was an abundance of food, and until the arrival of the Onkilons there had been no incentive to develop a better way of life.

From Amnundak the travellers learned that the Wampus had already borrowed a few practices from the Onkilons; formerly they even did not know how to make a fire and wintered near the hot springs, building stone shelters. When they learned to make fires, they began to spend the winters in caves, which afforded better protection from the cold and snow. They began to roast meat, although they still ate it raw as well; they learned to make rough wooden cups and to sew skin blankets and cloaks for the cold season; they also made bone spearheads, but still preferred to use flint for the purpose because it was more reliable.

Amnundak could not give Ordin a reply when he was asked where the Wampus got their flint from; the Onkilons did not know, he said; they used either bone or the bigger pieces of chalcedony, agate or sard which they got from the basalt along the fringe of the valley. It took a long time to make spearheads from this material and that work was usually done during the long arctic night by the light of a fire in the dwellings. There was no flint in the basalt and the travellers were led to believe that in the domain of the Wampus there were some other rocks, for example, limestone or chalk, which often contain deposits of flint. That prompted them to think of undertaking another expedition, deep into Wampu territory this time.

Finishing their inspection of the cave, the travellers and Amnundak rejoined the waiting warriors; the chief dismissed them and some, whose camps were nearby, dispersed to their homes, while others, who lived farther south, went with Amnundak along the edge of the valley. That gave the travellers a chance to see new places. On the whole, the road was monotonous but this monotony was broken now and again by some distinguishing feature: now the precipice, towering to a dizzy height, formed an almost sheer wall at the bottom of which lay heaps of melting snow that from time to time were replenished by avalanches; now the precipice broke up into ledges of varying loftiness and provided shelters for the brown mountain sheep that showed themselves for brief moments here and there; now a narrow crevice, forming a frowning corridor between the overhanging cliffs, peaked prominences, and boulders shaped fantastically by rain and wind, stretched from the bottom up. But these crevices were only accessible to mountain sheep and no human could even venture to climb them. Here and there, a huge mass of rock with water streaming down its sides bulged out like the stomach of some monster. At an elevation of hundreds of metres, a silvery waterfall, fed by snow from the peaks, arched out of a hole in the steep wall and, forming into spray, dropped to the ground below. There was nothing but basalt everywhere—now almost solid, now porous in the shape of lava, now ashy, now filled with the beautifully coloured stones the Onkilons prized so much for women's ornaments and for weapons.

Gorokhov noticed a mountain sheep outlined against a black rock on a narrow ledge about two hundred metres from the ground; the animal was feeling perfectly safe from the two-legged creatures crawling far below.

"Which of your warriors can bring that sheep down with his bow?" Gorokhov asked Amnundak.

The chief shook his head and said:

"It is beyond the reach of our arrows."

"But not of our lightnings. We'll have a sheep for dinner."

Amnundak measured the distance with his eye and again shook his head.

"Well, Nikita, you'd better make good your boast," Goryunov said in an encouraging tone.

Gorokhov loaded his gun, dropped on one knee and to make sure of his aim rested the barrel on a forked branch in a bush; the sheep seemed only a brown spot and was no easy target. Amnundak and his warriors crowded round Gorokhov in expectation. The Yakut took a long time sighting his gun and, at last, fired, the report echoing and re-echoing in the cliffs. The brown spot swayed, darted forward, and tore off the ledge. The sheep hurtled down, hitting the juts in the cliffs with its horns and bouncing off them like a ball; the enormous horns and bent legs flashed in the air; finally, the sheep crashed to the ground at the foot of the cliff. With a shout, the Onkilons ran to fetch it.

"The lightnings of the white men strike far and nobody can save himself from them," Amnundak said. "If the Onkilons had ten such lightnings there would not be a single Wampu in our land by the time the sun hides for the winter."

On the way, party after party of Onkilons turned into the forest towards their respective camps; finally, the last party took their leave and, passing the mudhouse of the shaman to whom they presented the head of the sheep, the travellers reached the clearing where their dwelling stood. Annuir, who had been with them all the time, ran to the mudhouse in order to meet her husband on the threshold together with the other women as the custom of the Onkilons required.

HUNTING HUNTERS

The travellers spent more than a week in their dwelling, resting after the expedition to the Wampus and learning the language of the Onkilons; with the women to chat to that was not difficult and the lessons around the blazing fire over a cup of tea or a pipe resolved into hours of merriment with jests and laughter; in their turn, the women learned to speak Russian and by the end of the week both sides understood each other quite well. Attracted by the laughter, Amnundak frequently went to see the white men, but in his presence the women comported themselves with decorum and the travellers upheld their dignity.

It was already the beginning of June and the sun no longer disappeared beyond the horizon; but, hanging over the northern outskirts at midnight, it hid for an hour or two behind a curtain of what looked like white clouds or a dense fog, bringing on twilight. The travellers were usually asleep at this time, but one day Goryunov went outside, noticed thes phenomenon, and called his friends.

The women told them that they were quite accustomed to it, explaining: "Big steam comes from the land as from a vessel in which soup is boiling or as from a kettle." That intrigued the travellers and redoubled their determination to penetrate into the land of the Wampus and discover the cause.

But at first they had to visit Nikiforov; everybody went except Annuen, who was left in charge of the dwelling. Nikiforov did not find his solitude boring; in addition to looking after the dogs and feeding them, he stocked up firewood and meat and when it was sunny he cured meat, hanging it on leather thongs and guarding it against birds and the dogs, whom he allowed to roam about freely during the daytime. Frequently, the Cossack amused himself by shooting a daring eagle which snatched up a piece of meat and hanging the bird up in the space it made on the thong; it was as good food as any for the dogs.

The snow-drifts had settled noticeably and a crust of ice formed on their surface so that it was impossible to reach the top without first cutting steps in the ice. Nikiforov took the trouble to do that and climbed to the crest from time to time to observe the condition of the sea. It had changed considerably in the month the travellers were in Sannikov Land; the stretch of ice-free water had widened and was close enough to be seen. There was often a fog hanging over it, but on a clear or windy day the fog dispersed and the tip of Kotelny was visible on the horizon. The island still had its blanket of snow and thawed patches showed through only here and there.

When the women, who had never seen the environs of the land they lived in, climbed to the top they were terrified by the desert of snow and ice lying before them in all its majesty, and felt genuinely sorry for the white men who had to live there most of the year.

"That is why you are so white," they decided.

"Tell me, Annuir, will you come with me when I leave your land?" Ordin asked.

Annuir energetically shook her head.

"No, it is too cold there, only snow and ice. Look, in my land it is summer and warm, but here it is winter."

"Then I shall go without you and you will be a widow."

"No, you will not go. All of you will live here as Amnundak said. Besides, you have promised."

They soon descended to the base for the sharp breeze blowing from the ice-field seemed very cold to the women, who were lightly clothed, and they were glad to find themselves by the fire, around which they spent the night. For climbing the snow-drift, the women were rewarded with strings of beads and mirrors, which the travellers found in their stores.

This time they took back with them many more things, brought in case of a meeting with the Onkilons, planning to give them away in Amnundak's camp. These included beads, mirrors, needles, shining buttons, bright ribbons, brass rings, and ear-rings with paste diamonds, a coral necklace for Amnundak's wife, which, they were sure, would enrapture the other women, a few knives, an axe, and a handsaw—to satisfy the men and induce Amnundak to give them a strong escort for their trip deep into Wampu territory.

Returning to their dwelling, they stayed there for another three days at the end of which time they talked the chief into giving his consent for an excursion to the northern part of the valley.

"Your lightnings," Amnundak said, "kill birds, beasts and men, but the Wampus are very cunning and may attack you from ambush or at night when there is a mist. Therefore, you shall have twelve of my bravest young warriors as your companions and they will guard your sleep, carry your baggage, and find the safest paths."

On the following day, a party made up of fifteen well-armed men and a woman left the camp; Annuir persuaded Ordin to take her with him and also armed herself with a spear, a bow and a quiver of arrows, ignoring the derision of the men and the apprehensions of the women. But she was determined to see new places, while Ordin wanted to train her to travel so as later to take her away to the mainland; he liked her very much and Annuir had fallen in love with him.

On the first day, the party reached the camp that had been raided by Wampus. The dwelling was already rebuilt and life was coming into its own; the women were busy with the household chores and the children were playing happily. Spending the night there, they went farther north. Meadows with lakes in them alternated with forests, which grew sparser, and there were fewer wild animals. They stopped for the night in a clearing on the bank of a lake, in whose centre a huge bubble rose every ten minutes. The water was so warm that the travellers decided to have a wash. While the warriors lit the fire and sliced the meat for dinner, they undressed and dived into the lake. The splashes attracted the warriors' attention and they sprang to their feet in alarm. They did not have such an aversion for water as Mongols, for example, who never washed, but like the other people of the North, where the water was too cold, they were unaccustomed to bathing. That was why they thought that the white magicians, who were entrusted to their care, wanted to leave the land of the Onkilons and for that purpose had changed themselves into fish or seals.

"Annu, look, your husband and the other magicians are disappearing. They have gone into the lake!" they shouted.

Annuir, who was busy cooking, jumped up and ran to the bank, the warriors following her. The travellers were already swimming and only their heads showed above the surface.

"There, they have already changed themselves into seals, look, look!" the warriors cried.

But Annuir knew more about the travellers than the others. She stopped worrying when she recognized Ordin in the water and laughed at the warriors. Incidentally, there was a bigger surprise in store for them. When the travellers climbed back to the bank they rubbed their bodies and heads and were soon covered with something white that resembled snow. The warriors had never seen soap before and were astounded.

"Look now. The water is freezing on the magicians and turning into snow!" they said to each other.

This time, too, Annuir, who knew what soap was, calmed them, explaining what the travellers were doing. But their fears were completely allayed only when the travellers dressed and returned to the fire, where all the warriors stole glances at them to see if there was any change.

While the men ate, Annuir took the cake of soap and also ran to bathe in the lake, choosing a secluded spot. Unable to swim, she did not go far into the water and washed herself by the bank. When she returned, the warriors made fun of her.

"You rubbed yourself with snow to become white like your husband! You were not scared to climb into the water where the water spirit could seize you by your foot and drag you down. But you are as dark as ever!" her fellow tribesmen jeered.

Later, Annuir admitted to Ordin that she was terribly frightened; that all the time she was in the water she thought someone would catch her by her foot and pull her under. Like all Onkilons, she believed there were evil spirits living in water, the forests, and the caves, and was quite sure that mists and snow-storms were also the handiwork of demons. It was only the desire to imitate him that made her enter the lake.

"Next time I shall go with you. But you must show me what you do to swim like a seal," she declared.

During the night, the warriors kept watch in pairs together with Krot and Belukha. The dogs had already grown used to the Onkilons, who gave them half-picked bones and pieces of meat. The warriors valued the dogs' vigilance and regretted that their forefathers had not taken a few of these animals from the Chukchis.

"Why can't they catch and tame wolf-cubs?" Gorokhov asked.

"A wolf can never be tamed," Goryunov explained. "The only thing I can recommend is to catch a she-wolf and cross her with our dogs. Pity we haven't any bitches in our pack."

The warriors doubted the wisdom of this suggestion, but said that it was not difficult to catch a wolf.

All day the party pushed on northwards; the woods were very sparse, the trees low and in the meadows there was only a thin covering of grass; the few oxen and horses that were seen were very cautious: hunted by the Wampus, they had learned to mistrust human beings. On the other hand, the travellers saw more and more rhinoceroses, who themselves terrified the Wampus and were not afraid of their spears and clubs.

Just before evening, the scouts who were in the lead with the dogs stopped the party with the news that there were Wampus in the clearing ahead. The travellers and the warriors hid in the bushes and watched.

A few oxen were grazing in the clearing; one of them was standing apart from the others and apparently dozing and chewing the cud.

Five or six Wampus were slowly crawling up to it from behind through the grass.

When the leading Wampu was about twenty paces from the ox, he jerked upright and threw two spears; the others, springing to their feet, ran to the sides of the ox, raising their spears and preparing to throw them. One of the spears caught the animal in the sacrum and pierced the skin. The ox bellowed with fright and pain and, noticing its enemies, charged at them, lowering its head, its formidable horns thrust forward; the Wampus leaped out of its way and the animal thundered past them, receiving a spear in each side. But the flint did not go deep into the tough skin and the spears fell on the ground. Snorting with anger, the ox wheeled round, overtook one of the hunters and with a throw of its head tossed him high in the air; but the other Wampus again hurled their spears and distracted the animal's attention.

Seeing that it was being attacked on all sides, the ox sought safety in flight and galloped across the clearing to join the herd; the Wampus started off in pursuit, but despite their speed they fell behind and the spears they threw made no impression on the fleeing animal.

"That was a bit of hard luck for them," Goryunov said. "Now we'll shoot the animal, but not for them, of course."

The ox was about two hundred paces away and the four Wampus thirty paces behind it; the fifth savage lay where he had fallen. The Wampus were running with great strides, their bodies bent far forward; their dishevelled hair fluttered in the wind; each had only a spear left. They hoped the ox would grow weak from loss of blood and allow itself to be overtaken. Suddenly, it stopped in its tracks and dropped dead on the ground. In the heat of the chase, the Wampus had either not heard the report of the gun or did not understand what had happened. With a roar of triumph they ran up to the animal and began a victory dance around it.

"We'll have to scare them off," Ordin said. "Otherwise we'll never see that meat."

"Yes, and in general we must clear a road for ourselves to the north and force the savages to keep to their caves."

Gorokhov raised his gun and fired. At first the Wampus froze to the ground, but a moment later they cried out in terror and rushed back across the clearing; the savage who had been thrown by the ox rose and limped after them. Instantly, the Onkilons showed themselves in the clearing and shouted their war-cry so that the Wampus would associate it with the report of a gun.

"We'll stay here for the night," Goryunov announced. "We have plenty of food and the Wampus will not dare to return."

While the warriors gutted the ox, the travellers walked about the clearing and discovered a little lake, a pool to be more exact, which had no outlet. The water in it was warmish and the steep sides gave the impression that it was very deep. The party encamped here, the warriors bringing big pieces of meat, leaving the rest for the eagles and wolves. The camp-fire burned cheerfully and everybody helped to cook the dinner. Ordin went to the little lake with a pot; the water was so low that to scoop up some of it he had to lie on the ground. Stretching for it he thought he saw the level rising; he raised the pot slowly and the water rose after it as though attracted by a magnet.

It kept rising until it reached the level of the ground.

"The lake is overflowing," Ordin shouted to his friends, jumping to his feet.

His cry brought everybody to the lake and they gazed dumbfoundedly at the water.

"We must collect our things and move away from here," Kostyakov said.

The Onkilons exchanged whispers and stared at the water with superstitious awe, expecting some monster to show its head. Fear and laughter mingled in the expression on Annuir's face, because glancing at Ordin she noticed that he was smiling. By now she had arrived at the conclusion that the white men knew everything, could do anything, and feared nothing.

But before the Onkilons decided upon flight, the water began to subside and in a few minutes dropped to its initial level. Gorokhov sighed with relief.

"It's gone, gone back. We've frightened it," he muttered.

Ordin, Goryunov, and Kostyakov burst out laughing; they had realized that this was a new kind of lake with a subterranean source; apparently, on its bottom there was a deep opening filled with water; from time to time vapours and gases raised the water and escaped into some side crack and not through the water as in other lakes. That was what made the water fall. All that now remained to assure themselves that their surmise was correct was to time the frequency of this phenomenon. Ordin took out his watch.

"Now I understand how animals use this lake," Goryunov said. "They wait until the water reaches the banks."

"Yes, and I was puzzled when I saw tracks on that sheer bank with nothing to show how the animals got to the water," Ordin said.

"Imagine what some of the animals feel when the water recedes under their very noses before they can drink their fill. They can do nothing but wait."

A long time passed before the water mounted again; the dinner was cooked and eaten before any movement was observed. The interval lasted nearly an hour.

No sooner did the sun hide behind the screen of vapour

rising from the northern end of the valley than a thick mist advanced from that direction and it became quite dark. However, the travellers had heaped up enough firewood for the night and it was bright and warm around the fire. The conversation centred around the lakes in this strange land with their periodic eruptions, which the Onkilons explained as a game of the water spirits. They said that in the north there was a place called the Valley of a Thousand Smokes, where smoke poured out of the ground, which was so hot that it scorched the foot even when boots were worn. They had never been there themselves but had heard about it from old men, who in their youth had participated in a great raid organized against the Wampus by Amnundak's grandfather.

Formerly, the Wampus wintered in that valley.

The conversation was interrupted by a drawn-out howl coming from the forest. Krot and Belukha barked angrily in reply.

"Wolves," Gorokhov said. "They've scented carrion."

"Here's our chance to catch a she-wolf or two," Goryunov said.

The warriors declared that that was easy to do; in winter they hunted wolves which molested the deer herds, driving the killers into the clearings with torches. Happily, one of the warriors had a net with which to catch the she-wolves; it was woven from thin thongs and used for moulting geese. They began to prepare for the hunt. From the piles of firewood laid in for the night they selected resinous saplings cut into pieces about half a metre long and tied them to spears; torches were made for everybody and put into the fire. Meanwhile, the wolves were growling round the remains of the ox and they could be heard gnawing the bones; the pack was banqueting under cover of darkness.

When the torches were lighted, the Onkilons and the travellers with a torch in one hand and a spear or a gun in the other quickly surrounded the wolves and, holding the torches close to the ground and swinging them to the right and left, closed in towards the centre, forming a moving circle of fire. Soon, through the mist, they discerned the pack of grey beasts bunched round the carcass of the ox; their tails between their legs, their teeth bared, they stood in confusion, unable to see a way out of the swinging and relentlessly advancing circle of flame. The wolves howled, dashed this way and that, getting into each other's way and, at last, mad with fear, rushed in different directions in twos and threes.

But very few escaped; the Onkilons deftly stabbed them with spears or, hitting them on their snouts with the torches, drove them back. The warrior with the net threw it over a she-wolf, which tried to break through the circle; it got entangled in the meshes and fell on its side. The remaining wolves returned to the carcass, trembling, huddling together, and snapping their teeth; they no longer tried to break away. A few shots finished them off. Raising their torches, the warriors put an end to the wolves lying where the spears had pinned them to the ground. Among the wounded animals they found another she-wolf. They covered its head with a jacket, bound its legs, and carried it away on a spear.

The dead wolves, of which there were eleven, were picked up and taken to the fire, where the warriors began to skin them.

Three stakes were driven into the ground for each of the she-wolves. The front and hind legs were tied to two of the stakes and the head to the third stake. That placed the thongs out of reach of the animals' teeth. When the excitement of this remarkable hunt died down, everybody went to sleep, as usual leaving two warriors to keep watch and to see that the she-wolves were not attacked by Krot and Belukha. It took a long time to pacify the dogs.

VALLEY OF A THOUSAND SMOKES

At their morning meal, which they ate in a thick mist, the travellers and the warriors discussed how to take the she-wolves with them; some of the warriors said they would carry them on their shoulders by turns, others proposed using the skin of the ox as a stretcher. The simplest solution would have been to force them to use their own feet, but there was no chain or wire with which to make a leash that their sharp teeth could not bite through.

Finally, they solved the problem by making wide leather collars and muzzles; the collars were fastened to the ramrod of Gorokhov's gun to which a lead was also tied. That forced the she-wolves to walk side by side like yoked oxen; one warrior pulled them by the lead and another urged them on from behind. At first the animals refused to budge and lay on the ground, but when the dogs were set on them and bit their flanks they yielded and followed their captors with their tails between their legs.

The party continued their journey as soon as the mist began to rise. The vegetation was more and more stunted and they passed whole belts of dwarf trees. In the clearings, there were pieces of ground with sparse grass alternating with patches of bare and weathered basalt. A few kilometres away the travellers came across a crevice with light smoke rising from it.

Ordin bent down, put his hand to the crevice, but drew

it back quickly—the air coming from it was scorching hot. They came upon more of these crevices the farther they went. The air grew hotter and it seemed to the travellers that they were in a strongly heated bath-house; the vapours spreading over the entire neighbourhood like a light mist intensified that impression. The Onkilons had already bared themselves to the waist, throwing off their jackets, and the travellers, unable to stand the heat, now followed their example. Finally, Annuir, too, took off her garment and remained in her loin-cloth, announcing with some embarrassment that it was as hot as in a dwelling where a good fire was burning.

The area where the mist was thickest drew the travellers' attention. There, from a few cracks, clouds of steam were issuing with a light whistle that sounded more like a sigh.

"These are real fumaroles," Ordin said.

The farther they went the more they found the bare, undulating surface of black lava pitted with these holes. It looked as though beneath their feet the ground was smouldering and belching smoke; they could feel the warmth through their boots.

When they had covered a kilometre or two of this terrain, they stopped to rest and to look round. The picture was extraordinary. From all sides, from different places, columns of vapour rose and curled in the still air, little rainbows flashing in them in the slanting rays of the sun. One might think that it was smoke from the chimneys of an invisible town as it rises into the air on a clear, frosty morning. The towering precipices on the fringe of the valley, which was only some five or six kilometres away, loomed black through the gaps between the white columns in the north, east, and west. Here and there the travellers caught glimpses of sharp-pointed peaks with strips and patches of snow sparkling in the sunlight. The snow and the white columns of vapour on the one hand and the black precipice and black soil on the other presented a rare combination of two opposite colours.

The silence was frequently disturbed now by a sharp whistle, now by a rumble in one of the holes.

"A black, smoking waste!" Goryunov exclaimed.

"Here it is, the Valley of a Thousand Smokes," Ordin said.

"The abode of evil spirits," declared the leader of the warriors. "The smoke is from their fires in underground caves."

With different feelings they contemplated this uncommon scene; the travellers—with interest, the Onkilons—with superstitious dread. Before them they saw a column of vapour that was thicker than the rest and when they went up to it they found that it was rising from a pool that was only about six metres in diameter. The water gurgled as in a big boiler.

Goryunov took a piece of raw meat from his knapsack, tied it to the end of a strap and lowered it into the pool. Tossed by streams of boiling water, the meat whirled and plunged and was cooked in a few minutes.

"What a wonderful place for a camp," Ordin remarked. "There is no firewood, but to make up for that there is a 'pot' in which to cook dinner and where we can get boiling water for tea."

Farther north, they saw a few more boiling pools. The smallest, one or two metres in diameter, boiled peacefully, liberating a multitude of tiny bubbles; in the bigger pools, the entire surface seethed and frothed. The travellers noted that on the sheer sides overhanging the surface of

207

the water and on the soil around the pools there were places with a thin white coating as of snow. With the water boiling, this was absurd. They took a sample and found that it was some kind of extremely bitter salt.

"But if the water discharges salt," Goryunov said, "it must be salty and unfit for tea."

They tasted the water. It was not altogether fresh but quite suitable for drinking.

Pushing on between the boiling pools and smoking holes they stopped at a big hollow when they were already quite close to the outskirts of the valley. The hollow was about two hundred metres in diameter and from fifteen to twenty metres deep.

The bottom was convex and the whole resembled a huge cup. But there was no water. Peering through the light mist hovering above the bottom, they noticed little blue flames shooting out of the cracks in the ground. Ordin wanted to take a closer look and began to descend into the hollow. He only took a few steps down when he turned and hurried back, his hands clamped over his nose and mouth. He said he felt he was beginning to choke from the sulphur and chlorine fumes that filled the air which was as hot as in a furnace.

Through field-glasses it was possible to see thick yellow and white deposits of what apparently was sulphur and sal-ammoniac lying in stripes and spots on the black surface.

"Well, Pavel," Ordin said to Kostyakov after recovering his breath, "now even you cannot deny that Sannikov Land is the crater of a colossal volcano that is not quite extinct."

"Nobody will deny it now! These basalt cliffs on all sides, the geysers, and the bubbling lakes in the south, the boiling pools and the fumaroles here, in the north, leave not the slightest doubt about it," Goryunov concurred with him.

"But the Onkilons," Kostyakov disputed, "have been living on this island for the last four hundred years, while the Wampus and animals have been here much longer. There is luxuriant vegetation in the southern half and that shows that the volcano has been inactive for a very long time."

"Undoubtedly. But it is also clear that the volcano stopped its activity gradually from south to north because the signs here are much more distinct. Perhaps when the first Wampus were settling in the southern part of the island lava was still pouring out in the north."

"That activity stopped by the time the Onkilons got here," Ordin added. "All they can tell us is that the smoke is the work of 'underground spirits.'"

"Is it possible that one fine day the volcano will awaken from its long sleep and make a lot of trouble?" Goryunov asked.

"I think so. Only volcanoes that have been inactive for whole geological periods and have been more or less destroyed may be called extinct. Nobody can vouch for the others and the correct description would be to say that they are dormant, for there is always the chance of them waking up. We know of cases when volcanoes that were regarded as extinct suddenly erupted. Take Vesuvius. It had a dense forest in its crater and Spartacus, the leader in the gladiatorial war against Rome, sought refuge there. Nobody thought the mountain was a volcano, and even legends had nothing to say about it. Yet it erupted in A.D. 79 and buried Herculaneum and Pompeii, and has been active ever since."

"Then there's Mont Pelé in Martinique," Goryunov recalled. "It slumbered until the middle of the 18th century and the natives knew nothing of its past activity. Then it began to wake up, taking a century and a half to do so and giving hardly any signs of life. It was only at the beginning of the 20th century that there was a terrible eruption and the city of St. Pierre and thirty thousand lives were destroyed in a few minutes."

"There have been many similar instances in both North and South America, the Sunda Islands, and Kamchatka," Ordin said.

"The awakening of this volcano," Kostyakov noted, "would be a calamity for the Onkilons."

"Depends on how and where it renews its activity. If the eruption is weak and is limited to the northern end of the valley, which is barren and unpopulated, the Onkilons will go on living in peace near the volcano. But if the eruption starts in the southern half, then the worst may be expected."

"It seems to me," Ordin said, "that this abundance of fumaroles, geysers, and boiling pools indicates that there may be a resumption of volcanic activity today, tomorrow, in short, at any time, although this condition has lasted for hundreds of years, according to the Onkilons. But then they seldom come to this place and their testimony is unreliable. Accurate observations are needed."

"Let's hope," Goryunov said, "that nothing happens while we are here and that Sannikov Land and its living fossils enjoy many more centuries of life."

Making a circuit round the asphyxiating hollow, the travellers soon reached the northern extremity of the valley, seeing the same sheer or stepped basalt precipices as in other places; they estimated that these precipices were at least a thousand metres high. The total absence of vegetation, even of lichens, in this wilderness emphasized its desolation. At a little distance from the foot of the black precipices stretched the withe wall of the Valley of a Thousand Smokes into which from afar the columns of vapour merged. The wall was not immobile; it tossed and rolled and in the rays of the low-hanging sun there was a rainbow-like play of colours in its billowy top.

There was a long white stripe along part of the foot of one of the precipices.

"Strange. Could it be snow from the top?" Goryunov said.

"No, it is not snow," Ordin told him, looking through his field-glasses. "It is a deposit of some white rock. And it is full of holes as though it's been nibbled at. I wonder if that is where the Wampus get their flint from?"

They hurried to the spot and found that there the basalt lay on crumbling snow-white marble protruding about two or three metres above the floor of the valley over a distance of two to three hundred metres. Black, grey, and dirty-white flint was imbedded in the marble in separate pieces, in clusters or in layers; the face of the marble was dented, which was evidence that the Wampus had been at work here with spearheads and scrapers.

"This is the very discovery we needed to determine the age of the volcano," Ordin said, examining the rock. "Here are a few fossils. I'll admit they're second-rate but they show that this stratum belongs to the upper cretaceous period. Consequently, this volcano dates back to not earlier than the Tertiary period, when basalt flowed to the surface in various parts of North Siberia. But we must look for something better to go by."

With these words, Ordin climbed into one of the deeper

niches in the precipice and set to work with his hammer; the others searched in the heaps of white sand on the ground; even the Onkilons joined them when they were shown one of the shells Ordin found and were told what it was. The hammering stopped and soon Ordin jumped to the ground, saying:

"There's a proper hell's kitchen deep underground. Keep quiet and put your ears to the precipice and listen. You can hear it best in that niche up there."

Goryunov and Kostyakov climbed into the niche and pressed their ears to the wall. The sound of hammering, the blows coming thick and fast one moment and slowly the next, could be heard as though somewhere in the depths of the earth titanic forges were at work; it seemed that sledge hammers were striking hard metal. The rock trembled slightly and crystals of limespar, of which the marble consisted, broke away from the face of the rock from time to time.

"The devil's at work in there," said Goryunov, coming out of the niche.

"Don't you think we ought to clear out while the clearing's good?" Kostyakov said with a note of anxiety in his voice.

"Don't worry. What you heard is not a sign that the volcano will erupt soon," Ordin laughed. "If we had been here before and did not hear those sounds, it would have meant an itensification of underground activity. But even that is no cause for anxiety for the volcano may take days, weeks, months, or even years to awaken."

"I'd say centuries, as Mont Pelé did," Goryunov added.

Learning what the travellers were talking about, the Onkilons climbed into the niche by turns and emerged with troubled faces. Now, more than ever, they were sure that evil spirits lived under the ground. In the aggregate, these blows, the trembling of the rocks, the tongues of flame in the hollow, the thousand smokes, the boiling pools, and the complete desolation frightened them and they insisted on leaving this terrible wilderness at once, before nightfall.

But it was already late in the evening. The sun hid behind the tall northern precipices, throwing an intense shadow. In addition, a big, black cloud was advancing from the west and it could be expected that the mist would be particularly dense here. What with fog and darkness enveloping the valley, it did not need much to wander off the path and fall into a crevice or a boiling pool.

Indeed, when they were only a kilometre from the precipice, the sky grew overcast and a light rain began to fall, cooling the vapours rising from the ground and draping the entire valley in a mist; it grew quite dark and, willy-nilly, the party had to stop in the neighbourhood of the sinister hollow by a boiling pool, where they could at least cook their meal and boil some tea for there was no fuel anywhere. The composure of the travellers influenced the Onkilons and all of them lay on the bank, immersing pieces of meat fixed to spears or tied to a thong. But they spoke in whispers. Gorokhov thought of cooking soup; he put some meat into a pot, added salt and groats, scooped water into it and half-immersed it in the pool. The soup proved to be quite good, especially the meat, which tasted better than the pieces cooked directly in the pool. The tea was quite drinkable.

Posting sentries, the warriors went to sleep after the meal, huddling close together under their shields to keep out of the rain. For the travellers, they had made a tent from the ox-skin, pinning the ends down with spears. But the latter wanted to see the lights of the hollow at night and they left the camp quietly, without disturbing the sleeping warriors.

Thanks to the warmth coming from the depths, there was no mist over the hollow and what they saw was a black hole with its bottom criss-crossed by restless lines of little blue flames which barely flickered one moment and burned brightly the next. It was a very strange and interesting spectacle.

To get a better view, the four friends stretched themselves on the ground at the edge of the hollow when suddenly they felt a sharp tremor—the ground shook under them.

"It's an earthquake," Kostyakov cried, jumping up. But he had to lie down again for the vibrations made it difficult to stand. A rumble was heard, while in the hollow the fires fluttered, rising and falling. From all over the valley came the crash of falling stones. In the darkness and mist these sounds produced terrifying sensations.

From the camp, which was about a hundred paces away they heard cries of dismay to which were added the wails of Annuir, who woke up and found that Ordin and the other white men were nowhere to be seen. The Onkilons thought that the white magicians had forsaken them in this gruesome land. The dogs and the she-wolves howled, coupling their voices with those of the Onkilons and raising an infernal uproar. The superstitious warriors were at their wit's end and did not know what to do.

When the tremors grew weaker and it was possible to get up, the travellers hurried back to the camp, which in spite of the inky blackness they found easily by the cries. The appearance of the travellers reassured the Onkilons and when Goryunov explained where they had been, the warriors even felt ashamed of themselves. Annuir put her arms round Ordin and hid her tear-stained face on his breast. Nobody thought of sleep any longer and Goryunov took advantage of this to question the warriors and find out if there had been earthquakes before. It turned out that this phenomenon was familiar to the Onkilons. Sometimes, usually in winter, they felt the ground shake slightly; the beams in their dwellings creaked and loose earth fell on their heads through the cracks.

"That is exactly what is happening now," Goryunov told them.

"No, it is not," one of the warriors said. "We have never known the land to shake so much that we could not stand. That is what frightened us and when we found that you were gone we thought you had abandoned us in this horrible place and that the underground spirits, which shake the earth, would leap out of the cracks and take us away to their kingdom of darkness."

The tremors stopped and the travellers returned to their tent, which had to be re-erected; the first shock had set the spears at an angle and the skin had dropped on Annuir, awakening and frightening her.

As for the Onkilons, they could not fall asleep; they had no camp-fire and that increased their superstitious fear. Besides, a thunderstorm, a rare phenomenon in Sannikov Land, had broken out over the southern part of the valley; there lightning flashed with dazzling brilliance and thunder pealed, echoing and re-echoing in the tall precipices. Huddling close together, the warriors, who feared no foe they could see, mumbled incantations until the wind dispersed the clouds and the mist and it began to grow light. Only then did they fall asleep.

GODS OF THE WAMPUS

That morning the air was cool after the rain, and there was no mist, which enabled the travellers to set out on their return journey earlier than they had expected. The Onkilons were particularly glad. However, they had to make use of the boiling pool once more in order to cook some meat and fortify themselves for the long march ahead of them. Before leaving, the warriors threw a few pieces of meat into the pool and bowed three times.

"They are thanking the underground spirits for having only frightened them without causing any harm," Annuir explained.

Without stopping at the pools and cracks they had seen the day before, the party passed through the Valley of a Thousand Smokes by midday and when they came across the first patches of vegetation the faces of the Onkilons underwent a transformation, regaining their former friendly, cheerful look. It was evident that in escorting the strangers into the terrible valley at their chief's orders they had made a great sacrifice and expected the worst. But they had to make another sacrifice, for when the party entered the forest belt, the travellers set their minds on going into Wampu country again and seeing the queer animals with "a fifth leg on their heads," which the savages regarded as gods. Inquiries showed that these animals lived somewhere in the vicinity of the Valley of a Thousand Smokes.

There was nothing they could do but head south-eastwards. Three scouts and the dogs were sent in front. A landscape they were familiar with stretched before them—meadows with lakes and more or less broad tracts of forest land where the trees were taller and grew in denser clumps. After about six kilometres, the scouts stopped the party with the information that "gods" were grazing in a glade ahead of them. Picking their way carefully, they approached the glade and a hundred steps from the edge of the forest saw four big animals. It was not difficult to recognize them as representatives of the elephant family. They had had a meal and were standing motionless, resting in the afternoon sun, their trunks lowered and now and then wagging their short tails or flapping their enormous ears. They had a coat of long but sparse brownish-red fur. One pair was bigger than the other. The smaller animals had different tusks; they were short and straight, while the tusks of the adult animals curved upwards.

"There is no doubt that these animals are mammoths," Goryunov said.

"I should like to see these monsters run," Kostyakov said. "The elephants we see in zoos are cooped up in enclosures where they have no room to run about."

"That would be interesting, of course. But how can we make them run?"

"We could scare them by firing a few shots."

"I don't think that will work because they don't know what effect firearms have. And, moreover, that might attract their custodians, who probably live somewhere close by."

"Pooh, the firing will scare the Wampus more than the mammoths, because they already know what it means."

"Quiet. Speak of the devil," Goryunov said, pointing to the opposite side of the glade.

Two adults and a boy, carrying something in their hands, came out of the forest. When they were close to the mammoths, they put their burdens on the ground, went

down on their knees and bowed to the animals. The mammoths came out of their doze and approached the Wampus, waving their trunks and emitting a sound that was suggestive of loud grunts. When the Wampus finished their obeisances, they loosened their packs, which turned out to be skins filled with roots; these they spread on the grass in front of the mammoths, which lazily picked up two or three roots at a time with their trunks and con-

veyed them to their mouths. One of the Wampus was a
woman; she unfolded her offerings before the two young
mammoths. The man and the boy fed the adult animals.
The mammoths soon finished the roots and demanded
more, grunting lustily and stretching their trunks out to
the savages. The latter resumed their bows and, suddenly,
snatching up the skins, darted off towards the forest as
fast as their legs could carry them. What Kostyakov wanted
to see happened next; the mammoths trotted heavily after
the Wampus, their trunks curled in front of them, their
ears outspread and their little tails raised. But evidently
this was simply a sign of gratitude for the food, for had

they wanted to they could have overtaken and crushed the Wampus; but all they did was to see the savages to the edge of the forest after which they staidly turned back, trumpeting sonorously.

While the savages had been bowing and feeding the mammoths, the travellers and their Onkilon escort watched with interest, but when the Wampus disappeared in the forest the warriors begged Goryunov and his friends to shoot a mammoth. The thick skin was very highly prized as material for shields, while excellent knives and heads for spears and arrows were made from the tusks. They seldom had a chance to kill a mammoth; the Wampus guarded their gods jealously and a mammoth hunt was possible only during a big war against the savages but even then the animals were practically invulnerable to spears and arrows and managed to escape. But here was an opportunity they did not want to miss; the travellers could help them with their terrible, death-dealing lightnings.

Ordin seconded the entreaties of the Onkilons; he wanted to examine a mammoth closely and to measure it.

Kostyakov remembered reading in childhood that elephant's trunk was delicious and also sided with the warriors.

"But the Wampus will retaliate if we kill one of their gods," Goryunov protested. "The custodians will gather the entire horde and attack us."

"They'll quickly change their minds after they hear a few shots. I think the risk is worth while both for the sake of science and to please our faithful companions," Ordin replied.

"An explosive bullet is not enough for that pachyderm;

it'll only madden it and we'll have more on our hands than we're bargaining for."

"All right, so we'll let it have two or three bullets. That shouldn't stop us."

Very reluctantly, Goryunov gave his consent to the killing of a rare and almost tame animal, but he did not raise his gun. The Onkilons were overjoyed and with bated breath watched what effect the white men's lightnings would have on a god of the Wampus. Ordin and Kostyakov fired simultaneously at the nearest adult mammoth, which was standing with its side to them and getting ready to doze off again. The animal reeled, took a step forward, turned, and, with a roar that resounded all over the glade, sank to its knees and then slowly rolled over on its side. Frightened by the reports, the three other mammoths ran off a little way, stopped and turned, waiting for the animal that had fallen for no reason they could understand to rise and join them; they called to it, trumpeting loudly.

The travellers and the warriors ran to the wounded mammoth, which was still moving its trunk and legs; when the men approached it it made an effort to raise its head but slumped back with a heavy sigh. Its little black eyes seemed to be full of reproach. But soon the eyes grew dull and the voice was still. Ordin took out his tape-line and started measuring the mammoth, Kostyakov helped and made notes, while the Onkilons surrounded the carcass and watched these manipulations with awe, suspecting that this was the white men's way of propitiating the spirit of the killed god. The dogs wasted no time to lick the blood gushing from the big wound and streaming down the belly on to the grass.

Everybody was so engrossed that, unnoticed, the three

remaining mammoths approached to within about forty paces and stopped, gazing at the strange two-legged creatures around their comrade, who seemed to have no desire to get up. The dogs were the first to sense their closeness and rushed at them, barking angrily. The men looked round and could not at once decide what to do—to retreat to the forest before the mammoths attacked or to attack the animals themselves. Krot and Belukha stopped at about ten paces from the animals, barking and yelping at the top of their voices. But their tails were between their legs and they did not try to get closer. The mammoths looked with amazement at these impudent midgets who dared to plague them with their noises. At last, apparently sick of the barking, they turned and with stately tread went to the opposite end of the glade, where they began to eat, tearing off branches from the trees.

The warriors calmed down and when Ordin finished measuring the mammoth and closed his notebook they began to skin it and to cut off pieces of meat. Meanwhile, the scouts, who had been sent after the Wampus, returned and said that in the neighbouring meadow there was a camp which had just been abandoned. Goryunov wanted to see it and taking Gorokhov and one of the scouts with him left the others to dress the carcass.

The camp was situated around a big, branchy poplar in the middle of a small meadow. The grass was beaten flat and on the ground were a few skins, roughly cut wooden cups, two heavy clubs and a number of spears. The fire was not altogether out and over it were some sticks with half-burnt pieces of meat. Terrified by the reports, the Wampus had made off, leaving behind a half-eaten meal; the ground was strewn with picked bones, while on a bough hung the hind leg of an animal—of a horse, judging from the fresh skin spread on the grass.

Goryunov took one of the cups as a sample of the artefacts of the Wampus and was about to leave when the Onkilon scout drew his attention to a Wampu "nest" in the tree, in which the custodians of the gods might be hiding. But that supposition was unfounded, for the Wampus would not have left their weapons and the meat on the ground. The nest was empty, of course. Goryunov and his two companions climbed into it; this was easy to do because of the thick foliage. The nest was almost on the very crown, where the trunk branched out into several thick boughs; on these the Wampus had laid thin logs with a floor of poles to make a kind of platform; part of this platform was protected from rain by a roof woven from branches and reeds. Beneath the roof were some skins—the bedding and blankets of the Wampus. A pair of clubs, a skin sling, a heap of stones and a few spears comprised the furnishings of this shelter in which primitive man hid from nocturnal beasts of prey. A few holes made in the foliage gave a view of the vicinity, including the glade in which the mammoths grazed; a part of that glade could be seen now and Goryunov made out the group of Onkilons bustling round the carcass.

While they were inspecting the nest and peering through the holes in the foliage, a Wampu stepped out of the bushes near the forest, looked round and waved his arm, calling other Wampus out of hiding. A woman and two children responded to the signal, and all four went towards the tree. Just then Gorokhov noticed them and asked in a nervous whisper:

"The custodians of the gods are returning, what are we to do? Fire at them?"

223

The Onkilon had already taken an arrow from his quiver and was about to pull the string of his bow when Goryunov stopped him with a movement of his hand.

"Let's sit quietly and watch them," he said to Gorokhov.

"But what if they climb up?"

"They've got nothing to do here during the day and then their food's down there!"

"But how'll we get out?"

"By frightening them away with our guns. Damn it, I've left mine on the ground!"

"Now we're in a fix! They'll find it and spoil it."

"We shan't let them. You've got your gun, haven't you? Mine is on the far side of the trunk; they might not even see it."

The men trapped in the tree lay down on the skins around a hole in the floor through which they could see the camp. The Wampu family squatted round the fire; the woman had a baby in her arms; the boy, who was about twelve, already had a stick pierced through his nostrils, but the girl, who was not more than six, was not yet disfigured. Seeing the half-burnt meat, the man made a few jerky sounds that had nothing in common with human speech but which the boy understood, for he ran to the forest and returned with an armful of brushwood. Meanwhile, the woman raked up the ashes, freed the smouldering coals and, covering them with twigs, started the fire. The girl took a stick with meat, picked off the burnt crust and ate the rest. The man found a piece of flint among the scattered bones and, using it as a knife, cut strips of meat from the horse's leg hanging on the bough and threw them to the woman; he sliced a few small pieces and ate them raw. The woman strung the meat on sticks, biting off a piece now and then, while the boy stuck the sticks into the ground by the fire and watched them. The baby, which was lying on the grass, began to cry; the woman picked it off the ground, wedged it between her knees, thrust the black nipple of her sagging breast into its mouth, and went on busying herself with the meat.

Suddenly, the man stopped working and listened, then muttered something and pointed in the direction of the glade of the mammoths; the woman raised her head, apparently in alarm, and the children sprang up. Evidently, the Wampu heard the shouts of the Onkilons. He threw down the flint and ran to the other side of the tree, intending to climb to the nest. There he saw Goryunov's gun hanging on a bough. He gave a loud cry of astonishment and the woman and children ran up to him. The object did not look like a snake, for it was motionless and made no sound; that emboldened the Wampu and he stretched out his hand, but the woman was horrified and stopped him. An argument began. Finally, the Wampu roughly pushed the woman away, took the gun down with trembling hands and, carrying it gingerly to the fire, squatted and began to examine it. The woman and the children came up for they were satisfied that the strange object did not bite but was lying immovably across the man's knees. By degrees, the Wampu grew bolder, stroked the shining barrel and butt, even blew into the muzzle, then fingered the cock and the trigger—and, without notice, the gun went off.

With a shriek, the woman fell on her back; the baby rolled on the grass, one of its little hands got into the fire and it screamed; the children backed away; the man hurled the gun as far as he could. The next moment the children took to their heels and the woman, seizing the baby up and holding one of her hands to her head (she had probably bruised herself), hastened after them, sobbing all the while. The Wampu ran a few steps, then stopped.

Everything was quiet; the fire was blazing and the object that had frightened them so much was stationary on the ground near the tree. Step by step, the Wampu returned to the fire; his dinner had been interrupted a second time and the meat on the fire was burning. He went to the fire and stretched out his hand to take the sticks with the meat when there was an ear-splitting report overhead and something crashed into the fire, scattering coals and smouldering brands.

Now, the man, too, lost his nerve; with wild cries, he rushed to the forest, where the woman and children were waiting irresolutely. However, when they saw the man in full flight, they disappeared in the bushes.

"Well, they won't come back for a long time now," Gorokhov said; he had sent an explosive bullet into the fire. "From now on they'll think this tree is bewitched."

The Onkilon laughed till his eyes filled with tears. Goryunov also laughed. The three men climbed down the tree and recovered the gun. But before leaving, the Onkilon set the nest on fire and threw all the clubs and spears into the camp-fire. Gorokhov stuck the sticks with the meat into the bark of the tree high above the ground and, finding a human skull among the bones, set it on the horse's leg, which he took down from the tree and stood against the trunk; he placed the flint, with which the Wampu had sliced meat, on the crown and put coals into the eye-sockets.

"If they pluck up enough courage and come back soon," he said, "they'll attribute all these jokes to some supernatural force and will be even more afraid of our guns than before."

The three men returned to the glade of the mammoths and rejoined the rest of the party, which was already hurrying to their rescue. When Ordin and Kostyakov heard the first report and then the second and the cries of the Wampus, they called the Onkilons away from their work, thinking that their friends had been attacked. Learning what had really happened, everybody had a hearty laugh over the incident with the gun.

Camp-fires were already burning in the glade and Annuir was cooking dinner; the mammoth's trunk was indeed a delectable dish, but the sirloin steaks were a little tough, perhaps because the meat had not been given a chance to cool. But there was enough left for the experiment to be repeated later.

Next day, heavily loaded with the skin, the tusks, and meat, the party directed their steps towards Amnundak's camp, which they reached only late in the evening.

The chief was already assembling a big war party to go in search of the travellers. The earthquake had stupefied the Onkilons. So far as they could remember, nothing like it had ever happened before. In some of the dwellings, the cross-beams had slipped out of their sockets and had fallen to the ground together with the turf, injuring many people and killing some children. Rushing out of the dwellings, the startled Onkilons saw trees swaying and heard the rumble of landslides; the tremors knocked them off their feet; then a thunderstorm broke out such as none of the old men could recall, while the torrential rain that followed drenched the people, who were afraid to return to their shelters, washed away the doors of the dwellings and soaked beddings and clothes.

Drawing a parallel between this calamity and the recent Wampu raid, the Onkilons began to think that the misfortunes the great shaman said would befall them with the coming of white men had started. The travellers had disappeared and nobody knew if they would vanish as mysteriously as they had appeared. A search party sent to the Valley of a Thousand Smokes from the northernmost Onkilon camp at a signal passed on by drums had returned empty-handed. Amnundak was seriously worried; the search had to be carried to Wampu territory and all the warriors had to be assembled for that. The return of the missing party assuaged the Onkilons' fears, while the skin, tusks, and meat of the mammoth redoubled their joy.

The travellers' mudhouse, thanks to its better construction, had hardly suffered at all during the earthquake and part of the chief's clan lived in it for two days while their own half-ruined dwelling was repaired.

THE SACRED LAKE

The shaman told Amnundak that a sacrifice had to be made to the gods at the sacred lake to mark the safe return of the travellers, who had not deserted the Onkilons during their hour of trial. Learning that all the waters of the valley flowed to this lake, the travellers were glad of this opportunity of visiting it and elucidating where the water went from there. The thanksgiving was set for the second day after their return.

All the warriors of the clan headed by Amnundak and the travellers started out early in the morning, heading south-westwards; the shaman and his pupil, beating a drum and chanting incantations, walked on either side of a white reindeer, which was led in the rear of the procession. In about two hours, passing through a number of meadows and the forests lying between them, the procession arrived at a small lake on the very fringe of the valley. On two sides, its banks consisted of black basalt rocks of various sizes, beneath which could be heard the gurgling of the water flowing into the lake from out of the pebble-covered ground; on the two other sides, the lake was flanked by steep basalt cliffs rising to a height of a few hundred metres and reflected in the undisturbed water together with a bit of the blue sky. Even in summer, this deep semi-well was lit up by the rays of the sun for only two or three hours in the early morning, when the sun was in the northeast; for the rest of the day the lake was wrapped in deep shadow. The soaring black cliffs, the black boulders on the bank and the black water combined to make a dreary picture and no wonder the Onkilons thought the lake was inhabited by spirits.

A big flat rock, towering a little above the others at the water's edge served as the altar; the shaman and his pupil climbed on it, dragging the reindeer after them. Amnundak, the travellers, and the warriors stood in a semicircle round the rock. The shaman raised his drum and began to beat a slow tattoo, which was echoed and re-echoed by the overhanging cliffs. Not knowing what echoes were, the Onkilons thought that from all sides the spirits were answering the drumbeats. When the shaman finished his invocations, he drew a short but sharp chalcedony knife from his belt; looking more like a dagger, it had a carved bone handle and was only used for sacrifices. The pupil seized the reindeer by its antlers and pulled its head to the ground, while with a powerful swing the shaman dealt a fatal wound on the back of its head. The tattoo was resumed over the dying deer and while the shaman was thus engaged two warriors brought a light raft made from four thin logs and lowered it into the lake at the end of the rock. Aided by the shaman's pupil, they dropped the deer on the raft and pushed it away from the bank. The shaman continued to beat on his drum; his lips moved as though he were praying or uttering incantations, but they made no sound for it was blasphemy to talk on the banks of the sacred lake.

Caught by an invisible current, the raft slowly sailed towards the middle of the lake. Finally, it reached almost the foot of the cliff and began to circle in one spot.

The chief and the warriors watched the raft in reverent silence. A rumble came from the black water, the surface of the lake rippled and a hole began to form in it as though some huge monster, hidden in its depths, was sucking the water into its mouth. The hole gradually deepened, the rumble increased in volume, a wheeze was heard, and the raft, held in the grip of the whirling water, disappeared in the gulf; the watchers caught glimpses of the ends of the logs and of the reindeer's antlers, and then the hole closed, leaving a hollow for a minute or two, after which the surface regained its mirror-like smoothness and lay as undisturbed as before.

As soon as the raft disappeared into the black sucking eddy, the shaman stopped beating his drum and announced in a toneless whisper:

"The sacred water has accepted the sacrifice!"

He bowed to the lake and descended from the rock and the whole party started on the return journey. Now the travellers could exchange impressions. The lake clearly showed them where the waters of the valley went: they collected in the lake and at regular intervals were sucked into a subterranean channel through which they flowed to the sea.

"Why is the lake held sacred?" Goryunov asked Amnundak as they walked back to camp.

"The shaman who led our forefathers to this land said it was sacred. He discovered the lake and on its banks the spirits spoke and revealed the future to him. Before he died, he ordered the people to bury him in the sacred waters, and ever since it has been the burial ground of our shamans."

"How are they buried?"

"A deceased shaman is put on a raft, like the one you saw, with a drum in his hands; a cup with gifts is placed at his feet and the head of a sacrificial reindeer at his head. His body is covered with a skin. The new shaman stands on the altar and prays in the presence of the warriors of the whole tribe. The raft moves back and forth on the water, which means that the shaman is bidding his people farewell. Then the water seizes him and drags him under."

"And it never throws back anything? Doesn't the skin, the drum or any of the logs rise back to the surface?"

"No. Everything passes out of sight. And if the water threw anything back it would mean that the shaman had failed to please the spirits or had done something evil in his lifetime."

"What do you do if a shaman dies in winter? I suppose the lake freezes?"

"The sacred lake never freezes. Snow lies on the banks but no ice forms on the water."

The only explanation that Goryunov could think of

was that when the water was periodically sucked into the subterranean channel it took away with it the thin ice forming on its surface in the intervals.

Returning to the camp, the travellers spent almost a month in and about their mudhouse because Amnundak refused to let them go on a long expedition. They had to rest content with walks to the nearby meadows in the company of a few warriors. During these walks they studied the vegetation and the habits of animals or fished in the lakes in order to acquaint themselves with the species of fish living in them. Incidentally, the weather was not favourable for long excursions; in Sannikov Land the first summer month was the rainiest; the sky was frequently overcast and there was an annoying drizzle. But even on inclement days, the travellers did not find time hanging on their hands; the five young women in their mudhouse saw to that; a knowledge of the Onkilon language, which they improved by constantly chatting with the women, enabled them to converse unconstrainedly and learn many facts about the customs, habits, way of life, and beliefs of the Onkilons.

The tribe had no written language, but there were many legends and fables worth recording. When they felt they knew enough of the language, the travellers invited old men and women from the neighbouring camps to them or went to see them themselves. They were also interested in the tribe's religious views and the shaman, as the guardian of the cult, could have told more about them than anybody else; but he categorically refused to do that and, on the whole, was covertly hostile to the travellers. The laymen had only the haziest and even contradictory notions which boiled down to a belief in the existence of good spirits in heaven—in the air, the clouds, and the heavenly bodies—and of evil spirits in water and under the ground.

In the course of that month, two of the travellers paid a visit to Nikiforov, who continued living as a hermit with the dogs amid the snow. He hunted, cured meat, and cut firewood for the winter. In order to be able to exchange urgent messages, the travellers left Belukha with Nikiforov and took Pestrushka from him. In the event of extreme danger, Nikiforov was to light a big fire on the ledge above the snow-drift; the smoke and flames would be noticed in Amnundak's camp.

In view of their intention to winter in Sannikov Land, the travellers, naturally, were interested to learn what to expect and questioned the Onkilons accordingly. They were told that beginning with September, autumn sets in rapidly; there is daylight in the valley only for six or seven hours and the sun hardly rises above the mountains in the south; the leaves on the trees turn yellow and fall off. That is when the Onkilons do double duty cutting wood. The weather often changes for the worse and snow falls. At the beginning of October, the sun no longer penetrates into the valley, but there are still a few hours of daylight around noon. Southern winds bring snow-storms, but when it blows from the north, rain falls and there is a heavy mist. At this time the Onkilons are busy with the last hunts to replenish the winter stores. There is no daylight beginning with the latter half of October, only an hour or two of twilight; bad weather becomes frequent, keeping the Onkilons indoors. The polar night sets in at the beginning of November and lasts until the end of January; it is illumined only by the moon when the sky is clear and by the northern lights, which the Onkilons ascribe to the souls of the dead. During these months a south wind means cold and clear weather, an east or west wind—a snow-storm, and a north wind—thaw and rain (writing that down, Goryunov added: it is obvious that in the winter this warmth comes from the boiling pools and fumaroles in the northern part of the valley). That is why snow cannot accumulate and the reindeer and the wild animals find grass in the meadows. Snow piles up mostly along the outskirts beneath the cliffs, where it lies until late spring. So far as the Onkilons are concerned these three dark months are the most tedious, for they have to keep to their dwellings during the snow-storms and the rain. When there is a bright moon in the sky they go hunting, especially for wolves which prey upon the reindeer.

Light appears in the south at the beginning of February, but the sun peeps into the valley only in March; the day swiftly grows longer, the weather becomes warmer and by the end of the month spring firmly establishes itself: the snow melts, grass begins to grow and all nature comes to life; towards the middle of April the forests break into leaf.

HUNTING MOULTING BIRDS

By the beginning of July, the young birds living in and about the lakes are strong enough to look after themselves and the geese and ducks begin to shed their feathers. At this period they lose their ability to fly and hide among the rushes and reeds. All the northern peoples take advantage of this to catch the birds en masse and the Onkilons were no exception. Each clan had two or three lakes as its own exclusive preserve. Enclosures are put up on the banks of the lakes well in advance. These consist of parallel fences of thin poles driven into the ground and spaced so that a duck would not get through. A hundred paces apart at the water's edge, the fences converge to form a narrow corridor leading to a quadrangle with a wall of stouter poles around it.

On the appointed day, the entire clan, with the exception of the babies and small children, armed themselves with sticks and surrounded the lake early in the morning, beating the birds out of the rushes with as much noise as they could raise.

"Hey, geese and ducks," one of them cried, "come out of your hiding places. It is time to take a swim!"

"Come out, you lazy birds," somebody else shouted. "Worms and fish are waiting for you in the water!"

"Our sticks are also waiting," another yelled, "to stroke your heads!"

The drumming, the shouts, and the excited cries of the children, for whom this was a gala event, combined to make an incredible din. The frightened birds rushed to the lake and everywhere the grass and the reeds swayed a few steps ahead of the beaters, showing where the ducks and geese were fleeing through the overgrowth. Some tried to fly only to fall back on the ground again, their wings flapping. The quacking of the ducks and the harsh cackling of the geese merged with the noise made by the beaters. Woodcocks, snipe, lapwings, curlews, and ruffs, which had shed their feathers earlier than the water birds, took to the air singly and in little flocks and flew across the lake and the meadow with shrill cries, tearing through the light mist that was still hanging over the water. The lake was swarming with ducks and geese by the time the beaters got to the banks. Only in the space between the two fences was the bank free of people. In the marshy places, the beaters put on snow-shoes made from skin stretched tautly over a frame of wood with fur on the underside; though meant for the winter, these shoes enabled the beaters to walk on boggy soil without sinking.

After surrounding the lake, the Onkilons brought out four birch-bark canoes, which they had taken to the lake beforehand, and launched them on the side opposite the enclosure; two men got into each canoe, one with an oar and the other with a clapper and a thong. The canoes quickly separated and the thongs which they dragged over the water stretched out in the space between them. The oarsmen rowed slowly and the men in the bows made the water splash with their thongs, frightening the birds and gradually heading them towards the enclosure. On the banks, the beaters kept up the din and the wall of splashes was accompanied by the cries of the boatmen. The birds did not know which way to go; some turned back when the thongs disappeared in the water; others tried to get to the banks, but when they came too near, the beaters shot them with arrows and the birds thrashed about on the water, increasing the panic.

Thus, step by step, hundreds of birds were driven to the end of the lake; the beaters on the shore kept pace with the canoes; some were already near the enclosure, but there they stopped making a noise and hid in the grass. When the birds were near the end of the lake, the men in the canoes redoubled their efforts for now the success of the hunt depended on them; the birds were concentrated in a small area. It was essential to keep churning the water up continuously with the thongs, otherwise the whole mass might swing round and everything would have to be started all over again.

At last, the advance flocks reached the bank and began

to climb on to the grass, moving forward; the rest followed suit and a solid stream of ducks and geese surged deep into the enclosure, quacking and cackling. As soon as the last of the birds were out of the water, the boatmen scrambled up the bank and, joined by the beaters closest to them, chased the birds on, making all the noise they could. Finally, the entire flock crowded into the quadrangle, where the grass had been trampled down. The beaters waiting around the quadrangle as well as the men who had followed the ducks and the geese in now fell upon the birds; from all sides dozens of sticks rained blows on the hapless victims; the cries of the excited hunters, the dull thud of the sticks as they landed on the birds, the flapping of wings and the frantic quacking and cackling mingled in a wild tumult. Blood-stained sticks flashed up and down and the piles of killed and quivering birds grew with tremendous speed. Only a few birds managed to escape between the legs of the beaters or through the gaps in the fence and return to the lake or the meadow.

Eventually, all the birds were killed, save the few that had got away, and lay in heaps in the quadrangle. The noise stopped, the fence was thrown down and the last stage of the hunt began; the birds were tied together in twos by their feet and slung over the sticks with which they had been slaughtered; the men worked in pairs, shouldering two sticks with thirty to forty brace of ducks or fifteen to twenty brace of geese; the children also helped, carrying lighter loads on their sticks.

At the camp, the birds were thrown on the ground in heaps and all the members of the clan set themselves to plucking and drawing them; the down was collected in skin bags and the giblets were dumped on sheets of bark. Fires were lit and stones heated; all the wooden pots were ready; the clan prepared for a giblet soup feast. The air was filled with the hum of voices and the shrill laughter of the children, who got into everybody's way through their enthusiasm to lend a hand. The boatmen returned, bearing armfuls of birds, having retrieved them on the lake where they had been shot down with arrows.

Towards evening, the Onkilons began smoke-drying the birds; this was their only way of preserving the meat as they had neither salt nor the necessary utensils. Bark huts were erected and the cleaned birds were hung on poles beneath the roofs; smoke fires were lighted in the huts and these had to be kept burning for a few days. The work and the giblet soup feast ended late in the evening. A similar hunt was scheduled for the next day on the second lake and for the morning after that on the third lake. There was no time to be lost. The birds grew wing feathers quickly and, though badly at first, they nevertheless could fly. The enclosures would be useless then.

Goryunov and his friends shared in these hunts but without any special enjoyment; they, too, needed winter stores. Their wives, however, helped willingly. But these three days were like a nightmare for the travellers; the fuss, the noise, the wanton slaughter of helpless creatures, the mountains of dead birds, the fires, the gluttony of all the participants, their greed and their eagerness to kill as many of the birds as possible were unpleasant to see and the travellers were glad when it was all over.

During these hunts no attention was paid to bigger game that sometimes showed themselves—their turn was still to come. A small number of wild boars lived in the rushes by each lake; pressed by the beaters, they gathered together and led by an old and ferocious boar charged the hunters. They were allowed to pass and only an odd young animal, which fell behind the adults or strayed from the herd, was speared or clubbed. These animals were hunted late in the autumn, when the rushes withered and dropped from the frost and the marshes were covered with ice; the boars were fatter and roamed about the meadows and forests. Beaten out of the undergrowth, they were speared or shot with arrows from behind shelters, in which the hunters were safe against their tusks. The cold enabled the Onkilons to preserve the meat; it was hung on trees where it stayed frozen. Later, after the first snow-fall, the Onkilons hunted hares, great numbers of which lived in the valley.

WARNING SIGNALS

At the close of July, the sun began to set not only beyond the crest of mountains on the northern outskirts but also beyond the horizon; the nights were dark and rapidly grew longer. The first indications of autumn appeared as well; the martins nesting in the cliffs were gathering in huge flocks and their young were practising flying in preparation for their long journey to the south. The surviving geese and ducks were likewise assembling and flying from one lake to another. The night mists were getting denser and hung longer over the valley in the mornings.

The travellers had definitely decided to winter in Sannikov Land. They replenished their food stocks by hunting and the women smoked and cured the meat and melted the fat, which they stored in gut sacks. But something happened at the end of the first week in August which heralded a whole series of emergencies that had grave consequences. On the night of August 7, the travellers were awakened by a violent underground tremor; at first, half-awake, they thought somebody was trying to open the door of their mudhouse; then they heard a rumble as though a heavy train were passing by.

"Another earthquake!" Ordin cried, realizing what was happening.

The dwelling was dimly lit by the dying embers in the fire; the wavering light fell on the alarmed faces of men and women rising from their beds.

The ground shook again. The beams grated and creaked and earth trickled through the gaps. The fire burned fitfully; everything hanging on poles or suspended from the beams began to swing; an ominous hissing rose from the ground.

"Our house is stronger than the others but we've got to get out into the open just the same," Goryunov said, seizing his clothes.

With trembling hands, the women tied their loin-cloths, and, gathering up their clothes, rushed out; the men, dressing as they went, followed them.

The night was unusually warm and bright thanks to a strong north wind which blew the mist away. The meadow was illumined by the moon hanging over the western outskirts of the valley. In spite of the wind, the rustling of the leaves in the forest and the crash of boulders falling from the precipices could be heard to right and left.

From the chief's dwelling came the shouts of women, the crying of children and the exclamations of men. Part of its population was already in the open and dressing. Soon these were joined by the others and together they crowded near the entrance, gazing with apprehension at the sky and exchanging remarks. Amnundak went up to the travellers; he was very frightened.

"The land is shaking again, white men," he said reproachfully. "The great shaman was right when he said misfortunes would begin for the Onkilons with the coming of white men. After you came the land shook twice and the Wampus attacked us."

"But the Wampus have always been your enemies and the land shook more than once before," Goryunov said.

"But never like this! And look how red the moon is! It is an ill omen," replied Amnundak.

Another sharp tremor made him stagger; many of the Onkilons fell. The women shrieked and the children cried. Before everybody's eyes one of the walls of Amnundak's dwelling crumbled and a column of thick dust rose in the air. The trees began to sway.

"Did everybody get out of the dwelling?" the chief exclaimed.

"Yes, yes," came the reply.

"No, not everybody," a woman's voice said. "My mother, Matu, who is sick, is still there. She said she does not care where she dies."

"Well, she is sure to be dead now," a man added. "The wall fell on her."

"Get the turf and the logs out of the way and free the woman," Amnundak ordered. "Bring firewood and build a fire."

But the Onkilons were afraid to go into the dwelling; they started tearing the turf from the fallen wall, keeping an anxious eye on the logs that were still standing. Annuir bravely went into her mudhouse and brought a heap of burning coals on a board. Ordin and Goryunov brought firewood and soon a crackling fire relieved the tension somewhat and everybody gathered around it, except the warriors assigned to clear the debris. The tremors continued and each time the ground shook the Onkilons backed away although there was no longer anything that could fall on them. There was a continuous rumble in the ground and the trees rocked; everybody sat down for it was almost impossible to stand upright. The clatter of falling stones did not cease.

"A great misfortune has come upon the Onkilons," Amnundak whispered, watching the fire flicker every time the earth trembled. The travellers had already noticed quite a few hostile sidelong glances from the warriors and especially from the women.

Annuen, who was sitting beside Ordin, got up in the interval between the shocks and joined the women on the opposite side of the fire. Goryunov's and Kostyakov's wives followed her and only Annuir and Raku kept their places.

"Seems as though we're being treated as lepers," Goryunov said in a half-tone, addressing his friends.

"Pay no attention," Kostyakov replied light-heartedly. "When the sun rises everybody will calm down and forget their fears."

"The moon is redder than it was before," Ordin observed. "The landslides must have raised quite a bit of dust."

A particularly violent shock shook the valley with a loud roar, throwing up even the wood in the fire and scattering it in all directions. Again there were panic-stricken cries; some people, who had been squatting, toppled over. The dogs howled piteously. The dwelling of the chief collapsed and only the central posts, surrounded by a cloud of dust, remained standing. The warriors clearing away the turf and broken timber fell to the ground, then got to their feet and ran away.

"We are perishing. The ground is crumbling under us. This is the end of our tribe," groaned the men and women; the latter pressed the crying children to their breasts; all eyes were wide open and on every face there was an expression of stark terror.

When the rumbling of the landslides died away, a terrible silence descended on the meadow, for the wind had stopped blowing. Everybody involuntarily listened. In a few moments the silence was broken by a distant but distinct beat of a drum. It had a magic effect on the Onkilons. Faces relaxed, eyes regained their normal size, and some people audibly sighed.

"Our shaman is alive! He is propitiating the spirits of the earth!" people cried happily.

That was indeed the last violent tremor and though there were a few weak shocks after that, nobody paid any attention to them. The people round the fire began to doze. They were roused by a war-drum from the neighbouring camp, the beats, now short, now long, sounding clearly in the stillness of the night; fainter drumbeats came from the more distant camps. When this ominous music stopped, Amnundak turned to Goryunov and said with a note of censure in his voice:

"Many of our dwellings were destroyed this night. Some women and children lost their lives, the bones of many were broken, and utensils and weapons were lost. This is a great misfortune, white men! You did nothing to prevent it. Your dwelling is whole, but mine lies in ruins."

"Because it was very badly built," Goryunov replied angrily. "Make a better job of it and your dwellings will not fall on you."

"Many generations have lived in our dwellings and nobody ever heard of them falling," the chief said. "No. When misfortune comes nothing helps. We are not magicians."

He wanted to add "like you" and though he stopped himself, the travellers understood him quite well.

The warriors at last cleared away the wall that had collapsed first and dragged old Matu out; she was dead. Her daughter and two other women lit a separate fire, laid her out near it and began to mourn by ritual, eulogizing her virtues. The others dozed peacefully round the big camp-fire. Amnundak told the drummer to inform the other camps of the destruction of his dwelling and of the death of Matu.

Around daybreak, the travellers began to feel sleepy; the earthquake had stopped and the intervals between the weak tremors grew longer. The traveller's mudhouse had stood the test and they could return to it. Talking it over among themselves, they got up and went to their dwelling, followed by envious and unfriendly glances from the Onkilons who were awake. Amnundak slept with his head on drawn-up knees. Only Annuir and Raku went with the travellers; Matu and Papu stayed with the other women, while Annuen had joined the mourners. Goryunov and Kostyakov found themselves in the role of deserted husbands.

Worn out by the anxiety they had experienced, everybody slept till late in the morning; sunlight was streaming in through the chinks in the door when they woke up. A bright fire was burning and Matu, Papu, and Annuen were cooking breakfast as though nothing had happened. During the meal the men had it out with them. The women said that when the ground started to shake they were terribly frightened and thought it would open up and the white men would take them down to their underground kingdom. That was why they had stayed with the chief's clan. The explanation was silly but it was plausible so far as they were concerned and Goryunov was compelled to explain again that he and his friends were neither magicians nor underground spirits. However, by the expressions on the faces of the three young women, it was obvious that they did not believe what he said.

They also informed the travellers that the shaman had visited Amnundak and told him that on the way from his dwelling he had seen a crack in the ground and had jumped over it with difficulty. His mudhouse had not collapsed; the good spirits had protected their minister.

This news prompted the travellers to examine the vicinity. All the warriors were busy taking the ruins apart and restoring the dwelling, and the travellers knew they would not have the usual annoying convoy, which was especially unpleasant now, after the events of the night. Taking their guns and leaving Gorokhov near the mudhouse to allay suspicion, they went along the path leading to the dwelling of the shaman and soon came across the crack he had described to the chief; it stretched from east to west and was nearly two metres wide; on its bottom the earth had settled together with bushes and trees; where the crack passed under thick trees, the latter were torn asunder from the roots up to a few metres of the trunk, with one half resting on one side of the crack and the second half on the other like the feet of a man standing over a ditch. Near the crack, some parts of the ground were covered with wet, black sand that had been thrown up during the earthquake.

From there they turned south-westwards to the sacred

lake in order to examine it without witnesses. They passed close on thirty cracks of varying width; some could be stepped over, others had to be crossed with a running jump. Many were not deep, but there were some with gradually converging sides whose bottom could not be seen and stones thrown into them showed that there was water at a depth of a few metres. The ground beneath the precipices fringing the valley was covered with rocks and stones that had fallen during the night. In one place they found a mountain sheep, which had evidently been thrown off a high ledge by one of the tremors. The travellers took it with them with the intention of showing it to the chief in order to justify their excursion without a convoy.

At the bank of the sacred lake they stopped in amazement; there was no water in it. Instead, they saw a big hollow shaped as a flat, irregular funnel strewn with pieces of slimy black lava; here and there water brought by the lake's tributaries, which had contracted considerably, gurgled under these rocks. Carefully stepping over the slippery ground, the travellers got to the mouth, which was close to the foot of the precipice; it was two or three metres in diameter and slanted steeply as it disappeared beneath the precipice; the water rising from beneath the rocks flowed into it in a tiny stream.

"Well, what do you say to this?" Kostyakov asked when all three of them stopped and gazed at the black, yawning mouth receding into mysterious depths.

"I think," Ordin said, "the earthquake destroyed the obstacle, say a knee-shaped bend, that was letting the water out of the lake periodically as it accumulated."

"But isn't this sharp decrease in the amount of water flowing into the lake the reason for its disappearance?" Goryunov asked. "Water is supposed to collect here from all over the valley and then, if you'll remember, the last time we were here we saw a big stream coming from the forest and disappearing into the ground. All the lake is getting now is a rivulet a metre wide and half a metre deep."

"Some cracks in the ground are probably preventing the water from getting here," Ordin replied.

"If these cracks are not bottomless, then isn't it possible that after they are filled with water the streams will be restored and flow into this lake as before?" Goryunov asked.

"I suppose so."

"Well, I hope that happens and the quicker the better because if the Onkilons learn that their sacred lake has dried up it will frighten them more than anything else and they'll attribute this calamity to the white magicians."

"Naturally, we'll not say a word about it to them."

"And see that you don't tell the women where we've been."

"Of course. Gorokhov need not know either. We'll say we went hunting, bagged a mountain sheep and saw the crack—nothing more."

They turned homeward and followed the line of the precipices for some distance. An enormous heap of white boulders lying at the base of one of the precipices attracted their attention. They proved to be broken ice, which the tremors had shaken off the top of the mountains; that showed that there were small glaciers around the valley. Much more important and interesting was the discovery of a crack at the very foot of a precipice; it stretched in both directions as far as the eye could see, now narrowing, now widening, and was filled with water to a depth of about five or six metres.

The travellers went up to the precipice at three other

places and everywhere they found the crack; apparently, the floor of the valley was separated from its western fringe along a distance of at least ten kilometres.

They returned to the camp only after midday and found that their absence had been noticed. But the mountain sheep settled all doubts and Amnundak regretted that he had taken some of the warriors away from their work and sent them in search of the strangers. The ruins of the dwelling had already been taken away, the space cleared and Onkilons were putting up the frame, using the old posts and beams. The travellers ate their dinner and appeared with axes, offering to help strengthen the frame so that the dwelling would not collapse on the heads of the inhabitants every time there was an earthquake. But to their surprise the Onkilons flatly refused their assistance.

"Our forefathers taught us how to build dwellings," Amnundak said, "and we have lived in them peacefully for many generations. We shall not build them in any other way. You had better see that the land does not shake any more, white men; then our dwellings will not collapse."

Nothing the travellers said was of any avail and the example of their mudhouse had no effect.

"If Onkilons and not white magicians lived in your dwelling, it would have been destroyed, too," said one of the warriors standing around the travellers as they talked to the chief.

The others nodded and cried:

"Yes, yes! That is true!"

The travellers had to return to their mudhouse but they could not discuss the situation—the women understood Russian sufficiently well and they could not talk freely in their presence for everything they said would instantly be known to the Onkilons.

To see whose side the women would take, the travellers told them of their offer of assistance and of the refusal and its motives.

"Amnundak did quite right," Annuen said.

The others upheld her. Annuir alone took the side of the travellers and, pointing out the strength of their dwelling, said that it was foolish to turn down the assistance of cleverer people.

"They are not cleverer. They are magicians," Annuen exclaimed vexedly. "Before they came to us, our dwellings never collapsed and the land never shook as it did last night. They have only to wish it and the land will never shake again."

This was the first fierce argument between the young women, and Annuir's ignorant and superstitious opponents began to say such nonsensical things that the travellers were sorry they ever started this conversation. However, it was fortunate that they did, as we shall see later.

To calm the women down, Ordin told Annuir that he wanted her to go with him and gather berries in the forest. The other women instantly announced that it was time to store berries for the winter and taking *tuyases*—cylindrical bark vessels with a lid, which fits tightly and has a handle for carrying the vessel—also went to the forest, choosing a different direction. Goryunov, Kostyakov, and Gorokhov stayed behind and used this opportunity for a talk.

"It seems to me," Goryunov said, "that we'll not spend the winter here, after all. The Onkilons are clearly becoming unfriendly."

"Yes," Kostyakov agreed, "and if anything nasty were to happen again, say, another earthquake, a storm or a raid by the Wampus, our wisest course would be to show a clean pair of heels."

"There's really nothing to worry about," Gorokhov put in. "Everything will be all right. It's not every day that the land shakes."

"Nikita likes it here," Kostyakov said in a mocking tone.

"You can bet your boots that I do. I think it's wonderful! We've got all the food we want and we'll soon marry our lovely brides."

"I see!" Goryunov drawled and fell silent. It was clear that if a conflict should arise, Gorokhov would probably side with the Onkilons or choose to stay out of it. There was an oppressive silence. Presently, Gorokhov rose and went out of the mudhouse.

"I'm afraid," Goryunov said, "that if we shall have to get out quickly and in secret, Nikita may not want to go with us and may give us away to the Onkilons."

"I don't think so. What put that into your head?" Kostyakov asked in surprise. "Don't forget the Onkilons think he's a magician, too, and if it gets too hot for us he'll also be in danger."

"Not quite. I've noticed that the Onkilons treat him differently. He is dark like they are, is more closely related to them and speaks their language. You can't call him white, can you?"

"I suppose not. But he came with us, lives with us, and, like us, has thunder and lightning and other remarkable things."

"And yet his position is somewhat different. Ordin drew my attention to that and he got it from Annuir. In any case, it won't do us any harm if we are not quite open with Nikita."

"You're right. And it's just struck me that today's clash among the women shows that we have an ally in Annuir."

"Yes, she's madly in love with Ordin and through her we can learn the plans of the Onkilons. That might be very useful."

"It would be interesting to know if, in case we'll have to go away in a hurry, she'd come along with us. Remember, Ordin asked her when we were on the ledge and looking at the sea and she said she wouldn't."

"Well, that was then. Now, I think, she'll follow him to the ends of the earth."

Gorokhov's return made them stop the conversation. They went outside to see what progress was being made with the dwelling.

The frame was already in position and the women had begun covering it with turf salvaged from the ruins or cut anew. The dwelling would probably be ready for habitation by nightfall.

Annuen, Matu, Papu, and Raku returned in the evening, their *tuyases* filled with wild raspberries and bilberries.

Soon Ordin and Annuir also made their appearance. Annuir had few berries in her *tuyas* and her eyes were red from weeping; when the other women saw how few berries she had, they sniggered and asked what she did in the forest.

"I scolded her for quarrelling with Annuen," Ordin said.

Annuir looked up at him in astonishment and flushed. Annuen was flattered and peace was restored in the mud-house.

When at twilight the women went to milk the deer, Ordin wanted to discuss the day's events but Goryunov stopped him with a whisper, pointing to Gorokhov, who was sitting on his bed.

THE SITUATION GROWS COMPLICATED

The familiar drawn-out wail of the Onkilons, repeated a few times, filled the air. Then the war-drum sounded. Alarmed, the travellers ran out of their mudhouse and saw warriors, women and children grouping near Amnundak's dwelling: the twilight and the gathering mist prevented them from seeing what they were doing, while the sinister roll of the drum drowned all sounds. They were about to join the Onkilons when they saw Annuir running towards them. Breathless, she said quickly:

"Don't go there. Go back to our dwelling while the women are away."

She ran ahead and the travellers followed her. In the mudhouse, Annuir told them that the warriors sent to look for them earlier in the day had found that the sacred lake had disappeared and discovered the footprints left on the drying bed by Goryunov and his friends. The footprints in the soft mud could not have escaped the attention of experienced pathfinders. They hurried back and informed Amnundak that the white magicians had been to the sacred lake and had dried it. That had been the reason for the wails while the drum passed the terrible news on to the other camps.

"It was wrong of you to go there without warriors," the agitated Gorokhov said with reproach. "Now they'll never believe that you did not dry the lake."

"What are they going to do?" Ordin asked.

"They don't know themselves," Annuir replied. "They are frightened. The warriors also saw the cracks in the ground. The chief has already sent for the shaman and ordered a sacrificial deer to be prepared."

"That means night rites and supplications to the spirits,"

Goryunov said. "And there's no telling what advice the shaman will get from the spirits. He might want us to be sacrificed to appease them."

"The Onkilons do not make human sacrifices," Gorokhov declared. "We have got nothing to fear on that score. I think the shaman will say that we must leave this land."

"That's not the hardest knock he can give us. We can go even though it's not the right time to cross the ice. There's too much ice-free water," Goryunov said.

"Yes, it is not the right time and I don't think we should go anywhere," Gorokhov added. "I'll go and have a talk with them and maybe I'll be able to settle things somehow."

He went out; Annuir, after waiting for a while, ran out after him, for Ordin had whispered something in her ear.

Taking advantage of the absence of Gorokhov and the women, Goryunov told Ordin what he and Kostyakov had decided about Nikita. Ordin, in his turn, told his friends that he had indeed scolded Annuir for siding so openly with the travellers and quarrelling with the other women. He made her understand that in the interests of the travellers she was not to quarrel with her fellow tribeswomen, otherwise they would not take her into their confidence; in view of the Onkilons' hostility, the travellers needed somebody they could trust to keep them abreast of the tribe's intentions and plans.

Annuir had wept not because of the scolding, which she knew she had earned, but because the travellers would soon leave. She was still wavering: the ties that bound her to the tribe were still strong and the thought of going to a strange land was frightening.

"She'll think it over," Ordin said in conclusion, "get

253

used to the idea and come with us. We love each other and it would be very hard for us to part."

"But Gorokhov won't go, I'm afraid," Goryunov added. "This free and easy life is very much to his liking."

"Well, if things develop the way I expect them to there won't be any free and easy life worth talking about," Ordin said.

"What do you think will happen?"

"Do you know where Annuir and I have been to? We went to one of the nearby meadows where the lake bubbles every half-hour. We sat there for more than an hour and there was no bubble or vapour in all that time."

"So that's it!"

"Comparing that with the numerous cracks in the ground and the disappearance of the sacred lake, it's not difficult to draw the conclusion that the earthquake has drastically changed the underground conditions of this valley. And I feel as though I'm sitting on a keg of gunpowder. . . ."

"Like the Onkilons," Kostyakov interrupted him with a laugh. "I doubt that it makes much difference if one lake has dried up and another's stopped bubbling. Nothing else has changed."

"I wouldn't laugh so soon if I were you. It may make all the difference for us," Ordin continued gravely. "On what does the warm, wonderful climate of this valley depend; solely on the heat from the bosom of an inactive volcano. Without that the valley would have been completely buried by masses of ice formed by the gradually accumulating snow."

"O-oh!" Kostyakov drawled, a sober expression on his face.

"Yes! And because of the earthquake, that stopped up

254

the crevices through which that warmth escaped from the bowels of the earth, the climate may change radically in the immediate future...."

"And bring an end to all animals, plants and people," Goryunov interposed.

"Yes, and already in the course of the coming winter. We know that here the winters were so mild that animals could find food beneath the snow."

"But most of the heat comes from the northern part of the valley and not from the bubbling lakes. Perhaps nothing has changed there?"

"I doubt it. For that was where we experienced the first earthquake. It's possible that not all the crevices giving an outlet for the boiling water and the steam have closed. In that event, the climate will not change so radically. But who can guarantee that the next earthquake will not complete the work?"

"Do you know, I think we ought to go to the Valley of a Thousand Smokes once more and find out what happened there."

"Yes, that would be useful. But I'm afraid Amnundak won't let us."

"Why not?"

"Because the first earthquake took place when we were there. What with their superstitions, the Onkilons...."

"I understand. But we could go there without telling anyone. It won't make matters any worse than they are now since we're already alienated."

"But it's a little frightening to go without a convoy. We might meet Wampus," Kostyakov said.

"They'll run away at the first shot and the dogs will warn us of danger night and day. If we travel lightly we can make the journey in two days and spend the night near the farthest lake. We don't need to go deep into the Valley of a Thousand Smokes—we'll see at once if vapours and boiling water are being discharged."

"Quite right," Goryunov declared. "We'll start out early tomorrow—without Gorokhov."

"I'd like Annuir to go with us."

"What for? She'll only encumber us."

"Not a bit. She's a good walker, and if we go alone we might arouse the suspicions of the Onkilons through whose camps we'll have to pass. Annuir will be our convoy."

"A woman as a convoy for three men," Kostyakov laughed.

"Well, a guide, a spy of the Onkilons, or whatever else you please. The Onkilons in those camps don't know that our relations with Amnundak are strained. Moreover, she knows the way to the northernmost camp, for she comes from that clan, and will ready be a guide and save us a lot of time."

"You're right again. Well, it's decided then: we'll leave at daybreak tomorrow. And tell Annuir on the sly to put some food together for the journey."

"And not a word to Gorokhov. Let's pack our knapsacks and get our guns ready while no one is around."

No sooner did the travellers do that than Annuir breathlessly rushed into the mudhouse.

"Nikita spoke for a long time to Amnundak and the warriors," she said hurriedly. "He told them the land will not shake or crack any more, that the waters of the sacred lake will return and that everything will be as it was before. The Onkilons were angry and wanted to know why the white men are doing all this. 'We gave them everything—a dwelling, food, and young wives, but they do not wish to do anything good for us.' And the women shouted:

'Take away their thunder and lightning and let them go back from where they came. We lived in peace without them.' And Nikita spoke again, but they would not listen to him. Amnundak decided that they would wait for the shaman to invoke the spirits and tell them what to do."

"Nikita imprudently promised them what might never happen," Goryunov said.

"And in the final count the matter will be decided by the shaman, regardless of these promises of Nikita's," Kostyakov added.

"I think the shaman, too, heeds to *vox populi*," Ordin noted. "He's a crafty old beggar. When he went through his act on the day of our arrival, you'll remember he spoke in the name of the spirits and said that misfortunes *might not* begin while the white men lived with the Onkilons. He left a loophole for himself and proved to be right."

Gorokhov came in and said:

"I've calmed them down a little, but at first they were very angry, especially the women: 'Chase them (that's us) away,' they shouted. 'We gave them a place to live in, food, all kinds of utensils, and the best of our maidens, and look what they are doing to us!' And you should have heard them go on and on. It was about all Amnundak could do to pacify them, saying the shaman would come and determine what they should do about the white men. The shaman's just come and I was told to go."

"We were hoping we'd be present at the rites," Goryunov said.

"That's out of the question," Gorokhov replied. "The minute the shaman came and saw me, he told Amnundak he didn't want any of the white men around."

"In other words, the trial will be held without the

accused," Kostyakov said with a sardonic grin. "But can the women go?"

"They're there already. They'll tell us what the shaman will say."

Gorokhov had not noticed Annuir when he entered the dwelling; without his seeing her, she ran out as soon as he said that the shaman had arrived and ordered him to leave.

"And do you know how cold it is outside?" Gorokhov added, sitting down by the fire and stretching his hands out towards it. "I was frozen stiff while I spoke. There's a dense mist and it's so cold that I thought I was back in Kazachye."

Ordin exchanged meaningful looks with Goryunov and they went outside.

A cold they had not experienced for a long time seized them in its embrace; the temperature was probably just above zero. And the gloom was so dense that nothing could be seen. The light from the fire shining through the smoke hole was hardly visible at all through the thick mist hanging in the air.

From the dwelling of the chief came the beats of a drum and the deep voice of the shaman.

The dogs, sensing their masters, ran up and yelped in the hope they would be let into the mudhouse.

"Oh-ho, they've grown to dislike the cold, too," Ordin said. "Never mind, start getting used to it, you'll soon return to your cold homeland."

"But aren't we going north tomorrow?" Goryunov asked.

"We must first find out what the gods will tell the shaman. We might have to make a getaway tonight under cover of the mist."

"It's unlikely that we'll find the way at night."

"But what are the dogs for! They'll show us the way," Ordin replied, stroking Krot, who was nuzzling against his feet.

In the mudhouse, Gorokhov was getting under his blankets and preparing to sleep for want of something better to do. Goryunov and Ordin waited until he began to snore and then discussed with Kostyakov the possibility of fleeing that same night, after which they packed a few things they thought they should take with them. Then they sat down by the fire and waited anxiously for the women.

At last, Annuir appeared, sat down by the fire and, staring at it, said with tears welling up in her eyes:

"There will be much trouble for the Onkilons, the shaman said. Frost, water, fire. The prophecy of our forefathers is coming true. White men came and misfortunes began. The white men will go away but the misfortunes will remain. If they can, let them help. We shall pray and make sacrifices. He said bad things, spoke incoherently. He got the prayers straight only after the third try. Now he's lying as though he is dead, and the Onkilons are waiting, hoping he'll say something to reassure them."

But the travellers were pleased with the results of the divination. At least there was no direct accusation that they had caused the calamities and no demand that they should stop them or that they should be driven out of Sannikov Land. And if nothing happened in the next few weeks or months, the Onkilons would forget their fears and the travellers would be able to wait peacefully and leave whenever it suited them.

"Annuir," Ordin said, "early, early tomorrow morning we shall go to the Valley of a Thousand Smokes and I want you to come with us. But don't tell the others."

"Why are you going to that evil place again?"

"To see what's happening there and find out if the misfortunes of the Onkilons will stop soon."

"How will you find that out? The shaman doesn't know but you know!"

"You'll come with us and see for yourself. I'll explain everything to you. We'll go past the camp of your clan. Do you know the shortest way?"

"Of course."

"And you'll find it in the mist?"

"I'll try. I'll do anything you ask me."

"All right. Now go to sleep. We'll have to get up early."

Shortly after they went to sleep, the other four women appeared.

The mudhouse looked deserted and for a moment they were alarmed, thinking the white men had secretly fled; but they soon noticed the sleepers and, after sitting by the fire to get warm, they went to their beds where they carried on a whispered conversation. The travellers later learned that when the shaman had regained concsiousness he said the white men must not go, otherwise there would be even worse misfortunes.

BLACK WASTE

At the first flush of dawn, the three travellers and Annuir, putting on warm clothes and taking the knapsacks and guns, quitted the mudhouse, leaving a note for Gorokhov telling him that they were off on a tour of the lakes and would be back not earlier than the next day, adding that they were leaving him as a hostage with the Onkilons. The mist was very dense, but Annuir quickly found the path to the northern camps and confidently guided her

companions. The cold made them walk at a fast pace; the grass was covered with hoarfrost and one of the lakes, past which they went, had a thin sheet of ice along its banks.

"It was never so cold at this time of the year," Annuir said when she saw the ice.

"That is why we are going to the Valley of a Thousand Smokes. We want to know the reason for the cold," Ordin explained to her.

The mist dispersed only towards midday, when the travellers reached the camp of Annuir's clan. They stopped there for a meal. Here, too, the dwelling had collapsed during the earthquake, but already it was almost completely rebuilt. Its inhabitants gave the travellers a friendly reception; as yet they knew nothing of the sentiments and suspicions that had developed in Amnundak's clan the night before. They knew that the sacred lake had disappeared, but there had been nothing in the terrible news conveyed by the drums to indicate that the travellers were being blamed.

The presence of Annuir, who was a favourite with the clan, banished any idea they might have had that the travellers were fleeing, and when they were told where the white men were going three warriors offered to act as convoys and their offer was not refused; that made them dismiss all thought that the travellers had absented themselves without the chief's knowledge.

After a short rest, the travellers resumed their journey. It was already getting warm, but the impression was that it was autumn rather than summer. They took the shortest cut to the north and in three hours found themselves amid sparsely growing vegetation, which was quickly superseded by total desolation. The changes that had taken place in the valley could be seen from afar—no columns of white vapour were visible on the horizon and the black wall along the outskirts loomed distinctly. They were amazed by what met their eyes when they entered the Valley of a Thousand Smokes. Not one of the thousands of billowing, iridescent columns was left; in the once boiling pools, the water had either disappeared altogether or was motionless though still hot. Everywhere, as far as the eye could see, stretched a bare, barren waste of black lava with its scoriaceous surface criss-crossed by cracks; a dry heat was now coming from it and every gust of wind, like the breath of a huge bakery or a metallurgical furnace, raised the black dust and whirled it about the dead plain. The hot air streamed across the surface, losing its transparency, so that the black precipices on the outskirts seemed to be sailing in a vast lake and assumed fantastic lines. It looked as though there was a big city on the other side of this lake.

Lost in wonder, the travellers and the warriors contemplated the transformed basin. The three Onkilons had been here before, having accompanied the travellers the first time as part of their escort and they were appalled by what they saw. They whispered among themselves and at last asked:

"Where are the thousand smokes that we saw here? Where are the pools in which we cooked meat? What does it all mean? Tell us, white men. Why have the underground spirits stopped cooking and why are their fires no longer burning in the depths? Have they died? Are they asleep? Or have they gone elsewhere?"

With Annuir's help, Goryunov explained that it was all the result of the earthquake. They understood only half of what he said and drew an unexpected but correct conclusion:

"Therefore, we need not go far like the last time?"

In point of fact, there was no necessity to penetrate deep into the black waste and, besides, that would have been hard to do. It was difficult to breathe in the heated air. When they were here before, the steam evaporating in the atmosphere had somewhat reduced the temperature; and though it was hot as in a bath-house it was bearable.

Throwing a last glance at the lifeless waste and at the fantastic "city" towering in the distance, the travellers and their escort turned back and at sundown stopped for the night at the first lake where the dense forests began. It was still warm here—the north wind carried the heat from the black wilderness. After lighting a fire and roasting some meat, they discussed the situation. Annuir conversed with her fellow clansmen and the travellers could talk freely; they were alarmed.

"What do you make of it all?" Goryunov asked.

"I think the situation is very grave," Ordin replied. "My guess that the earthquake has radically changed the underground conditions of the valley has, unfortunately, turned out to be correct and Sannikov Land's heater, as the Valley of a Thousand Smokes may be called, has gone out of commission. The soil there is still hot but it will soon cool and this oasis in the polar ice will vanish quickly."

"And is there nothing else to be expected? Is that the only possible outcome?" Kostyakov asked.

"No, that would have been the only possible outcome if the post-volcanic activity, represented by the fumaroles, the boiling pools and the bubbling lakes, had died a natural death through progressive weakening. In that case life would be quenched very slowly, over long decades; the winters would gradually grow colder and longer, the animals, plants, and people would resist the deteriorating conditions of life for a long time."

"But now they are doomed to perish in the course of a single winter. Is that it?"

"Yes, if the heater is not restored within the next few weeks or months."

"Do you think it can be restored?"

"In my opinion, it not only can, but it must. The earthquake has closed the crevices that had been letting out the vapours and gases discharged in great quantities by the extinct or dormant—we don't know which—volcano. This discharge has not stopped, only the outlets have been blocked; the vapours and gases are amassing deep in the ground and, sooner or later, they must find a way to the surface; the later that happens, the more catastrophic the eruption will be. That is why we must hope there is another earthquake soon which would open the old vents for the vapours and gases or produce new ones; that would be the most painless solution of the crisis, because if, after accumulating to a bursting point, the vapours and gases break through to the surface themselves it might result in the restoration of the volcano and the population will perish not from frost but from fire."

"A pretty pass, I must say!" Kostyakov exclaimed. "I'm sorry for the Onkilons. They'll perish one way or another."

"Their only salvation is in another earthquake," Goryunov said. "And yet they are praying to their gods, hoping the earth never trembles again."

"The faster it does, the better, because if that happens only next spring, it will be too late; most of the animals will not survive in frosts of 40-50 degrees below zero and the long snow-storms; the Onkilons may live through the winter in their dwellings—they've got enough firewood, but next summer they'll begin to die out from hunger, because there'll be no big game left."

"What about migratory birds, water chestnuts, mushrooms, berries, and roots? You're taking a far too gloomy view of it."

"I don't think so. Anyway, they will have to eat less and their diet will be poorer than ever. They could, of course, begin to grow corn and vegetables and to breed fish and livestock. But to do that they'll need seeds and implements and someone to teach them."

"Does that mean that when we get back to camp we should tell the shaman and Amnundak they must pray for an earthquake; what if it produces new outlets in the southern half of the valley?"

"That will be worse, because it will destroy the vegetation over a more or less extensive area, which might include the deer pastures, the meadows and the dwellings. Still, that would be better than death from the cold."

"But what are we to do?" Kostyakov asked.

"We must stay in the valley as long as we can and leave only at the last extremity," Ordin replied.

"Time will show us what to do, but in the meantime we'll wait and see what happens next, how the weather will change and what the mood of the Onkilons will be like. By staying, we'll run a smaller risk than by pulling out prematurely," Goryunov said.

Tired by the long walk, the travellers were soon sound asleep.

The Onkilons took turns to keep watch.

THE SACRIFICE

Next day, the travellers returned home quite early. Near Amnundak's dwelling, the Onkilons were standing in a circle round some warriors from the neighbouring camp who had just arrived with a captive Wampu.

They said that when they went hunting that morning they came upon five Wampus, apparently scouts, spying out if it was possible to steal a few deer. The Onkilons came to grips with them near the herd; two of the Wampus were killed, two escaped, and the fifth, who was wounded, was taken prisoner and brought as a gift to the travellers. The warriors knew that they were collecting the skins and skulls of wild animals, and that during the excursion to the Valley of a Thousand Smokes they had taken away with them the skull and bones of a Wampu who had been

266

eaten by wolves; the Onkilons decided that a live Wampu would be even more useful to the white men. The prisoner was standing with his hands tied securely behind his back. He was covered with blood, which was still oozing from several spear and arrow wounds, and was hardly able to keep on his feet. The women and children, who seldom got a chance to take a close look at a Wampu, crowded round him, for now they could gaze all they wanted at a live savage.

When the travellers said the Wampu interested them only while he was alive, Amnundak ordered the warriors to tie him to a tree. Goryunov and his friends determined to take the savage's measurements and to photograph him at once and then to ask Amnundak to release him.

The prisoner was quite young and he was powerfully built like all the other Wampus. It was impossible to measure his head because of his matted mop of mud-filled hair, and Goryunov decided to give him a hair-cut then and there. He went up to the Wampu with a shining pair of scissors in his hand, but the latter thought he was going to be killed and let out a wild yell. All the Onkilons watched Goryunov working away with the scissors; they had never seen him do that before and the scissors intrigued them. The prisoner thought it was a prelude to some torture and tried to bite his tormentor's hand with his strong teeth, with the result that he had to be gagged. The shining skull measurer made him tremble with fear; he imagined that the manipulations with that instrument and the tape, with which his body was measured, were some kind of sorcery that would end dreadfully for him. When the travellers brought a black object and set it up on a glossy tripod and he heard the shutter click, he closed his eyes, expecting to be struck down by a thunderbolt. So it was

a great surprise to him when, unharmed, he was finally left in peace.

The Onkilons watched all these operations with tremendous interest; they had seen head and body measurements taken on previous occasions, for first women and then a few warriors and children were measured and the process had invariably ended with the clicking in the black box on the shinig tripod, whose use they could not understand.

When everything was finished, Goryunov asked the chief to release the prisoner but received a categorical refusal.

"Tonight we shall pray again and the spirits will tell the shaman whether the Wampu must die or not," Amnundak declared. "We have never released prisoners before."

Twilight was already gathering and the travellers, who were exhausted after the long excursion and the business with the prisoner, were glad to return to their clean mudhouse and sit round the crackling fire. The fog was already becoming denser and it was growing cold. Gorokhov told them that the mist had held until midday for two days running and that, though the sun could be seen, it had been cold "as in Kazachye at this time of the year." That day it was noticed that the martins were starting their migration to the south, while the geese and ducks, prompted by the cold, were preparing to fly away. The Onkilons were surprised, saying that they usually had such mists and frosts a month later, and that the birds were starting south much earlier than usual. The cold was the reason for the rites that evening.

When it grew dark, Gorokhov went to find out if the shaman had arrived and whether the white men would be permitted to be present; he came back with the news that this time the rites would be held in the presence of warriors only, and that all the women and children would be told to leave the dwelling.

In view of the cold, Amnundak asked the travellers to let the women and children into their mudhouse while the rites were held.

"I think they are cooking up some mischief," Ordin said when Gorokhov finished speaking. "They're sending the women away so that we'll be unable to learn anything through them."

"That's quite possible," Goryunov replied. "But there's nothing we can do to stop them and our only recourse is to be careful. Here, ask Annuir, if women have ever been barred from rites before."

Annuir informed them that such rites had been held when the tribe took the war-path against the Wampus.

Soon the mudhouse was crowded with women and children. Many of them had been in the dwelling of the white men before, especially in their absence, but now that they were all here they bore themselves with greater freedom, bringing meat and pancakes and cooking dinner. The dwelling was filled with their laughter and jokes, with the shrieks of the children, and the screams of the babies. Gazing at these happy and carefree people, who had only recently wanted to drive the white men away and blamed them for their misfortunes, the travellers could not help thinking of what they had seen the day before in the black wilderness and that this stone-age tribe was threatened with immediate extinction if the situation did not change.

"I can't for the life of me decide," Goryunov said to Ordin, who had followed him to a corner of the dwelling when the laughter and jokes of the women began to bore them, "whether we ought to tell the Onkilons of the danger hanging over their heads and suggest that they go south with us."

"I've been thinking of that, too," Ordin replied. "My opinion is that it's still too early to say anything. The sea is open and they'll get nowhere without boats. Besides, nobody can say if my fears are justified and how things will shape if they are; if the heater is restored one way or another, everything may change for the better, perhaps for decades to come."

"What if it isn't restored and winter sets in before our very eyes?"

"Even then we ought to keep our mouths shut. How can they go across the ice in the darkness of the polar night without an adequate supply of warm clothing, fuel, or reindeer, which will perish from the frost on the very first lap of the journey? No, they'll have to live through this winter somehow and in the spring, when they'll see that the snow is not melting and that all the animals have died, they'll realize that their only chance of surviving is to quit this land."

"I suppose you're right. In the spring we can return with a big expedition, which the Academy will fit out to study this land and its population before it is completely buried by snow. It will be easier to arrange for the departure of the Onkilons, for by that time they will want to leave themselves."

"While now they will only demand that we stop the calamity."

At Gorokhov's request, the women danced after dinner. They made the children and the old women sit along the walls, threw off their clothes, joined hands and began to circle round the fire. They hopped, alternately raising their right and left feet and swaying their bodies to the accompaniment of a simple melody, which they chanted. With these dances they amused themselves and the men during the long polar night, whenever they grew tired of sitting in their dwellings. At first, the chanting and the movements were slow, as though the dancers were going through the motions unwillingly, but the dance gradually livened up until finally the women gyrated so swiftly that the spectators grew dizzy watching them and their ears rang with the stamping of feet, clapping of hands and shrill yells. The dark bodies of the women twisted in a mad dance, their braids whirled in the air, their necklaces bounced on their breasts, their bracelets flashed backwards and forwards, their eyes burned, and their lips parted, revealing pearl-white teeth. At last, utterly exhausted, they dropped to the ground and stretched out round the fire each in a different pose, breathing heavily and adjusting the loin-cloth. The blue-black markings stood out with especial sharpness on the sweating bodies: fanciful patterns, flowers, leaves, the sun, and the heads of animals were portrayed with all the fantasy that the primitive artists could summon up. These artists were old women, who spent the seemingly endless polar night tattooing the bodies of girls and trying to outdo one another in the intricacy of the design. We have already described the markings of Amnundak's second wife—the woman with the snakes. Annuir's markings were different; the front part of her body was covered with leaves and flowers of various shape, while between her shoulders there shone a sun, the rays of which radiated to her neck, shoulders, and the small of her back; below that were two crescents facing each other. Raku had zigzag lines in front and wavy lines on her back; on the shoulder-blades and below her waist these lines ended in spirals. The girls were proud of their intricate tattooing and displayed it boastfully, while at the bride-show during the spring festival, these tattooings influenced the young warriors when they chose their brides.

After a rest, the women sat in a semicircle opposite the travellers and started a game; the woman on the extreme right slapped her neighbour on the back with her left hand and cried "first"; the slap was passed on to the next woman with the cry "second"; that went on until the wave of slaps reached the woman on the extreme left. If anybody lost count, she was slapped from the right and left amid general laughter. From the extreme left the slaps were passed back, this time with the right hand. The players again kept count, beginning with one, but in the centre of the semicircle they crossed with a new wave of slaps coming from the right; thus it was easy to lose count, which gave rise to frequent tussles, much to everybody's delight. When the women grew tired of this game, they started another. From a squatting position they stretched their arms forward, at the same time throwing out their right feet towards the fire and quickly drawing them back and throwing out their left feet; if anybody was slow to do that or threw out the wrong foot, her neighbours pushed her and she toppled over, her legs flashing in the air and everybody enjoying the sight. Excitement soon reached such a pitch that the women began to push each other over without any reason at all and it ended with all of them lying on the ground with their feet towards the fire and laughing uproariously.

"These dances and games," Goryunov remarked, "are splendid exercise and help the women overcome the pins and needles that they get in winter from sitting for a long time."

"Yes, the men have plenty of exercise hunting, herding deer or splitting firewood, but the women stay indoors and have nothing to do except a few household chores," Ordin said.

"The first game they played is called 'necklace,' the second—'frogs.' There's another which they call 'trial'; it's a quiet game," Gorokhov told the travellers. Turning to the women, he said:

"Show us 'trial.'"

The women squatted.

"Who was the most enduring among us last winter?" one of them asked. "You, Annu?"

"Yes," Annuen declared emphatically.

"And I was the most enduring in my clan," Annuir announced.

"We don't know you here and must see for ourselves if what you say is true. Then lie down first," the women decided.

They brought a skin and spread it on the ground in the centre of the semicircle near the fire and Annuir lay down on it on her back. Annuen took a cup, filled it with water and put it on Annuir's stomach. Then she sat down at her feet and began to tickle her heels. The other women began to count. The woman undergoing the trial had to lie so still as not to spill a drop of water until the count of ten; to do that she even had to hold her breath. Although the heels of the women were rough from walking barefoot, only a few could stand the test, the more so since the on-lookers counted slowly on purpose. The woman passing the trial received the title of enduring and the right to tickle the heels of those who failed.

This time Annuir could not restrain herself and burst out laughing at the count of nine; true, her rival for Ordin's love had tickled her very expertly.

"There, you lied!" the latter declared spitefully. "You never were enduring."

"Perhaps you never were, either!" Annuir protested passionately.

"The others can tell you. If you don't believe it, you can test me yourself and I don't care if it's the great trial," Annuen said proudly.

"She can do that, too," the others put in.

"Come, show us, Annuen," Ordin said.

Annuen took Annuir's place on the skin and the latter refilled the cup, placed it higher on her stomach, near the breasts, and began to tickle the stomach around the navel, which is the most sensitive part of the body. But Annuen lay like a stone and bore the torture.

"Try and stand that!" she said derisively, getting up and throwing the water out of the cup full into Annuir's face. That was the prerogative of anyone passing the great trial; Annuir silently wiped herself and stepped back in humiliation.

One after another, the women lay down for the test and Annuen forced them all to laugh, some sooner, others later, and drenched them with water before they could rise, thus adding to the general merriment.

The women dried themselves by the fire and laughed, watching while someone else went through the same

274

ordeal. Only one other woman stood the test and when everybody had had their turn, Annuir said she wanted to be tested again but with the condition that she be tickled by the woman who had been successful. Annuen protested, but the others, knowing their rivalry, found that because Annuir had passed the trial once before she had a right to a second try. Annuir even agreed to be subjected to the great trial and bravely endured it, but she did not use her privilege to pour water over her torturer. Oh, if it had only been Annuen! She would have got all the water there was in the cup.

"Well, now you've got two super-enduring brides," Coryunov said, congratulating Ordin.

"And jealous ones at that," Kostyakov added.

"Exactly as it should be," Ordin laughed. He was glad that Annuir had redeemed her reputation.

They sat chatting by the fire for a little longer, but soon an old man appeared and told the women they could return to Amnundak's dwelling. The rites were over.

"What did the shaman say? What did the gods reveal to him? What's going to happen to us?" he was asked.

"You'll know everything tomorrow, but now return to your home and go to sleep," the old man said evasively and walked out.

The women dressed, picked up the children, who were sleeping in the corners, and trooped out of the white men's dwelling. Outside, they could be heard exclaiming: "It is cold again! Oh, how cold it is. What a mist! Hold hands or you'll lose the way!"

Annuir went with the others to try and learn the results of the rites. Presently she returned and said:

"Amnundak and all the warriors have gone somewhere —perhaps to see the shaman off; there is nobody in the dwelling except two old men and one of them upbraided me for asking questions."

"As I see it," Goryunov said, "the best thing we can do is to go to sleep. We'll not find out anything until tomorrow."

Had the travellers known what the spirits had ordered the shaman to do and where the Onkilons had gone they would not have been able to lie down and peacefully fall asleep.

Soon after the rites were completed, all the warriors present in the chief's dwelling started out in a south-westerly direction regardless of the mist and the frost; the procession was led by torch-bearers, followed by Am-nundak, the shaman, the shaman's pupil, and four On-kilons, who bore the captive Wampu on a stretcher; the other warriors, fully armed, marched in the rear in deathly silence. The only sounds were the light tramp of feet, the rattle of the arrows in the quivers, and the creaking of the stretcher. Picking their way unerringly in the mist, the torch-bearers led this bizarre procession to the sacred lake through forests and across meadows. At the lake, the prisoner, whose hands and feet were tied, was put on the sacrificial slab. The shaman stood at his head and the pupil—at his feet. Amnundak and the warriors stood round the slab in a close semicircle facing the lake, which was still dry. All the warriors lit torches and held them above their heads; the shaman took his drum, and the sacrificial ceremony began. The torches threw a flickering red light on the black slab, on the hairy, naked man stretched on it, on the shaman in his weird robes, on the raised drum dancing in his hands, and on the semicircle of armed men with eagles' plumes in their hair, their stern faces lifted towards the shaman in reverent contemplation. All around hung a heavy mist, which tore into shreds every now and then to reveal the dark cliffs and the stone-strewn bottom of the lake with its black mouth. In such circumstances, this nocturnal rite made a profound impression on the Onkilons; it would have affected anybody else much in the same way. The prisoner evidently guessed what was coming, for he rolled his eyes wildly and his whole body twitched. After the prelude on the drum, the purpose of which was to call out the spirits and draw their attention, the shaman lowered his arms, lifted his thin, wrinkle-lined face heavenwards, fixing his gaze on the swelling mist, and began to invoke the spirits in a hollow voice:

"Ommolon, Amnungem, Irgani!" he called, repeating these names over and over again. "Rulers of the kingdom of the underground, I call upon you. We have brought you a human sacrifice, a sacrifice with red, smoking blood. Accept it. Do not shake our land. Close the cracks. Return the water to this lake. Ommolon, Amnungem, Irgani! Hear us. We are calling to you!"

When the shaman called out the names of the spirits he raised his voice to a shout, and these strange names were echoed and re-echoed by the cliffs around the lake. It seemed as though the spirits of the underground were giving answer, repeating their own names. At the last ejaculation, the shaman suddenly pulled his stone sacrificial knife out of his belt and, bending quickly, drove it up to its hilt into the chest of the Wampu. The savage uttered a terrible cry, which, likewise, was echoed by the cliffs. Leaving the knife in the wound, the shaman stepped on the face of his victim and again beat on his drum.

When the convulsions stopped, the shaman freed his knife, wiped it on the Wampu's hairy skin, and said:

"Take the sacrifice and throw it deep into the entrance to the kingdom of the underground."

Six warriors carefully raised the corpse and carried it across the slippery, inclining stones to the mouth, while other warriors lit the way for them in front and on the sides. Near the hole, the warriors cried out in surprise and joy:

"Water! There's water!"

Indeed, the hole, which a moment before was only a black, yawning mouth reaching deep into the earth, was filling to the brim with gurgling water.

"The spirits of the underground have accepted our sacrifice," the shaman announced. "Behold, water is coming back to the sacred lake. Hurry and tie a stone to the feet of the sacrifice and throw it into the hole."

Lowering the corpse on to the stones, the warriors freed the hands and with the same thong tied a big stone to the feet. Lifting the corpse, they swung it in their arms and hurled it into the hole, out of which water was already streaming over the bed of the lake. Black ripples, which reflected the red, trembling light of the torches, closed over the head of the savage.

"Bring a sacrificial deer!" the shaman ordered. "We shall offer a sacrifice to the good spirits of heaven."

Moving apart the line of torch-bearers, two warriors pushed forward, leading a white reindeer by its antlers. The antlers were festooned with coloured ribbons made from skin, and the fur was spotted with red ochre. Frightened by the torches, the animal pulled in the opposite direction and bellowed. It was dragged to the slab, raised on it and pushed over on its side at the shaman's feet.

Once again the drum rolled, and the shaman invoked the good spirits of heaven, begging them to restore the warm weather, to stop the frost, and to preserve the herds of reindeer. Once again the sacrificial knife flashed, piercing the reindeer's neck; scarlet blood spurted out, staining the white wool, and the animal stretched out and grew still. It was left on the slab; only the head, which always went to the shaman, was cut off.

The lake was filling rapidly and when the shaman, after bowing to the sacred waters that were returning from the kingdom of the underground, climbed off the slab, the deepest part of the bed was already concealed. In the former order, with only the head of the reindeer on the stretcher, the procession retraced its steps.

THE LAST DAYS WITH THE ONKILONS

On the following morning, the travellers learnt with surprise that there had been an earthquake during the night and that the sacred lake was once again full of water. The latter could be explained by the former, but why had they not felt it? It turned out that the earthquake was felt only by the two old men who had remained behind in Amnundak's dwelling after the departure of the warriors; they fell asleep and were awakened by quite a strong tremor and ran outside, but finding that everything was quiet and that the land was trembling only slightly, they soon returned because of the frost.

"Why didn't we feel anything?" Goryunov wanted to know. "Could the old boys have dreamt it? We had a lot of people in our mudhouse and yet nobody noticed the quake."

"Hold on!" Ordin cried. "Could it have happened when our mudhouse shook with the dancing?"

"That's it! A tremor, if it wasn't too strong, could easily have passed unnoticed."

279

"But which, nevertheless, restored the link of the sacred lake with. . . ." Ordin faltered.

"With what?"

"I wanted to say with the sea, but recollected that the lake had an outlet to the sea before and had dried up not because that outlet was blocked but because of a considerable decrease in water flowing to it from the valley itself."

"We must investigate that. It's very important to establish why water appeared. The Onkilons say it rose out of the hole."

"If we go there and the water disappears again, we'll be blamed and that will land us in trouble. No, we'd better wait and go there together with Amnundak," Kostyakov said.

The travellers learnt of something else that had happened that night. The captive Wampu, they were told, bad freed himself and escaped while the warrior guarding him dozed by the fire.

This news was brought by Annuir, who was the first to return from the morning milking.

"When did the Onkilons learn that there's water in the lake and see it rising?" Ordin asked in wonder.

"They held rites by the sacred lake at night. Amnundak, the shaman, and all the warriors went there. They sacrificed a white deer and now the water is rising," Annuir said with a happy look, apparently believing in the efficacy of the rites and the sacrifice.

"A sacrifice," Goryunov drawled and fell silent. He connected the mysterious sacrifice at night, which was preceded by the expulsion of all the women and children from the chief's dwelling, with the disappearance of the prisoner, and suspected what had really happened.

Later, taking advantage of the absence of all the women and Gorokhov, he told his two friends of his suspicions.

"We must find out if what I think is true," he concluded. "Because if they've started on human sacrifices, then, having begun with the Wampu, they might pass on to us if their misfortunes continue."

But it was impossible to learn anything. The warriors willingly told them that at midnight, while invoking the spirits, the shaman was ordered to offer the usual sacrifice—a white reindeer—by the sacred lake and that as a result water appeared out of the hole and flooded the entire bed of the lake. They denied that there was an earthquake; evidently, they had not noticed it on the way to the lake or during the rites on the bank.

A few days passed; it was only the beginning of August, but it felt as though it were late autumn; the nights were cold, with mist and hoarfrost; the leaves were falling off the trees without turning yellow. The grass was fading and withering. The migratory birds had flown away and the lakes were deserted, and ice, which formed during the night, held for the greater part of the day. More often than not the sun hid behind lowering clouds and gave out hardly any warmth. The women brought the winter clothing out of the chests and hastily got down to mending them. The men spent all their time chopping firewood. Once more, the travellers began to notice hostile glances thrown in their direction, and the women, with the exception of Annuir, again began to absent themselves and stay in Amnundak's dwelling. Ordin asked Annuir to act like the others because that would make it easier for her to learn the plans of the Onkilons.

On the 15th of August, a stiff north wind rose and a real snow-storm broke out; it snowed heavily and the temperature fell to a few degrees below zero. By midday, the snow stopped falling and when the travellers emerged from their mudhouse they saw Sannikov Land in its winter finery; the meadows lay under a thick blanket of snow and the trees in the forests were bare and adorned with snow. The Onkilons also came out of their dwelling and looked about them; they were joined by the travellers' wives.

At twilight, Amnundak went to see the travellers; he had not visited them since the falling out after the earthquake, which destroyed his dwelling. He sat down by the fire and, warming his hands and staring fixedly at the flames, said:

"What is going to happen to us, white men? Winter has come a full moon earlier than usual. The trees froze before they could turn yellow. The birds have flown away and the sun is cold. If snow continues to fall all our deer will perish. The oxen, horses, and rhinoceroses will also die. What will the Onkilons live on then?"

The travellers listened in silence; they knew the reason for the untimely frost and they knew that while the subterranean channels through which the valley had received its warmth stayed blocked up there was no hope for any improvement. But who could say when these channels would clear. And what could they say to give Amnundak any hope?

Seeing that no answer was forthcoming, the chief got up and, raising his arm in a threatening gesture, said:

"You are responsible for it all. You came to us from a land of snow and frost and brought the snow and frost with you, because you like them, because you like to live in a white land, white men! You want to kill all the Onkilons with your frost and snow in order to occupy our land. The Chukchis made our forefathers come here, and you, mighty white magicians, want to kill us altogether!"

He turned sharply on his heel and strode out of the dwelling. The travellers exchanged troubled looks and when the chief went out Goryunov said:

"We can't afford to dally now. We must leave early tomorrow; there's a north wind, the lakes are frozen, there won't be a mist and the snow isn't deep."

"Yes, and if there is another fall we'll have a hard time without skis," Kostyakov added.

"And we haven't got any winter clothing. Everything's at the base," Ordin put in.

"Do as you wish but I'm staying with the Onkilons," Gorokhov said resolutely. "This frost will soon pass and everything will return to normal. I don't think you'll ever reach Kotelny across the ice."

Nothing the others said could make him change his mind and he kept on insisting that in Sannikov Land it was better than in Kazachye; food was more plentiful; he had a good wife and the dwelling was warm—there was nothing to grumble about, he said.

"What if you are killed like the Wampu was? What if they sacrifice you to their gods to get the frosts to stop?" Goryunov demanded.

"You're talking nonsense. The Wampu escaped. Onkilons do not slaughter people. If they did, they'd have finished us off long ago instead of talking to us like Amnundak just did. They'll plead with us but they will certainly not offer us up to their gods."

There was a painful silence.

Presently, Gorokhov rose and went out. A few minutes later Annuir appeared.

"Amnundak has just come back from your dwelling and told us that you will not have Onkilon wives any more.

He said that until you stop the frost and snow we are to live in his dwelling and that we are not to go to you under pain of punishment. And all the men and women shouted: 'We should have done that long ago! Let them live without wives, without milk, without cakes.' I asked to be allowed to go for my blanket. He said: 'Go, but come back at once!'"

Annuir took her fur blanket and whispered in Ordin's ear:

"At night, when everybody is asleep I shall come to you and tell you everything I find out. I feel all this will lead to great trouble."

She ran away, leaving the travellers feeling oppressed.

"We'll have to go tomorrow at the crack of dawn," Kostyakov said. "Obviously, this is only the first of the measures to compel us to turn back the early winter."

"And if we dawdle, we'll find ourselves prisoners with a guard at our door. Then it won't be so easy to fly," Goryunov added.

"Let's get everything ready while Gorokhov is away," Ordin said. "However, it would be interesting to know where he is. I wonder if he went to Amnundak to tell him of our plans?"

Gorokhov and the women did not return that evening. The travellers cooked supper for themselves, packed their knapsacks, and then sat up late, discussing the situation. It looked as though Gorokhov was spending the night in Amnundak's dwelling.

At midnight, Ordin was awakened by Annuir.

"You must go away as quickly as you can," she whispered. "The warriors are saying that the spirits of the underground returned the water to the sacred lake only after a Wampu was sacrificed to them. The spirits of heaven were only offered a deer; that angered them and they sent frost and snow to the land of the Onkilons. They must be offered a better sacrifice. Nothing definite was said but I think they mean you."

"Did Nikita hear this?"

"No. That happened before he came. They said nothing in his presence. He came and told them that he wants to become an Onkilon, that he will leave you and live with them. He said he did not wish to do anything to harm the Onkilons. He spoke all evening about how bad it is in your land. Now the Onkilons know why you came here: you are looking for a good land for your tribe. Amnundak said: 'They are spies then! But we'll not let them out, otherwise they will return with a big party of warriors and begin a war against us with lightnings. That would be the end of the Onkilons!' "

"Did Nikita say anything about us wanting to leave tomorrow?"

"No. He only spoke about himself. And Amnundak praised him and returned his wife to him. Then he told the warriors to call the shaman tomorrow. They will hold a rite in the evening and I think it will be about you and the snow."

"Well, Annuir, we're leaving at dawn. What will you do? Will you come with me?"

"I'll go anywhere with you, if there, in your land, I will be your chief wife," Annuir replied.

"You'll not be my chief but my one and only wife."

They spoke for a long time and when Ordin's watch showed that dawn was near, they woke the others and after a quick breakfast, when day was just breaking, they quitted their cosy dwelling for ever. They left a note for Gorokhov, asking him to inform Amnundak that they had gone for warm clothes and would be back on the following day. If he wanted to catch up with them, there was still time for him to do that as they would wait for two days on the outskirts of the valley. They warned him that the winter in Sannikov Land would be terrible and that it would not be better than in Kazachye. They wrote that he could come later with the Onkilons for the stock of meat prepared by Nikiforov, since it was more than they needed for their journey.

A fire was left burning in the mudhouse so that for a while at least the smoke would allay any suspicions that the Onkilons might have; they fixed up their beddings in a way that would make anyone looking in think they were fast asleep; Annuir alone took along her blankets and all the clothes she possessed.

The light snow quickly obliterated their tracks. They relied on Nikita preventing any pursuit, till the evening, at any rate, and left him Pestrushka, locking the dog up in the mudhouse.

When day broke they were already a few kilometres from the camp, in the neighbouring meadow, which they scarcely recognized. How everything had changed in four months! Then there had been novel impressions, the excitement of discovering a land replete with mysteries that needed to be explained, and the pleasure of finding awakening nature draping itself in young greenery. Now there was nothing but naked forests and snowed-up meadows; they were fleeing from an ignorant people; before them lay a monotonous, dangerous and long journey to the mainland; one of their number, who until then had shared all their joys and troubles, had betrayed them, but they were worried about what would happen to him; and, last but not least, there were the women, whom they had grown to like but had been forced to leave behind. Only

Ordin was light-hearted, for striding cheerfully by his side was Annuir, who for his sake had broken away from her kith and kin and the life she had been brought up in and was leaving her home without a single backward look and going to a world that for her was strange and fearful.

They arrived at the base by evening and gladdened Nikiforov, who had not had news of them for a long time. At the base everything was in order; there was a goodly supply of meat and firewood; the dogs were well fed and happy, and only one was missing—it was crushed by a bear during a hunt. The Cossack was surprised when he was told that the expedition was quitting this bounteous land.

"I've been sweating all for nothing," he said ruefully. "What did I strain myself for, hunted, dragged, dried, smoked? What did I shoot so many animals for? What did I cut firewood for? So that all should be left for the bears, damn them!"

"Don't mourn, Kapiton. People and not bears will eat that meat. Gorokhov will come here with the Onkilons and take everything to their camp."

"What? Isn't Gorokhov here with you?" the Cossack asked in amazement.

"No. He decided to stay. He's in love and says that it's better here than in Kazachye."

"You don't say! The son of a gun. He's got a wife in Kazachye. True, she's old and shrewish."

"While the one here is young and kind. He'll be something of a prince in this land."

"But who is this? Someone to see you off?" the Cossack asked, indicating Annuir.

"No. This is my wife," Ordin replied. "She is going to the mainland with us."

"I see!" Nikiforov drawled, throwing a curious glance

at the embarrassed Annuir, who could not follow this rapid interchange of words but realized that the men were talking about her.

"So instead of Nikita a woman of the local tribe is going away with us. I don't know how we're going to manage with the dogs; she can't replace Nikita and probably never saw dogs before to say nothing of knowing how to drive a sledge. Oh, what a nuisance."

Nikiforov went on philosophizing in this strain for a long time, sitting by the fire around which the travellers had gathered. The proficiency with which Annuir cooked the dinner somewhat reconciled him to the change, and towards the close of the evening he even said:

"You've got a nice, hard-working little wife, Semyon Petrovich. And she must love you a lot if she made up her mind to leave her people and go to a strange country beyond the sea. What about your wives?" he turned to the others. "Didn't they want to come?"

"No," Goryunov said and briefly told the Cossack what had prompted them to leave this interesting land in a hurry.

"If everything goes well, we'll come back next spring," he concluded.

During dinner, Nikiforov said that they could not leave the valley immediately, because the snow-drift had sunk a good deal in the course of the summer and no longer reached to the edge of the crest; it gave access only to the topmost ledge, from which they had to clamber up rocks for something like another fifteen metres. It was necessary to clear a way and cut steps before the sledges and the rest of the equipment could be dragged to the top. The snow-drift itself likewise needed attention; it had a thick coating of ice and steps had to be hewn in it along its entire length.

"But I don't think we'll manage everything in one day," he wound up.

"We've got two days," Goryunov said. "We promised Nikita that we'd wait that long. Perhaps he'll change his mind and join us."

FLOOD

The travellers spent the night in Nikiforov's tent. It still stood in the ice cave, which had been made considerably bigger by the summer thaw. In the morning, they began to cut steps along the top of the snow-drift.

Everybody worked with a will and by evening they found themselves on the ledge. It was from four to ten metres wide and stretched for about a hundred metres on either side of the snow-drift; farther on it narrowed down and could be negotiated only by a mountain sheep. Over it rose a sheer wall, whose lowest point was at least ten metres high; it consisted of separate high and low ledges along which an experienced mountain-climber could reach the top. However, they were too high for the dogs and for men carrying a heavy load, and the travellers had to fashion intermediate ledges, which because of the flakiness of the basalt was not too troublesome a task. In any case, there was enough to keep them busy all day.

Looking round the ledge, Goryunov said:

"Do you think we ought to raise all our things and the sledges up here today?"

"What for?" Kostyakov asked. "It's much more comfortable to sleep down below; besides, it's easy to roll off when you're half awake."

"We'll sleep at the base, but it'll be better if we took the entire load up today and here is the reason. We're supposed to be back at Amnundak's camp this evening, as, according to our note, Gorokhov must tell the chief. But when he finds that we're not showing up he may send his warriors after us. The Onkilons know the way. They'll be here early in the morning and if we leave the sledges and everything else at the base, we'll be caught—I don't think we'd have the heart to shoot. But if we bring everything to this ledge, it will take us very little time to climb up and to destroy the steps. Look, it will be enough to level say a dozen metres of the ridge of the snow-drift to put us out of their reach."

"I suppose you're right," Kostyakov agreed.

"Yes, but what about the dogs?" Nikiforov asked. "They'll be crowded up here."

"They can stay in their caves. It'll be no trouble to get them to run up quickly."

Acting on this decision, they began to raise their equipment, but that proved to be no easy job. In spite of the steps cut in the ice, the dogs were unable to pull the heavily loaded sledges up the steep slope. The load was therefore lightened and each team had to make several trips. That kept them busy till nightfall and in the end everything, including a supply of meat and firewood, was safely on the ledge; only the sleeping-bags and the dinner and tea things were left at the base.

There was so much firewood that they could use it generously for the fires in order to keep the bears at a respectful distance. Nikiforov said that they had been frequent visitors during the summer and that only the cave saved him from their embrace and kept the meat stores, which attracted them, from being sacked.

Belukha had always awakened him in time and gave him the opportunity to hide behind the ice in the entrance and shoot any nocturnal visitors who tried to tear out the lumps of ice with which the meat stores were sealed.

The Cossack told the hunters that the two earthquakes had given him quite a scare; both times he had rushed out of his cave for fear it would fall in. Nearby, the stones had rained down from the precipices "like hail" and the ground had cracked.

Tired out by the work, the travellers turned in early, lying down between four fires, and fell sound asleep with Krot and Belukha keeping watch. Around midnight they were awakened by a vigorous underground tremor. Frightened, they raised themselves on their elbows and listened; from under the ground came a distinct rumble as though heavy carts were being driven over a broken road; soon to this rumble was added the crash of rocks falling off the precipices; the earth beneath the travellers trembled. Presently, all these sounds were drowned by the frenzied howling of the dogs locked up in the ice caves.

The travellers were in the open and quite far from the foot of the precipice and there was no need for them to run anywhere. They stayed in their sleeping-bags, alarmed by what was happening.

There was a second tremor, which was more violent than the first; the travellers felt themselves thrown lightly in the air; the flames of the dying fires bobbed up and down, and smouldering brands and coals scattered around them. Somewhere close by there was a crash, and Goryunov, who was nearest to the entrance of the cave in which the tent had recently been standing and in which the travellers had slept the night before, saw a few big lumps of ice fall out of the arched ceiling.

"It's our luck that we are here and not in there," he

cried, "or we would never have seen the light of day again."

"Are the dogs safe?" Ordin said in alarm.

"I think so. The caves are small and are in the highest and thickest portion of the snow-drift."

"If we let them out, they'll scatter," Nikiforov declared. "And there's nothing to tie them to; the sledges are on the ledge. Let them stay where they are."

But a new series of violent shocks made the travellers change their minds. The dogs howled so piteously, evidently sensing danger, that Nikiforov, an axe in his hands and staggering as though he were on the deck of a rolling ship, ran to the caves, tore out the lumps of ice blocking the entrance and let the dogs out. In the open they stopped whining and began to leap over each other with joy. They ran only a short way off from the cave, then collected in a bunch and gazed at their teamster, wagging their tails. Nikiforov tied them in teams and made them lie on the ground near the fire. Then he glanced into all the three caves and, returning, said:

"The huskies had a good reason for their panic. The ice over their heads has cracked and the hole is so big you can put your fist in it. I'm afraid the ice may tumble down any minute."

"It's quite likely that all the dwellings of the Onkilons have collapsed again," Goryunov said.

"Now they'll attribute this new calamity to our departure," Kostyakov noted.

"Or to the fact that one of us has remained behind," Ordin added. "Now it'll be difficult for Gorokhov to give them the slip."

Annuir listened in silence, but her eyes were filled with tears. This was another calamity for her clan and for all her people and although it did not affect her she was deeply saddened.

"Perhaps this earthquake will make things better," Ordin said in an effort to comfort her. "If it restores the underground channels for the hot water and vapours the climate may be warm again and the life of the Onkilons will run on as before. As for the dwellings, it is not difficult to rebuild them."

Annuir already knew why the frost had set in so early and Ordin's surmise calmed her; she gave him a grateful look and timidly stroked his hand.

"And why shouldn't they build their dwellings like ours? I'm sure it hasn't collapsed," she said, breaking her silence.

"Maybe after our departure they'll begin to build differently. The 'magicians' have gone but nothing happened to their dwelling is what they'll say to themselves," Goryunov remarked.

"Do you think there may be an eruption in the northern part of the valley?" Kostyakov asked.

Involuntarily, everybody turned to the north. But the overcast sky was black and did not have a single red reflection to show that lava had begun to pour out somewhere.

The tremors continued but were much weaker and at last fatigue overcame the travellers and they fell asleep.

But they had little rest. First one, then another woke up, rose on their elbows and looked round anxiously, but seeing that all was peaceful, that the snow-drifts were not breaking up and that the fires were burning, again lowered their heads and dozed off. Nikiforov got up a few times to throw wood on to the fires. The hours of this terrible night dragged on.

At last, in the east the clouds grew lighter and then became streaked with the reddish rays of the still invisible sun. The peaks of the nearby moutains could be seen faintly traced against the background of the clouds, and the white strips of snow came into view. In the north, they could see the dark outlines of the forests; the snow-drifts seemed to be higher and whiter than before and the light from the fires grew dim. The cold that precedes dawn awoke the sleepers.

"Let's boil some tea while it's still dark," Goryunov suggested, "and then get down to work before any search party arrives."

"That's what I think, too," Nikiforov said, getting to his feet. "If we're set on going, we'd better move off while we can!"

"But if the heater of Sannikov Land comes to life again we might not have to go," Ordin thought aloud.

"We'll see if anything like that happens in the course of the day; if it grows warm and the snow melts, then your supposition will turn out to be right. But we'll have to make a way out for ourselves all the same," Goryunov decided.

It grew lighter. Brilliant colours tinted the torn clouds in the east and the dark forest stood out sharply in the north. The black wall formed by the precipices encircling the valley extended on either side and seemed unchanged in spite of the masses of rocks and boulders that had fallen off during the night.

Nikiforov saw to the fires, took the kettle, and went to the end of the snow-drift out of which water was trickling and collecting in a little pool where it could be scooped up. No sooner did the Cossack get round the snow-drift than he was heard crying out in alarm:

"Good Lord, there's nothing but water everywhere!"

The travellers ran to join him, going past the fires, whose smoke and flames hid the surrounding landscape. They stopped in amazement, for a hundred metres from the base of the snow-drift, where the day before the stone-strewn ground had been lying beneath a heavy covering of snow, there was a sheet of smooth, turbid water stretching to the edge of the shrubbery, which likewise was inundated. This new lake, which had appeared in the night, extended on both sides as far as the eye could see, to the very foot of the mountains, it seemed, and only the southern corner of the valley, where the snow-drifts stood, was not flooded. The water trickling out from under the snow-drift, about ten paces from its end, murmured softly as it flowed into this lake, which had cut the travellers off from the rest of the valley.

"How d'you like it, instead of lava we've got a flood after an earthquake!" Kostyakov said, interrupting the silence.

"But look! The water seems to be creeping towards us," Ordin cried. "It's rising!"

They went to the water's edge and saw that that was true; the snow lying on the ground was becoming wet, settling and breaking up, and the water which took its place was full of melting lumps.

"Well, comrades, we haven't got any time to lose!" Goryunov exclaimed. "Let's get our things and hurry to the ledge. Our camp will be under water in half an hour."

"But we can't go on from there!" Kostyakov protested. "We'll be trapped."

"Are you afraid the ledge will be flooded, too? We'll clear a road to the crest before that happens. Don't forget it's at least a hundred metres above the floor of this valley."

"What a good thing we took the sledges and collections up yesterday! We'd never have managed it now," Ordin said.

Returning to the fires, they quickly folded their sleeping-bags and took them to the top of the snow-drift. Then, from the storehouse, which was also threatened with inundation, they took a big supply of meat and as much firewood as they could, piling it all on the steps cut into the snow-drift—from there they could carry it to the top without hurry. By the time they came down for the last few armfuls, the water had already reached the snow-drift and they had to wade through it.

"Now for the dogs," Nikiforov said.

The dogs were restless and were endeavouring to run up the steep side of the snow-drift, but slipped and fell, howling their disappointment. Nikiforov, Ordin, and Kostyakov each took a team and drove them up the steps; Goryunov and Annuir went in front, carrying the sleeping-bags. At the top, the travellers were dumbfounded by what they saw. The day before the snow had lain almost on the same level as the ledge, but now they were separated from it by a wall that was almost

a metre high. During the earthquake, either the snow-drift had split and settled or the floor of the valley had sunk. The men had to scramble up to the ledge. The first team of dogs stopped before this wall. One by one, the dogs were picked up and put on the ledge. There they rushed back and forth, edging towards the sledge loaded with meat. It was all Nikiforov could do to round them up and tie them down in one place. The other men went down for the supplies, and Annuir busied herself with the tea; the ledge was covered with new-fallen snow, which she melted in the kettle.

When everything was safely on the ledge, the travellers looked round them while they waited for their breakfast. From the ledge they could see far into the valley; there was water wherever they looked; all the meadows had become lakes and the forests between them looked like islands and isthmuses. Beneath the rays of the sun peeping over the mountains the water glistened with a silvery light and there was nothing terrifying in the scene; within the frame of black precipices, which were encircled by a white ribbon of ledges and crowned with snow-capped crags, there was a huge lake with numerous islands and peninsulas.

But it was terrible to think that only yesterday this had been a land inhabited by a big tribe of people and countless animals. Had they all been drowned? The people could still find a temporary shelter in the trees, but for how long? If the water went on rising, it would swallow them up sooner or later; but even if it did not rise, they would die of hunger and cold. The animals had nowhere to go—the sheer walls around the valley were accessible only to birds and mountain sheep. Sannikov Land had become a gigantic snare from which there was no escape.

These thoughts filled the minds of the travellers as, with field-glasses, they carefully scanned the valley in the hope of seeing people in the trees. They saw nobody, while far away the forests overlapped and the distance was too great.

"Do you know what?' Ordin cried. "We can use our canoe and try and rescue Gorokhov and any of the Onkilons we find."

No sooner were the words out of his mouth than a soft arm wound itself round his neck and Annuir put her cheek close to his and whispered:

"Yes, yes, go and rescue my people. They will not harm you now."

"But how will we get across the forests in our canoe?" Kostyakov asked.

"The animal trails have probably become canals by now and, then, look, the bare ground along the fringe of the valley has changed into a wide stretch of water," Goryunov said.

Gulping down their breakfast, they took the canoe off one of the sledges, assembled it, put in the rudder, a boat-hook, oars, smoked meat, a bottle of spirits, some biscuits from their meagre supply, ropes, and an axe.

"Of course, there's no need for all of us to go," Goryunov said. "Two will be quite enough, otherwise there'll not be much room for anybody we might find. One of us will steer and the other will row and we'll keep changing places. Who wants to go?"

Nikiforov was needed to look after the dogs. Annuir could not row and the choice was between the three travellers. They decided that Kostyakov would stay behind. "There's plenty to do here," Ordin said. "You'll have to cut steps from this ledge up across the boulder."

The canoe was lowered with ropes. The water was already nearly a metre deep. Goryunov took the helm, Ordin got down to the oars and the light craft pushed off across the muddy waters flooding Sannikov Land.

THE VOYAGE

With only two passengers in it, the light and fast canoe could develop a speed of up to ten kilometres an hour, and it was possible to reach Amnundak's camp in something like three hours. Goryunov and Ordin went along the outskirts of the valley but kept to the line of forests instead of hugging the precipice, where there was greater danger of running against a rock and ripping the thin bottom. They glided rapidly over the muddy water, which was full of dry leaves, twigs, branches, and dead insects—the entire refuse of many years that had lain on the ground and had now risen to the surface and made the water turbid. From time to time Goryunov sounded the depth with the boat-hook and found that it was more than a metre. This led him and Ordin to the thought that the bigger animals might also have perished if they had not escaped to places where the water was not so deep or where there was no water at all, assuming that there were such places. This question occupied the minds of the travellers.

"I can't for the life of me understand where all this water came from," Ordin said. "Do you think the temporarily blocked subterranean river is responsible for the flood?"

"What about the possibility of its being sea-water?" Goryunov suggested. "The sea is close by and the hole in the sacred lake is as good a communication as any."

"Then it must be salty. Try it."

Goryunov scooped up some water, tried it, and spat.

"It's bitter," he said, "but still it's not like the water in the sea."

"We can understand that. It's been diluted by the water from the lakes and by melted snow. But one thing is clear and that is if sea-water could penetrate here it must mean that the floor of the valley has sunk quite a bit."

"In that case the water can't rise very much higher, or can it?"

"That depends on how far the floor has dropped and on the ratio between the diameter of the hole in the sacred lake and the area of the valley; the hole is narrow and the valley is huge and therefore it will take a long time before the water rises to the level of the sea. And then we don't know how far the valley sank. I don't think the entire floor fell in like a pancake; I should say that it sank unevenly, to varying depths."

300

"That would mean that some places are above the water-line and are affording a refuge for people and animals."

"Let's hope that that is so; it would be very fortunate for the population of Sannikov Land."

The canoe was slipping past the border of the shrubbery, which was also almost completely submerged; to the right, the shrubs were taller and gave way to a forest; to the left there was a smooth sheet of water stretching to the foot of the precipices with the bigger boulders standing out on it like islands. There were mountain sheep on some of the ledges; they were either standing quietly and gazing down at the water or rushing to and fro. Small animals—pikas that lived amidst the stones, rats and mice—were stranded on the rocks and bits of high land; here and there among them was a hare, which seemed a giant by comparison. Huddling together, these little animals were doomed to death by starvation. When the travellers drew near to one of the rocks, they saw an eagle dropping from the sky like a stone, seizing a hare and carrying it aloft and, at the same time, frightening the smaller animals so much that some of them plunged into the water. Other birds of prey were also circling in the air, seeking out easy victims. But it was a picnic that would not last long and they, too, were fated to die of hunger. There was a mixed pack of wolves and foxes on one of the bigger islands; some of the animals were lying on the ground, others were standing and following the two men with their eyes.

After sailing for about two hours, they came within sight of the sacred lake, which they recognized by the semi-well formed by cliffs on two of its sides. As the canoe approached, Goryunov, who was at the oars, felt the going getting harder. The two men stopped the boat and saw that they had been moving against a current; here the water was saltier and much cleaner. In the lake itself, the current was even stronger, while over the hole the water was rising in a flat mound.

"You see, there is still quite a strong inflow," Ordin said.

He lowered the boat-hook and just managed to touch the bottom; the boat-hook was three metres long.

"The sacrificial slab is completely under water," Goryunov pointed out, "and, if you remember, it was about two metres above the level of the lake."

Along the edge of the valley, the travellers found a narrow stretch of water receding deep into a forest in the direction they needed. In the forest, this channel was narrower and the canoe slid between trees. It was strange to see this flooded forest; the bare deciduous trees and the evergreens rose out of the water which was covered with leaves, twigs, and branches; dead birds and small animals also floated on the surface. Little birds flitted in the trees with plaintive chirps. Polecats, weasels, and martens took refuge on boughs side by side with rats and mice which ordinarily they hunted. The sun, frequently breaking through the clouds, illumined this unusual and gruesome picture.

In the forest, the travellers had to be careful not to run their canoe against a snag or a sharp bough. However, it soon grew lighter and in front of them, instead of a meadow, they saw open water. They stopped and regarded the scene before them, wondering if this was the meadow where Amnundak's camp had been situated. The outline of the forest looked unfamiliar. Suddenly, the water began to swell in the middle of the lake near them. It rose in a bubble from which a cloud of vapour escaped.

"This is not the meadow where we lived," Goryunov exclaimed. "There the lake did not bubble."

"That's what I say, too. It's the one that lay to the south of us," Ordin said. "Anyway, now we know for certain that this water is coming not only from the sea but also from the restored underground sources. It must be fresh here," he added and, feeling thirsty, scooped some of it up with his hand. "It's almost fresh and quite warm," he remarked, quenching his thirst somehow.

"It won't do our canoe any good to sail in hot water," Goryunov said, "the tar and impregnation may suffer. We'll have to keep away from the bubbles."

They headed northwards along a narrow canal and soon arrived in the meadow where the Onkilons had lived, recognizing it by the clearings in the surrounding forest.

"And there's our mudhouse," Ordin cried.

On the opposite side of the lake a small portion of the central part of the dwelling was above the water; on it lay the remains of the melted snow and a piece of bark that they had used for closing the smoke hole at night. They came alongside this little island; Ordin got out of the canoe and peered into the hole.

"There's a mass of things floating inside," he said, salvaging a skin blanket, a pillow, a few women's jackets with pantaloons, a wooden cup, and charred logs.

"We'll take the pillow and blanket back with us," he said. "Here, let's wring them out; they'll come in useful for Annuir."

Ordin got back into the canoe and the friends rowed to where the chief's dwelling stood. Only the four central posts and part of the roof could be seen. With the boathook, they found the turf and the beams beneath it.

"But not a sign of people. We mayn't have noticed them among the trees, but they should have seen us and called out," Goryunov said. "Let's call out ourselves."

They shouted out the names of Amnundak, Nikita, and of some of the women they knew, but nobody answered. The stillness was complete.

"All of them could not have been drowned! I'm sure some could have climbed a tree or the roof of our mud-house," Ordin said.

"They probably had time to leave; we must look for them deeper in the valley. Perhaps the water rose so slowly that they had plenty of time to withdraw," Goryunov suggested.

"Doesn't look like it," Ordin said. "If that had been the case they would not have left clothes and blankets —things they need most now that winter's here."

They rowed along the canal to the neighbouring camp, which was about two kilometres away. They found the dwelling. It was badly damaged but more than half of it was above the water. Goryunov sounded the depth; it was not more than a metre and a half.

"Well, nobody could drown here," he said. "The water is shallower in this part of the valley."

Rowing up to the dwelling, they looked over one of the ruined walls; there were rags, bits of wood, and rubbish on the water, but no clothes.

"The clan had time to carry away everything that was of any value," Ordin said.

Around the trees standing nearest to the camp, they called out again, but only the crows huddled on the branches, waiting for the water to retreat, cawed in reply.

In the next two camps, the dwellings were either destroyed or half ruined, but there were no people to be seen; the water was only a metre deep; in the canals, the canoe scraped against some of the fallen trees and the travellers had to row with redoubled care.

"I think we can stop searching," Goryunov said. "All the Onkilons are safe and have gone to the northern portion of the valley, which, apparently, is not submerged. Consequently, nobody needs our help, and if we get to dry land and meet the Onkilons the situation may be very unpleasant for us."

"Perhaps farther on the water is deeper and we'll find people trapped by the flood and requiring assistance," Ordin said. "Let's do a thorough job so that nothing pricks our consciences later on."

Goryunov yielded and they pressed forward. In the next meadow the canoe got stranded a few times and the tips of grass, reeds, and rushes rose above the water, showing where formerly there had been a lake. In the canal beyond the meadow, the water was only half a metre deep and in front the ground was almost dry.

"We may come across the Onkilons any minute now," Goryunov warned.

"Looks like you're right," Ordin said. "That smoke is from a camp-fire and proves that they're on dry land. We'll be hearing voices next."

They stopped rowing and listened; from where the smoke was rising came the sound of human voices.

"The earthquake and the flood have forced the Onkilons to move to the northern half of the valley, where they'll continue to live in peace," Goryunov said.

"And now that the heater is working again, as the

two bubbling lakes we saw showed, we need not worry about them," Ordin added.

"But it would be unwise to return to them. In case anything else were to happen, they'll be suspicious again and we'll run the risk of being made prisoners."

"If there is too much open water to allow a crossing to the mainland we can stay on the ledge and wait for the frost. We have plenty of food and fuel and there's a stretch of water between us and the Onkilons. The only thing is that we're leaving Gorokhov to the mercy of fate; I expect he's thought better of it by now and wants to join us."

"Nikita might already be on the ledge, waiting for us," Goryunov said. "If the flood caused him to change his mind about it being a rich life here he could have taken one of the Onkilons' birch-bark canoes in the general panic and gone off alone or together with his wife. He knows where the canoes are hidden on the lake, because he's used them often for his fishing trips. We'll wait for him until tomorrow morning as we've arranged."

After a short rest, they turned back, taking an easier and shorter route along the edge of the valley. Nevertheless, the journey lasted four hours. They passed the site of the sacred lake. Water was still coming from the hole, but the flow was very much less; the flood must have reached its highest level. It was more than three metres deep here, for the travellers could not touch the bottom with their boat-hook. During their absence, the water level near the snow-drift had risen considerably and was now over two metres high.

Goryunov and Ordin found the others waiting for them at the bottom of the ice steps in order to help land any survivors.

"What, didn't you find anyone?" Kostyakov exclaimed with surprise.

"A waste of time, eh?" Nikiforov added.

"Have they all—all been drowned?" Annuir whispered, turning pale.

Ordin calmed her.

"Here are the only drowned things we found," Goryunov joked, pulling the women's costumes out of the canoe and handing them to Annuir.

Together, they pulled the canoe up the steps but they had some trouble getting it on to the ledge, because the distance between it and the snow-drift was now nearly two and a half metres, either because, washed by the water, the snow-drift was crumbling or the floor of the valley was slowly sinking. To make communication easier they shaped a staircase out of lumps of ice.

During lunch, they told each other of the happenings of the day. Annuir, Kostyakov, and Nikiforov had worked hard all day, cutting steps in the cliff above the ledge, and had already been to the top and seen the open sea, which was quite near. Soon after Goryunov and Ordin had pushed off in their canoe, two huge bears had come out of the water at the foot of the snow-drift and climbed up, fleeing from the flood. Such neighbours were very undesirable and the clumsy beasts were met with guns; one fell and rolled down the snow-drift into the water, the other was killed on the ledge. This unexpected supply of fresh meat for the journey was very welcome.

The blanket and women's garments that Ordin had fished out of their dwelling were Annuen's, Annuir said.

CATASTROPHE

Before sunset, Goryunov and Ordin went to the top of the cliff to see what was happening outside the valley, the walls of which had limited their field of vision all summer. Snow lay everywhere as though there had never been summer. The southern slope of Sannikov Land slanted gently towards the sea, which was still ice-bound for above five kilometres from the foot of the mountain. But beyond that and up to the very horizon there was open water with floes and whole fields of ice floating on it. The stretch was too wide for a crossing in the canoe, which in any case could not carry the entire party, the supplies, equipment, and dogs. The expedition either had to wait for the autumn frosts to freeze the sea and narrow down the open water or go eastwards in the hope that there the ice extended farther south and was close enough to Kotelny Island to make it possible to take the expedition across in two trips.

"We're like shipwrecked mariners on a desert island," Ordin said, "with water at the back and front of us and fire and destruction in the centre. It's exactly like a fairy tale."

"There's no fire yet, but there's enough water and destruction," Goryunov replied. "Look behind you."

Sannikov Land did indeed resemble a huge lake. Through field-glasses it was possible to distinguish geysers spurting from the ground in a few places in the central part of the valley. Only the day before the meadows and forests had been wearing their winter garb, but now water had replaced the snow, while the warm north wind showed that the land's heater had been restored.

"Still, the best portion of the valley is gone," Ordin said, "and all its inhabitants, both two-legged and four-legged, are massed in the north, half of which is barren."

"Yes, it will be close for them there, especially for the people," Goryunov added. "The Onkilons will probably start a war of extermination against the savages so as to be rid of such dangerous neighbours."

"This is when our thunder and lightnings would have stood them in good stead. They'll feel sorry they let us give them the slip."

"Well, Gorokhov has a gun."

"Here's what! You know that spare gun we wanted to give Amnundak as a parting present, well, I've just remembered that we left it in our mudhouse. Gorokhov can give it to the chief and make peace with the Onkilons."

When the blood-red setting sun disappeared behind the mist hanging in the distance over the sea, the travellers went down to the ledge and sat down by the fire, talking late into the night. All were in low spirits; they had become enamoured of Sannikov Land and this was their last night in it. They recalled the evening when from the mountains along its border they had first set eyes on this land of mystery, heard sounds coming from below, and tried to guess what they would see. They saw much more than they had expected, made many wonderful discoveries, and found a unique world of extinct animals and primitive people locked up in this extraordinary warm oasis in a desert of ice. The expedition had been marvellously successful, all its members were safe and sound, yet instead of joy and satisfaction they were full of alarm because of the events of the past few days which threatened this wonderful valley and its population with destruction.

The night was quite warm and the travellers economized on fuel by not leaving a fire burning over night. They felt secure on the high ledge with the great expanse of water placing them out of the reach of wild animals, the Wampus or the Onkilons. One of the sledges was loaded, covered with skins, and tied with thongs. It held all the natural history and ethnographical collections, photographs, and diaries; the load was bulky but not heavy and the sledge stood apart from the others near the brink of the ledge; Kostyakov lay down beside it to keep the dogs away from the fresh meat that was put on it for the night. The other two sledges, which were only partly loaded, stood closer to the dogs lengthwise across the ledge and the rest of the party arranged themselves near them in their sleeping-bags.

Goryunov woke up after midnight from a light nudge in his side. He thought somebody was waking him up, and opened his eyes. There was no one near him and he was just about to doze off again when he heard something that sounded like a far-away peal of thunder.

"Rain is something we definitely don't want now. You can't fix a tent on this rock," he told himself, rising on his elbow and looking round. The sky was unclouded and the moon was riding high in the sky, illumining the whole valley. He put his ear to the ground and distinctly heard a hollow rumble.

"Is it an earthquake again?" he thought. "It was quiet during the day and it seemed that the earthquake ended with the sinking of the valley and the flood. Or was that only the prelude?"

His thoughts were interrupted by a tremor that was so sharp that it tossed him up in his sleeping-bag.

"It's shaking again!" Ordin said sleepily.

Goryunov sat up in his bag and looked at the lake below; disturbed by the earthquake, the water was rising in waves that spread in circles, foaming and breaking; the sides of the waves facing the moon, sparkled in long arcs as though they were streams of shining quicksilver. Goryunov heard the boom of the rollers along the base of the precipices and the splashing of the water as boulders dropped into it.

A few more violent tremors followed one another in quick succession and suddenly Goryunov heard a sharp crack, as though a gun had been fired in his ear, and with a horror that paralyzed him saw a black crevice forming a few steps away from him as the part of the ledge on which Kostyakov was lying dipped over, then turned and crashed into the water below. A desperate cry mingled with the splashing of the water and the cracking of the boulders that burst asunder against each other; a column of dust soared into the air. All this took only a few seconds. The plash of the waves raised by the fall of the huge mass of rock gradually subsided.

With difficulty, his whole body shaking, Goryunov got out of his sleeping-bag. His voice refused to obey him and only trembling sounds flew out of his throat. Two steps from him instead of the eastern part of the ledge there was the black, newly-broken line of the precipice with a gaping chasm beyond it. He crawled to the brink and looked down—a pile of boulders loomed above the water that was still turbulent; in the snow-drift with the steps there was a deep hole that had evidently been made by one of the boulders.

"What's the matter? What happened?" came the voice of Ordin, who slept so soundly that only the crack and rumble of the landslide caused him to wake up.

"L-l-landslide!... Kostyakov... the sledge... fell off...." Goryunov forced himself to say without taking his eyes off the dark waters below.

The terrible news brought Ordin to his feet.

311

"Then we must help and drag him up! Quickly!" he shouted, freeing himself from the sleeping-bag. "Hey, Nikiforov, get up! Come here! Where's the canoe?"

"Impossible!" Goryunov said hopelessly. "We can't lower the canoe. The snow-drift's gone and Kostyakov's dead."

"How do you know?"

"He was in his bag and when the ledge tilted over he slid down the side together with the sledge before the whole mass collapsed on him; he and the sledge were buried by the landslide."

Ordin went to the edge and looked down.

"You won't see anything there except water and the rocks," Goryunov said. "The sleeping-bag would have brought Kostyakov up to the surface like a bubble if nothing had been pinning him down."

"What an awful thing to have happened!" Ordin groaned. "He perished with us right next to him and there's nothing we can do."

One glance at the snow-drift showed him that it was impossible to descend to the bottom without long preparations; a hole about fifteen metres wide and ten metres deep stretched along the top.

"But can't we get to the water with ropes?" he asked.

"The ropes we have won't get us half way; it's more than eighty metres to the bottom," Goryunov replied.

"And two men are not enough to support anybody that distance down," added Nikiforov, who joined them at the edge.

"But besides Kostyakov all the results of our expedition are gone!" Ordin cried.

"Yes, they're gone," Goryunov said despondently.

"At least we ought to try and light up the place where the rocks fell. It's in shadow and can hardly be seen. It's possible that Kostyakov had been thrown out of the way of the landslide and that he is lying insensible somewhere."

Nikiforov brought a big bundle of brushwood from their supply of fuel, tied a rope round it, lit it and, fastening the other end of the rope to the boat-hook from the canoe, let it dangle in the abyss. Ordin and Goryunov lay down on the edge, so as not to be dazzled by the light and peered down. All they could see between the snow-drift with the steps and the lower snow-drift next to it were the disturbed water and the heaps of basalt rocks rising from it. There was no sign at all of Kostyakov, the sledge or the load that was on it. The landslide had taken everything along with it. The rope end tied round the boat-hook burned through and the bundle of flaming brushwood flew down, falling on a pile of rocks, and, in the few moments it took to go out, brightly lit up the whole area of the disaster. But nothing could be seen.

Another underground shock made Ordin and Goryunov spring to their feet; a few rocks tore off the brink of the ledge and dropped into the water below.

"Get the sledges away from the edge!" Goryunov said. "There'll be another catastrophe if we don't look out."

The three men, helped by Annuir, who had been standing silently and watching them, dragged the sledges farther away from the new edge of the precipice, to the steps leading down to the snow-drift, and moved away their sleeping-bags. With its mass of ice, the snow-drift was bolstering up the sheer wall of basalt and it seemed that there it was less dangerous. Deep in the ledge, at the foot of the overhanging cliff, it was not very safe either; a few stones had already hurtled down from the cliff.

A distant rumble again filled the air and made the travellers turn their eyes to the north. There, over the northern part of the valley, were wreathing columns of smoke or vapour interspersed with a sinister red light; deafening explosions followed one another and were echoed repeatedly by the cliffs fringing the valley. The ledge shook lightly with every explosion.

"The volcano is coming to life," Ordin muttered.

"And the people, the unhappy people who thought they'd be safe there from the flood, what's going to happen to them?" Goryunov cried. "One of our friends was killed here a moment ago, and another will die there and again there's nothing we can do to help!"

Annuir pressed close to Ordin and looked into the distance; tears were running down her cheeks and she shook as she fought to check her sobs.

"Is this the end of Sannikov Land?" Nikiforov asked in bewilderment. "Just look what's happening there, with all that smoke and fire belching from the ground!"

There was not just a column but a whole colonnade of intermingling black smoke and white vapour and it was rising to a height of over three thousand metres, which was higher than the mountains around the valley: here and there white hot stones shot out of this colonnade and, rocket-like, flew in fiery arcs. Every now and then a cloud of vapour, accompanied by a series of explosions that sounded like an artillery barrage, tore away from the ground and floated in the air, broadening out as it rose. The glow on the clouds above this colonnade grew brighter; molten lava was evidently flowing out of the ground somewhere. A mournful moon was slowly sinking, illumining the valley as before and throwing a ghostly light on the waters of the lakes, which were growing turbulent.

"Yes, this looks like the end of Sannikov Land," Ordin

said through his teeth. "We discovered it and now we're witnessing its destruction."

"When it grows light let's see if we can lower our canoe somehow and do what we can to rescue any survivors," Goryunov said.

Goryunov, Ordin, and Annuir, who kept close to Ordin all the time, sat on their sleeping-bags till dawn, watching the eruption develop and exchanging remarks about it and their lost friend. Nikiforov watched for a while and then went back to sleep.

At last, the terrible night ended. There was a rosy glint in the east and it grew steadily lighter. Annuir lit a fire and set the kettle to boil. Ordin and Goryunov could now examine the damage done to the ledge during the night. The entire eastern part had disappeared and in its stead there was a chasm, while what remained of the platform resembled a wedge with the sharp end pointing downwards. Apparently it had broken off along the cracks that had existed before and the earthquake had only provided the impulse which overcame the inertia of the mass and caused it to fall partly on the snow-drift and partly into the water, where it crumbled into rocks. In the huge dent made in the snow-drift, the ice was covered with black dust, stones, and rocks; below, rocks, scattered chaotically, towered above the water. The mud had settled in the course of the night, making it possible to see the bottom; but even with field-glasses the travellers noticed nothing except the basalt rocks and boulders. Yet these very rocks and boulders had buried Kostyakov and all the achievements of the expedition.

The travellers examined the dent in the snow-drift and saw that before they could cross it they would have to cut steps into the steep ice on both sides.

"We can have that job done by lunch-time," Goryunov said. "We'll lower the canoe in parts with ropes and then pull it up on the other side. Well, let's have something to eat and get started."

In the north of the valley, the eruption continued to develop behind a screen of vapour and smoke; the ledge shook at every explosion. The curtain of vapour and smoke hid the catastrophe from the travellers, and all that they could see in the daylight was this curtain stretched across the entire valley. A fire suddenly appeared in front of it and spread swiftly in two directions. A belt of forest was burning, as a look through field-glasses showed.

"It's all up with the Onkilons," Ordin said. "Obviously, the eruption started not in the northern end of the valley but in the middle, approximately where we were yesterday —where the Onkilons saved themselves from the flood. It might be that the whole northern part is affected, too."

The two men returned to the sledges; the tea was ready. Nikiforov took some cured meat and went to feed the dogs, which were tied together in the western corner of the ledge, but he stopped short before reaching them.

"Come here!" he shouted. "Something's wrong."

Goryunov, Ordin, and Annuir, who were already squatting by the kettle, jumped up and hurried to join the Cossack. He was standing near a crack; it was about as wide as the palm of a hand and ran obliquely across the ledge from the new brink formed by the landslide to the western end. The sledges and the travellers were between this crack and the outer edge; the dogs were on the other side.

"This crack wasn't here yesterday," Nikiforov said.

"This is a bad business," Goryunov put in. "It's got the makings of another landslide."

"Which will start the minute the ground gets a good

shake," Ordin added. "The snow-drift's apparently holding it up or it would have collapsed last night and taken us down with it."

"Much as we hate to do it, we'll have to leave as quickly as we can," Goryunov muttered, "otherwise we'll find ourselves joining Kostyakov."

"First, let's take all our things to the other side."

When that was done, they sat down to their breakfast, but kept their eyes on the crack, expecting it to begin widening at any moment and another landslide starting, with the stones crashing on to the snow-drift this time. The crack was only three steps away from them.

After the meal, they set to work; two of the men went up the steps taking ropes with them, and the third stayed below; when everything was hauled up, the dogs were untied and driven up the steps.

Goryunov, who was the last to leave the ill-fated ledge, went to the brink and whispered a farewell to Kostyakov.

NIKITA'S ADVENTURES

The day his friends left, Gorokhov woke up quite late; he was awakened by the voices of women:

"Where is Annuir? She must have run away to her husband during the night. She disobeyed the chief."

"Go and bring her here," Nikita heard Amnundak say.

"Drag her by her hair if she won't come," a woman added.

Here Gorokhov remembered that his friends had intended to leave that night, and he felt a weight upon his heart. He dressed quickly in order to go and find out if they were gone. But before he finished, Annuen and two other women, who had been sent for Annuir, returned and said in a disappointed tone:

"The dwelling is empty. Annuir and the white magicians have disappeared. Only one of the dogs is still there."

"Have you looked properly?" Gorokhov asked. "They're probably asleep under their blankets."

"We wanted to go in but the dog growled at us. We shouted but nobody answered. Perhaps they're dead."

"I'll go and see," Gorokhov said, making for the exit.

"Bring Annuir back," the chief shouted after him.

On the way to the mudhouse, Gorokhov no longer doubted that his friends were gone. But he hoped to find some instructions which would help him to explain their absence to the Onkilons; in any case, he wanted time in which to think over what to tell Amnundak so that his own position would not be endangered. In the dwelling, Pestrushka fawned upon him. Gorokhov's eye was instantly caught by a piece of paper nailed to one of the posts. He read it a few times syllable by syllable, memorizing the words, and returned to Amnundak's dwelling.

"Where is Annuir?" Annuen demanded, rushing up to him.

"Wait. Let me put in a word. The white men have gone to their base for warm clothes. There is snow on the ground and it is cold, all their warm clothes are there. They promised to bring warm clothes for me as well. They will be back by sunset tomorrow."

"How do you know all this if they are gone?" Amnundak asked.

"It is written on this paper. They left me a letter. Read it," Gorokhov said, suppressing his laughter and giving the piece of paper to the chief.

Amnundak turned it over in his hand, saw some black signs, and declared:

"I shall send this to the shaman. He will know if you are telling the truth."

"But why did Annuir go? All her warm clothes are here," the jealous Annuen persisted.

"Because her love is greater than yours," Gorokhov cut her short.

"The chief forbade me to love my husband and I obeyed him."

"Exactly. But Annuir did not obey because she loves him more."

"She is only his second wife, she thrust herself on him. . . ."

"Enough of this, woman," Amnundak stopped her. He still had the paper in his hands and did not know what to do: to send his warriors in pursuit of the travellers or to believe Gorokhov and wait. One of the strangers was here, in his power, and it seemed to him that the others would not desert their comrade.

Suddenly, he was struck by the thought that the white magicians might have gone to the sacred lake again to dry its waters like they did the last time when they went without Gorokhov.

He dressed and went outside, calling three warriors out with him and ordering them to go to the sacred lake and see if the travellers were there. Going back into the dwelling, he said to Gorokhov:

"You stay here, in my dwelling, until the others return."

At midday, the warriors came back and in worried tones said to Amnundak:

"The white men are not at the sacred lake, but they have been there. We saw their tracks in the snow—three big tracks and a smaller one."

"Now then, either you lied to me or they lied to you in

their letter," Amnundak said angrily to Gorokhov, and then, turning to the warriors, asked:

"Is the sacred lake dry again?"

"No, great chief, it is not dry. It is even deeper than before. The water is higher than the banks and we could not get near the sacrificial stone."

Amnundak frowned: he could not say whether the overflowing of the lake was a good omen or not. And, as was always the case when he found himself with a difficult decision to make, he relied on the shaman to help him.

"Go and tell the shaman what you saw. Wait! How did you know the tracks were left by the white men? Have you seen the boots they wear?"

"Properly speaking, the tracks were left by bears," replied the senior warrior, "but we believe that the white magicians turned themselves into bears so that we could not tell where they went."

Gorokhov burst out laughing. The Onkilons looked at him with surprise, while Amnundak asked irately:

"Why are you laughing?"

The Yakut hunter realized that it would do him no good if the Onkilons began to doubt the might of his friends and replied:

"I thought it funny that they turned even Annuir into a bear; there are only three of them but the warriors saw four tracks."

"That is right, and the fourth track was smaller and evidently a woman's," the warriors said.

"All right. Go for the shaman," Amnundak decided.

The messengers presently returned and said that the shaman would first go to the sacred lake and then come to the chief's dwelling for the rites, and that he wanted the Onkilons to prepare a sacrificial deer.

Gorokhov, who was watched closely by warriors assigned to this task by Amnundak, was lying on his deer skin and thinking if he had done right by staying behind with the Onkilons. If anything happened again, they would blame it on him or on the departure of his friends or on one or the other. They might even demand things from him that were beyond his power and threaten him; there was no telling what might enter the heads of these people!

Perhaps he ought to go, too? His friends had promised to wait for two days. Only now he was virtually a prisoner and it would not be so easy to get away. And then it was impossible to guess what the shaman would say after the evening rites. Gorokhov's spirits sank and only his wife, Raku, who came to sit by him, diverted him with her chatter.

The shaman arrived after twilight had set in and had a whispered conversation with Amnundak. Then he squatted by the fire to warm his bony hands; he stared at the flames and his lips moved soundlessly. After a while he raised his head and said:

"It is time."

"Women, take your children and go to the dwelling of the white men. It is empty. Stay there until you are called," the chief ordered.

Fear clutched at Gorokhov's heart. The last time, too, the women were sent out of the dwelling during the rites, which ended with a bloody nocturnal sacrifice by the sacred lake. He had only heard about it today from his wife, when she thoughtlessly let the secret out. It would be terrible if the shaman decided that a human sacrifice would help to keep the waters of the sacred lake within their banks and that he, Gorokhov, would be chosen as the victim. A cold sweat broke out on his brow and he felt his heart stop beating.

"Go to your dwelling with the women," Amnundak said to him. "Women, see that he goes nowhere. You shall be responsible for him."

That somewhat reassured Gorokhov. If they wanted to sacrifice him to their gods, he reasoned, they would not have let him out of the dwelling alone with the women.

Had he known that after his departure Amnundak would order two warriors to stand outside the door of the mud-house, he would not have been so calm.

The women filled the empty mudhouse with their laughter and chatter; they lit a fire and sat around it. Gorokhov lay down on his bed and stretched his hand out for his gun, which he always kept near the wall. But there was no gun. Who had taken it? Surely not his friends? No, they would never dream of taking that mighty weapon from him. But if they had, they would have taken the ammunition as well; he rummaged in his knapsack and found a whole packet. Evidently, on Amnundak's orders, the Onkilons had searched his bedding some time during the day and had taken the terrible stick that sent forth thunder and lightning so as to deprive him of the means of defending himself. The situation was critical and he was sure the Onkilons were up to mischief.

He called Raku to him and, while the other women merrily chatted away among themselves, asked in a round-about way about the intentions of her fellow tribesmen. But she could tell him nothing definite and only repeated the foolish things the women were saying about the might and pernicious influence of the white magicians.

Suddenly, Gorokhov remembered that when the travellers visited their base the last time they brought back a new, spare gun that they wanted to present to Amnundak before their departure. Did they leave it? What luck if

322

they did! Goryunov had kept it disassembled and packed
at the head of his cot and the Onkilons could not be
expected to guess that that package was also a lightning
stick. Then and there Gorokhov wanted to make sure that
the gun was in its place, for after the rites he might need it
to defend his life. He let Raku join the other women and,
waiting for a few minutes, crossed to Goryunov's cot, saying that it was the place of honour in the dwelling and
much more cheerful than his corner. He lay down and
carefully began to rummage deep under the skins at the
head. His fingers came into contact with the package; it
was lying beneath some hay. But how was he to untie it
and assemble the gun without arousing the suspicions of
the women? If only he could divert their attention. But,
then, why not do everything in front of them as though it
were a trick and make an impression upon them? That
would be the best thing to do, Gorokhov decided, and they
would see a terrible stick grow out of paper and pieces of
metal and wood.

Pulling the package out of its hiding place, Gorokhov
sat on the edge of the cot and said he would turn "this
club taken from the cannibals into a stick that throws out
thunder and lightning." Some of the women cried, "Oh,
don't," but the curiosity of most of them triumphed.
Gorokhov untied the parcel, which had been packed in a
shop in the capital; undoing the strings, he gave them to
the women, who had never seen anything like them before.
They were passed from hand to hand and examined. Then
Gorokhov unfolded the big sheets of wrapping paper,
which were likewise something new for the women; the
"thin, yellow skins" fascinated them and when one of the
sheets, which was held too close to the fire, caught alight
and burned with a bright flame, there were cries of fear

and astonishment, for they had never known skins to burn like that. While all eyes were on the flaming sheet, Gorokhov quickly assembled the gun—it was a centre-fire double-barrelled piece with one of the barrels rifled for bullets—brought it up to his shoulder and exclaimed:

"Here now, the stick is ready!"

The women sitting closest to him started back with screams, imagining that lightning would flash out at them from the shining stick. But Gorokhov laughed and said:

"Do not be afraid. The lightning will strike only those who wish to hurt me, but all of you are kind."

The "trick" made a profound impression; some of the women knew that the death-dealing lightning stick of the "half-white" magician—as the Onkilons called Gorokhov because of his swarthy skin—had been taken away that day to make him helpless. And now, before their very eyes, he had turned a club into a lightning stick. They would be sure to tell the men about it.

Gorokhov put the packet of ammunition that went with the gun into his pocket, meaning to load the gun when and if the necessity arose. Now that he had a weapon, he calmed down and his good mood returned to him. Holding the gun, he said:

"And now, women, dance as you did the last time you were in our dwelling. You can have these strings and the skin, but dance while the shaman is invoking the spirits in the chief's dwelling."

The women felt they had to obey the magician, especially since he was in possession of a lightning stick. However, they always danced willingly, particularly during the long winter night, and now it was already winter with snow lying fast on the ground. So those who had not yet undressed when they entered the mudhouse, did so now. The women began to dance round the merrily crackling fire and Gorokhov, half-lying on Goryunov's cot, his gun in his hands, and a pipe between his teeth, watched them.

But this time the women did not dance till they were exhausted; a warrior entered the mudhouse and said that the rites were finished and that the women could return to their dwelling.

"Raku will stay here," Gorokhov declared. "Raku, do you hear me?"

"Amnundak said that you were to go to his dwelling, too," the warrior said.

"Tell Amnundak that I shall sleep in my own dwelling and that Raku will stay with me," Gorokhov said in a resolute tone of voice.

"Amnundak ordered. . . ." the warrior began again.

"I am not an Onkilon and do not have to obey Amnundak," Gorokhov interrupted him. "He cannot order me about. Raku, come here."

The other women were already dressed and whispering among themselves and exchanging looks of surprise; the warrior was astonished. Never before had any of the white magicians pronounced such words; they had always tried to please the chief even though secretly they harmed the Onkilons by bringing them misfortunes. And here, in spite of his being all alone, this half-white magician was taking such an unheard of liberty. Raku did not know what to do—to go with the other women or to stay with Gorokhov.

"Raku, I'm telling you, do not dress but come here to me!" Gorokhov thundered. His determined tone took effect and Raku, who had only put on her pantaloons, went to his side, holding them to her waist.

"Sit here! We'll have our supper when the others clear out."

The women picked up their children and followed one another out of the mudhouse. The warrior stood irresolutely for a minute or two and then went out. Raku sat down and said:

"Amnundak will be very angry and will punish me for staying here."

"Don't be afraid, he will not dare to do anything to you. You'll see. But now, set the water to boil."

The hunter's calmness communicated itself to Raku and she returned to her household duties. They ate their supper in peace and were getting ready to go to bed when the door opened and four armed warriors entered; the senior warrior declared:

"Amnundak said that if you do not wish to be a guest in his dwelling you can stay here. But he ordered us to go to you and protect you. We shall sleep here. There is plenty of room."

"He's wriggled out of the difficulty, the fox," Gorokhov thought and said loudly: "It was wise of Amnundak to do this! Two of you can sleep there," he pointed to Ordin's cot, "and two there," he indicated his own corner. "I shall occupy the place of honour until the other white men come back."

Three of the warriors lay down without undressing; the fourth squatted by the fire.

"They are here to see that you do not run away secretly like the other white men," Raku said in a frightened whisper.

"They came to protect us against the Wampus, bears, and underground spirits, you silly girl," calmly declared Gorokhov, who, of course, realized what Amnundak's intentions were. When he lay down he took the precaution of putting his gun between the wall and himself and loading one barrel with a bullet and the other with buck-shot; he made Pestrushka lie down at his feet, knowing that the dog would not let anyone approach its sleeping master.

Nothing happened during the night; the warriors took turns sitting by the fire, and the man on watch kept the fire burning and dozed, leaning against one of the posts with his spear in his hand. Gorokhov slept soundly, but Raku was restless all night; she was worried about what Amnundak would do the next day.

In the morning, the warriors went away, but their place was taken by Annuen and two other women; Gorokhov was still asleep, but Raku got up and asked them to tell her what the spirits had revealed to the shaman and how the chief had taken Gorokhov's refusal and her disobedience. But the women had apparently been instructed, for they said:

"We do not know what the spirits said. Amnundak heard the warrior out and said what the men sent to your dwelling passed on to you; he said nothing about you."

That set Raku's mind at ease, but Gorokhov, who woke up and learned what she had been told, was dissatisfied; it was important for him to know what the shaman had conjured up, and, in the course of the day, which he spent in and about his mudhouse, he sent Raku a few times to the dwelling of the chief to see if she could get him the information he wanted, but she achieved nothing. The first time she went she trembled with fear, thinking that Amnundak would get the women to seize her, take off her clothes and flog her, which was the usual punishment for quarrelling, laziness or disobedience. But Amnundak paid no attention when she came in.

That evening, the chief came to Gorokhov, sat down by the fire and said:

"You did not wish to be my guest so I have come to you. Yesterday you told me that the white men would be back today. It is already night, but they have not returned. What do you say about this?"

Gorokhov, who had had all day in which to think of an answer to such a question, composedly replied:

"There is snow on the ground and it is difficult to walk. They have no snow-shoes and that is why they are slow in coming. They will be here late at night or in the morning."

"Why did they not take snow-shoes from the Onkilons?" asked Amnundak and, after a pause, added: "I shall wait till morning. If they do not come by then I shall send warriors to look for them and help in case anything happened to them."

He spent a little more time with Gorokhov, complaining that the snow was not melting and that winter had begun a full month earlier than usual; the Onkilons were uneasy about it, he said. Then he rose and went out. The wives of the absent travellers made ready to go, too. They had been in the dwelling the whole day. Leaving, they said:

"Raku, come and get your portion of milk and cakes."

Raku took a vessel and went out with them, but she did not return. Instead, four warriors appeared and made ready to spend the night in the mudhouse. Gorokhov stayed up late, waiting for Raku, and finally decided that the Onkilons were holding her back. He had carefully considered his own position and had come to the conclusion that it was fraught with danger. He realized that alone he would be unable to stand up against Amnundak for long and that he would be disarmed by force or guile. Then he would be at the mercy of the shaman. He could still overtake his friends, who had promised to wait for two days;

328

that meant he would have to join them by next evening at the latest. And he decided he would escape during the night.

FLIGHT

At the first hint of darkness, Gorokhov had cut away the turf on the outer side of the mudhouse opposite the head of his cot and filled the hole with snow. Now it would not be difficult noiselessly to pull out the few short, thin logs that had been sunk a short way into the ground and stood against the long poles sloping from the roof to form one of the sides of the dwelling. Before dawn, when sleep was most overpowering and the guard would be dozing, it would be an easy matter to climb quietly out through this hole. The knapsack was prepared and Raku was already wearing her winter clothes. Gorokhov hoped she would follow Annuir's example and go with him. Their absence would be noticed only in the morning, because they would leave their bedding and Pestrushka, who would follow in their trail later; they would stop up the hole on the outside. Before they would be missed they would be at least ten kilometres away; Gorokhov had concealed two pairs of women's snow-shoes in the snow under cover of twilight.

Raku's failure to return grieved the hunter; he had become attached to her and it was chiefly because of her that he had decided to live with the Onkilons. But now he was compelled to go without her. She might not, he told himself, want to go after all and might tell the chief. Perhaps it was for the better that she wasn't there.

Gorokhov turned in early, taking Pestrushka into the cot with him; now there was no point in leaving the dog behind. Covering himself with his blanket, he said in a loud voice so that the warriors sitting by the fire would hear him:

"Raku has not come back; the dog will wake me up in the morning."

Close on midnight, a severe underground tremor awoke the dozing guard and Gorokhov. The cross-beams creaked and earth poured through the cracks. All the warriors jumped to their feet and Gorokhov sat up in great alarm. If the earth shook again, the whole of Amnundak's clan would leave their dwelling and gather round fires in the open; he would never be able to slip away unnoticed then. He had to leave now, during the confusion.

While he was making his plans, the earth trembled again and the whole mudhouse shook; one of the beams was wrenched out of place and fell on the fire together with a pile of turf. Gorokhov hurriedly drew on his warm jacket, while the warriors ran out with cries of dismay. But when the trembling stopped and the Onkilons saw that the mudhouse was unaffected, one of them went in and took a few burning brands; apparently, they wanted to light a fire near the exit in order to carry on with their duties as guards.

"You had better go out of the dwelling," the warrior said to Gorokhov, who was sitting on his cot, "you may be crushed; half of Amnundak's dwelling has fallen."

"No, I shall stay here and sleep peacefully," Gorokhov replied. "My corner is quite safe."

The warrior shook his head and went out. That was just what the hunter was waiting for. He took Kostyakov's blanket, made a roll of it, and put it under his own blanket so that the first impression was that somebody was sleeping in the cot. Then he quickly made a hole in the wall by his cot, got his knapsack and gun through it, climbed out himself, called Pestrushka, blocked up the hole with snow and, carefully keeping within the shadow of the dwelling that hid him from the warriors around the fire, made for the nearest tree that stood some twenty paces away on the edge of the meadow. It was an old, branchy poplar, which had been spared by the Onkilons because they had no use for it either as firewood or as timber for their dwelling. Hiding Pestrushka and the knapsack in a hollow, Gorokhov climbed as high as he could and sat down on a thick bough close to the trunk. From there he could see the whole meadow and yet remain concealed by the boughs and branches in spite of their being already bare of leaves. He realized that it was impossible to cross the meadow now; it was illumined by the fires of the Onkilons, and against the white background of the snow his black figure would be instantly spotted by the people sitting up. He had to wait until they fell asleep by their fires. It would take too long to make a detour round the meadow and, moreover, if he did that he was afraid he might miss the trail leading to the base and lose his way.

From his point of vantage, he saw that part of Amnundak's dwelling had already collapsed; women were still bustling round the fires, busy with the children or with the things salvaged from the dwelling; the warriors were hurriedly bringing out the rest of their property. Soon after Gorokhov had settled down in his hiding place, another tremor shook the valley; he felt the poplar tremble and sway; another wall crashed in Amnundak's dwelling, while around the fires peoples reeled and some of them fell; again there were cries and wails, and from the outskirts of the valley came the thunder of landslides.

That same instant Gorokhov heard a loud crack coming from somewhere near the middle of the meadow; he turned in the direction of the noise and saw a black patch with numerous white spots flashing in it faintly outlined against the dark forest amidst the white sheet of snow.

"The ice in the lake has cracked!" he thought. "Damn it, now I can't go across it."

When the rumbling in the earth and the crashing of the landslides ceased, Gorokhov heard a gurgling and splashing coming from the dark patch and steadily increasing in volume.

"Is the lake overflowing its banks? If it is we'll probably all be drowned here. What a calamity! It will put all the fires out and leave the people in darkness. I had better get away from them. But where am I to go if the water is rising in the other meadows as well? Why the devil did I stay behind? If only I had a boat!"

No sooner did he say that than he remembered the birch-bark canoes that he had often used when he fished in the lake. When the lake began to freeze, the Onkilons had dragged the canoes out of the water and buried them in the snow at the back of his dwelling to protect them against the reindeer, which could damage the bottoms of these frail craft with their hoofs if they were left on the ground. That calmed him—the boats were near and he hoped to be able to get to one of them before the Onkilons.

In the meantime, the dark patch grew rapidly and its edge was already about thirty paces from the fires; the water was swallowing up the snow and advancing relentlessly. Just then it was noticed by the Onkilons; one of them ran to the dark patch, saw that it was in motion, and cried:

"Save yourselves! The water is advancing! You will all be drowned!"

There was a terrible panic; people screamed, wept, or rushed backwards and forwards. Some shouted: "Climb into the trees!" Others cried: "Where are the canoes! The canoes!" Still others wanted everybody to go into the dwelling of the travellers. The warriors grabbed whatever they could lay their hands on and the women took the children. Amnundak ran to the sentries by the fire in front of the travellers' mudhouse and shouted:

"Where is the white magician! Lead him out and let him stop the water! Or we shall kill him right here!"

But at that moment a drawn-out cry came from one of the trees:

"Onkilons, run quickly to the north! It is dry there! Save yourselves in the north, in the north! I, the spirit of heaven, am telling you this."

The frightened people repeated over and over again: "To the north, let us run to the north! Quickly!"

A crowd of warriors, weighted down with bedding, clothes, and utensils, moved in disorder towards the northern end of the meadow, together with the women and children and the herd of reindeer. The water was already putting out the outer line of fires, which threw up an acrid smoke and hissed; the brands were turning black and the flames were dying away.

Amnundak was still standing at the door of the travellers' mudhouse. The warriors, who had hurried in to fetch Gorokhov, returned quaking with fear:

"The white magician has vanished together with his dog. They flew out through the smoke-hole. The dwelling is empty."

Such was their report. Amnundak lifted his hands in

despair and rushed after his clansmen, followed by the guards. When the last of the Onkilons had left the meadow, Gorokhov climbed down from the tree and ran to his dwelling where he pulled one of the birch-bark canoes together with an oar off one of the sloping sides, shook the snow out and carried the light vessel to the poplar. He got Pestrushka to sit in the bow, put his knapsack and gun in the middle, then made himself comfortable in the stern, took the oar, and waited. The cries of the Onkilons were already dying away in the distance, the last of the fires had gone out and the water had reached the door of the mudhouse.

"Heck," thought Gorokhov, "I could have taken away one or two other things, say a fur blanket. My sleeping-bag has probably been given to Annuir. It's going to be cold sailing at night."

He ran to the mudhouse, but the entrance was already flooded. So he quickly went round to the hole he had made, pulled aside the logs, reached for a blanket and with the water close on his heels returned to the canoe.

"This way it will be better," he thought, sitting on one half of the blanket and covering his feet with the other half.

The water was already swirling, eating up the snow around the canoe; it grew darker and only a white mass that was the mudhouse stood out in the darkness. Presently, the canoe was afloat; Gorokhov got the oar out and headed towards the lake.

"Farewell, our dwelling!" he said as he rowed past the mudhouse. "We weren't destined to winter here and now nobody will. The water will spoil everything."

Rhythmically propelled by the double-bladed oar now from the right, now from the left, the light canoe glided

334

smoothly over the black water; Gorokhov's eyes grew accustomed to the darkness and he saw the receding line of forest and the white, hill-like contours of the two dwellings delineated against it. Directly in front was an open expanse from where the water gushed. Soon the hunter distinguished what looked like a flat mound and felt the current going against him. He guessed that this was the centre of the lake which was rising in a huge bubble and directed his vessel round it, struggling hard against the current; when he had skirted it the current came to his assistance and he soon reached the opposite side of the meadow. Now he had to find the trail to the south; the dwellings looming white against the background formed by the forest helped him to find his bearings; he remembered the direction in which the trail led from them. After that it did not take him long to find it and he guided his canoe along a narrow canal flowing through the forest.

It was very dark in the forest and the danger of a chance bough ripping the flimsy bottom of the canoe was extremely great. Gorokhov stopped rowing and let the current carry his light craft. But soon the current grew weaker and a new current flowing in the reverse direction stopped the canoe. Gorokhov had to take to his oar again; he measured the depth and found the water to be no more than knee-high.

He had scarcely started to row when he heard the sound of splashing, snorting, and bellowing in front of him. A herd of wild oxen were apparently moving along the trail and Gorokhov knew that he would be in great peril if he stayed in their path. Without hesitation, he headed his canoe into a thicket two or three metres from the trail, caught hold of the trunk of a tree with one hand, dug the oar into the ground with the other and waited. The splashing grew louder and very shortly a dark mass of big animals, panting, snorting, and bellowing, and pressing against each other in their hurried northward flight from the flood, moved along the water-bound trail past Gorokhov's place of refuge; they trotted laboriously, belly-deep in the water and throwing up fountains of splashes and starting waves, which lost themselves deep in the forest. If Gorokhov had not been grasping the tree and had not used the oar as a wedge, the waves would have overturned the canoe; the Yakut spent a few unpleasant minutes while the herd ran past, churning up the water.

When the waves subsided, Gorokhov continued his journey, but before he had covered a hundred metres a rapidly approaching noise was heard again; and again the hunter had to hide in a thicket. This time a few rhinos rushed past him, agitating the water so much that it was all Gorokhov could do to keep the canoe riding the waves; a fountain of splashes showered down upon him.

"The damned, clumsy beasts. I hope you drop down dead," he grumbled, wiping his face. "I won't get far this way. There's nothing to bail the water out with and, besides, it's pitch dark."

But as soon as it grew quiet, a herd of horses appeared and stirred the water even more than the rhinos did; they ran faster than the oxen, reared up on their hind legs, snorted and neighed and tried to overtake each other.

Before reaching the next meadow, Gorokhov had to hide again; a mixed herd of horses and oxen rushed by and were followed by a dozen or so bears. In the meadow, which was now a lake, the hunter headed his canoe towards the opposite fringe, making a detour round the middle, where the water was rising; when he was almost half-way across, huge foamy waves suddenly arose and nearly overturned the canoe. A rumbling and a splashing that came from the edge of the valley showed that the earthquake had struck again. Struggling against the waves, which took a long time to settle, Gorokhov at last got to the next forest where he found a canal and steered his craft along it. But very soon he stopped in bewilderment; the canal branched out in three directions and in the inky darkness it was impossible to tell which direction was the right one—the edge of the valley could not be distinguished; Gorokhov did not have a compass and there were no stars in the sky.

"There's nothing I can do except to wait for dawn," Gorokhov decided. "It can't be long. I've been hard at it on the water for quite some time now and the earthquake started after midnight."

THE SHAMAN'S LAST SPEECH

Gorokhov turned farther into a thicket where he was almost completely out of reach of the waves from the meadow and the canal; tying the canoe to a tree, he stretched out in it, tucked the blanket about him, and went to sleep, rocked lightly by the ripples on the water.

Pestrushka's whining awakened him late in the morning; opening his eyes, he saw that the water, which had risen during the night, was pressing the canoe up against the branches of the tree; the dog was squeezed so tightly that it could not move. To free it, Gorokhov had to hack off a few branches with his knife. He tried to measure the depth of the water, but could not touch the bottom with his oar, in spite of the fact that together with his arm it was over two metres long.

"A real flood," the Yakut thought. "I shan't be meeting any animals now; those that haven't escaped have been drowned."

Pestrushka, freed from the grip of the branches, sniffed at the knapsack, wagged its tail, and looked up at its master with a pleading look in its eyes.

"The poor thing is hungry," Gorokhov guessed. "As a matter of fact, it is time for a meal, only my stock is low and there's nowhere I can make some tea. The game's all gone, too."

From his knapsack he produced a pancake and a smoked goose, that he had taken from the abundant supply hanging beneath the roof of the dwelling, and began to eat it, letting the dog have unpicked bones and scraps.

"We're eating our one and only goose, Pestrushka," he said, addressing the dog. "All our supplies are under water by now and there was nobody to save them. What a pity!"

That reminded him of Raku and her solicitude for him, and he grew pensive. He thought of Kazachye and of his old and bad-tempered wife, whose irascibility had so often driven him out of his house to seek a night's lodging with friends or to hire himself out as a teamster to merchants making long journeys. And it struck him that perhaps he could yet succeed in getting Raku to go away with him; the Onkilons had probably stopped in the first dry meadow they found and were sound asleep after the harassing events of the night. He could go there, hide on the edge of the forest and wait until Raku appeared somewhere near, call her to him, and take her away in the canoe. The Onkilons could not pursue him over the water. His friends would wait until the evening, but even if they were gone they could not go very far in one day and he was sure he could quickly overtake them by following in

338

their tracks. Gorokhov was aware that he had not gone far during the night, three or four kilometres at the most, and that meant he had not far to go to get back to where the mudhouse stood.

Adopting this decision during the meal, the Yakut untied the canoe and rowed northwards; the sun had risen long ago and was warm whenever it appeared between the clouds; in daylight the picture of the flood did not make such a terrible impression as at night. The water sparkled as it swirled and the forest was reflected in it as in a mirror; Gorokhov was amazed by the amount of rubbish floating on the surface in the forest and the canals; only in the meadows, where the water issued in all directions, was the surface clear. Quickly reaching the meadow where Amnundak's clan had lived, he decided to get a supply of food. Coming alongside the mudhouse, which stood up to the top of the door in water, he climbed on the roof and through the smoke-hole caught hold of a few pairs of smoked birds hanging from one of the beams; he was so happy about it that he gave a whole duck to Pestrushka, who had had very little to eat that morning. The dog growled with pleasure as it lay down on the bottom of the canoe and began to gnaw at the bird.

He rowed in the direction taken by the Onkilous at night. Along the canal in the forest, the canoe pushed on through leaves, twigs and all sorts of other litter raised by the water. There were dead birds and small animals; a marten was hiding in one of the trees and Gorokhov, who hunted for the love of hunting, killed it with a blow of his oar.

"It's summer fur, but it'll do for a cap. It would have died of hunger anyway," he muttered, reaching out for the animal. Farther northwards, he noticed that the bubbles in the lakes were smaller and that the water was not so deep; he could reach the bottom with his oar.

"Ah, pity Matvei Ivanovich isn't here. He would have explained where so much water is coming from. The earth opened, as it says in the Scriptures, and the flood began. Thank God, it isn't pouring and flooding the land from above as well, for that would have put the lid on everything."

Around midday, Gorokhov found himself where the water was quite shallow in the canals and the meadows; he could see the tops of small bushes, while about the lakes in the meadows the rushes were in full view. The Yakut had to row carefully to avoid the tree-stumps. Then the canoe began to scrape the bottom and finally stopped. Gorokhov climbed out and went on by foot, dragging the canoe after him; soon he had to take Pestrushka down and to shoulder his knapsack in order to make the canoe as light as possible for there was hardly any water on the ground. At last, he got to the edge of a meadow, which was really nothing more than a wet glade with water shining only here and there in the hollows. It was full of animals: oxen, horses, reindeer, and a few families of rhinos; they were either feeding on the grass or lying on the ground and resting. From the shrubbery came the grunting of boars, who were hunting for food in the wet ground.

"It's a marvel how many there are here," Gorokhov thought. "They had a hard time of it, the poor things, wading through the water all night without rest. And there are the hunters!"

Wampus, stealing up to the nearest herd of horses, were crawling behind the bushes along the border of the forest. The animals were not as vigilant as usual, probably because there were so many of them, and the Wampus were already quite close. Gorokhov counted twenty of them. The nearest savage was about forty paces from the bush behind which Gorokhov was hiding with Pestrushka's jaws clamped in his hands to keep it from barking.

"Here, I'll give them a scare. Let them know that the thunder and lightnings are still here!" he decided and aimed his gun above the heads of the Wampus. When the smoke dispersed, the Wampus were nowhere to be seen, and only the swaying of the bushes showed that they had fled to the forest from where their yells, which gradually grew fainter, could be heard. The report started a commotion in the meadow as well; the animals that had been lying on the ground sprang to their feet, and the herds rushed to and fro.

"If there are Wampus around," Gorokhov told himself, "the Onkilons cannot be anywhere near. And it's a good thing I scared them off or I might have been attacked myself."

He dragged the canoe farther, but soon reached ground that was quite dry; on the trail there were stones which could damage the canoe. A tall, conspicuous poplar with a forked crown was growing on the edge of a meadow and Gorokhov decided to leave the canoe there; he sandwiched it between the forking boughs and left the knapsack and Pestrushka in it, tying the dog to the canoe by its collar. When he was about two kilometres away from the tree, he heard voices, and the smell of smoke assailed his nose. Cautiously gaining the fringe of the forest, he stopped to see what was ahead of him. In the meadow, Onkilons were standing, sitting or lying around fires; meat was being roasted and the smell pleasantly tickled the Yakut's nostrils. The whole tribe or most of it had evidently gathered here from the flooded areas and, as usual, each clan had its own fire. On the side where Gorokhov stood, a particularly large number of people were crowding round one of the fires. The Yakut hunter decided that that was Amnundak's clan and crawled closer along the fringe. When he was about thirty paces away, he recognized Amnundak. The chief was surrounded by the headmen of the other clans. The question they were discussing was whether the tribe should settle down in the dry meadows extending right up to the barren northern part of the valley and immediately start the building of dwellings in view of the closeness of winter or to wait for the water to retreat and return to their old haunts.

"What fools," Gorokhov thought, "they're still hoping the water will retreat. They don't know how much there is of it."

The Yakut's attention was arrested by the fact that there was no snow at all in the meadow as in the other places which were left dry after the flood. Apparently the snow had melted because the air was quite warm; the flood seemed to have brought the summer back to the valley.

Women and children were sitting on the far side of the fire. Gorokhov saw Annuen, Papu, and Matu, but Raku was not among them.

"I wonder if she joined her clan as a widow?" he thought, and took a good look at the women around the other fires; Raku's clan, who had lived closest to the clan of the chief, were sitting at the fire next to that of Amnundak's, but Raku was not there, either.

"Where can she be? Did she go somewhere or is she asleep? I'll wait. They'll soon begin to eat and everybody will be here."

Presently, the women shouted out that the meat was

ready; all the people who had been wandering about the meadow joined their clans and sat down around the fires; the women gave each a portion of roast meat and pancakes. But Raku did not appear either among Amnundak's or her own clan. This troubled Gorokhov. The thought crossed his mind that she might have been killed for disobeying the chief. The only other explanation he could give himself for her absence was that she might have been crushed when the chief's dwelling was brought down by the earthquake.

"This means that I've been on a wild-goose chase," he muttered. "I've come all this way for nothing. Now I've got to hurry back for the sun's already sinking in the west."

But before he could turn back, a group of armed warriors emerged from the forest close to where he was watching. They went up to Amnundak and made a pile of Wampu clubs and spears at his feet.

"You sent us, great chief, to search the place from where the sound of thunder came," said the senior warrior. "You thought that the white magicians had returned. But all we saw there were big animals, and found this," he pointed to the clubs and spears. "We did not find the white magicians or their tracks."

"I still think they are somewhere close by," Amnundak said. "The Wampus have no thunder and we all heard thunder distinctly."

"It's a good thing they've got no dogs," Gorokhov told himself, "or they'd have found me long ago."

But what Amnundak said next seriously alarmed him.

"Tell the headmen of the clans to send all the warriors to scour the forest around our meadow. The white magicians are near and have brought us more misfortunes."

The warriors went from one camp-fire to another, passing on the orders of the chief. Gorokhov realized that he would be unable to go sufficiently far to be safe and decided to climb a tree and wait till the end of the search. He ran deeper into the forest, chose a convenient tree, climbed as far up as was possible and found that he commanded a view of the entire meadow. Settling down between two boughs, he saw armed warriors leaving the fires and running to the edge of the forest. There they formed a chain and began to move forward. Part of that chain went past the tree Gorokhov was hiding in, but the warriors kept their eyes on the ground, pushed into thickets, stuck their spears into bushes, but none of them thought of looking up at the trees. But even if they had looked up they would have seen Gorokhov only if they knew the tree he was in, for the Yakut was wearing dark clothes and was sitting quite high above the ground, clinging to the boughs; although there was no foliage, the branches made a thick net around him.

The search lasted for about two hours and when the tired warriors began to return from all directions and sit by the fires to rest, the sun was already behind the mountains. Gorokhov climbed down the tree and again stole up to the edge of the forest, where he was within earshot of the chief's clan. Amnundak was sitting beside the shaman; he had just been informed of the futility of the search. He looked anxious and displeased.

"Tell the headmen of all the clans to come here. We must hold a council," the shaman said.

Amnundak gave the order and warriors ran to all the camp-fires.

"What else has that old scoundrel hatched up?" Gorokhov thought. "All the women are getting up to make room by the fire, but Raku isn't there; they're all here except her. It's a fact that they've put her to death."

When all the headmen had taken their places round the fire, the shaman rose, lifted his head, stretched out his arms, and said:

"Great misfortunes have befallen our tribe. How many times has the earth trembled and how many times have our dwellings collapsed since the day the white magicians set foot on our land, where we lived so peacefully before. They came and saw that life was good here, better than in their land, where snow never leaves the ground and the sun is cold. They saw the forests and the grass, the good pastures and the many wild animals. They saw our great herds of reindeer. And they planned our destruction in order to take possession of our land and our herds. They dried the sacred lake, but the waters returned after we offered a bloody sacrifice. They brought frost and made the winter begin a full month earlier, and kept the snow from melting. They thought we would freeze to death. But we did not freeze to death for we kept the fires burning in our dwellings and warmed ourselves. Then they decided to drive us out of our dwellings with a flood; again the earth shook, and water issued forth and flooded our meadows and dwellings. We saved ourselves. The voice of the spirits of heaven directed us here, where there is no water. But our dwellings are ruined and our herds scattered.

"Are we going to suffer this for long? Winter is at hand. We shall all die and the white magicians will seize our land. They are waiting for this. They are there, on the edge of the snows, sitting and waiting, and the one who remained behind is spying out where we are. He is here, near us, but we cannot find him."

345

The shaman stopped for breath; all eyes were tensely riveted on him.

"We must slay the white magicians. We received them as honoured guests. We gave them a dwelling, food, and young wives. They paid us back with calamities such as have never been seen before.

"Is all this not so, Onkilons?"

"Yes, yes, it is so," the headmen cried.

"We have already punished a woman who disobeyed us. She was one of the women we gave them. She wanted to betray her tribe, like the one who ran away with them to the snows. And the white magician, her husband, did not protect her; he fled although she called to him for assistance when she was drowning in the water, which the magicians had drawn from the earth.

"Now we must catch all the magicians and sacrifice them to the good spirits of our land. Tomorrow, a hundred of our bravest warriors will go forth to the snows; they will make rafts and sail across the water with our chief at their head; they have spears and arrows and he has thunder and lightning, which we took from the white magician. Now we are as well armed as they and there are many of us and only four of them. Surely they can be overcome by a hundred warriors! Let half fall in battle, but our land will be saved and we shall go on living as before. The water will not go back into the earth, our dwellings will stand in ruins, and our herds will remain scattered unless we sacrifice the white magicians. I have spoken!"

"Oh, you miserable old blackguard," Gorokhov muttered, listening to the shaman. "You drowned my Raku and now you want to catch and slaughter us like deer. But first I'll send you on your way to join your ancestors."

346

He raised his gun and aimed at the shaman, who was standing directly opposite him on the far side of the fire with his arms and head raised in the inspired pose of a prophet. In the gathering dusk the flames threw a bright light on his figure. A report rang out and the shaman dropped to the ground, falling face foremost into the fire. Struck dumb with horror, Amnundak and the headmen sat stone-still; the shaman's fur cap caught alight and the women standing close by shrieked. And suddenly, as if by command, all the men sitting round the fire raised their arms heavenwards, uttered a drawn-out cry and then covered their faces with their hands, repeating this dramatic gesture three times. Then Amnundak got up and said in solemn tones:

"The lightning of the white magicians has killed our shaman for urging us to harm them. They are all-powerful and we cannot struggle against them. Such was the prediction of the great shaman who led our forefathers to this land. Take the dead man away from the fire!"

GHASTLY NEIGHBOURS

After firing the gun, Gorokhov took to his heels, expecting that the ensuing confusion would prevent the Onkilons from giving immediate chase and that under cover of the night he would be able to hide himself on a tree as a last resort. Plunging into the shrubbery, he found the trail that had brought him here and did not stop running until he got to the poplar on which he had left his canoe and dog. If the Onkilons came this way, he told himself, he would climb the tree, where he had his knapsack, blanket, and provisions and spend the night quite comfortably. It was not likely that with such a load he would be able to cover the nearly two kilometres to the water's edge fast enough.

He stopped and listened; at first everything was quiet, but soon he heard voices and saw lights flashing in the distance; the Onkilons, lighting their way with torches, were hunting for him. Forthwith, Gorokhov climbed the tree, dragging the canoe still higher. Pestrushka, who could not sit still on a bough, gave him the most trouble. He had to fix the canoe between two thick branches and put the dog and knapsack in it. As soon as he had finished that task, a few Onkilons, bearing torches, appeared on a path near the poplar, and there were other warriors to the right and left of them. Going past the tree, they soon came upon the track left by the canoe on the wet soil and grass and with cries of joy they called the others to them and quickly followed the track, hoping to overtake the fugitive.

Gorokhov ate a smoked bird, fed Pestrushka, and lit a pipe, but there was no further sign of the Onkilons. He began to feel drowsy and decided to sleep until the moon showed itself; he tied himself to the trunk and was soon fast asleep.

He was awakened by a fierce rocking—he almost lost his balance and if he had not tied himself to the trunk he would have fallen off his perch; the canoe had to be held with both hands. He could not grasp what was happening; there was a deafening noise all around him; the moon, which had risen long before, was shining in the sky; all the trees were swaying but there was no wind. At last, it dawned upon him that the earth was shaking again; glancing in a northerly direction, he saw that something terrible was happening somewhere very close by; clouds of white and black smoke were rising from behind the forest and the rumble that came from there was so loud that Gorokhov's ears rang. Then a scorching wind arose and made it difficult to breathe.

"Mother of heaven, what's happening there? The ground is being torn apart and flames are shooting out," Gorokhov said in an awed whisper. "I must run, run and get to the water!"

Laboriously, he lowered the knapsack, canoe, and dog by turn because the tree swayed all the time. On the ground, he could scarcely keep on his feet; staggering as though he were drunk, he pulled the canoe along the ground and then over the shallow water. From time to time something heavy fell into the water now to the right, now to the left of him, shattering the branches of trees. The rumbling did not cease. The air was getting hotter and closer.

When, finally, the water was deep enough, Gorokhov got into the canoe and rowed with might and main to put as much distance as possible between him and the seat of the catastrophe; reaching a big meadow, he glanced back to the north and saw a reddish glow against a background of puffs of smoke streaked by flashes of red lightning.

"The poor Onkilons are dying in that hell," he thought, "and again putting the blame for everything on the white magicians and saying: they've killed the shaman and now they're destroying the whole tribe."

The water rippled slightly, but farther on, where it was deeper, the surface was rougher and the canoe was tossed from side to side. The battle with the waves over a stretch of about ten kilometres utterly exhausted Gorokhov and he decided to find a place of safety he could stay in until dawn. On the edge of a meadow, where the waves were particularly choppy, he saw the frame of a dwelling rising above the water; the earthquake had destroyed the walls before the flood, but the four central posts with part of the roof were left because they had been sunk into the ground and made fast with cross-beams. This platform was standing almost a metre above the water where it could not be reached by the waves.

"I can rest here," Gorokhov thought and directed his canoe to the platform. With difficulty, he took everything, including the dog, out of the canoe, climbed out himself and pulled up his light craft. Spreading the blanket on the wet turf, he promptly fell asleep in spite of the rumbling that reached him from the north and the plash of the waves.

He woke up at dawn and took stock of his surroundings, seeking out landmarks that would show him the way. In the course of the night the water had grown still and only tiny ripples disturbed the mirror-like surface from time to time. Rising above the water nearby was another little island in the shape of a green hillock. A tall poplar standing in the vicinity showed Gorokhov that this was the dwelling he and his friends had lived in; it was the poplar he had climbed the night of his flight; that meant that the platform he had slept on was the remains of Amnundak's dwelling.

Eating a quick meal, he lowered the canoe and called Pestrushka; the dog was standing near the smoke-hole in the centre of the platform, looking down at the water and yelping.

"What have you seen there? A fish or what?" Gorokhov asked and went to take the dog, who refused to answer his call. A glance into the smoke-hole made him shudder—

the fingers of two human hands were jutting out of the water by one of the posts supporting the platform.

"Good Lord and the saints above, there's a drowned man here!" he exclaimed. "Why didn't he climb up the post to the top?"

A silver ring that Gorokhov thought looked familiar showed on one of the fingers; none of the Onkilons had silver rings and only the wives of the travellers had received such rings as presents from their husbands and had been extremely proud of them.

"Oh, the murderers! It's Raku! All the other women were there, and the old dog said that they had drowned the traitress."

Gorokhov lowered himself into the canoe and rowed round the platform to where the hands could be seen; thongs held the wrists tightly to the post. He cut the tongs and pulled the body up by one of the stiff wrists; an arm rose slowly above the water, then the hair appeared and finally Gorokhov saw the face; the eyes were open and gazed at the Yakut with mute reproach. He screamed and started back; the wrist slipped out of his grasp and the head and arm disappeared in the muddy water.

"Unhappy girl!" the Yakut thought. "They tied her to this post for the night so that she would not run away to me. Then, when the water began to rise, they either forgot her in the dwelling or left her there on purpose, and she was drowned."

He pictured to himself what Raku must have suffered when the water burst into the dwelling and began to rise higher and higher up her body; how she struggled and cried for help, and the only answer was the splashing of water in the terrible darkness; how the water rose up to her breast, her neck and her mouth and finally stifled the last sounds in her throat. And he had been close by and could easily have saved her as soon as the Onkilons had fled. Evidently she started to shout only when the water penetrated into the dwelling and he was already on his way across the lake.

He wanted to get the body out of the water and bury it; but he had no boat-hook and, besides, even if he had, the only place where the body could be buried was in the snows beyond the valley. Heartsick, he put Pestrushka, who now obeyed his call, in the canoe, took his things and headed south. He rowed with all his strength, hoping he still had time to catch up with his friends, and the canoe virtually flew over the calm, deep waters of the lakes and canals.

The outskirts of the valley with white snow-drifts outlined against the dark cliffs came into view. Black and white clouds were still billowing in the sky in the north and every now and then he heard the rumble of explosions.

At last, Gorokhov reached the end of the belt of forest and before him he saw smooth water extending right up to the snow-drifts. Here, too, the land was flooded. Where were his comrades? Had they left? Were they drowned? There was nobody on the ledge above the snow-drifts where they had dug caves.

The figure of a man, silhouetted darkly against the bright sky, appeared high on a precipice. Gorokhov shouted at the top of his voice and waved his oar. Pestrushka barked.

He was seen! He was saved!

He rowed to the base of the snow-drift below the precipice, landed the dog, took his gun, knapsack, and blanket, and climbed the steps.

A chasm he did not expect to find opened before him

and he had to stop. Goryunov and Ordin were already standing on the other side.

"I've managed to overtake you, after all!" Gorokhov cried, throwing his load on the ice. "If you only knew what I had to go through!"

"Well, there's a long wait ahead of you while we cut steps down and up this chasm," Goryunov replied.

"Some hole, this! Fencing yourselves off from pursuit, or what? Hm, it won't be easy to get across," Gorokhov said, gazing at the hole, which was fringed by sheer walls of ice a few metres high. "It'll take too much time to cut the steps. Here's what. Bring a rope and throw one end over to me."

The travellers had a rope with them, having brought it in case it was needed. They tied a stone to one of the ends and threw it to Gorokhov. He pulled it over to his side of the chasm, and began to lower his things after folding the rope in two; when each item was on the floor of the chasm, he released one end of the rope and pulled it by the other, thus leaving the item on the ground and recovering the rope. In this manner he lowered the knapsack, blanket and, finally, Pestrushka, slipping the rope through its collar. The dog, hanging by its neck, choked and kicked in the air, but the operation took so little time that not much harm was done to it. Now Gorokhov had to lower himself. There was a basalt rock sitting firmly in the ice at the edge of the chasm. The Yakut wound the middle part of the rope round it and lowered himself down the side of the chasm; on the floor, he let one of the ends of the rope go, pulled it by the other end—and the rope fell at his feet.

The ascent did not present much difficulty. Gorokhov, Pestrushka, and the hunter's belongings were quickly pulled to the top by Goryunov and Ordin.

"Thank God, I made it! I was already thinking I'd find nobody here!"

As a matter of fact, Gorokhov would not have seen his comrades if he had emerged from the forest a few minutes later than he did. The two remaining sledges were already on the southern slope of the crest and while Nikiforov was tightening the ropes, Goryunov and Ordin returned to the crest to take a last look at Sannikov Land, where they had spent so many weeks exploring and which together with its population was being destroyed before their very eyes by flood and molten lava. They had amassed many valuable observations, but the results of this work were lost together with one of the members of the expedition during the last hours of their sojourn in this land when they were least prepared for it; another member of the expedition had remained behind voluntarily and they had every reason to believe that he had perished, too.

The land, which was now an enormous lake framed in black precipices and bristling with dark, forest-overgrown islands and isthmuses, glistened like silver in the rays of the low-hanging sun, while in the north, behind the tossing and pitching wall of vapours and smoke the last act of the drama of Sannikov Land and of the Onkilon tribe was playing itself out. Ordin used his last plate to photograph this painful picture—a picture of a little world of the remnants of mammoths, woolly rhinoceroses, and representatives of primitive humanity—a world only just discovered for science and already dying. After taking the photograph, he went to pack his camera, while Goryunov stayed for a moment longer and saw Gorokhov's canoe nosing its way out of the forest.

If it had not been for this piece of good fortune, the Yakut would have had a hard time overtaking his friends.

Climbing to the top, Gorokhov saw the deep crevice, learnt of Kostyakov's death and realized what a narrow escape he had had.

"It seems that I was born under a lucky star, Matvei Ivanovich," he said, stopping on the crest. "I've had one foot in the grave so many times in the course of these last two days, but here I am hale and hearty, while poor Raku, for whose sake I stayed behind, was drowned because of me. May her and Pavel Nikolayevich's memory live for ever!"

He took off his cap and bowed three times in the direction of Sannikov Land, which had become the grave of so many people.

That day the travellers went only a short distance and stopped at the foot of the southern slope of Sannikov Land. They tested the ice and found that it was too thin and could be broken by the first storm that arose. They had to move to the east in search of more reliable ice.

ACROSS SEA AND ICE

For a whole week, the travellers pressed eastwards, looking for a place that was suitable for a crossing; but everywhere the ice was weak. Although the summer was coming to a close and warm days constantly alternated with frosts, the latter, far from being strong enough to bind the sea, could not even strengthen the old ice-fields that had been loosened by thaw. The alternative was to wait for the beginning of winter, but that was only possible on Bennett Island, where stood the hut that had been built by Toll and where the travellers could gather drift-wood for their fires, and hunt bears and reindeer for food. Luckily, the ice between Sannikov Land and Bennett Island had not been broken that summer and the travellers, after making a short detour to the north, reached the island on the tenth day. And it was fortunate for them that they did: the supplies for the dogs, taken from Niki-forov's stocks, were giving out, and the travellers had had no firewood for three days.

After sunny Sannikov Land, gloomy, rocky and almost barren Bennett Island made a cheerless impression upon the travellers. But they were happy to get to Toll's hut; it stood in the mouth of a small valley on the eastern bank of a fresh-water stream along which it was possible to reach the flat highland occupying the entire island. There was plenty of drift-wood, but no game at all: they did not see any reindeer or bears. So they had to begin killing some of the dogs in order to feed the rest; the loss of one of the sledges left the travellers with an extra team, and it was these dogs that became meat for the others.

At the expiration of the tenth day on the island, the situation remained unchanged: summer was still holding its own even though it was the beginning of September and the ice continued to melt and break. The provisions for the travellers likewise began to give out. Every day, the four men left Annuir in charge of the hut and the dogs and searched the island for game—it is about sixteen kilometres long and eight kilometres wide in the east, which is its broadest part—but all they brought back was an occasional crow or gull.

"Now listen, friends," Goryunov said at the close of the tenth day, "we can't afford to wait any longer. If we do, we'll find ourselves without dogs by the time the sea freezes over and they're needed the most. For a few days the reading on the barometer has been remarkably high, the sea is calm and I doubt if there'll be a storm. Besides our warm clothing and guns, we've got very few things and only half of the dogs are left; if we reduce their number to five or six, there'll be room for all of us in the canoe. In this still weather, we should get to Kotelny in a day or two; there, if the weather changes for the worse, we've got enough food to tide us over the winter, and if it stays calm we'll go on along Kotelny and try and reach the mainland."

After discussing this plan, the travellers concluded that

it was quite practicable; the days were still sufficiently long—more than twelve hours; and, by taking turns with the oars, they could cover the distance across the sea from Bennett Island to Cape Vysoky on the nearest of the New Siberian Islands in one, or, at the most, in two days—in the latter event, they could spend the night on one of the ice-fields floating on the sea. Of course, a sudden storm could sink the canoe; but that was a risk they would have to take later in any case if they decided to cross over the newly-frozen sea—the difference was that then, in October, there would be no more than two or three hours of daylight and more frequent winds capable of smashing the ice.

Thus, it was decided that, providing the barometer held, they would kill the extra dogs, feed the others as much as they could eat, and set out at dawn, leaving their surplus equipment in the hut. For this purpose, they carefully went over the things packed on the sledges.

Towards evening, the barometer rose and, with heavy hearts, the travellers put to death a few of their faithful dogs. At the first hint of dawn, they left the hospitable hut and dragged the canoe over the ice for about two kilometres to the open sea; then at sunrise, they pushed off, heading due south. The canoe was heavily loaded and the travellers found that their progress was not as swift as they had hoped; towards sunset they were only a little more than half-way across. The number of ice-floes increased the farther they went and they realized that it would be very dangerous to continue their voyage at night. They stopped at an ice-field and set their tent up on it. By the light of the setting sun, Cape Vysoky could be seen on the horizon quite well.

At daybreak, they resumed their voyage. When it became

light, Nikiforov and Gorokhov, who were peering into the distance, exclaimed in unison:

"Here's a fine state of affairs. We've been shifted off our course quite a bit during the night!"

"How? Where to? Isn't there any land to be seen?" Ordin asked.

"We can see land, all right, but it's not the land we saw yesterday."

"Where could we have been carried away to?"

"Either to the east, in which case we're seeing the eastern part of the New Siberian Islands, or to the west, which means that Faddeyevsky or even Kotelny is lying ahead of us," Goryunov said.

"The horizon is still blurred," Gorokhov declared, "and it's impossible to see what land we're heading for."

"Whatever land it is," Ordin remarked, "let's get to it. The barometer began to fall during the night and we must hurry."

When the sun rose and the light mist hovering above the sea dispersed, Goryunov took his field-glasses, studied the land in front of them and said:

"Here, Gorokhov, you've got keen eyes. Can you tell us the name of that island?"

Gorokhov looked, shielding his eyes from the sun, and said:

"Kotelny!"

"Right! And the ice-field saved us from sailing past some nasty places along the islands. Now we'll make our canoe fast right opposite our storehouse."

Indeed, by midday, there were no longer any doubts that the island in view was Kotelny; they all recognized it by its outlines even though the snow that had covered it in spring had almost completely melted.

Towards evening, they landed on the ice-field encircling the island and pulled the sledges over the hummocks for five kilometres, a task which reminded them of their journey in spring. They reached the hut at the base of the northern cape when dusk began to gather.

In the hut, they found some of the stores missing; the hunters who came to the island in the course of the summer had evidently taken some of the provisions, particularly *yukola*. But there was a sufficient supply of it for the few remaining dogs.

On the following day, the weather was still clear, but the barometer fell sharply, foretelling a drastic change. The travellers felt they had tempted fate quite enough and decided to bide their time. Sure enough, a storm broke out in the evening and in the morning it began to snow, the weather grew frosty and winter made its appearance all at once. With short breaks, storms raged up to the end of September, but there was ample food for all and the travellers took their ease. They had a long journey before them, but the chief obstacle—the open sea—had been passed.

On one of the rare clear days, all of them climbed a bluff rising above the cape and looked at the peaks of Sannikov Land that could just be made out on the horizon. What was happening there? Had the volcano stopped erupting? Had the water drained out of the valley? Or, perhaps, everything living had perished and the forests, the last trace of fertile life amidst the ice of the north, would in a few years likewise disappear under water or snow. They looked sadly at the faraway land, where each, particularly Annuir, had left some object of affection. Annuir was unused to the intense frosts that she had to experience now and they caused her great discomfort in spite of Kostyakov's warm clothing, which fitted her excellently. She frequently brooded over the homeland she had forsaken, the accustomed conditions of life, and her lost kinsmen. Often, she asked the others:

"Is it always so cold with nothing but snow and ice over there, in your land, as well?"

In October, the frosty weather that had established itself allowed the travellers to start on the last stage of their journey. They pushed ahead on sledges. The heavier one was pulled by the dogs; the men took turns in pairs to pull the lighter sledge. The days were short and they pressed on at night as well, whenever there was moonlight. A storm began to rage when they reached Cape Medvezhy. They sought the shelter of the hut and when the storm abated they took a risk and crossed to Maly Lyakhov Island over the thin ice. On Bolshoi Lyakhov they were stopped twice by storms; their food supplies were extremely low, but that made the sledges lighter and enabled them to travel faster. At the end of October, utterly exhausted, with only three of the dogs left, they finally arrived in Kazachye.

AGAIN AT THE ACADEMICIAN'S

It took the travellers a whole week to recover from the hardships of the long journey; they spent that week sleeping in Nikiforov's hut, waking up only for their meals. Incidentally, the polar night and the severe frosts did not incline the rest of the population of that dismal territory to intense activity.

Little Kazachye, with its score of huts, impressed the naive Annuir as being a huge settlement; for the first time in her life she saw houses with roofs, stoves with chimneys, windows, tables, chairs, and beds, and learned that people did not have to sleep and sit on the ground or to eat on their knees; it was all novel and strange and she had to adjust herself to many things, although she thought some of them funny or unnecessary.

Upon its return to Kazachye, the expedition, which has made such a great discovery but lost one of its members and all its collections and notes, had every right to consider its mission as ended and Goryunov, after sending Academician Shenk a written report, could go where he pleased. But his respect for the scholar was too great for that; a man who could entrust instruments and a large sum of money to a total stranger for a near-fantastic enterprise deserved more. Goryunov wanted to see him personally and to have his story confirmed by one other member of the expedition. Moreover, the instruments and the money recovered from the sale of the sledges, the canoe, the guns, the tents and so forth had to be handed over to him. Most of the equipment was bought by Gorokhov and Nikiforov, who set a high store by good sledges and guns.

Collecting about a thousand rubles, which sum included the remainder of the money given by Shenk, Goryunov, Ordin, and Annuir set out for Yakutsk by way of Verkhoyansk. But there they came upon an obstacle; Ordin's term of exile was not yet up and the Governor refused him permission to leave, while Annuir did not want to go on without him as the long journey across the snow frightened her. Ordin was given permission to stay in Yakutsk, which Annuir thought was a great capital with countless wonders, beginning with cats, cows, and harnessed horses and ending with ball-dresses and gramophones.

Goryunov had to go on alone and rest content with a photograph of Annuir in her indoor costume, i. e., the tattooing and the loin-cloth. He took along with him a small collection of rocks found in Sannikov Land and on Bennett Island, and Ordin's last photograph of Sannikov Land which he took from a precipice on the day of their departure. He arrived in the capital at the close of December and at once went to see Shenk.

The academician had received a brief telegram informing him of the discovery of Sannikov Land and of the expedition's return, and he was impatiently awaiting Goryunov's arrival. He wanted to introduce the young man to the Academy and a few scientific societies where he could give a series of public lectures on his remarkable explorations. But Goryunov asked the academician first to listen to what he had to tell him in private.

And, so, one evening, Shenk listened to Goryunov's tale in the room in which he had received him a year ago and at the same table. When Goryunov reached the part about mammoths, rhinoceroses, wild oxen and other "living fossils," the academician beamed and said:

"You doubtlessly measured and photographed them and have some proof of this most astonishing discovery."

The fact that the expedition found the Onkilons and people of the Palaeolithic period amazed Shenk much as did the information Goryunov gave him about their life and customs.

Before going on to his painful reminiscences of the last days of Sannikov Land and its inhabitants, Goryunov made a pause. Shenk took that to mean that the story was finished and said:

"Of course, you've brought diaries, photographs, and perhaps even the skulls and skins of animals, and some artefacts of the Onkilons and the savages? We'll give a wonderful lecture and surprise all unbelivers."

"We had all that—but it—it was all lost."

"What are you saying? Do you mean—positively everything?"

Perturbed, Shenk listened to the end, examined the photograph of Sannikov Land and the samples of rock, and said:

"Well, from the testimony of four eye-witnesses, we now know that Sannikov Land exists, that it is situated approximately a hundred kilometres north of Kotelny Island, and is the huge crater of a volcano that recently became active again. On the basis of this data, I shall shortly try and persuade the Academy to fit out an expedition which will have all the necessary means and scientific personnel and go to this land to study what still remains of its population. Naturally, you and your friend will go along and contribute your experience to ensure the success of the enterprise."

"Of course! But what are we going to do about the report to the Academy and the scientific societies?" Goryunov asked.

"At the moment, it would only spoil things," Shenk said. "I think you will agree with me that all you have told me is so unusual, remarkable, and incredible that we must have convincing proofs. What you can show your listeners is too little. They'll say that the tattooed woman on this photograph is an Eskimo or a Chukchi; they, too, tattoo their bodies and wear only a loin-cloth in their dwellings, and, furthermore, the type is the same. Take this piece of basalt—how can you prove it's from the mountains of Sannikov Land and not from Bennett Island or St. Nos? And this photograph of the valley with the lake and erupting volcano—it hardly shows anything. Why didn't you take more and better photographs after the loss of the sledge with your collections and notes?"

"Because we used up all but one of our plates photographing people, animals, and nature. This woman was photographed in Yakutsk."

"Pity! If you had photographs of this land taken from the mountains as well as from Bennett Island, you would have had proof of what you say. As things are nobody will believe you."

"Don't *you* believe me?" exclaimed the disheartened Goryunov.

"Yes, I believe you," Shenk hastened to assure him. "It's impossible to have made up all that you told me. . . . But other people will be sceptical and say: that old blockhead gave his money to some exiles who came to him with a cock-and-bull story; the money was spent and the exiles invented an instructive tale for children about a fantastic land and its extraordinary population and took it to gullible Shenk to justify their expenses. No, we had better say nothing for the time being."

"For the time being? How long will that be?"

"Until, with your participation, a new expedition visits this land, finds this enormous crater, the flooded forests and the bones of animals and people. Then you can make your report, which, supported by documents and the accounts of the members of the new expedition, will be received with trust and will preserve for science a mass of information about the life and destruction of the population of this unhappy land."

"You're perfectly right," Goryunov said. "That is the best course to take. We do not wish to discredit you or ourselves."

"But," Shenk continued, "time passes and dims memories. Write a description—for me personally—of the whole journey now, while everything is still fresh in your mind. I shall keep it until a favourable opportunity turns up."

"I'll do that without fail. It's a duty I hold sacred. I made a few notes on Bennett Island, in the huts we stayed in, and in Yakutsk; I'll write a full and systematic report and let you have it in two or three weeks. Here is our expense sheet and what is left of the money you so generously gave us."

Shenk looked at the account but returned the money to Goryunov.

"You did not leave any reward either for yourself or for Ordin. That is not right. All labour must be paid for."

"But we brought you nothing except an extravagant story and some stones, and therefore deserve no reward."

"If I had any doubts about your honesty, the very fact that you returned a part of the money and took the trouble to journey ten thousand kilometres from Kazachye to bring these stones and your story to me would completely remove them. If you would like to know, you have carried out a very difficult task and it is not your fault that the results were lost. There have been many similar instances; ships carrying collections and reports have been lost time and again and the members of expeditions often barely escaped with their lives. In your case, you have suffered something in the nature of a shipwreck. As a matter of fact, collections sent by post are sometimes lost, too. No, no, you must be rewarded. Besides, you are going to write a report for me and will have to stay here because of that. Living is expensive in the capital. Take the money, as a fee for that report at least."

Not to offend Shenk, Goryunov had to take the money. Soon he gave his report to the academician and then enrolled in the University in order to be better prepared for the prospective expedition.

Unfortunately, it never took place. War broke out with Japan and the Academy was unable to obtain the necessary means. When the war ended, Shenk died before he was able to take any steps to realize the plan. Nobody else was interested in promoting explorations in North Siberia and the plan was shelved for a long time. After waiting in vain for news from Shenk, Goryunov and Ordin turned to other matters. But the report that was preserved among Shenk's papers in the Academy's archives served as material for this book. Perhaps it will awaken interest in Sannikov Land among the new generation and induce some of them to search for it amidst the icy expanses of the Arctic Ocean.

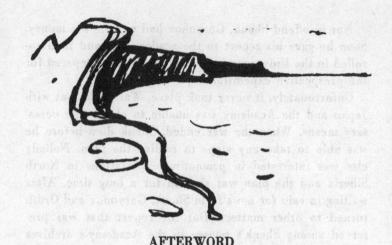

AFTERWORD

After turning over the last page of this description of the adventures of Goryunov and his companions in *Sannikov Land*, the young reader will be justified in asking the author if there really is such a land lost in the Arctic Ocean. After all, the young reader may say, isn't this only a scientific romance?

Yes, this is a scientific romance and the journey to this unknown land has been imagined.

The question of whether *Sannikov Land* exists today has been answered by new Soviet investigations of the Arctic. It is now believed that this land existed for more than a hundred years, as evidenced by the observations of Sannikov and Toll, but that it disappeared quite recently. Soviet polar explorers discovered floating islands in the eastern part of the Arctic Ocean. The new researches by Soviet scientists confirmed the conclusion drawn back in 1899 by Admiral Stepan Osipovich Makarov that there are drifting islands of ice in the Arctic Ocean. Sailing north of the big Spitsbergen Island, Makarov saw an unknown island amidst the ice. There, the admiral's companions found boulders and small stones; the water melted from the ice on the island turned out to be fresh. Makarov established that this was an enormous iceberg, which, apparently, had slided off Spitsbergen Island, where it had formed the tip of a glacier.

It is known that in the Arctic Ocean there are quite a few big, mountainous islands with glaciers slipping down to the sea. During the summer, when the ice breaks, the icebergs thus formed are borne from place to place by the currents. For instance, two big icebergs were noticed north of Henrietta Island in 1939, and in 1946, 1948, and 1950, Soviet polar airmen discovered three enormous floating islands of ice with ice hills and mountains as well as rivers and lakes, that came into existence when the ice and snow melted, and huge boulders—moraines. Soviet explorers have produced evidence to show that icebergs break off the glaciers on Franz Josef Land, Severnaya Zemlya, and the Canadian Archipelago and that currents carry them about for a few years until they melt.

We may make the surmise that *Sannikov Land*, too, was such an island of ice, which separated itself from a glacier on Severnaya Zemlya. Evidently, it ran aground north of the New Siberian Islands, remaining there for over seventy years, because in 1811 Yakov Sannikov noticed this island to the north-west of Kotelny, and on a clear day in 1886, in exactly the same spot, Edward Toll saw four flat-topped conical mountains with foot-hills abutting them on the east. It is possible, however, that what these two explorers saw was not one and the same island but two different ones that had run aground in approximately the same place in the different years they were formed.

Floating islands of ice such as these naturally could not have become the home of the Onkilons, who were driven from the northern coast of East Siberia by the Chukchis. No vegetation grows on floating islands.

Neither could these islands attract birds as a nesting ground. We may presume that migratory birds flying from the south seek to build their nests in more reliable places of which there was a sufficient number in the archipelagoes in the Arctic Ocean.

In general, there is a multitude of big and small islands throughout the region of the Arctic Ocean fringing the shores of Europe, Asia, and America. Young volcanic rocks may be found on many of these islands, while some of them, Iceland, for example, have active volcanoes. This shows that the author's hypothesis about the existence of *Sannikov Land* is not altogether unjustified.

Geological investigations showed that at the beginning of the Quaternary period the entire region of the Arctic Ocean from the Taimyr Peninsula to Wrangel Island and to the north up to the 80th parallel was part of North Siberia. This is confirmed by the remains of big mammals—mammoths, woolly rhinoceroses, oxen, and horses—in the soil of these islands. These remains would not have been there if at the beginning of the Quaternary period the islands had not been part of the mainland of Siberia. Explorations also revealed that on some of the islands there still are thick layers of ice, which are the remains of glaciers that had once lain on the higher sections of this mainland.

Numerous mammoths' tusks are buried in the fossil ice on Bolshoi Lyakhov Island. Hunters search for these tusks in the early spring when they are washed out of the ice by the sea. In the last century, fifteen to thirty tons of tusks were brought to the Yakutsk fair every year; this proves that hundreds of these big animals lived here in the beginning of the Quaternary period, when this area was part of the mainland. The explanation for this large number of mammoths on these small islands is that the latter were the higher portions of the former mainland and the mammoths sought refuge on them when the land began to sink beneath the level of the sea. Thus, we have proof that in this area there were volcanoes, glaciers, and great herds of mammoths and we can determine the time when this land sank beneath the sea. That happened during or at the close of the last glacial epoch, while the discovery of pictures of the mammoth drawn by primitive artists confirms that the land was inhabited by people as well.

Therefore, the supposition that mammoths and primitive people survived on a big isolated island, which was once the crater of a huge and not quite extinct volcano, is likewise not unfounded. Such a rich island amidst the polar ice could have been settled by the Onkilons, who, originating from Alaska and kindred to the American Indians, were forced to retreat to the islands in the Arctic Ocean by the Chukchis.

People known as Onkilons lived in North Siberia three or four hundred years ago. The remains of their unique dwellings were found on the New Siberian Islands, which fact proves that members of this tribe lived on these islands for some time. However, nothing else is known about them. Explorers of the 19th century did not find them on these islands and nobody can tell whether the Onkilons were wiped out by some epidemic or perished while crossing from one island to another in canoes or over newly-formed ice in autumn.

The question of birds flying to the north in spring and returning to the mainland in autumn, a subject dealt with in a number of papers, likewise remains unsettled. The migration of birds to the north, which was noticed back in 1938 by explorers wintering on Henrietta Island, proves that that year a land suitable as a nesting ground existed somewhere amidst the ice. But the position of this island in the east makes it doubtful that these birds flew to *Sannikov Land,* which was (if it existed in 1938) more to the west. Consequently, in 1938, there must have been land north of the De Long Archipelago, where birds could spend the summer. Perhaps one of the young readers of this book will, after becoming a polar flyer, set himself the aim of solving the riddle of *Sannikov Land,* discover it beneath the ice, explore it and tell us what it is like today.

1955